Please return/renew this item
by the last date shown.
Books may also be renewed by
phone or the Internet.

Tel: 01204 332384

www.bolton.gov.uk/libraries

COLD BAYOU

COLD BAYOU

Barbara Hambly

Severn House Large Print
London & New York

This first large print edition published 2019
in Great Britain and the USA by
SEVERN HOUSE PUBLISHERS LTD of
Eardley House, 4 Uxbridge Street, London W8 7SY.
First world regular print edition published 2018 by
Severn House Publishers Ltd.

British Library Cataloguing in Publication Data
A CIP catalogue record for this title is available from the British Library.

ISBN-13: 9780727893857

Severn House Publishers support the Forest Stewardship Council™
[FSC™], the leading international forest certification organisation. All
our titles that are printed on FSC certified paper carry the FSC logo.

Typeset by Palimpsest Book Production Ltd.,
Falkirk, Stirlingshire, Scotland.
Printed and bound in Great Britain by
T J International, Padstow, Cornwall.

For Eric
With many thanks

One

'I see blood, brother.' Olympia Snakebones raised her eyes from the bowl of ink on the table before her, and worry creased her brow. 'I see death.' She passed her hand across the top of the bowl, a shallow Queensware saucer she had found years ago on the bank of the river, miraculously intact; one shouldn't, she always said, turn down the gods when they handed you a gift. The small house on Rue Douane was silent in the dense heat of the early autumn afternoon, far enough back from the river that little sound that came from New Orleans's steamboat wharves. Little even from the gambling-hells along Rue du Levee and Rue Gallatin, which even in the depths of the September doldrums ran full-cock, day and night. Smoky daylight pierced the louvered shutters and crossed the narrow shelf, fixed up in a corner as an altar. A handful of marigolds. A cheap painted statue of the Virgin. A couple of cigars (the gods all liked tobacco) and some graveyard earth in an old perfume-jar. A circle of salt and mouse-bones.

A black-painted bottle that was always kept sealed.

'M'am L'Araignée say—' The voodooienne gestured toward the bottle with one long-fingered hand – 'there's blood waiting for you at Cold Bayou. Death in the water, she say. Death in the fire.'

1

Benjamin January was silent for a long time.

He should not believe his sister, he knew. Thirty-seven years of white man's school, of training as a surgeon at the Hôtel Dieu in Paris, of confession and prayer and devotion to the saints, all insisted that there was nothing in that bottle. Or if there was, it was a demon in service to Satan.

But the dream he had dreamed that morning lingered, like the black stain of poison.

He had waked from it to profound stillness. Even Baby Xander, not yet two months old, seemed to be settling at last into a rhythm of sleep, and it had felt to him for a time that the world outside his own house, that big old ramshackle dwelling on Rue Esplanade, had somehow slipped away into gray twilight. Though he was sharply and clearly awake, the veils of his dream still wrapped him, and he had had the strange feeling that if he'd risen from his bed, slipped from beneath the mosquito-netting and gone to the French doors that opened onto the gallery, he would have seen outside not the shaggy, tree-shaded neutral ground in the center of Rue Esplanade – not the cottages of the Metoyer Sisters and the Becques and Lalie Gouvert across that wide expanse of street – but yellow floodwaters. As he had seen in his dream.

Silent as death, in his dream the water had rushed past the gallery-rail, inexorably rising. He'd seen trees floating in it, ripped from their moorings by the weight of the flood. Whole lengths of fence, chicken-coops and the roofs of houses. The sight was one he had seen before,

2

and recalled clearly: he'd been six years old, sitting on the sill of one of the high windows in the stone sugar house on Bellefleur Plantation, where he and Olympe – Olympia Snakebones was what the voodoos called her – had been born. Every separate floating plank and gourd, every knot of snarled cane, he remembered distinctly from that evening thirty-eight years ago.

Yet in his dream he had been his present age. The house around him, his present house, not the sugar mill into which Michie Fourchet had been wont to lock all his slaves during the river's floods, lest they escape into the swamps in the confusion. In his dream he'd been conscious that Rose was asleep behind him, hidden by the gauzy scrim of mosquito-bar. That Xander lay curled in his crib. Conscious of his older son, not quite two years old, asleep also beyond the open door of his little nursery, and of his niece, his nephew – Olympe's children – sleeping upstairs. All unconscious as the waters rose around the house.

At the same time, in his dream, he'd smelled the smoke of fire.

'Death for me?' he asked at last.

Olympe's eyes – so like their mother's – focussed on him again, as if returning from a world far away. 'I don't know,' she said. 'What did you dream?' She hadn't let him tell her before she'd looked into the ink-bowl.

January hesitated, trying to put into words the deep horror that the vision had brought.

Waking from it, he had washed and dressed and gone to early Mass in the cathedral, with the men who worked the levee, and the marchandes

3

who sold milk and strawberries and watermelon in the streets. But the incense and the dim glow of the votive-lights had not brought him their accustomed comfort. Leaving the cathedral, he had made his way through the French Town, inland, to find his sister scrubbing the front step of her dark-red cottage with brick-dust in the clammy warmth of a September morning that would swiftly turn hot.

He stammered a little as he spoke of the dream, for the images of it frayed away from him, like very old cloth damaged by the sun. It was in any case impossible for him to convey to her the uneasy terror he had felt. In his actual life – in the actual childhood he had shared with Olympe – there had been no such fear. They had had real things to fear then, like Michie Fourchet when he got drunk (although sober he was no saint either), or the possibility of encountering an alligator or a puma when they'd run off to play in the ciprière. There was also the ever-present dread that one or the other of them, or their mother or their father, would be sold off . . .

Michie Fourchet locking everybody into the sugar mill during a flood was just an interesting adventure.

In real life – in the real flood he'd watched at the age of six – there had been no smell of smoke.

Old Mambo Jeanne, the wise-woman of that little African village that the white folks called 'the quarters', used to say of dreams, 'They're how God talks to you, when you get too smart to listen to anythin' else He says.'

Olympe rose from the table where she sat, and went to the shelf in the corner. She came back with a carved tray, a gourd and a bowl. From the gourd she scattered dust on the tray, from the bowl she took a handful of beans. These she shook over the tray, her fingers held half-open, so that the beans scattered on the wood.

Père Eugenius, January's confessor, would, January knew, have a thing or two to say to him at confession Saturday, when he got back from Cold Bayou.

Wagons rattled in the street outside, and an old woman's hoarse voice wavered over a sing-song chant:

I sell to the rich, I sell to the po'
Gonna sell to that lady standin' in that do'
Wa-a-a-a-a-a-termelon . . .

The last word dissolved into a melismatic wail, like the cry of a muezzin summoning the faithful to prayer.

On a day this sticky-hot, at the end of that gruesome summer of 1839, red sweet water-melon, reflected January, would itself be a form of prayer . . .

'Don't go to Cold Bayou, brother.' Olympe raised her head from a study of the dropped beans. 'Nuthin' good waitin' for you there.'

It wasn't the first time she'd said something of the kind to him since he'd been asked to play at the wedding of Veryl St-Chinian on Tuesday. As one of the best piano-players in New Orleans, January was delighted to get the job – summer

5

was the starving time for musicians, with all the planters, bankers, sugar brokers and merchants out of town on the lake. He knew he had his youngest sister Dominique to thank for the engagement. Her protector, Henri Viellard, was the nephew of the elderly groom, and St-Denis Janvier – Dominique's father and the man who'd purchased January's mother, freed her, and 'placed' her as his mistress – was a remote connection of that whole sprawling French Creole clan.

He had, in fact, had second thoughts about the job, but the money was too good to turn down. Their mother, the elegant Widow Levesque, had received an actual invitation to the ceremony, as had Dominique and a number of other free colored connections of the family: children and grandchildren of the St-Chinian or Viellard or Duquille sons and uncles by 'plaçeés' of their own. Their mother had been preening herself about it for weeks, casually inserting the phrase 'They look upon us as part of the family, you know', into every single one of her conversations with her friends in the free colored demimonde. Americans might be thrusting themselves into every corner of New Orleans, taking greater and greater shares of its trade, its businesses, its wealth, but it was the old French and Spanish families that were the true heart of the town. Among the free people of color – the *gens du couleur librés* – there were few greater distinctions than to be recognized for what they were: a part of those old families, albeit 'on the shady side of the street'.

Invitation to be at the wedding of the head of one of those great French land-owning families – even if it was only because she had once been plaçeé to a four-times-removed cousin – meant far more than presentation at the White House would have done, always supposing that a) *any* person of color would be received by the president's wife under any circumstances whatsoever and b) the president hadn't been a widower for the past twenty years. (January could almost hear his mother sniff, 'What's *she*, anyway? Some Dutch girl from New York.')

Olympe, who hadn't willingly spoken to their mother since 1816, would have been delighted had he refused to have anything to do with the wedding at Cold Bayou.

But to the marrow of his bones he knew that his sister wouldn't bend to such purposes the things she saw in the ink-bowl.

She gathered up the beans, one by one, and dropped them back into their dish. Tapped and patted the sides of the tray to shake the dust onto a clean newspaper, which she rolled into a neat funnel into the gourd again. Watching her, January was reminded strongly of their mother, who was tallish, like Olympe, and who, though fleshier, moved with the same light economy of motion which she had schooled into incomparable grace. Olympe lacked their mother's startling beauty, and, like January, was African-dark, a complexion not admired among the mixed-race librés: black was the color of the slavery they had themselves so recently escaped. He didn't know whether Olympe even remembered their father, who'd

7

been out in the fields when their mother had been sold to St-Denis Janvier. He recalled vividly, though, his sister spitting on Janvier's shoes, when their mother had informed them that Michie Janvier had purchased – and freed – not only herself, but her two children as well.

I won't have no white man buy me what I ought to be. I'll be what I was born, the child of my ancestors; the daughter of their gods. From the age of five, Olympe had held their mother in anger and contempt, clinging to her cane-patch French and the dark loa of African belief. When she was sixteen she'd run off to become a voodoo-ienne, and their mother – who had long before that transformed herself into the perfect plaçeé – had not even gone to look for her.

Yet January knew that what she'd said had nothing to do with the past.

He replied, after long silence, 'It's not that simple.'

Her wide mouth quirked. 'It's never simple for you, brother. You got no business goin' down to Plaquemines Parish to see some old white man marry a gal young enough to be his grand-daughter. The food afterwards ain't gonna be *that* good. You think Maman's gonna admit to anybody there you're her kin?'

'Maman's got nothing to do with me going.' He answered her expression with a grin as wry as her own. 'That was old M'am Janvier who asked her, since she's kin to the Duquilles and grew up with Madame Viellard's mother. She likes Maman, and she can't stand M'am Marie-Hélène—' He named the wife of their mother's

8

deceased protector – 'and didn't invite *her* to keep her company. So of course Maman's got to go, even if the place is the back-end of nowhere and Maman will complain the whole time about how hot it is and how she's gonna die of boredom. For me it's a job,' he finished. 'And if it wasn't, I'd go anyway. Rose was asked, by M'sieu St-Chinian himself.'

Olympe sniffed. 'Just 'cause your wife is kin to the family, through her mama or her grandmama sellin' herself for some white man's money—'

'It's not just kindred.' January shook his head, knowing his sister looked down upon the whole custom of plaçage – the 'custom of the country' – with scorn. 'Back in '34, Veryl St-Chinian hired her to tutor one of his nephews, when her school had closed and she was broke. Hired a *woman* to tutor science and mathematics. He put in money to help us re-open our school come October. And with every member of his family screaming bloody murder at this marriage of his, he wants to know at least that some of the people who'll be down at Cold Bayou for the wedding will genuinely wish him well.'

His sister rolled her eyes. 'He'll need it.'

'He will.' January replied as if her words had not been a jeer. 'Henri Viellard cares for him enough to do so—' Olympe sniffed again at the mention of the protector of their younger sister Dominique. That fat, indolent, and extremely wealthy planter's mother – Madame Viellard – was the aged groom's sister – 'even though he and his mama will lose their stranglehold on the family holdings, when Uncle Veryl brings a

9

wife into the family councils. And I know Minou—' He used their sister's family nickname – 'is very fond of the old man as well.'

Olympe made a face. As vividly as he recalled that flood in his childhood, January remembered their mother's attempt to push Olympe into a contract of plaçage with one of St-Denis Janvier's business associates when she was barely fifteen. In his sister's eyes he saw, too, the reflection of the other young women they knew, whose choice of 'protectors' had not been entirely free despite their legal status as librées.

'She must dote on that fat pudding Viellard if she's going down to a place like Cold Bayou just to hold his hand while he watches his uncle make a fool of himself.' In very few of the twenty-six states could Henri Viellard have married Dominique – who, as far as January knew, the podgy young planter genuinely loved – and a little to the surprise of both January and Olympe, Minou had made it clear that she loved Henri in return.

'And I suppose that cold little wife of his will be there as well.'

January nodded.

'I wonder if *she* wishes him happy?'

'Veryl St-Chinian is Madame Chloë's uncle,' returned January. 'And she's said to me that he was more a father to her than her own was. Which could just mean he let her read some of the more scandalous Latin authors in his library. But yes,' he added, 'I wonder, too. With César St-Chinian's death last year, Uncle Veryl and old Madame Aurelié Viellard are the only two members left, of the family's senior generation. They control I don't know how many plantations and town properties, and since Veryl's hopeless at anything concerning the real world, Chloë and Madame Aurelié have had a pretty free hand in running things as they choose. I know nothing against this girl—'

'She's an eighteen-year-old tavern slut who can't write her name,' retorted Olympe, and turned to replace the *ifa* tray on its shelf. 'What else do you need to know?'

In the bedroom, the voice of her youngest child, baby Zephine, rose in a fretful clucking. Olympe sighed, and knocked the last flecks of dust from her long fingers.

'I see bad things in the ink, brother,' she said, in a matter-of-fact voice. 'Bad things at Cold Bayou. Fire and water, and blood soaking into the earth. There's no need for you to be there.'

'If Rose is going to support Uncle Veryl,' he returned, 'and there is danger there, I do need to be there.' He leaned a massive shoulder against the bedroom door-jamb, as she bent over the crib. 'And they've asked me – Veryl, and Minou, and Henri – to be there, not just to play at the wedding, but because I'm the personal physician to Uncle Veryl's friend Michie Singletary – who'll probably be the only person present who truly wishes Veryl happy, unreservedly and with the whole of his heart. Or anyway the whole of his heart that isn't occupied with trisecting angles or squaring circles. He's frail, Olympe. He needs me with him.'

She turned from the crib-side, her baby in her arms, a whip-slim black Madonna with the five

11

points of her red-and-gold tignon that marked her as a voodooienne like an incongruous halo. The anger in her voice had turned to exasperation. 'To take care of this old white man's old white friend?'

'To take care of my family until Christmas—' January smiled – 'with the fifty dollars Uncle Veryl is going to pay me to look after his old white friend.'

She made a noise in her throat, for all the world like their mother when confronted with yet another example of January attempting to run his own life. Then she was silent for a time, regarding him with those velvet-brown eyes.

'Will you do something for me then, brother?' she said at last. 'Will you warn Minou of what I said?'

'I don't think it'll keep her from going.'

'Then at least warn her not to take their child. Tell her I'll look after Charmian. And you tell Rose to leave Baby Xander and Professor John here as well. I don't know what's in the shadows that I see at Cold Bayou, nor whether the blood I see is a sign for you or for some other there. But if blood's shed, and the "shady" side of the family are gonna be on hand for this fool weddin', you know who's gonna get the blame for sheddin' it.'

January sighed. 'Then it might be just as well that I'll be on hand.'

Two

'Mesel', ah mun bide here sooner nor go mixin' wi' yon cleckin' crowd.' Old Mr Selwyn Singletary sat back as January put away his stethoscope, and offered a fragile, bony wrist for the inspection of his pulse. A mathematician of some repute, the elderly gentleman had been mistakenly incarcerated in a madhouse for some months two years previously,* and heavily dosed with opium the whole time. His friend Veryl St-Chinian had offered him a home during his lengthy recuperation, and had retained January as a physician, the only white person to have paid for the services that had been, in fact, January's chosen career.

From the courtyard of the dilapidated Rue Bourbon townhouse, Veryl St-Chinian's slow, soft voice rose, against the counterpoint of Dominique's bright chatter, both muted by the thick moisture of the sweltering afternoon air. Now and then a child laughed: Charmian Viellard, five years old, Minou's daughter by her protector Henri.

January was relieved to see the smile in his patient's eyes at the sound of the child's voice. Along with its agonizing physical symptoms, the ordeal of weaning away from opiates had been accompanied by a crushing depression of spirits

* See *Good Man Friday*

which had frequently left Singletary barely able to eat or speak. Even for a recognized eccentric like Uncle Veryl it was considered inappropriate to introduce his friend to his nephew's quadroon mistress, much less to the five-year-old daughter of that illegitimate union. Yet January knew that there had been weeks when visits from 'Madame Minou', as Singletary called her, and little Charmian, were the only reason the old man would get out of bed.

'Veryl's Frenchy relations, wi' their skinny noses in t' air an' not a word o' decent English amongst 'em . . .' Singletary shook his head, and accepted his shirt back from the valet Uncle Veryl had hired for him, a hulking, grave-faced, gentle young man named Archibald.

With his nearly-incomprehensible Yorkshire speech, January reflected that Singletary had little business criticizing his friend's Frenchy relations.

'An' not a good word amongst 'em to say o' that poor lass that's made Veryl happy as a lad, like 'tis any business o' their'n who he weds. Ah couldna leave him frontin' that lot alone, think on, not for all t' relatives i' this benighted land. Nor her, poor lass.'

'Have you met her?' All January knew from his mother was that the entire interlocked tribe of St-Chinians, Viellards, Janviers, Duquilles and Aubins – whose senior members controlled nearly three hundred thousand acres of the finest sugar-producing land in Louisiana – was in an uproar at the thought of its eldest living member marrying a 'cheap Irish tavern-slut' – 'Not that I've ever encountered an expensive Irish tavern-slut, mind you,' had remarked his friend Hannibal Sefton, whose experience of Irish tavern-sluts was fairly comprehensive.

'Ah have an' all,' assented the old man. 'A fair sweet lass I thought her, soft-spoke as any doo. Speaks French a treat, she does, an' her English no more Irish than Mr Sefton's, though she can't read a word beyond her name. She come to this country a lass as young as Miss Charmian, an' her father, she says, tewed all his days keepin' books for some company in New York, an' fell sick only after comin' here to New Orleans. She'll call of an evenin', an' Veryl'll read to her, or I will. Veryl says when they're wed he'll have her taught proper.'

He frowned, buttoning his shirt and letting Archibald slip him into an extremely shabby silk waistcoat cut in a style that January recognized as having been popular in Napoleon's day. From the jungle of banana-trees and resurrection-fern that choked the courtyard, Dominique's voice raised in silvery exasperation, 'I honestly don't know which is worse, Rose: M'sieu Singletary and Uncle Veryl going on about people who've been dead for *thousands* of years, or Uncle Veryl and Henri going on about *bugs*!'

Singletary chuckled at this, like dry leaves rubbed together, as old M'sieu St-Chinian and his nephew protested in chorus that, strictly speaking, only members of the order Hemiptera could be classified as *bugs*, and that such creatures as the Lepidoptera and Hymenoptera were in fact no such thing . . .

15

'A grievous unregulated mind, Veryl,' sighed the Englishman. 'Small wonder he canna grasp t' basic principles of Pythagoras, think on, wi' his mind all flittin' off aboot if some attercop creepin' up t' wall's a Mygalomorphus or a Araneomorph. But why, after leavin' him much to his own for the whole o' his life here—' the gesture of one arthritic hand took in the crumbling Spanish townhouse around them, which for forty-odd years had been Veryl's home – 'they start fratchin' *now* aboot him tumblin' in love, has me reet flummoxed.'

'It's because of his brother's death,' said January, a little surprised that Singletary didn't know.

The old man's frown returned. 'What, Miss Chloë's da'?'

Miss Chloë – strictly speaking, Madame Chloë St-Chinian Viellard – was Henri Viellard's very young wife, a cold-blooded and bespectacled little scholar who had substantially increased the voting rights of the Viellard faction in the family corporation.

'It's Miss Chloë's grandfather, who was Veryl's brother,' January explained. 'And no – Gilbert St-Chinian, his wife, his son Raymond, and Raymond's wife all died of yellow fever in 1827, leaving Miss Chloë sole heir to Gilbert's share of the family holdings. César St-Chinian – the oldest of old Aimé St-Chinian's sons – died last year, leaving Uncle Veryl and Henri's mother, Aurelié St-Chinian Viellard, in control of most of the St-Chinian lands. Under Louisiana law,' he added, seeing the old man's frown deepen, 'land is left equally to all of a man's children,

16

not divided up. Most of the French planter families who control the sugar lands below Baton Rouge hold the property as shares in a joint family corporation, with all senior members having a vote on its administration . . . or its sale. Americans have been trying for decades to get the law changed, to make it easier to buy sugar plantations without the whole family having to agree to sell, because the old land grants were given under French law. It's what allows the French to continue their hold on the state government.'

'Ach.' Singletary nodded. 'So that's why, the one time I went wi' Veryl to them relatives of a Sunday dinner, t' whole o' the table got to slangin' an' shoutin'. Not knowin' a word o' Frogspeak I couldna follow, but Veryl did say, t'was land they was fratchin' aboot. This Brother César you speak of was there, think on, bellerin' loudest of all. A tall old yin wi' a beard on him like a holly-bush?'

'That would be him.' January recalled the old man well, from years of playing the piano at balls, weddings, and Mardi Gras festivities of the French and Spanish Creole elite. 'He died last year, after disinheriting both his son and his daughter. In Louisiana it's almost literally impossible to disinherit your children: the law requires a man to leave his children at least a third of his property if his wife survives him, half if she does not, and two-thirds if he has more than one child. I suspect,' he added wryly, 'that's because too many men were leaving property to the sons of their plaçeés. But Locoul St-Chinian – César's

17

son – struck his father in the course of an argu-ment, which is one of the handful of grounds for utterly disinheriting one's child. My mother claims that César baited his son into striking him, because Locoul had defied him about something else, I don't recall just what – at this point it scarcely matters. Fleurette, old César's daughter, married at the age of sixteen without her father's permission, which is another. What does matter is that there are now only two members of the older generation of St-Chinian landholders with a controlling interest in the family lands – and one of them is on the verge of taking a wife.'

'Not like they can forbid t' banns, think on,' agreed Singletary, with a rusty laugh. 'An' as Veryl's wife this lass'll come to havin' a voice i' runnin' t' whole shebang?'

'Exactly,' January said. 'The situation is usually dealt with by pushing the young men of the family into matrimony when they're still young enough to be bullied, bribed, or blackmailed by their seniors. Veryl is what? Nearly seventy?'

'Sixty-seven – an' no so great an age,' added the old man, poking an admonishing finger at January.

'No,' agreed January with a smile. 'The problem is that this young lady – what's her name, by the way?'

'Trask. Miss Elizabeth Trask.'

'The problem is that Mamzelle Trask will be Veryl's first wife, and therefore entitled to a share of the management of the family lands. Subsequent wives – *en second noces*, as it's called – don't have the same rights.'

'Dommed clever o' somebody,' grumbled the

18

old mathematician. 'An' still no manner o' their business, whate'er t' law says. Why, you've only t' look at t' lass t' see she's right an' sweet a child as' e'er you'd meet of a summer's day, think on! An' no more guile to her than a wee cuddy in a hedge.'

January stepped back as Archie helped his master to rise. 'How did M'sieu St-Chinian come to meet her?' he asked, well aware that old Mr Singletary – a lifelong bachelor who seldom lifted his nose from theoretical calculus – had slightly less experience of the world than Olympe's six-year-old son Ti-Paul.

'T'would break your heart, Mr J.' Singletary's silver brows pulled down over his great, hooked nose in real distress. 'All that poor lass has suffered, after her da' was took by fever. He'd been rentin' a couple o' rooms in St Mary's up t'river, an' when he passed, her hagwife landlady turned her out, an' took what little money he'd left in the place, sayin' as how he owed for the month, though poor Ellie knew he'd paid already. Ellie'd saved a little, sewin', an' hid it in t'back o' a drawer, but when she went t' look there, 'twas gone – taken, Ellie thought, when she was sleepin', so wore down she was wi' nursin' her poor da'. She'd walked the whole of the way from St Mary's to the place her da's sister lived, clear downriver in Chalmette, only to find the woman gone, an' t'rain pourin' down – t' fore-end o' July, this was – an' she turned the heel o' her poor little shoe an' twisted her ankle some-thin' cruel, an' took shelter from t'rain reet down in t' carriage-way there . . .'

He stepped out onto the little gallery outside his window, pointed his thin, shaky finger past the overgrown garden, to the arched tunnel that led out onto Rue Bourbon.

'Veryl found her, wi'evenin' comin' down, shiverin' wi' cold an' soaked to her skin an' faintin' wi' hunger. He took her in an' give her a little wine, an' a dollar to find her a place to stay the night, for she wouldna sleep t'night under a gentleman's roof, she said; her ma had raised her better nor that, she said. Then t'next day she come back, to return Veryl his money, havin' found a little sewin' work. An' by that time, you could say, Veryl felt as if she was in a way his own. She'd have died sure, had it not been for him.'

Times were hard, January knew. More than one young girl in New Orleans had genuinely found herself tramping the streets in quest of a fugitive aunt . . . And God knew there were hagwives aplenty who wouldn't turn a hair at ejecting a tennant's child after cheating her out of her father's remaining few coins.

And he supposed that pretty young ladies *did* sprain their ankles just outside the carriageways of unworldly old bachelors who had recently acquired control over several hundred thousand acres of sugar land, too.

''Twas but a few weeks ago,' Singletary went on, 'she'd come of an afternoon to ask how he did, an' he was took sick, an' she stayed on here, nursin' him turn an turn about wi' me, James an' Archie – though she'd all her own sewin' work to do as well, poor lass. Veryl's own daughter

20

couldna cared for him better. I don't ken what passed betwixt 'em, but 'twas a beautiful thing to see, him comin' back to strength an' her weepin' wi' joy at it.'

I'll bet. 'And it was then he asked her to marry him?'

Singletary nodded, lined face wreathed with tender happiness for his friend's sake. Just as if, thought January, herbs like so-called Indian tobacco didn't exist which would reduce a man to vomiting and weakness, so that a clever woman could 'nurse' him to health with simple tisanes and win his gratitude.

Particularly an inexperienced old scholar, separated from the affairs of business and family, in love for perhaps the first time in his life.

'Oh, M'sieu St-Chinian,' cooed a lovely voice down in the court below, 'please excuse me, I didn't know you had guests.'

It was the voice of a very young angel, her French just tinted with a slight Irish lilt.

'It's nothing, *mignonne*. M'sieu Janvier – M'sieu Singletary's physician, you know – was in the neighborhood . . .'

January stepped onto the gallery, and ascertained – without an atom of surprise – that Miss Ellie Trask was one of the most beautiful young women he had ever laid eyes on. Her hair, under a neat bonnet whose curtailed poke framed rather than concealed her face, was the mellow gold of evening sunlight, clustering in curls at her ears and trailing in fragile whisps around her temples. Even at this distance January could see the delicacy of her features, the perfect shape of her

21

mouth – wide and gentle with its suggestion of kindness and smiles – and the healthy (though slightly augmented) rosiness of her porcelain skin.

When he and Singletary descended to the court and he was presented to Mamzelle Trask, the eyes she raised to his were brown, doe-like under eyelashes whose natural length and thickness had been accentuated – he had watched his mother do it a thousand times in his childhood – by the skillful application of kohl.

Altogether she was enough to make the most austere saint in the calendar burn his books.

He found himself wondering how quickly she'd gotten over that sprained ankle. Quickly enough to return her benefactor's money to him the following day, anyhow.

'I'm ever so pleased to meet you, sir,' she cooed, when he bowed over her hand. Then she turned those tender eyes upon Veryl, filled with the adoration of a young girl. 'I do hope M'sieu Singletary is well?'

'Perfectly so, yes, Mamzelle.'

Rose was introduced to her as January's wife, Dominique as his sister, along with her child. Henri Viellard, fat and balding and bespectacled in a modishly cut green linen coat, remained at his uncle's side with the expression of a chance caller who had happened to arrive at the same time as the advent of the Janvier family party. Even Charmian – a vision in white gauze – knew, January noticed, at the tender age of five, to keep her distance from her father and cling to her mother's hand, seen and not heard, in the presence of a white stranger. The custom of the

22

country, as he'd said to Olympe. New Orleans was full of dusky-complexioned little girls and boys who knew from toddlerhood that they weren't to greet their fathers in the street unless spoken to first. But the knowledge that it had to be so, like the bitter gleam in Olympe's eye, lay sour on his tongue like the backtaste of poison.

A glance at the young planter's stolid face and unhappy eyes showed him that Henri Viellard tasted the poison, too.

Mamzelle Trask exclaimed over Charmian's prettiness, and stooped – with a dancer's suppleness – to admire the child. 'You must be so proud of her, Madame,' she said to Dominique, with such obvious enthusiasm that Minou, despite her initial reserve, smiled warmly back.

'I am, Mamzelle.'

'Do you go to school yet, pretty girl? So big a girl as you are?'

'I don't go to school,' replied Charmian in her soft, precise voice. 'But Maman is teaching me my letters. Would you like to hear them?'

'Oh, above all things, acushla!'

'Mamzelle, if you will excuse us,' January said, knowing his social duty. He held out his elbows, one to Rose, one to Dominique. 'I fear we must take our leave. It was truly a pleasure to meet you. Ladies . . .?'

Visitors of color did not linger when white guests put in an appearance.

Judging by the expression on Henri's plump face, he guessed that the son of Veryl's co-heir in the family property wouldn't remain for the refreshments that he heard Veryl calling for, even as he guided his lady-folk down the carriageway to the street.

September was hurricane season in New Orleans, fair and hot, but with quick gusts that spoke of clouds above the far-off Gulf. The cathedral bells chimed mellowly for the noon Mass, and in hundreds of low stucco cottages, ladies – white or *les femmes du couleur librées* – set out plates of creamy Queensware or exquisite blue and white porcelain. In the sweltering kitchens in hundreds of yards, servants checked étouffeés, gumbos, grillades in preparation for their owners' Sunday dinner. Rose propped her spectacles more firmly on her nose, and said, 'I hope she treats Uncle Veryl decently.'

Minou sniffed. 'For the money she'll be coming into when she weds him, she'd better.' The pink-and-celery silk of her skirts rustled as she drew them aside from an old Indian woman and her dog, peddling packets of filé from a basket. '*I* hope she isn't expecting any single one of the family to have one word to say to her, or that she'll be invited *anywhere* . . . Not that poor Uncle Veryl's going to fight very hard for invitations. I daresay he won't notice whether *he* gets them or not. "Sprained her ankle" in his very doorway, indeed!'

'Mamzelle didn't look like a bad lady,' ventured Charmian, glancing from her mother to her aunt.

'Of course she didn't, dearest,' said Minou. 'If she looked like a bad lady Uncle Veryl wouldn't want to marry her.'

The child's brow puckered with distress. 'Will she be mean to Uncle Veryl?'

24

Minou relented, as January picked up Charmian and held her, as lightly as a kitten, on one massive shoulder. 'Of course not, sweetheart,' she said. 'She just wants someone to take care of her without her having to work, that's all. I expect once Uncle Veryl gives her money, she won't see much of him at all.'

'One hopes that will be the case,' remarked Rose. 'Because Veryl really cares for the girl – and she'll be in a position to make his life very miserable indeed. If, in fact,' she added as an afterthought, 'his family lets him marry her at all.'

Like Mr Singletary, January observed, 'They can't very well forbid the banns.'

'If you think,' said Rose, 'that Aurelié Viellard and old Basile Aubin aren't perfectly capable of stopping the wedding between them, I suggest you go back and review everything you know about French Creole families, Benjamin. Personally, I'll bet you twenty-five cents that the wedding doesn't take place at all.'

'Done,' said Minou at once. 'Men can be *so* silly when it comes to beautiful young chickens. Benjamin?'

He thought for a long moment about the look that had come into Veryl St-Chinian's eyes when Ellie Trask had glanced at him across the green tangle of the garden. About what it felt like to be in love after one thought one was done with such things.

About Olympe's dark glance as she'd looked up from her ink-bowl.

He said quietly, 'Done.'

25

Three

'*Ellie Trask*?' Hannibal Sefton let out a hoot of laughter. 'Old Uncle Veryl is going to marry *Ellie Trask*?'

'I take it,' said January, 'you know her.' He handed his friend the sole shirt that occupied one of the broken shelves at the back of what had originally been either a toolshed or a prostitute's 'crib' behind a bathhouse on Perdidio Street – Hannibal's current residence.

'Every man in Natchez,' returned the fiddler, 'knows her,' and there was a world of Biblical implication in his coffee-black eyes.

'Yourself included?'

'A backstage acquaintance only.' Hannibal tucked the shirt into his much-worn music-satchel, along with other items of linen equally threadbare, and three waistcoats of faded silk nearly as outdated as Singletary's. 'I dealt poker at the High Water tavern owned by her father for three weeks in the summer of '34, when I'd managed to annoy that fellow Roarke that used to own the Jolly Boatman on Gallatin Street and needed to be out of town. *Abiit, excessit, evasit, erupit* . . .' In his drinking days the fiddler had slept in any of a dozen hideouts in the Swamp – that insalubrious district at the back of town where sailors, flatboat-men, and river rats went to get drunk, laid, and systematically stripped of their pay. More recently the proprietors of several of these dens continued to offer him shelter in return for his not-inconsiderable talents as a house musician: these days, a young lady known locally as Kate the Gouger, who ran the bathhouse and its gamier subsidaries. Besides his few items of clothing, always kept scrupulously clean, the fiddler had only a dozen books. Those, January knew, he would leave on the shelf until his return from playing at the wedding at Cold Bayou Plantation.

Nobody in the Swamp would steal books.

'Ellie worked at the bar and sang for the customers,' continued Hannibal, wrapping his shaving-things in an old-style, foot-wide linen cravat, 'to my accompaniment, and a very pretty voice she has, too. I hadn't the price that her father asked for a night with her, not that I've ever had the desire to sleep with a thirteen-year-old girl. She passed for anything from eleven on up to sixteen, depending on the customer's proclivities, and I have no doubt she'll surrender her virginity on her wedding-night as convincingly as she did on about a hundred occasions that summer. By all accounts she does it very well. A sweet girl,' he added, with a slight reminiscent frown at some memory. 'She was always very kind to me, even when she could see no profit in it.'

'So I take it—' January moved his feet out of the way as Hannibal took down his violin from the shelf – 'that her poor old father didn't work himself to death and his landlady stole his small savings?'

Hannibal drew himself up in theatrical indignation. 'There's nothing to say a whoremaster and moneylender doesn't work as hard as other men! Well, almost as hard.' He checked his fiddle, re-wrapped it tenderly in its nest of faded silk scarves and replaced it in its battered case. '*Absque sudore et labore nullum opus perfectum est.* He did die – back in '37, I think – but if anybody got his small savings I expect it was Ellie herself, along with his boots and the gold fillings from his teeth. Would you like me to speak to Uncle Veryl on the subject?'

'If you would.' It wasn't that Veryl St-Chinian himself would take personal offense at a black man – or a woman of color like Rose – bringing him the news that his intended was, to put it mildly, unchaste. But most of the St-Chinian and Viellard families, while rejoicing in the news itself, would have had January arrested and whipped for saying such things about a white woman.

The two men stepped out of the crib – its door had no lock – and into the harsh sunlight of the bathhouse yard, where a slave was filling a wheeled water-butt from the cistern behind the bathhouse itself. Three other shacks stood among the rough clumps of palmetto and tupelo at the edge of the open mud of the yard, doors agape to the muggy forenoon. The girls who worked the place sat together on the doorsill of one of them, drinking coffee, and called out lazy greetings to both Hannibal and January. It was shortly after eleven, on Monday morning, and the stale heat was already suffocating. The steamboat *Illinois* was leaving – supposedly – for Plaquemines Parish at three: January had long ago learned to allow plenty of time to get the fiddler out of bed. The Swamp wouldn't really come alive until almost dark, when the queer, sultry heat of the early autumn abated and it got too dark to work on the river wharves or those of the Basin canal. The back of town was quiet at this hour, the girls still waking up, snaggle-haired and tousled. The gamblers and grifters and shills, if they were out of bed at all, slumped over grillades and grits at whichever taverns served food as well as liquor, or negotiated with mulatto laundresses about the clean, starched linen that marked them as gentlemen in those parts.

It was the time of day, January had found, that was safest for a black man to walk about the Swamp without risk of being robbed, beaten up by an aggressive drunk, kidnapped by the slave stealers who haunted the district, or killed for the contents of his pockets. He'd approached the Swamp through the actual swamp – the ciprière of marshy puddles, crotch-high weeds, small bayous and moss-draped cypress and oak that lay behind and between the makeshift tents and saloons. But once Hannibal was with him – a white man, no matter how shabby – he was at least not likely to find himself up against a couple of up-river ruffians demanding to know, 'What you think you're doin' around here, boy?'

'I hate to do it to him,' said January, as they made their way down Common Avenue toward the river. 'I saw his eyes, when he looked at her yesterday afternoon. According to Rose, he's always been the "queer old duck" of the St-Chinian family: scholarly, shy, disregarded by his brothers and sisters because it was obvious he was never going to be of any use in the family business. He was generally low on the list of eligible bachelors because every mother in town could see that he was going to let his siblings control his interest in the family property rather than listen to the family of a wife.'

'We had those at Oxford.' Hannibal hopped neatly over the brimming gutter of Rampart Street – the 'improvements' by the Council of the Second Municipality didn't extend to the back of town and the 'islands', as they were sometimes called, of buildings were still surrounded by yard-wide ditches rank with weeds and creeping with small wildlife. 'Sometimes for a rag the choicer spirits would take them out, get them drunk, and couple them up with the local white-aprons, which I should imagine would be enough to put one off the female sex for good. Brilliant scholars, many of them – there was a fellow on our staircase who could translate from Greek to Arabic in his head – but they learned pretty early to stick with their books.'

'Old Aimé St-Chinian arranged for his son to get a mistress at some point,' said January. He paused, frowned, and made a move toward the body of a man lying in the gutter in front of the Turkey Buzzard saloon, then stopped when a second glance told him the man was dead. Old Swipes, the barkeep, emerged on the saloon's doorsill at that moment and looked at the corpse in exasperation, then proceeded to sweep the step.

'If he doesn't care,' pointed out Hannibal quietly, 'I'm sure you needn't,' and January knew he was right. It was a common enough sight in the Swamp. But something pinched him inside, at the reflection that this was the world in which he was raising his sons.

In time he went on, 'I gather from Minou – who had it from Henri, but my mother corroborates it – that the girl took a lover out of sheer exasperation with Veryl's awkwardness and neglect. Eventually the pair of them sold everything in the house he'd given her and ran off to Europe together. There was a terrific scandal and Veryl was the laughing-stock of the town for years – this was when I was in Paris myself – and I daresay that was the last time he looked seriously at a woman.'

'And I daresay,' concluded Hannibal regretfully, 'that Miss Ellie learned all about that – particularly after César St-Chinian's death left Uncle Veryl with substantial interest in twenty-eight sugar plantations.'

They walked in silence for a time, dodging from one side of the street to the other depending on whether the scattered buildings had sidewalks or *abat-vents* to offer some shade from the sun. Common Avenue fed into Canal Street, rattling with drays and goods-wagons coming and going from the levee, despite the blistering sun. The air began to be gritty with the soot of the boats, whose tall stacks loomed above the ten-foot rise of the ground.

Beyond the levee, most of the boats drawn up to the wharves were the small stern-wheelers,

31

that could hug the banks on a low river and chug their way up the maze of bayous of Jefferson and Plaquemines Parish. The river was low, and the wide stretch of muddy gravel exposed between the wharves was scattered with crates and bales, barrels and boxes, and sacks of mail for the overseers of the downriver plantations: communication and instruction from the owners who were, for the most part, still taking refuge along the shores of Lake Pontchartrain or in the milder climates of Vermont or Paris. At a distance January descried the gaudy red trim of the *Illinois'* pilot house. A moment later he identified the other musicians who'd been hired to play at the wedding, clustered on the stern-deck with their instrument-cases: Jacques Bichet with his flute and his white-haired old uncle with his bass fiddle, enormous Cochon Gardinier and dandified Philippe duCoudreau. With them was Rose, shading her eyes as she scanned the levee for sight of January.

And at the sight of her, his heart lifted.

Slender, gawky, scholarly, with her spectacles flashing in the sun and her close-wrapped white tignon and plain pink dress the antithesis of the gaudy market-women moving around her, the sight of her still moved the bones of his body with delight.

'I'm sure we'll have the whole family behind us,' sighed Hannibal, as he followed January down the steps of the levee, and they threaded their way through the piles of boxes, makeshift pens of hogs, the groups of stevedores and deckhands. 'But I'll bet you ten cents that at least one member

32

of the family complains because stopping the wedding will cancel the wedding-breakfast.'

'No takers,' said January, with a grin. Then he sobered, and said quietly, 'But telling him the truth about her will break the old man's heart.'

'Yes.' Uncle Veryl folded white, long-fingered hands around one bony knee. 'Yes, Ellie – Madamoiselle Trask – told me of her . . . her terrible past.'

January, Hannibal, and Rose exchanged a startled glance. Outside, in the thickening twilight, the plantation bell clanged in the quarters, calling the work-gangs in from the fields. From the top of the levee, as he and the other musicians had disembarked from the *Illinois*, January had seen one field downstream being dug up and re-planted, back-breaking work. The upstream fields were being rattooned – a second or third crop grown from a planting a year or two ago – and were, as usual for this time of year, shoulder-deep in weeds that had to be patiently chopped and cleared by the 'second gang' of youngsters, older men, and those women who weren't in the final months of pregnancy.

Cold Bayou – named for its original owner, a man named Alexandre Froide – for all its isolation and small size, still paid its share of the family expenses.

The footsteps of the servants, who Madame Viellard had brought from town, creaked in the parlor and the pantry of the 'big house', and in the smaller chamber next door which had been assigned to Henri Viellard: making beds with linen also brought from town, laying down fresh straw matting over bleached, scrubbed plank floors. Like most French and Spanish Creole plantations, Cold Bayou had been strictly a place of business, one of a score of plantations in Alexandre Froide's original French landgrant. The 'big house' was little more than a field-office, simply furnished and inhabited by its owners for barely a fortnight out of the year. For families like the St-Chinians and Viellards, one's 'home' was the townhouse in New Orleans. To hold a family wedding at so obscure a place was considered profoundly eccentric, and entailed horrendous efforts at cleaning, fixing, and providing sleeping-quarters for far more guests than it could easily hold.

Cautiously, Rose asked, 'What did she tell you, sir?'

'That her father was a brute, who forced her to work in a low tavern. That she had been . . . dishonored . . . against her will.' The old man's dark eyes travelled gravely from Hannibal's face – it was Hannibal who had told the sorry tale – to that of Rose, and then to January's. 'Do you honestly believe that I, or any gentleman, would hold such things against an innocent girl?'

Hannibal drew breath – probably, January guessed, to take issue with the adjective – but said nothing. The set of Uncle Veryl's mouth – stubborn, angry, struggling with emotional pain – was the only answer he'd give to any further argument. *I love her and I believe her story over anything you will say.*

And why not? January recalled the three sluts

34

in the doorway at Kate the Gouger's bathhouse that afternoon, the dead man in the gutter. The stink of the Swamp. To the marrow of his bones, he knew that no girl raised in such a place had the choice to be anything but a whore. In the Swamp, *choice* was not even a word.

Of course she'd use any wits or wiles she possessed, to secure herself a wealthy protector. Including, if necessary, targeting the most vulnerable prospect in advance and telling him whatever pitiful tale she thought he'd fall for. Before the Blue Ribbon balls, where the *librée* girls sought protectors of their own, he'd heard plaçée mothers coach their daughters in much the same techniques.

What to say. How to present themselves as brave but well-bred heroines in need of a strong man's rescue.

'You're probably going to ask me,' continued Uncle Veryl, 'why I don't simply take the girl as my – er – *pallaca.*' He glanced apologetically at Rose, covering the word *mistress* with a veneer of Latin which he knew Rose knew perfectly well. 'I won't do that,' he went on, with a sort of humble dignity. 'I won't further debase a girl who has been debased sufficiently in her life. I seek to raise her up. "Wedded love, mysterious law", as Milton says – what God declares pure . . . I want to show our love to the world.'

There was silence, in which voices echoed from the house's front gallery, outside the long French windows of the old man's bedroom: 'Well, where do you propose to put her?' demanded a woman

35

whose crystal-pure French identified her, to January's ear, as Madame Sidonie Janvier, the mother of his own mother's late 'protector'.

The trumpeting voice of Madame Aurelié Viellard retorted, 'The little slut can sleep in the quarters for all I care.'

Veryl's sparse white brows pinched down over his nose. 'I haven't spoken to anyone,' he said, 'of what my precious bird has told me. I hope that I may count on your silence as well?'

Hannibal bowed at once and said, 'Of course.'

'M'sieu,' spoke up Rose. 'Please bear in mind that M'sieu Sefton may not be the only man here who has encountered Mamzelle Trask in her former life.'

Uncle Veryl's frown deepened at this colossal understatement. While crossing from the former plantation weaving house in which guests of color were being put up – crammed now to the rafters with the musicians, January's mother Livia (and her maid), Minou and her daughter Charmian (and Minou's maid and Charmian's nurse), plus the mistresses of Henri Viellard's brother-in-law M'sieu Miragouin, of the Viellard family lawyer and more yet to come – January had mentally tallied the number of white male guests likely to have encountered Mamzelle Trask in the High Water Tavern in Natchez. Even had they not been entertained – in one fashion or another – by the bride, they would almost certainly have heard her name.

'It's one reason,' went on the old man, 'that I wanted a small wedding, here.'

By French Creole standards, some thirty white

guests and almost that many 'crocodile eggs' – as the French Creoles described those 'from the other side of the family' – did constitute a small wedding, and January winced to think of the snubs the bride would have received in town. Even among the plaçeés, and the free artisans of color, she would not have been accepted. He knew full well that like his own mother, the Aubin and St-Chinian ladies of color had come only because of the prestige of being considered 'one of the family' and not because any of them would have so much as admitted Ellie Trask to her house.

'I beg you not to think,' he lied tactfully, 'that we hold Mamzelle Trask's past against her. But we are concerned for you, sir. M'sieu Singletary tells me that you've known the young lady for just under ten weeks . . .'

'Would it not be better to wait,' took up Rose, who as a former employee of St-Chinian's had a certain degree of license, 'and perhaps learn a little more of her antecedents—' *And her possible present connections*, added January mentally – 'before committing any irrevocable step—'

'My dearest Rose.' Veryl stood, and stepping across the little room – even the chief bedroom on the men's side of the plantation house was barely ten feet wide – and took her hands. 'To do so would be to put weapons in the hands of my foes: *Acerrima proximorun odia* . . . Why do you think my sister has brought along her lawyer? And that dreadful cousin of hers has hers in tow? The only thing to do was to present them with a

37

fait accompli: to steal a march, in the words of the immortal Xenophon.'

He looked gravely into Rose's face, and tightened his grip reassuringly on her hands. 'I know my Ellie. I feel as if we have known each other since . . . since our childhoods.'

January could just hear his mother pointing out that Uncle Veryl's childhood had taken place several decades before Mamzelle Trask's.

'I thank you for your concern,' continued the old man, and smiled. 'But what is love without trust?'

Four

'I was afraid he'd say that.' Chloë Viellard, straight as a little soldier in her pale severe frock, frowned in the direction of the building that January had heard referred to as the Casita. That slightly ramshackle dower-house stood a hundred yards inland from the big house, surrounded by a shaggy copse of pecan trees, and about twice that from the old plantation weaving house on whose gallery January had found the younger Madame Viellard, sitting arm-in-arm with her husband's plaçeé Minou.

Torches and lanterns moved around the Casita in the darkness, as the elder Madame Viellard's house servants cleaned it, swept it, and carried bedding along the shell-path through the vegetable garden to install in its four airy rooms.

Evidently, January guessed, wiser councils had

38

prevailed over Madame Aurelié's wish that Ellie Trask be put up in the slave quarters.

He could well imagine the comments being exchanged by the Viellard servants as they prepared that neglected dwelling for immediate occupation, at half an hour's notice, in the dark.

'But he's right.' Dominique turned on the rough bench at the end of the gallery, and frowned in protest. 'Loving someone means trusting them.'

'Does it?' Candlelight from within the long weaving house glinted on the round lenses of Chloë's spectacles as she raised colorless brows. 'Given what I've seen of love, I must say that's an extremely unwise attitude to adopt. I am not, however, certain that it's true.'

'It should be.'

'And I'm sure it is,' put in Hannibal, 'depending on the limitations one puts upon the definition of "trust". *Initium sapientiae verbis definitionem*, as the philosophers say. I love my beautiful Rose—' he gallantly kissed Rose's hand – 'yet were I to desire a soufflé for my dinner, I'm not sure that I could trust her . . .'

Rose yanked her hand free in mock indignation – she was notoriously maladroit in the kitchen – and Minou admonished gravely, 'You know what I mean.'

'I know what you mean, *bellissima*.' The fiddler bowed to her again, and to the two ladies – bronze and ivory – on the bench between the smouldering cressets of tobacco and lemongrass. 'In the circumstances, I should say that the odds are good that Uncle Veryl's wholehearted trust in Miss Trask might well be . . . unwise.'

'It is said,' remarked Chloë, 'that even the gods find it impossible to love and be wise. The question is, what can we do?' Her wide blue gaze, cold as pale aquamarine, went from Hannibal to January, from Rose to Dominique.

The old weaving house, now pressed into service as a guest house, dated from the earliest days of Cold Bayou plantation, older than either the Casita or the big house itself. A long building perched on six-foot brick piers, it had for years been given over to storage: barrels of nails, bales of moss harvested from the cypress marshes that stretched away behind the cultivated sugar fields, bolts of cheap cloth for the garments of the slaves. At some point it had been divided into five small chambers, and through the shut jalousies January could hear acrimonious voices as the various members of the family 'from the shady side of the street' strove to establish their rights to sleeping-places for the night.

'I quite understand your position in the family,' came the light, precise voice of Sylvestre St-Chinian – a small planter from Avoyelles Parish on the Red River and the son of old Granpere Aimé by his lifelong plaçeé Andromache Courtois. 'But the fact remains that your father is only Uncle Gilbert's brother-in-law, and M'am Laetitia is Uncle Veryl's sister . . .'

'So what am I to do, then?' wailed a woman's operatic contralto. 'Take my poor baby boy and sleep in the quarters? Or up in the loft with the servants and the musicians?' The tone could just as easily have been applied to cockroaches and spiders – of which the loft, January had already

40

discovered, had an ample population. A moment's mental calculation allowed January to place her as Solange Aubin, the half-sister of one of the removed cousins who as he recalled was seeking to marry one of the Viellard sisters. 'You'd like that, wouldn't you?' Solange added spitefully. 'I know your side of the family always hated my father . . .'

'No surprise,' chipped in the dark, sweet Virginia drawl of Mamzelle Ellie's maid. 'Everythin' I ever saw of him, your father was a hateful man.'

'You jumped-up little tart—'

'Ladies!' pleaded Sylvestre, 'Ladies—!'

Glad for the moment that he was outside and not in, mosquitoes notwithstanding, January turned back to Madame Chloë. 'Madame, if I may be permitted to say so, I don't think there's much you – or anyone – can do. M'sieu St-Chinian is well and truly of age.'

'And if *I* may be permitted to say so,' added Hannibal diffidently, 'is it really our business if he wants to commit an act which will almost certainly make him miserable?'

'I'm very much afraid,' returned the girl in her sharp, silvery voice, 'that it is. Americans have been trying for years to introduce a bill in the State legislature to change the constitution so that family lands can be more easily divided, so that they can purchase land in the old French and Spanish landgrants without the entire families of the original grantees having to consent. This girl's marriage to my uncle – since it's his first – will give her equal voice in the disposal of the St-Chinian lands. Due to

41

Uncle César disinheriting both his children, that leaves only the three of them – Uncle Veryl, Madame Aurelié, and now – or tomorrow, anyway – Madame Ellie St-Chinian – with rights over a substantial percentage of the St-Chinian lands. Since we can assume Veryl's going to vote as Ellie tells him to . . .'

Hannibal said, 'Ah.'

'And, I might add,' the young woman went on, 'in the event of Veryl's death, two-thirds of the rights to his share of the lands will pass to her even if he makes no will . . . And I must say I would feel a great deal better were I sure that the girl is working only for herself, and not for members of her family.'

'But she has no family,' protested the soft-hearted Minou.

'Oh, *please*, darling!'

The fiddler thought about that one. He said again, 'Ah,' in a different tone.

'I should say our best course of action,' said January, 'is to convince M'sieu St-Chinian to postpone the wedding, if we can. At least until we can learn something of Mamzelle Ellie's family and background. Perhaps if you added your voice to ours? I'll be seeing M'sieu Singletary as soon as he's settled in his room—'

'I'll see if I can convince him to talk to Uncle Veryl as well.' Chloë half-rose from the bench. 'I've known M'sieu Singletary since I was eleven – well, we corresponded, anyway, which is more than either of my parents ever bothered to do while I was at school in the convent. For a man who's spent the whole of his life with his head

42

in Newton's *Principia*, he does have flashes of common sense—'

'And I would suggest,' added Rose, who'd been listening with one ear to the escalating uproar in the weaving house, 'that one of us – you or I, Minou – see what we can learn from . . . Valla, is it? Madamoiselle Ellie's maid?'

'I think that had probably better be you, Rose,' said January.

He was thinking only in terms of the fine gradations of social standing – maidservants often found the plaçeés intimidating – but his sister rolled her beautiful eyes and exclaimed, '*Honestly*, P'tit, I don't think I *could* stand to hold two minutes' talk with that *pichouette*! Please don't think I'm haughty, because I'm not, I'm honestly not . . . But that girl Valla thinks the sun rises and sets on her because she's nearly white – musterfino, she says, though anybody can see . . . Well. And when all's said the *only* reason Uncle Veryl gave her to Mamzelle Ellie is because Valla was the *only* girl on this place who knows how to iron clothing and fix hair – she was Madame Molina's housemaid, you know – the overseer's wife, though the way Madame Molina's hair looked this evening at the landing I'm guessing she's not much of a judge! But Valla seems to think it was because she was *so* special and *so* genteel—'

Movement in the twilight behind them – January glanced along the gallery as a woman mounted the steps. He knew her by sight from the Blue Ribbon Balls in town: Isabelle Valverde, whose protector was the husband of the eldest of Henri

43

Viellard's four sisters. The husband – Florentin Miragouin – was some twenty years older than Euphémie Viellard, and the plaçeé Isabelle, a handsome woman in her mid-thirties, whose present stoutness detracted little from what must have been dazzling beauty in her youth. Behind her trailed a maid burdened with luggage, and a girl of ten or so, carefully dressed in white linen with green ribbons in her curly brown hair. Her daughter, January guessed, who by her grown-up dress and graceful deportment was undoubtedly being trained to be a plaçeé in her turn.

When Isabelle opened the French door into one of the weaving house chambers, January saw within the maid Valla – fair-complexioned as a Spaniard, delicate-featured and blue-eyed, and clothed in a dress of yellow-striped muslin which had clearly been cut and fitted for her rather than handed on from someone else. His first wife had been a dressmaker, and the significance of the new garment wasn't lost on him: *Is Mamzelle Ellie so grateful at having a maid of her own that she has a dress that fine made for her? Or is she already a confidante?*

The gold cross at her throat and the gold bracelet on her wrist looked genuine as well.

'Is it true that Henri's maman is suing Uncle Veryl to have that girl returned to the overseer here?' asked Minou. 'As property of the family, of course, he should have asked permission, but *really*, she can't be *that* valuable even if she *was* a lady's maid back in Virginia or Carolina or wherever it is she comes from.'

Looking at Valla's beautiful, discontented face,

44

January reflected that if Madame Molina got her maidservant back – and overseers on small plantations like Cold Bayou rarely had more than one house-servant to help with all their cleaning, cooking, and laundry – she'd find the victory more trouble than it was worth. Those sharply intelligent eyes betokened the ability to cause a great deal of trouble for anyone who took her away from the more comfortable duties of looking after one pretty and generous girl in a wealthy house.

It might, of course, he thought, be that the one who wanted her back at Cold Bayou was the overseer himself – a stout, powerful man who had been among those who'd met them at the landing, and whose tawny complexion and Nubian nose spoke of a mother or grandmother who had been a plaçeé herself.

'I suppose Mamzelle will go to the Casita the minute her own room there is in order.' Rose's soft voice drew his attention back to the group at the end of the gallery. 'I'll walk over tonight and ask if she has everything she needs. Minou, thank you beyond what I can say, for offering me shelter in your room for the night—'

The Casita, built as the result of some long-ago feud between lesser branches of the family who twenty years previously had been dividing the overseeing tasks between them, was rickety, but its four rooms were given over wholly to the bride and her maid. On the other hand, chambers in the old weaving house were at a premium.

'Of *course*, darling!' Minou cried. 'It's absolutely *barbaric* that they have simply *noplace* to put people, because they have to know that everybody *always* brings extra people to these affairs! They can't seriously expect you to sleep in the loft with the musicians, although they're perfectly sweet people and of course that's where they've put Benjamin . . . For one thing, the place is *festooned* with cobwebs and hasn't been swept in *decades*! And Aunt Laetitia has just been telling me – Laetitia St-Chinian, you know, old Grandpere Aimé's youngest daughter – Aunt Laetitia has been telling me that she's heard that Aristide DuPage – the Janvier family lawyer – is coming down on the next boat, the *Evelyn B*, tonight, bringing *his* plaçeé – that would be Nanette Picard, I think, a *horrid* woman who laughs like a donkey! – and Leonard Bossuet, who's been courting Henri's sister Sophie although not very enthusiastically since all this uproar about Uncle Veryl's marriage started, and if he brings Constance Trepagnier with him – you know he bought her a house and settled an annuity of *eight hundred dollars* on her just last year? His mother is grass-biting furious over it . . .'

Through the open door January could also see his mother, sitting close to the candles and working at embroidery, something she only did in company – she had her maid do the boring parts when no one was around. Now he saw her sit up, her eyes blazing. 'And what makes you think *you* have the right to a room of your own?' she demanded in a voice that could have razored flesh from bone.

January muttered, 'Oh, Lord . . .'

'What right?' retorted Isabelle Valverde. 'I suppose, as a member of the family . . .'

'Florentin Miragouin's *cocotte*?' The Widow Levesque's eyebrows shot up, as if she'd been confronted by a savage in warpaint claiming a place at a diplomatic dinner. 'His – what are you? His third in five years—'

'M'sieu Miragouin,' Isabelle's voice was deadly, 'has done me the honor to keep company with me for five years now—'

'Oh, an *eternity*! He's slowing down,' Livia added judiciously. 'I scarcely think that qualifies you to displace someone who has been a member of the family for nearly forty.'

'The Janviers,' returned Isabelle coldly, 'are scarcely *family*—'

'No more than the Miragouins—'

'And if they were I doubt they'd boast of the connection. What'll you do, Madame Levesque? Get your voodoo daughter to put a cross on me?'

Livia Levesque was on her feet now and tossed her embroidery aside, and January stepped through the door just as the silver-haired Sylvestre came up beside Isabelle, who looked as if she were getting ready to defend her right to a room with her fingernails. 'Now, Maman,' said January, 'we all have to put up with inconveniences—'

'*Inconveniences*?' His mother turned upon him like an affronted queen. 'Do you call having our rightful place pilfered out from under us by a woman who's been through six different "protectors", if you can call them that—'

January had the impression that, though Isabelle's

47

face remained frozen, beneath her beautifully-wrapped gold-and-russet tignon every hair of her head stood on end with rage.

'I'm sure Solange would be happy to share—' began Sylvestre placatingly, and Solange Aubin recoiled.

'That fat *harpy* and her wretched daughter in the same room with my poor little Stanislas?' Solange clutched her son to her, a sturdy four-year-old whose silky curls hung in lovelocks down to his wide collar, and glared daggers at Isabelle's daughter. 'The girl's been scratching since she came into this room . . .'

Isabelle swung with an inarticulate cry of fury upon the younger woman and both January and Sylvestre stepped in to head her off.

'I'm sure something can be worked out,' said January, a sentence which had served him often in good stead at meetings of the Faubourg Tremé Free Colored Militia and Burial Society, but the affronted Isabelle ignored him as if he were a roach on the wall.

'Fine words,' she jeered, with a haughty stare at Livia, 'from a woman who was Simon Fourchet's cane-hand!' She swept from the room, across the gallery, past her over-laden maid and down the steps, her daughter trotting meekly at her heels. Presumably, reflected January, on her way to take the matter up with Michie Florentin Miragouin, who undoubtedly had troubles of his own.

'And I suspect,' he added with a sigh, as he descended the fifteen plank steps to ground level a few minutes later and held out a hand to steady Madame Chloë over the uneven path, 'you're

48

going to find the same kind of argument going on at the big house, if I may be so bold as to make a guess.' He frowned at the dark bulk of the building, counting windows, sulfurous with candlelight in the blackness. 'I wonder if we shouldn't send Hannibal after her,' he added after a moment's thought. 'He could probably talk her into a better frame of mind.'

'Hannibal could probably have talked Medea into a better frame of mind,' agreed the tiny woman thoughtfully. 'And thereby reduced Euripides' play from a tragedy to a drawing-room farce. But I wouldn't advise him going after Isabelle Valverde: Florentin Miragouin is rather given to calling people out over trifles. More to build up a reputation as a swordsman than because he really cares who dallies with Isabelle, or with any of his sisters, I think. I heard him say – he came down on the same boat with Henri and myself – that his mother and sisters were talking of coming for the wedding tomorrow. Heaven only knows where my mother-in-law is going to put them.'

Looking around him at the dense, threatening line of the cipriére, the dark isolation of the cane-fields and the dim smudges of the few lights in the big house, January thought again of what the wedding would have been like had it taken place, like most big French Creole weddings, in town, during the Carnival season that followed the sugar harvest. Not only would it have featured the cruel social ostracism of the bride, but a constant uproar of admonitions from cousins, nephews, connections and the connections of connections – not

to speak of harangues by those families –
like the Aubins – whose sons had been courting
the three unmarried Viellard girls and now stood
to lose a substantial portion of their prospective
doweries.

It did not do to speculate aloud on any of this,
however, so he followed Chloë Viellard across
the kitchen yard towards the house in thoughtful
silence.

Rose, with very real heroism, had volunteered
to remain at the weaving house with Dominique
and work at smoothing down her mother-in-law's
bristling feathers, while January went with Chloë
to confer with Singletary. Hannibal remained
behind as well, partly because he was being
lodged in the building's attic with the other musicians and partly because January's mother had a
soft spot in her heart for the fiddler. Most women
did.

As January had feared, acrimonious voices
could be heard before he and his companion were
halfway to the big house, and against the needles
of ruddy light that leaked through the jalousies,
dark forms moved like agitated ghosts. There
were, he knew, in addition to the four official
'bedchambers' in the big house itself, three more
rooms that could be pressed into service as such,
plus three rooms in each of the wings that
extended from the back of the house, which in
the usual Caribbean fashion formed a long U
which funnelled the river breeze. Counting up
Henri's sisters and mother, Florentin Miragouin
and his ten-year-old son, old Basile Aubin –
Chloë's uncle through the Duquilles (*And thank*

God they're *hermits that never go anywhere!*)
– and his son Evard, who had been somewhat
provisionally courting Charlotte, the youngest of
the Viellard girls, the situation didn't look
promising.

And that wasn't even counting the white
'friends of the family': Madame Aurelié's dear
friend and twice-removed cousin old Madame
Janvier, Selwyn Singletary, and at least two
family lawyers . . .

And the situation in the attics, where everybody's valets and maids would be dossing down
on pallets among trunks in the trapped, baking
heat, must be nightmarish.

'Ah been in big houses in England, think on,
an' in France an' Belgium too, where they'd put
t'menservants up one side o' t'house an' t'lasses
in t'other,' remarked Singletary, shaking his head
as January and Chloë climbed the high steps of
the gallery outside his room in the upstream wing.
''Tis t'first I been where they divvies up t'guests
as well. Makes a man think t'Frenchies are no
gentlemen.'

Across the yard, in the other wing, candles
flitted along the covered gallery that fronted the
rooms given to Henri's various sisters and to old
Sidonie Janvier. Madame Janvier's pug Thisbe
barked excitedly, and elsewhere a shrill voice
lifted in a protesting wail, 'But what are we going
to *do*? You saw how Etienne's mama looked
through me yesterday, as if I weren't *there*! I just
know she's going to call off our betrothal!'

The old man frowned at this, though January
wasn't surprised. Few provident parents would

51

ally their son's fortunes with a clan whose inner councils were about to be invaded by an American who had no idea how things were properly done. His frown deepened when they went into his room, and Chloë broached the subject of urging Veryl to postpone the wedding. 'We thrashed this a mickle times afore, nor like. Why you can't leave t' poor chap alone . . .'

'The problem is not that we mistrust the girl.' Chloë brought out this lie with the earnest innocence acquired by spending far too much time dealing with high French Creole society. 'But the fact is that as Veryl's *first* wife, she would be entitled, on his death, to complete control of his interest in the St-Chinian family assets – and thus in a position to put considerable pressure on Aurelié and myself to sell to a third party.'

'Ah know, ah know! But . . .'

'It may indicate an unladylike attitude of suspicion on my part,' she continued, 'but personally, I'd like to have time to be certain that Madamoiselle Ellie is really as isolated as she appears. To know there's no father or uncle or brother who might think she's more useful to him as Veryl's widow, than as Veryl's wife.'

Singletary cogitated on this for a time. 'Ah see where you're drivin', think on,' he agreed at length, as January read his pulse, and gently tapped his joints. 'But t'will stir a rare puther, callin' a halt now, wi' parson on his way an' t' garlands all goin' up. Veryl, he's had it to here—' he touched his sparse white eyebrows – 'wi' folk pullin' an' clackin' at him. 'Tis why he come here to wed t'lass in t'first place.'

He stepped to the French door of his little chamber, and looked down the gallery toward the main house. Where the back gallery of the larger building joined the wing, January could just make out two forms sitting on a bench. In the dense shadow the blur of an old man's long white hair was just discernable. Less visible still, the murky glow of a couple of mosquito-smudges caught the woman's blonde curls and the perfect oval of her face.

'He been reet good to me,' said the Yorkshireman in a softer voice. 'Takin' me in when I was that poorly, an' seein' to it I had you t' look to me, Mr J. Last thing he needs is me of all people tellin' him to put t'lass aside, same as all t'others. An' her so sweet an' pretty. She'd ne'er do him a wrong.'

'I'm sure she wouldn't.' Chloë handed the old man his shabby red silk waistcoat, and held it for him like a valet as he slipped his arms through the holes. 'But in truth, the last thing he needs is a wife he deeply loves either betraying him with a lover – if she's been put up to this by some family we don't know about – or, God forbid, triggering his murder. There are monstrous people in the world, M'sieu. You know this.'

He was silent for a time. Remembering – January guessed – the innocent-looking young woman who'd drugged him and committed him to a madhouse for months to keep him out of the way of her own schemes.

And who had poisoned him there.

'Ah know't,' sighed the old man at last. 'Ah, lassie.' He put a thin arm around Chloë's shoulders.

'Best we wait til they got yon dower-house redded, an' Miss Trask gone over to't.' He nodded at the ant-like stream of grumbling servants who, through the entire conversation, had been coming and going along the crushed shell path that led back from the yard through the darkness toward the Casita's candle-lit bulk. 'I'll not tell Veryl we think t'girl's lyin', not whilst she's standin' there—'

'Of course not.'

'Will ye come let me know, Mr J?' Singletary turned to him, and waved aside the coat January held out to him. 'Shippin' down-river, an' comin' here, has wore me out, an' that's a fact. I think I'd be t' better for lyin' down a bit—'

'I was just going to suggest that, sir.' Though the candle-gleam in the room behind them warmed the old man's face somewhat, January still thought he looked haggard. A breath of clammy wind, stirring in from the Gulf, shook the cypresses around the house and made the curtains belly eerily. Rain coming, he guessed. Rose, brought up in the Barataria further south, had said earlier that it spoke of storms at sea. 'I'm sorry this has to be done tonight,' he added quietly. 'But I'm afraid I agree with Madame Chloë. I'm very fond of Michie Veryl, and I should hate to see him hurt. I'll let you know, as soon as I see them go over.'

As he descended the steps he had to stand aside to let the overseer Molina pass, like an overgrown, sullen boar in his rough coat of mustard-colored tweed. He was trailed by four slaves, in the coarse rags of field hands, burdened with tubs of water from the cistern. 'Get on there, you lazy niggers, we ain't got all the night!'

The men had undoubtedly been in the cane-fields since sun-up. One of them had a blotted line of blood soaking through the back of his shirt.

The first spatters of rain flecked January's cheek. Candle-flame crept and crawled from window to window of the Casita in the darkness, like the last glowing ember-worms in a near-dead hearth, and in the women's wing a girl's voice lifted again, 'If he marries that *puta*, *nobody* is going to marry any of us!'

Loudly enough, January guessed, for the couple sitting in the dark of the gallery nearby to hear.

And won't that *improve Veryl's readiness to postpone the wedding* . . .

Far-off thunder rumbled in the tarry darkness.

It would be, he reflected, a very long night.

Five

The conflict at the weaving house had calmed down by the time January climbed its steps again. In only one room were candles still burning, and by the pallets set along the walls he guessed that this had been turned into a sort of dormitory for a number of the plaçeés. Around a small table near the open French doors sat January's mother, Hannibal, old Laetitia St-Chinian, and Solange Aubin, playing whist. Isabelle Valverde had returned and was sitting on one of the pallets with a slender, handsome young woman whom January guessed to be Nicolette Charpentier, the mistress of the Viellard family lawyer, complaining – rather loudly – about the thieving ways of their maids and playing écarté.

The maidservant Valla stood just inside the doorway, a willow basket on her hip and an expression of bitter annoyance on her face.

'I'm so sorry, dear,' said Dominique, making tea over a little chafing-dish that January guessed she'd brought in her luggage. Judging by the paper sack near the hearth beside her, she'd brought the charcoal for this operation as well. 'Ordinarily, of course my dear, Bergette would be *delighted* to help you, but poor Charmian is being a complete little wretch tonight, and it's more than poor silly Musette – the nurse, you know – is able to cope with.'

'And I hope you don't think I'm going to lend you Mirelle,' put in Solange Aubin, with a malicious glance at the infuriated maid. 'Quite apart from the fact that others besides your mistress need hot water and assistance in brushing their clothes and hair, like dear little Charmian, my precious Stanislas can not get to sleep unless Mirelle is with him . . . And his physician said that sleep is absolutely vital to one of his delicate constitution.'

With artful insouciance, she adjusted a fold of her purple silk tignon.

'We will of course,' added Livia sweetly, 'lend you a couple of pitchers to fetch water from the cistern.'

Valla's mouth opened to snap some reply, then at the sound of January's step behind her she swung around and thrust the basket into his hands. 'You,' she said brusquely. 'Make yourself useful. Fetch me some charcoal from the stores, and a couple of pails of water—'

She clearly took him for somebody's valet. January put the basket on his arm, and half-bowed. 'At your service, m'am.' He glanced sidelong at his mother, wryly entertained by the conflict plain on her face: the satisfaction of putting down an 'uppity' maid would of course involve admitting that she had a son who had flecks of gray in his short-cropped hair, but whose ebony complexion announced that at some point in her life she'd had sexual congress with an African-born field hand.

But it was Dominique who said, 'Valla, dearest, I don't think you've met *my brother* Benjamin? P'tit—' this to January – 'you can go sleep up in the attic with the musicians if you want to, but you'd be perfectly welcome in the next room with Sylvestre and his sons, you know.'

Livia Levesque sorted her cards with the air of one who has no connection whatsoever with the conversation around her, but Solange and Isabelle hid snickers at Valla's startled chagrin. The maid-servant snatched the basket back, but made no effort to apologize to January for mistaking him for a servant. Like many of the fair-complexioned plaçeés, she seemed to assume that anyone that much darker than herself *should* have been a slave.

Another step sounded on the gallery, and as

57

January looked behind him to see who it was – a man's step, he thought it might be Sylvestre – Valla brushed past him and snapped, 'Luc, you take that water over to the Casita for Madamoiselle Ellie.' Her French was good, but it was white folks' French, not the half-African patois of the Louisiana slaves. 'Then I want you to get charcoal from the stores and start up a fire in the pantry, and look sharp about it.'

The voice from the darkness that responded, 'Yes, Valla,' was young, but there was a note of exhaustion in it. January recalled Michie Molina's harsh commands, and the spots of blood on the back of one of the water-bearers.

'That water was brought for *us*, girl,' cut in Livia angrily. 'As members of the family we are entitled to *some* consideration,' and January politely retrieved the basket from Valla's arm, forestalling her next remark.

'No reason I can't fetch your mistress' charcoal for you, Madamoiselle,' he said to her, in his best English, furthering her discomfiture (and causing his mother to smile smugly). He removed his coat, laid it over the back of the kitchen-chair in which his mother sat, and stepped out into the darkness of the gallery once more.

The tall bulk of the water-carrier moved aside from him – nearly his own great height, and smelling of the sweat and earth of the cane-field – and that soft youthful voice murmured, 'Thank you, Michie. But you don't gotta—'

'Don't be silly,' retorted January, reverting to cane-patch French. 'Quicker we gets that place fixed up the quicker everybody can get to bed.

Who do I ask about the charcoal? Where's it kept?'

'M'am Molina got the sto'house keys. You take the path toward the landin' an Michie Molina's house there on your left.'

It never hurt, January had long ago learned, to establish friendly relations with the servants, though in Valla's case it was clear that Dominique was right: the girl definitely shared the common plaçeé attitude that her fair complexion put her well above those as dark as himself and Luc.

Which would have put an extra layer of tension, he guessed, on her dealings with the overseer and his wife. Molina was a little darker than she, though he could still have passed himself off as a Spaniard if it hadn't been for his features. Madame Molina, still arrayed – when he reached the overseer's cottage – in what was obviously her Sunday-best puce silk frock, was definitely of African parentage, though in defiance of custom she wore her thick, slightly frizzy honey-blonde hair like a white woman's rather than in a tignon. The daughter or granddaughter of a plaçeé, January guessed, either here or on Sainte-Domingue before the Rebellion, and not pretty enough to aspire to plaçage herself. Despite African features her eyes, by the light of her kitchen lamp, were bright blue.

She clicked her tongue that a guest of the family should undertake so menial a chore as fetching charcoal. 'And for such a one!' She shook her head as she led him to the storehouses behind the plain little dwelling, mounted like everything else in Plaquemines Parish on six-foot brick piers.

59

'Who knows what scandal that *Irlandaise* is going to bring to the family, eh?'

In the shadows among the piers beneath the storehouse, January made out a large number of hogsheads, the huge barrels in which sugar was taken to market. The first two rows of these were filled with what appeared to be branches of oak and cypress. Only when Madame Molina's lantern-light played across them did January see that the boughs were twined with ribbon, and punctuated with over-large satin bows.

'Coming down here all in a clap,' Madame went on, leading the way across the yard, 'and holding a wedding – and such a wedding, my God! As well none of the family are here . . .'

By the exasperation in her voice January guessed that either Guillaume Molina or his wife was also 'one of the family'. The position of overseer was a not uncommon way of providing for the sons of cousins or uncles or brothers, if they weren't closely enough related – like old Sylvestre – for land to be turned over to them outright. As overseer of Cold Bayou plantation, Molina would have a position for life, if he proved efficient and trustworthy. Sugar was a hellishly hard crop, and it took a hard man to control those forced to labor in the fields.

'We have had no time to get ready for them, no time to build up proper supplies or send for what's required from town! Do you know how many eggs alone are needed for a decent wedding-cake?'

'I had never thought of that,' exclaimed January – mendaciously, as it happened, but he knew how people enjoy relating such details and listened with genuine interest to the little woman's outraged recital of the trials involved in putting on a wedding-feast for thirty-some guests, plus providing for their valets, maids, nursemaids. 'And that parcel of stuck-up town servants that came with M'am Aurelié – and the musicians, though if you will permit me to say so, sir, I except you from among them.'

'I assure you, we are perfectly decent folk, m'am,' January said with a bow and a smile.

Her lips stretched in a tight expression of reply, but her sapphire eyes still snapped as she climbed the plank steps of the storehouse, and unlocked its door.

'And for why?' She shook her head. 'Why to this place, eh? It's prepostrous! So far from town. We go from one year to the next here, and the family never comes near us, except maybe Michie Henri and that . . .' She bit off an opinion about Henri's bride that was clearly more authentic than tactful, and corrected herself. 'And Madame Chloë, now. And that is as we like it, M'sieu. Guillaume does a good job. So long as they get their sugar crop every year, why should they care how things are done down here?'

With a huge tin scoop she shoveled hunks of charcoal from the bin, as January held the lantern high.

'And then that senile old detritus just walks in and takes my girl from me! Just like that, without a by-your-leave! Not that she isn't stuck-up as the Devil and light-fingered, too.' She turned to lock the door behind them again. 'Well, at least

I can go to bed each night without having to weigh the coffee, if you understand me. I never could catch her at it, but I swear she was selling anything she thought I wouldn't miss. There's a trader that comes along the bayou when the moon is bright – that wicked old False River Jones, encouraging niggers to steal.'

As they came down the steps again Molina himself appeared from the direction of the Casita, still with his little work-gang of exhausted men. 'I want you to get those barrels up to the house tonight, so we can make a good start in the morning,' he rasped. Beneath the brim of his black high-crowned hat, January saw the dark glint of his eyes, soulless as beads, and the skirt of his mustard-colored coat half-covered the whip that hung coiled from his belt. When January glanced at Madame's face, he saw there a tight expression, hatred deeper than pilfered coffee or petty theft.

But she only whispered, 'Well,' and turned her eyes aside. Then she called out, 'Antoine!' and a slim young man emerged from the cottage, and jogged across to the storehouse steps. 'You take this charcoal up to the Casita—'

'It ain't that heavy,' said January, dividing the load with the young slave. 'I been kicking my heels on that steamboat all afternoon. Lord, what a fuss!' he added, looking back in the direction of the house where the work-gang was rolling the barrels of greenery.

Antoine shook his head. 'All them white folks gonna be sorry if the weather turns inland.'

'You think it's fixing to?' Wind moaned sharply

around the house-eaves, and the trees that surrounded the Casita hissed like an ocean of snakes.

'That's what the old aunties say in the quarters.' By his speech – and his clothing, which was considerably less ragged than those who worked the fields – January guessed the young man was the 'house nigger' for the Molinas: the one who carried in the firewood and water, and did the heavy work. Now that Valla had gone on to bigger things, he was probably the only regular indoor servant on the place.

This suspicion was confirmed when they climbed the steps to the Casita's gallery. Madame Aurelié's kingly butler Visigoth stood in the light of several large cressets, giving orders to a small party of footmen and maids who had been brought from the Viellard townhouse in New Orleans. Every French door in the little dwelling had been thrown open and its four rooms were redolent of wet flooring and damp straw mats. The footmen, aided by a couple of very tired field hands, were just carrying in the last of the furniture as January and Antoine ascended the gallery steps, with the basket of charcoal between them. Despite the cressets, and a multitude of candles inside, the rooms were thick with shadow, in which Valla's pale dress gave her the look of a haughty ghost.

'You unpack those boxes in the pantry,' she commanded Alicia – one of Madame Aurelié's housemaids from town – and got a murderous glare in response. 'And wipe the bottles 'fore you put them on the shelves. Antoine . . .' she said, startled, as she turned and found herself face to face with the young man.

For a very long moment they stood, looking into one another's eyes. Then she turned quickly away, and said, 'Take that charcoal into the kitchen. There was no call for you to help with that, Michie Janvier,' she added, a little stiffly. 'And I'm sorry I spoke to you as I did.'

'The sooner the work is done, the sooner to bed for everyone,' he repeated, still in his most perfect English.

Visigoth's wife Hecuba emerged from the bedroom, the slave Luc trailing her with a couple of branches of candles, and Valla swung around. 'Is that the only armoire there is in this place?' She looked about her as if she expected to find an unnoticed wardrobe or two in the parlor where they stood. 'I've seen bigger bathtubs! It won't hold half of Madamoiselle's things—'

'It's all we got here.' Hecuba wheeled and set her fists on her hips. 'How much clothes your Mamzelle need for a night or two, girl?'

'You think that's any affair of yours . . .' began Valla, and beside January, big Luc shook his head with a shy half-grin.

'We better clear out of here, sir. Valla been tryin' to come over Hecky all afternoon, goin' on about how they did things this way back in Virginia an' that way back in Virginia. Couple hours ago I thought they was gonna kill each other! An' for all that, 'fore Michie Molina give her to M'am Molina to help in the house, what- ever she been back in Virginia she was just a field hand here like ever'body else.'

'Was she indeed?' said January, wondering what the girl had done in her former place that had gotten her sold as a field hand rather than a maid.

A couch was brought in – simple local work with cushions that looked as if they'd once been the skirt of somebody's Sunday dress – and Valla disappeared into the dim bedchamber behind her, re-emerging a moment later with one of the most extravagant dresses January had ever seen, draped over one arm, and a frothing snowstorm of petticoats over the other. 'Well, I'm not going to have Madamoiselle's wedding-clothes crushed in that miserable little coffin!'

January was familiar from long acquaintance with Dominique with the logistics of petticoats, but even so, he was impressed at the sheer volume of those that Valla laid on the table. The wedding dress was draped across the couch, layer on layer of rose-pink silk ruffles, seven-inch festoons of lace on hem, sleeve, bosom. As he departed, he passed the other two Viellard housemaids – Lila and Reinette – in the door, grumbling and laden with wicker hampers of linen sheets: from Madame Aurelié's private store, beyond a doubt. January's mother – wise in the ways of small and isolated plantations – had brought her own, as had Minou and probably every other guest, white or colored, as well.

'That dress contains a hundred dollars worth of silk alone,' he remarked, later, to Rose, in the darkness of the weaving-house gallery. 'Not to speak of the lace.' He handed Rose's spyglass back to her.

65

The firefly lights around the Casita had at last retreated to the big house. The weaving house had settled into silence, its shut jalousies dark. Even the musicians and the servants up in the attic had gone to their pallets, all the bickering downstairs stilled as the common hand of sleep gathered the combatants in.

Tar-black clouds had covered the white half-moon. With the wind rattling around the eaves, it was as if they stood alone on the deck of a ghost-ship, driven through night toward a darkness deeper still.

'If, as Michie Singletary says, the girl was destitute when Uncle Veryl so touchingly found her in his carriage-way in July,' he went on, 'it must be he who paid for it. And the rest of her wardrobe, I daresay. I got glimpses of it as the maids hauled most of it up to the attic. She – or rather Veryl – must have spent thousands on it.'

'Do *you* think she's been sent in by family who want to lay hands on his share of the St-Chinian property?' Rose lowered the spyglass, and pushed her disarrayed spectacles back into place. 'Or that she just saw the chance of bettering her own situation, and took it?'

January was silent, weighing his words and his thoughts. 'It feels very *planned*,' he said at length. 'Completely aside from what Hannibal has told us, it's a *very* striking co-incidence that a young woman left on her own that way would cross the path of an old man that vulnerable, and that wealthy, so *promptly* after the death of one of the main controllers of the family holdings. I think there has to be someone behind her.'

'Hannibal was fairly certain Old Man Trask did die last year. He said he heard it from Mr Tavish of the minstrel-show you traveled with in June – a man who knew the river well.'

'Doesn't mean she doesn't have uncles and cousins – maybe even a husband – who plan to use her.'

'Can't be a husband,' said Rose judiciously. 'If someone is behind it, they'll know there'll be legal trouble. And she seems a very sweet girl.'

'So did Delphine Lalaurie.' January grimly named the respectable New Orleans matron who had imprisoned, tortured, and murdered slaves in the attic of her town mansion on Rue Royale. 'That's the last of them,' he added, as the lights of the cressets detached themselves from the Casita's front gallery, and made their way toward the big house. 'Late as it is, we'd best catch Uncle Veryl as soon as Mamzelle leaves him.'

'I wonder if poor Michie Singletary will walk with them back to the Casita.'

'It'll save us waking him up, poor man.'

He lit a stub of candle at the smudge-pot on the gallery rail, and she took his hand, and followed him down the steps of the weaving-house gallery, and along the rough shell-path that led in the direction of the big house.

'There's going to be real trouble if it rains tomorrow for the wedding,' she remarked, as he released her fingers to shield the candle-flame.

'There's going to be real trouble before that,' he amended wryly. 'The cane comes to within

67

yards of the trees around the Casita, and the ciprière's barely a dozen yards behind it. Every rat in the Parish has to be living in the attic.'

'I wonder if Madame Aurelié was aware of that possibility, when she assigned it as Mamzelle's residence?'

He laughed at that, the weariness of travel – the weariness of negotiating with squabbling hordes of wedding-guests – dissolving, in the joy of being with her in this blowing darkness.

After nearly four years of marriage, there was nothing that gave him greater pleasure than the sound of her voice, the grip of her hand on his sleeve in the blackness. In three weeks, the first of the students would be arriving at Rose's school. With the return of cooler weather he'd be teaching music again. *That* was what mattered. It had been a difficult and frightening summer, but the summer was over. Even if Madamoiselle Ellie murdered Uncle Veryl – though it would be grievous and terrible, of course – it didn't really touch *them*. Touch himself and Rose. Touch Professor John and Baby Xander, tucked up in bed at home with Gabriel and Zizi-Marie watching over them, hearing this same wind stream over the shingles of the roof.

Like a shard of those far-off storm-winds, Olympe's words passed through his mind, and at the same moment he stopped in his tracks.

Another tiny apple-seed of candle-flame showed near the back of the Casita.

Rose whispered, 'What . . .?' and she pressed close against him.

January shook his head, though he was well

aware that even a shout would have been drowned in the rattling sea-surge of the canes.

They were within a hundred feet of the Casita. The other candle showed up much closer to the building, coming swiftly from the concealment of the woods behind.

Candles burned in the pantry and enough light seeped out when the pantry door was briefly opened to show a cloaked figure slipping through.

He turned his head quickly, marked the retreat of the last of the servants and the swaying dots of lantern-light emerging from the long downstream wing of the big house. Ellie Trask – almost certainly accompanied by Uncle Veryl and his valet.

'If you're going to steal something,' murmured Rose, 'I suppose now's the time to do it, when everything's at sixes and sevens. Valla should be on the porch, meeting her mistress . . .'

January shivered, remembering one of the maids on Bellefleur, whom Michie Fourchet had beaten to death for pilfering coffee beans. 'Not something I'd want to do.'

'Is there anyone lives in the woods?' she asked. 'The fields don't go back more than a mile from the river, and it's all overgrown where Cold Bayou itself cuts through upstream of the house. When I was little they'd talk about escaped slaves hiding out in the woods.'

'There's not as much of that as there was,' said January. 'There may be a maroon village back there still in the swamp, but it's easier now to escape up-river, and harder now to remain unde-tected, even in the deep woods.' He had returned

69

his attention to the back gallery of the house, knowing that between the utter darkness and the threshing of the wind, the intruder could slip from the pantry door and vanish down the steps in an eye-blink. 'More likely it's someone from the house or the quarters. I'd be surprised if a trader like False River Jones didn't come down here specially, knowing there'd be a wedding.'

But no one emerged. Rose whispered at one point, 'Someone can slip out one of the windows on that side and we wouldn't see them. Should we . . .?'

'Not our business,' returned January. 'Luc – one of the men here – mentioned they've seen bears in the woods, or cougar. I'm not going to risk you meeting one – or running into a slave dealer like Captain Chamoflet, who operates in these parts – just to get a look at who's stealing Mamzelle Ellie's hairbrushes.'

They remained standing in the darkness until the lanterns from the big house mounted the tall steps of the Casita's front gallery, and saw no sign of the intruder's departure. Yet neither was there any trace of untoward excitement when the shadows of the bride and her escorts moved back and forth across the dull-gold slits of the jalousies. The light in the pantry went out ('So they're not in the pantry anymore.' 'Nonsense, Benjamin, with only a couple of candles in the room you could be sitting under the table and nobody would see you in the shadows, if you kept still.')

After a time, lanterns came back out onto the gallery, and down the steps, retreating along the shell-path to the big house.

Rose had taken out her spyglass again, and trained it on the lights. 'Uncle Veryl,' she reported. 'James. Archie. Madame Aurelié's footman Jacques-Ange. No sign of Michie Singletary.'

January took the glass from her, handed her his candle and walked a little ways – carefully – through the rough weeds and maiden-cane until he could see past the downstream wing of the big house to the windows of the upstream wing where the male guests slept. All its windows were dark.

He folded up the polished brass tube, returned it to her and took his silver watch from his pocket, held it to the candle flame. 'Eleven,' he said quietly. 'Let's go back. Tomorrow will be plenty of time to enlist Singletary's help on this, and I don't think we'd do the old man any favors by waking him for this.'

She slid her arm through his, and handed him his candle again. 'I agree. Although I'm dying to learn who that is, snooping about the Casita at this hour.'

'Not our business,' said January again. The light in the little dwelling's parlor dimmed with the snuffing of the candles there, one by one. The wind strengthened, the trees behind the weaving house hissing like the thunder of the sea. January guided Rose back along the lumpy, crooked path toward the weaving house: silent before them, all those people who weren't supposed to exist – sons and daughters by women the white men couldn't marry – the 'crocodile eggs'.

There's someone still in the Casita . . .

Is *there someone still in the Casita?*

71

Do we tell someone?

Wake them up at this hour, to admit we were spying on our betters?

When he looked back he saw a smudge of light on the planks of the gallery, thrown by the window of Madamoiselle Ellie's room. Another, on the other side of the house, shone in the little chamber where Valla would sleep.

The one went out.

Then the other.

They were mounting the steps of the weaving house when he looked back and saw, somewhere in the blackness behind them, movement – another seed of light. They were too far away, and the night too dark, for him to identify positively whether it crossed the back gallery of the Casita.

By the time he turned to Rose to get the spyglass from her again, whatever it was had disappeared into the dark.

Six

'Someone is trying to kill me . . .'

Ellie's voice was barely a whisper, and she pressed her face to Uncle Veryl's sleeve.

January, who tried to live by his confessor's dictum that God does not hold anyone accountable for their first thought in any unexpected situation, nevertheless felt a stab of guilt at thinking, *Damn it, I should have come back here last night and talked to Veryl no matter how late it was.*

In the old man's set face he saw that nothing would persuade him to postpone the wedding now.

Uncle Veryl's arms tightened comfortingly around the girl's trembling shoulders. Servants hanging great swags of ribbons and greenery on the front gallery did their best not to look like they were peeking through the French doors into the bedroom. Ellie had run all the way from the Casita in her chemise and dressing-gown, her blonde hair tumbled loose on her shoulders, and looked very fetching indeed. In the parlor next door, muffled voices whispered and babbled intently in the early-morning quiet, and January could hear even through several intervening rooms Madame Aurelié's strident voice demanding what on earth was going on.

'It's all right.' Veryl folded the shivering girl close against his narrow chest. 'I swear to you, my beloved, nothing will harm you.' His eyes went to January, and then past him as M'sieu Singletary – also in severe déshabillé – appeared behind him in the doorway. 'Do you know what happened?'

January shook his head. Knowing his patient Singletary to be an early riser, he had crossed to the big house as soon as it was full daylight: thank God for the custom that forbids the bride-groom to see the bride before the wedding. Early as it was, Missy – Madame Aurelié's town cook – had been in the kitchen behind the house, bossing the plantation cook and working in a patient frenzy to prepare pigeons and partridges, compotes and custards, not only for the thirty-some white guests but for the other 'members of the family' as well.

The quarters, too, had been in a bustle, the smoke of a pit-buried roast pig puffing white among the cabins, while the men tacked lesser garlands on everything in sight. January had seen Archie emerge from the laundry – beside the kitchen – with a fresh-ironed shirt, and had calculated there was enough time to beg a cup of coffee from Missy before going to Singletary.

Then he'd seen Ellie emerge from the Casita – white gauze dressing-gown billowing around her like a cloud of angel-wings – and run toward the big house with every appearance of terror.

He'd reached Uncle Veryl's room only seconds after she had, in time to see her throw herself into her bridegroom's arms.

Now she raised her face – white with shock and fright – and looked from Uncle Veryl to January to Singletary, her beautiful eyes pleading. 'They hate me,' she gasped. 'They don't mean to let you marry me, and oh, Mr St-Chinian, please don't leave me! I'm afraid . . .'

'What happened?' asked January.

The girl's face twisted. 'They put something horrible in my dress.'

'Who did?'

'I don't know! A *pisesog* – the Devil's marks! I locked all the doors last night and they still got in!'

'Now, lass,' soothed Singletary, 'you're not

74

believin' in hocus-pocus an' hags ridin' broomsticks across t'sky, are you? 'Tis all granny-tales—'

'It's not!' She clung tighter to Uncle Veryl's nightshirt. 'Not here. Not always. The Negroes . . .'

'What was in your dress?' January was fairly sure he knew.

'A claw.' She shuddered, and hid her face again. 'A wrinkled-up, awful little claw, sewn into the waist where I wouldn't see it. And there was dirt smeared on the inside of the skirt. It's voodoo—'

Unfortunately, January had to agree that it certainly sounded like it.

Ellie refused to go back to the Casita, but January walked up the shell-path, turning over in his mind what he had seen last night. Valla had moved the elaborate wedding dress to a table on the back gallery and was making up her mistress' bed, her beautiful mouth vexed and angry. 'Bitches,' she said, when January asked to see the dress. 'I'll bet you gold to goober-peas it was one of Mr Viellard's stuck-up sisters! Whining and crying about how the old man marrying Miss Ellie's gonna turn away every one of those worthless boys that's out to marry them for their money. I never heard such belly-aching in my life!'

'Was the Casita locked up last night?' January followed the young woman out onto the rear gallery, turned up the skirts of rose-pink silk with their festoons of Belgian lace.

The severed foot of a pigeon, tiny and pink and curled on itself like a wicked little clawed hand, had been sewed among the tight cartridge-pleating at the back of the waist.

75

'I locked it up myself, sir.' The maid's dark-blue eyes narrowed in contempt. 'Locked the doors and bolted the shutters. I knew those girls would likely be up to something.'

Even though, like Singletary, January didn't believe in hocus-pocus and witches, he still wrapped his handkerchief around his fingers before he took hold of the little gris-gris, and with a penknife gently cut the threads that held it. He told himself this was because the tiny thing may have been imbued with poison of some kind, like the wedding-robe the sorceress Medea had sent to her rival – although stitched where it was, it would have rested against not only the waist-bands of seven petticoats, but the lower part of a stoutly-laced corset as well.

The stitches were small and neat, executed in white silk thread.

This hadn't been done in a hurry.

'What time did you lock up?'

'When Miss Ellie went to bed.' Valla's lips tightened at the sight of the brownish smudges that marked the pale silk lining of the skirt. X's, crudely-drawn serpents, the elaborate crosses of Marinette of the Dry Arms. 'I don't know what time that might have been, sir. There's no clock in that house. Mr Veryl came back here with her from the big house, and it was just on eleven. I made coffee for him.'

January hoped she'd had the decency to give Archie, James, and Jacques-Ange coffee while they waited on the porch, but didn't ask.

'I sat in my room, waitin' for the men to leave so I could unlace Miss Ellie an' brush out her hair. She walked around the house with me while I locked up. Then we both went to bed.'

He followed Valla back into the house. There was a little pantry, though of course any real meals would be taken in the big house, and a stair leading from it up to the attics. To the left of the back door as he came in he noted that the shelf above the tin bathtub and tin coal-scuttle was stocked with three bottles of plum brandy and two of Hooper's Female Elixir, a compound of laudanum and sherry whose very smell – he knew from experience – was enough to put a horse into a coma.

The window that opened from the pantry into the rear gallery – and, he recalled, the window from the small back bedroom behind the stairs as well – were of the small sash type, and the back bedroom had no door out onto the gallery. The only egress from the rear of the house was the back door from the pantry.

'Did you look around the rooms before you locked up?' he asked. 'Check to see that nobody had slipped in the back while you were opening the parlor doors for Mamzelle?'

'Shit. Sir,' she added, her beautiful eyes glinting dangerously. 'Fucken . . . You mean whoever did this was hiding inside the house while we were locking up?' No fear in her voice. Just rage.

'I mean they could have been.' January climbed to the attic, up a stair so steep it bore more than a little resemblance to a ladder. Under the high pitch of the roof he could almost stand up straight, even at his height, and the space beneath the rafters was thickly cluttered with wicker clothes-hampers of the kind women stored their dresses in, dessicated now and falling apart, though everything still smelled faintly of talcum powder and orris-root as well as rat-piss. The hampers had been pushed aside to make room for three new trunks – Madamoiselle Ellie's, presumably – and four large hatboxes. 'Anyone could have slipped in through the back door while you were opening the front for Mamzelle.'

The long room was lit by four dormer windows and would have been an abyss of shadows last night. A smaller room – a servant's at one time – had been partitioned at the attic's upstream end.

You could have hid Leonidas' Three Hundred Spartans among the trunks and still had room for Macbeth's witches and Snow White and her dwarfs.

'You sleep with your door open, don't you?' he asked, following Valla down the stairs again. 'You'd have to,' he added, with a glance at the small, shut door cattercorner across the parlor from that of Ellie's spacious chamber.

Valla didn't reply immediately. Her eyes shifted: trying to read his face, January realized. Trying to determine what he wanted to hear.

He knew the expression, the hurried guessing. He'd done the same, a thousand times, in his childhood: *What can I say that the master will believe that'll spare me a beating?*

'Yes,' she said, as if she could see where this was going. Her bedroom door, if open, would have looked straight into the parlor where the wedding dress had lain. 'Of course. But I sleep heavy,' she added quickly. 'And with all that rushing around getting this place ready, after the trip down-river . . .'

She's hiding something . . .

Was it *she* who went out last night after Mamzelle was settled?

'May I?' He walked toward the narrow door to her chamber, and was aware of her intake of breath. As if she would have forbidden him to go in had she not been afraid that he'd wonder why she wouldn't let him. 'The stair to the attic goes right up over your room,' he explained, watching her face as he said it. 'Would you climb up to the attic, and then come back down again? It creaks pretty badly – I want to see how loud it is in your room.'

This wasn't entirely the truth at this point, but Valla couldn't very well do anything but obey. In truth, once January was in the small, tidy rear bedroom he could easily hear the steps groan and squeak under the maidservant's ascending – and then descending – weight. But he wasn't sitting still to listen. He was swiftly checking the wicker laundry-hamper in the armoire, and the skirt and the sleeves of the yellow-and-white-striped frock he recalled Valla had worn yesterday evening, the yellow silk flowers from her tignon all piled in a heap.

Skirt and sleeves were heavily spotted with dripped wax, as they would have been had the wearer been walking in the windy darkness last night. A badly-guttered candle-stub lay in the armoire's bottom drawer.

So she was outside.

And the intruder would have departed later, after carefully sewing that nasty little curse in Mamzelle's wedding dress.

Where was she going? To meet whom?

'To tell you the truth, sir . . .'

Valla came to the door of her bedroom even as January, with the casual air of a man who has done nothing but listen to the stairs creak, reached it.

'Mamzelle doesn't often wake in the night. She's a sound sleeper. And she keeps her door shut. Last night I was worn out with one thing and another, getting this place ready, though I'd have waked if she'd rung for me. She's got a bell, beside her bed,' she explained, nodding toward the larger door of her mistress' bedroom.

'May I see?'

Valla stepped quickly in his way. 'Why? They wouldn't have gone in there, whoever they were.'

January raised his brows. From the gallery outside came the voices of Visigoth and half a dozen other men, bearing baskets among them, pink silk ribbons fluttering in the breeze.

He recognized the young house-man Antoine among them. Observed how his eyes went to Valla; how the maid averted her face from his glance.

'Give us another minute,' she called out, as Visigoth tapped at the side of the doorway. 'Antoine, take those garlands around to the back.' Then to January, in a lower voice, she murmured, 'They wouldn't have gone into her room, sir. If she'd waked, she would have seen them – she had a night-light burning. They're trying to stop

80

the wedding. Trying to scare Mamzelle away.'
Possessiveness tinged her voice. *And why not?*
reflected January. Mamzelle was the reason she
wasn't still stuck down here on an isolated plantation cleaning chamberpots for the wife of the
man who raped her every other night. 'They
wouldn't have let her see them.'

'Hmn.' January crossed to the chair where the
white silk petticoats were piled. Moving them to
reveal – as he'd suspected – more curse-marks
and crosses, spots of blood and black wax, he
shook loose also a faint whispering patter of salt
from their folds.

'It'll be all right, once she's wed.' Valla followed
him, though she drew back a little from the salt.
'Père Eugenius will be on the *Vermillion* coming
down from New Orleans this morning, and they'll
be married, whatever those stuck-up Frenchies
can say or do. They'll have to quit pecking on
her then.'

But even as she said the words she shivered,
and glanced around the parlor, as if seeing it as
it had been last night, every window shuttered
tight, black as the abysses of Hell.

As if seeing, thought January, the glimmer of
a single candle by which someone had sewn that
nasty little clenched claw into the dress. By which
someone had drawn those neat, vindictive signs
of snakes and Xs with a finger ground in graveyard earth. By which someone could just as easily
have walked through Ellie Trask's door with a
rag soaked in paste and held it over the young
woman's nose and mouth until she quit struggling, until she quit breathing.

Leaving Valla to be handed back to Michie Molina, and the life she had known before.

'Well, I know all that curse business is just silly.' Hair dressed, cheeks rouged, clothed in a gown of blue-and-ivory print that made her look as neat and cool as a piece of Dresden china, Ellie sipped a cup of coffee in the corner of the big house's front gallery. But her soft brown eyes were haunted as they traveled from January to Veryl to Rose. 'There's no such thing, for all what Ma told me when I was little. Ma believed in it – witches and *piseogs* and leaving out milk for the pookas. But that's not what scares me, Mr J. Somebody really did get into the house last night, while I was sleeping – while Valla was sleeping. And neither of us heard a thing. And I know – well, wasn't there some old tale, that Mr St-Chinian read me, about a wicked witch in the old times who killed the girl her sweetheart was fixing to marry by soaking the wedding dress in poison? And another who did something – poisoned a needle and broke off the tip of it in the seam of a glove or something? I know they hate me.'

'Beloved, no one would—'

She reached across the little table to take Veryl's hand, and the old man gripped hers tight. 'Mr St-Chinian, I've seen how they look at me. Your sister, and old M'am Janvier. Mr Aubin and Mr Miragouin and those lawyers they have with them. Like I'm – not even a cat. Can't we leave tonight?' She turned swimming eyes back to Veryl. 'Right after the ceremony is over? Just go away, back to New Orleans, away from them all . . .'

'Of course we can, *mignonne* . . .'

'Not unless there's a steamboat bound up-river on its way past this afternoon, Mamzelle,' pointed out January, careful to keep his tone diffident. Behind them in the parlor furniture thumped and grumbled as it was moved into the bedrooms, and every chair in the house was arranged around a makeshift podium in the dining room, under a canopy of moss, cypress-boughs, and ribbons. On the lawn below, trestles were being set up, tabletops borne out of storage. Visigoth's wife Hecuba came bustling around the corner of the house – even on so small a plantation the rule about slaves never cutting through the house was evidently as strict as it had been on Bellefleur in his childhood – with her arms full of Madame Aurelié's second-best table linen.

Hurrying to be ready, before the priest arrived.

From behind the house the smell of smoke drifted from the barbeque pits and ten-year-old Gérard Miragouin's voice asked in a clear treble, 'Can I help you with that, m'am?'

'Can't we take the carriage?' Ellie's eyes widened in consternation. 'I know it's a long way up the river road to town, but . . .'

'There's no carriage here at Cold Bayou,' explained Rose. 'It isn't as if any of the family lived here full-time, you know.'

'We'll have a flag out on the landing the moment the ceremony is over, *ma mie*,' promised Uncle Veryl, patting the small, lace-mitted fingers. 'I promise.'

*　*　*

83

'Oh, I can just hear the uproar there'll be over *that*!' Rose shook her head as she and January descended the steps and made their way through the confusion of trestle tables beneath the trees in front of the house. 'Say an up-river boat does come through just after the ceremony . . . or in the middle of it . . .'

She sidestepped Old Madame Janvier's lively little pug-dog Thisbe, chasing the kitchen cat.

'Do you honestly think Madame Aurelié will permit her brother and his new bride to get on it and leave nearly sixty guests before they have so much as received a bridal toast? Or that she – or old M'am Janvier – won't storm down to the levee and tell the pilot to take the steamboat off?'

'Or tell him he can wait with his hold full of cargo and passengers until the wedding luncheon is over?' speculated January, enchanted by the thought of the battle royal that would ensue.

Rose's quicksilver smile flashed into existence for a moment at that. 'I can just hear your mother on the subject. And I can't say I entirely blame her. With more people coming down for the wedding this morning the big house is going to be bursting at the seams, and if everybody is forced to spend another night – *after* the bride and groom have run off and left everyone . . .'

The smile vanished as quickly as it had come, and she propped her spectacles onto the bridge of her nose. 'It would be funnier,' she added quietly, 'if we hadn't seen somebody slip into the Casita. Without wanting to insult anyone, Benjamin, I honestly wouldn't . . . wouldn't . . .'

84

She couldn't say the words, and January finished for her, 'Wouldn't put it past some members of the Viellard clan to slip "inheritance powder" into the nuptial champagne?'

'It sounds so horrible—'

'It is horrible,' he agreed quietly. 'But so – I'm sure any of Henri's three unmarried sisters would assure you – is having all your suitors desert you because their parents doubt that control of the St-Chinian property is going to pass intact to the Viellard side of the family. I don't know the girls well,' he added, as Rose made a protesting noise in her throat. 'As far as I know they're perfectly innocent, well-bred Creole French damsels who would no more think of harming another person than they'd consider robbing the poor box in the church. But so, I expect, was that woman in Bremen about ten years ago who was beheaded for poisoning her relatives with arsenic for no apparent reason. Or that painter in Britain who was supposed to have poisoned his sister-in-law, uncle, mother-in-law, and a friend for their insurance money.'

'Yes, but . . .'

'People get frightened at the prospect of losing money they think is going to be theirs, my nightingale. And frightened people act out of impulse – especially if they don't consider the person who's taking the money is quite human.'

'An "American animal",' Rose quoted her mother-in-law and any number of Uncle Veryl's relatives. 'An "Irlandaise".'

She frowned to herself as they edged between the tables. Those on the upstream side of the

85

house, where the shade was better, were – to judge by the chairs at the heads of them – for the white relatives and friends. On the downstream side, benches would obviously do for 'the other side of the family'.

'That's worse than your speculations last night about Mamzelle herself,' Rose remarked after a time. She paused again, this time to let the housemaid Lila pass her, arms weighted with napkins. In addition to Madame Aurelié's three housemaids, the ladies' maids of nearly every female guest had been pressed into service, and there had already been a number of sharp quarrels between Madame Aurelié and her daughters over whether Gayla and Etta should be pressing out frocks and petticoats or polishing silver. 'It might almost lead one to suspect that you paid heed to Olympe's dark warnings of evil seen in the ink-bowl.'

'It might,' January agreed. Rose – a naturalist to her fingertips – shared Ellie Trask's perfect skepticism. For himself, it was harder to say, that dream was just a dream.

The slaves Luc and Antoine appeared around the corner of the house, carrying benches. January and Rose were far enough along the path that led back to the weaving house that they could see Valla hurrying down from the Casita. Antoine said a word to Luc and set down his end of the burden, almost running to meet her. The maid stepped back from him and the manservant reached to take her hands.

Not the gesture, January thought, of a man asking for instructions about seating arrangements and the stringing of garlands.

What was said he could not hear, but the young woman gestured emphatically, and Antoine violently shook his head.

'In any case,' Rose's voice went on, 'I challenge you to tell me how poison could be slipped into the nuptial champagne without doing away with poor Uncle Veryl and half the wedding guests as well.'

January returned his attention to her. 'Nothing simpler. In the pantry I saw two bottles of Hooper's Female Elixir – something a great number of females take a great deal more often than they should. This is probably the only occasion on which Madamoiselle Ellie's household goods are going to be easily accessible to those members of the family to whose property she will very shortly have legal claim. If it were me, I'd put something in it.'

His eyes met Rose's again, thinking of that cloaked form glimpsed on the rear gallery of the Casita in last night's windy darkness.

'Female Elixir,' mused Rose, as they resumed their stroll toward the weaving house, 'if it contains as much laudanum as those nostrums generally do is the one medicine that I'll wager Madamoiselle Ellie isn't going to throw away on anyone's advice. It might do to have a quiet word with Uncle Veryl – and with Ellie – on the subject, after the wedding and before they get on that steamboat.'

Seven

'Well, about damn time.' Old Uncle Bichet – born in the rose-red city of Timbuktu but who had now, for forty years, played bass fiddle for the well-off white folks of New Orleans – walked to the end of the weaving-house gallery, from which a fair view could be had of the long yellow reach of the Mississippi between Wills Point and English Turn. The moist, spooky winds of the night and the early morning had utterly died, and the sun blasted the dark-green cane-fields like a molten hammer. The cane-hands, scrubbed and clothed in their least-tattered and cleanest garments, had been loitering around the big house and its environs for two hours.

The *Vermillion* from New Orleans, which was calculated to have arrived at ten, was late.

'That her?' January rose from among the other musicians and walked to join him, shading his eyes to descry the distant smokestacks.

The old man's grin flashed all the myriad gaps in his teeth. 'If it ain't, gonna be some perturbed folks in the big house.'

'If it ain't—' January sank his voice to exclude everyone but the little circle of musicians who had, with Rose and Nicolette Charpentier, been playing Black Peter for most of the morning with Hannibal's worn-out pack of cards – 'does anyone want to help me cook and eat Stanislas Aubin?'

Hands were eagerly raised amid stifled guffaws. After a night and a morning in the environs of the weaving house, everyone was heartily sick of Madame Solange's whining and ill-mannered four-year-old, whose rude faces and ruder remarks his doting mother considered evidence of a wit to rival Walpole and Voltaire. From within the weaving house, Solange's voice wailed shrilly, 'How *can* you?' and the usually saintly old Laetitia St-Chinian snapped, 'Well, it's perfectly true . . .'

'Ladies.' admonished Sylvestre St-Chinian (for the thousandth time since yesterday afternoon). 'Ladies . . .'

Solange's non-stop panagyrics of her offspring, and his mother's caustic commentary, notwithstanding (though January was ready to drown both of them in the rain-barrel at this point), he felt a certain degree of sympathy for them. The wedding was to be followed by a 'breakfast' – currently reposing in decorative state under an army of miniature gauze pavilions on trestles behind the kitchen, under guard – but it followed that nobody was going to partake of this meal before the ceremony, which was now two hours overdue. Laetitia St-Chinian's daughter Marcellite had fainted twice and Bergette – Dominique's maid – had had hysterics. According to Chloë (who had quietly sneaked Dominique a couple of slightly stale batter-cakes pilfered while 'inspecting' the Molina kitchen) the situation was worse in the big house. There had been a screaming fight already between two of the Viellard girls, Madame Aurelié had slapped her

89

maid, and the Viellard and Janvier lawyers – who were sharing a room – had had to be forcibly separated from calling one another out over whether the father of the current King of France had been a traitorous dog or a patriot.

January had arranged through Luc to purchase a quantity of hoecakes from a couple of the slave women in the quarters. Under other circumstances he'd have assumed that the several quiet conversations he had glimpsed between Valla and Antoine involved similar negotiations, but no, had said Luc, that wasn't the case. Valla scorned slave rations – 'An' anyways,' Luc had added, 'I doubt she'd do anything that'd put her beholden to Antoine. They was sweethearts, back when they was both Michie Molina's house-niggers. Thought she was too good for him.' The young man shrugged. 'Far's I could tell, she thought she was too good for Michie Molina. But that's why he been pushin' to get a word with her now she's back. I don't think she'd buy bread from him if she was starvin'.'

January had divided his hoe-cakes with Rose, ungallantly glad that pretty much everybody else in the weaving house, like Valla, considered themselves too good to partake of slave rations. 'More for us,' he'd said.

But that had been an hour and a half ago and he'd definitely added his voice to the chorus who had – just before Uncle Bichet had spotted the approach of the *Vermillion* – been urging Hannibal to go up to the kitchen and prostitute himself to the cook. Thus it was not entirely from any sense of rejoicing in a family occasion that January and Rose joined the throng of plantation guests and personnel half an hour later as everyone gathered at the landing to welcome the vessel to shore.

The river being reasonably high for early September, the *Vermillion* – a medium-sized stern-wheeler of the sort which could nose its way up the shallower water of bayous – was able to dock at the long pier which extended into the river. Up-river and down from the landing, the yellow water was dotted with snags and towheads where washed-down branches – whole trees, sometimes – lurked underwater, but a glance showed January that Michie Molina had used the low-water months of summer to have work-gangs keep the vicinity of the landing clear, a horrible task which he remembered all too well from his early childhood.

Although Madamoiselle Ellie remained at the Casita, as befit a bride on her wedding-day, January glimpsed Valla, resplendent in yet another new dress – this one pale green muslin starred with pink flowers with a tignon nearly a foot and a half tall to match – among the house servants. On the fringe of the group of house servants – and he recalled just how firmly the caste-lines were drawn among the bondsmen and -women as to who was equal to whom – he saw Antoine, his long, handsome face several shades darker than Valla's but still lighter than the lightest of the field hands, watching the maid with a kind of aching intensity. Sweethearts, back when they was both Michie Molina's house-niggers, Luc had said.

91

Love? January wondered. *Or simply expedience on one hand and proximity on the other?*

And – given the probable cost of the midnight blue silk frock Madame Molina wore (*an appeasement gift?*), and of the ivory cameo at her throat – presumably a triangular affair of which the overseer had not been aware.

Or maybe he had.

Maybe he just didn't care.

A young man leaped lightly from the steamboat's deck up onto the pier. His honey-colored hair and long, rectangular features reminded January instantly of Solange Aubin, and indeed, the next moment Chloë's uncle Basile Aubin detached himself from the white portion of the group on the levee and strode forward to meet him. Evard, January recalled from his mother's airy recital of the more tangled ramifications of the St-Chinian/Viellard family tree. Who was courting one of the Viellard girls. Charlotte?

Yes, Charlotte: the youngest of Henri's sisters surged forward on Basile Aubin's heels, with a glad cry of 'Evard!' and a lace handkerchief fluttering in welcome.

But Evard, trailed not only by his valet but by an older white man whom January guessed was yet another family lawyer, and *his* valet, went at once to his father and barely gave the girl a glance. Charlotte fell back an uncertain step, hand to lips in distress, and her brother put an arm around her shoulder with, January guessed, re-assuring words.

Old Laetitia, at January's other side, gasped, 'Good Heavens!' at the sight of the next group coming down the pier, led by the man whom January recognized as Locoul St-Chinian – that disinherited son whose father's death last year had left Veryl with a substantially increased interest in the St-Chinian property in the first place. The man who hurried to keep pace with him was big and thickset, with the remains of a florid handsomeness and tobacco-stains on his too-gaudy waistcoat. St-Chinian had yet another family lawyer in his wake – January knew this one by sight also, an American named Loudermilk – and both men were trailed by women who kept as far apart from one another as the width of the pier allowed. St-Chinian's wife – his second, January recalled – was French Creole, as his first had been, but (according to his mother) of much lower social standing. The other man's, trailed by a younger couple who were clearly her children, was almost certainly that Fleurette whom old César had disinherited for marrying an American.

'The *nerve*!' breathed old Laetitia. 'I'll dare swear *they* were never invited – my goodness, Locoul's gotten stout! He used to be thin as a broom-handle! So that's Gloyne Cowley! Mama always said he was handsome enough to die for – or at least to be disinherited for . . .'

'That was nearly thirty years ago,' Rose reminded her, wrinkling her nose a little as the florid American spit tobacco on the pier, then stuck out his hand to receive Veryl's welcome. '*Ou sont les nieges t'antan*?'

Aurelié, at Veryl's side, drew back in pained indignation. The lawyer Loudermilk strode over to break into the discussion among the Aubin men (That settles it, surmised January, the third man has to be their lawyer) and all three drew back from him as if he'd pissed on their shoes.

The usual reaction, he knew, to three French Creoles when approached by an American.

All eyes went to the deck of the *Vermillion*, searching for the tall, rather rawboned, bespectacled form of Père Eugenius, one of the junior priests who served at the St Louis Cathedral in town.

Instead, another group of men disembarked, even more American – if that were possible – than the lawyer Loudermilk and the tobacco-spitting Gloyne Cowley. The man who strode in front was somewhat above middle height, though he gave an impression of bulk and power: wide-shouldered, his once-handsome face a roadmap of most of the circles of Hell, his dyed-black hair shiny with pomade that flashed nearly as bright as the six-carat diamond stuck in his neck-cloth. The inevitable valet that followed him was so much darker than the usual house servants purchased by Southerners that January guessed he had to be a free man, and dressed with such excrutiatingly modest good taste as to be nearly invisible. The other men, ranged like a wall between chief and valet, were of a type that January had seen on the waterfronts of New Orleans or driving goods-wagons in Washington City: unclean frock-coats of exaggerated cut and cheap manufacture, trousers tucked into heavy boots, gaudy silk neck-cloths and gaudier shirts. Beneath their high plug hats, their hair was cut close at the back, its anterior length plastered to the temples in extravagant, curling locks glued down with dried soap.

Their chief strode straight up to Uncle Veryl – who had scarcely recovered from his polite dismay at encountering Locoul St-Chinian and family – shifted the cigar over to one side of his rat-trap mouth, and introduced himself, in bad French but a not-unpleasant baritone: 'Mick Trask, at your service, sir. You'll be Mon-soor St-Chinian, I take it? That's to wed my little Ellie? Pleased to make your acquaintance.'

He grasped Uncle Veryl's kid-gloved fingers in a crushing grip.

Understandably appalled beyond speaking, Madame Aurelié – and every other member of the group on the landing, black, white, and in between – turned as one toward the *Vermillion*, seeking the reassurance of the priest's appearance.

But the only persons now on the pier were a couple of half-naked stevedores engaged in tossing the ropes back onto the deck. They leaped nimbly back across the widening yellow water, and picked up poles to shove the boat towards the river's main channel. With a loud hissing of steam, the engine engaged, and the great stern wheel began to rotate.

The *Vermillion* surged on its way down toward Willis' Point.

Luncheon was served soon after.

'Thank God for small favors, anyway,' remarked Hannibal, when he strolled back to the weaving house, upon whose gallery trestle tables, hastily

95

removed from the front lawn, had been set up for the benefit of the shady side of the family. (A mere meal, as opposed to a wedding feast, being deemed insufficiently festive to include 'crocodile eggs' dining in the same area). '*Malum quidem nullum esse sine aliquo bono*, though I can't say food will improve anyone's mood over at the big house, given the additional guests that have to be accommodated. But Mr Trask – he's Ellie's uncle, by the way, her father's brother – brought a newspaper with him from town which proves conclusively there won't be another down-river boat today. And believe me, the schedule was studied with the intensity of a treasure map. So there really was no point in waiting.

'Thank you, no,' he added, as Nicolette, Dominique, and January's mother all moved toward the makeshift serving-tables at the far end of the gallery, with offers to provide him with nourishment. 'I was seated with Trask's "boys" and a mixed assortment of family lawyers – a feast more reminiscent of Beowulf than of Trimalchio, I may say, in its potential outcome as well as its conversation. Between being ignored by the legal fraternity and glowered upon by the Irish brotherhood for being an Orangeman, I was pleased to shovel most of my meal into my pockets when nobody was looking and beat a retreat. Thank you,' he said again, as Nicolette scooted sideways on the bench (crowding Sylvestre's sons and old Laetitia almost off the end) to make room for him.

'He led the goddess to the sovereign seat,
Her feet supported with a stool of state
(A purple carpet spread the pavement
wide);
Then drew his seat, familiar, to her
side . . .

'That's most kind of you.' He proceeded to extract from his pocket several layers of napkin which contained a quantity of barbequed pork, a white roll, and a stuffed tomato artfully swaddled in lettuce leaves.

With a coquettish smile, Livia Levesque fetched him a clean fork and spoon. Not to be outdone, Isabelle Valverde brought a glass of lemonade.

'What happened to Père Eugenius?' asked Rose, and the fiddler shook his head.

'Not the whisper of a clue,' he said. 'But everyone agrees that he wasn't on the boat. Half a dozen passengers disembarked at English Turn, but no priest. Of that all were certain.'

'Anyone want to bet that M'am Aurelié bribed him to stop at home?' old Sylvestre suggested.

'You can't bribe a priest!' cried Solange indignantly, and Livia cackled with laughter.

'Oh, can't you just?'

'I wouldn't put it past her to try.' Minou's brow furrowed thoughtfully.

'More likely,' theorized January, 'she paid someone else to delay him.'

'Assault him in an alley?' inquired Rose, interested. 'Leave him bound hand and foot in his own confessional?'

Solange and Laetitia looked horrified at this,

and January said, 'More likely manufacture an emergency of some kind to make him miss the boat. Did Madame Aurelié look surprised at all by his absence, Hannibal?'

'I overheard her say that it was a judgement of God, a remark to which Mr Trask took instant exception. Trask took his lunch at the Casita, by the way, waited upon by his valet – St-Ives is his name – and accompanied by Madame Chloë, who offered to see what Ellie might need. The Viellard girls were visibly repenting that they'd so vocally established themselves as Ellie's enemies and thus couldn't go along and hear whatever plans might be exchanged. All except Madamoiselle Charlotte, who never took her eyes from Evard Aubin and was heard to express the wish that Madamoiselle Trask would choke on a chicken-bone and die. So far as I could tell, no one spoke to either Locoul St-Chinian or his sister, nor to their respective spouses – Locoul's wife's name is Josèphe, by the way, and she is known as Madame Pepa, though Mesdames Aurelié, Janvier, and Miragouin called her other things as well. I must say I am deeply curious as to whether the good Father will put in an appearance tomorrow, and if not, what will happen then.'

Half an hour later the ringing of the plantation bell summoned all the field hands – who had not been invited to partake of any feast whatsoever – to the overseer's house. The libré contingent on the weaving-house gallery, just concluding a dessert of sweet-potato pie and the rather soupy ice-cream that had been intended for the wedding

98

feast, had a good view of them, and of Michie Molina, sweating in his mustard-colored coat and top hat, giving out instructions, though he was slightly too distant to be heard. It was clear within minutes what he'd said, though, for men and women both were already forming up into work-gangs as they walked back to the quarters. They emerged very shortly thereafter, dressed in the ragged frocks or trousers of everyday labor. A few retired to exhume their own pig from the roasting-pit, but most of them moved back out toward the fields.

'That isn't fair!' protested young Marianne Valverde. 'They were supposed to get the rest of the day off to celebrate the wedding—'

'But there hasn't been any wedding, dear,' explained old Laetitia. 'And it isn't good for darkies to be idle.'

'All the same,' commented Rose, as she, January, and Hannibal walked back to the big house an hour later, 'in the circumstances, I should be miffed.'

Mentally, January sighed. For all her quirky wisdom, her scientific erudition and her sympathetic understanding of human nature, Rose was every inch the daughter of a plaçeé. 'All the things those folk have to trouble them,' he said, 'getting let off work, and then put back on again, is the least of their worries.'

She nodded, seeing his point. 'Yes, of course.'

She had never grown up, as January had, not knowing if she'd wake up some morning to be informed that her mother or father, friend or brother, had been sold off in the night, never to be seen again. And that, January reflected wryly, was the *easy* part of being a slave, if your master also didn't happen to be a drunken lunatic.

What that did to you, Rose – much as he adored her – would probably never completely understand.

Luncheon at the big house had finished, and the tables were being cleared up, disassembled, and carried to shelter under the house. The warm Gulf wind had kicked up again bringing the smells of storm and sea. Deprived of a wedding, the guests clustered on the gallery, waiting for Visigoth and Antoine to carry out chairs from the parlor ('Are they going to put all those chairs back where they came from and re-assemble them again tomorrow?' wondered Rose, and Hannibal returned, '*Sufficit diei malitia sua.*')

'I suppose that depends on whether they believe that Père Eugenius is going to be on the next boat tomorrow,' said January. A gust of wind tore loose one end of the porch garland, making it thresh like an angry snake and shower the front steps with glossy oval leaves. 'You didn't happen to read if there *is* a boat tomorrow, did you?'

'The *City of Nashville*, and the *Democrat*. The *Sarah Jane* and the *Phoenix* should be passing up-river sometime this afternoon. But I'd be willing to bet, at this point, nobody's going to hail them.'

January had already noticed that no flag flew from the landing.

'I doubt even Madamoiselle Ellie will insist on it,' agreed Rose. 'For fear of missing Père

100

Eugenius on his way down-river, if for no other reason – although there is something rather enchanting about the thought of the bridal party and the officiant chasing one another up and down the Mississippi for three days. At what point do we call it a loss and you pay up twenty-five cents to myself and Minou?'

'With this many lawyers in attendance I can't see anyone running the risk of being left out of . . . Well!' Hannibal's voice took on a note of pleased surprise. 'The lawyers must be making some headway after all.'

Above them, on the downstream corner of the front gallery, Charlotte Viellard and the handsome Evard Aubin stood in conversation, as if oblivious to Florentin Miragouin and his young son Gérard standing in conversation with M'sieu Brinvilliers – the Viellard attorney – a few feet away.

'Not ready to approach her seriously,' added the fiddler judiciously, pausing to study the tête-à-tête like a connoisseur examining a suspiciously fresh-looking Rembrandt. 'He's a good six inches too far from her for a declaration of love. But by the look on her face, at least he's come up with a believable reason for snubbing her at the landing, other than the fact that she may be heiress to a far smaller holding than she was originally advertised to be . . .'

'You leave them alone!' Rose poked him sharply in the arm. 'Don't treat the poor girl's humiliation like a scene from a play.'

'*Mea culpa – absit invidio*.' Hannibal executed a deep bow of apology. 'All the world's a stage . . .'

But January had to admit – studying the couple – that his friend was probably accurate in his reading of the situation. The girl's strained expression as she studied the younger Aubin's handsome face seemed to corroborate the assertion that Evard was hedging his bets, not committing himself until the lawyers had had their chance to sit Veryl and Aurelié down before the wedding and work out a settlement.

'Père Eugenius' absence does seem to be rather fortuitous,' he murmured.

'Are you certain the good Father didn't embark at New Orleans?' inquired Rose, as they moved to circle toward the long U between the wings at the rear of the house, where steps led up to the gallery of the downstream wing – suitable for non-whites, given the number of family members gathered at the front of the house. 'Perhaps a couple of hired bravos tipped him overboard?'

'Had he been aboard,' surmised Hannibal airily, 'I'm certain Mr Trask's "boys" would have guarded him with—'

He turned his head, at the sudden soft drum of hoofbeats on the shell road that ran along the river's edge. A single rider on a black horse, black hair flicked back from his brow with the wind of a light canter.

'Oh, good,' said Hannibal. '*More* guests.'

Rose nudged him indignantly.

'No lawyer,' January observed.

'You *men*—'

'Jules!' Charlotte gasped, as the young man drew rein before the front gallery steps. Face aglow with joy, she slipped past Evard Aubin

102

and ran, as lightly as a girl of her podgy build could scamper, down the front steps and into 'Jules's' arms.

Evard, left standing on the gallery watched them – January observed – with smouldering fury in his eyes.

Eight

Continuing their circle to the rear yard of the big house, January and his companions encountered Madame Chloë as she came past the kitchen on her way from the Casita. 'Is Uncle Veryl in his room?' she asked.

Heads were shaken – 'We've only just got here ourselves,' explained Hannibal.

'I don't suppose Aurelié is in there with him?' went on Madame Chloë.

'She's on the front gallery,' provided the fiddler. 'With all the lawyers. *Devil with devil/damnéd concourse holds* . . .'

'Getting ready for a frontal assault, I should think,' said Rose, as they all fell into step with the girl and climbed the rear steps of the gallery, stepping carefully around Antoine and Visigoth, who were setting up a ladder to remove the garlands. They passed through the rear doors into the house, to find the vacant dining room and parlor still filled with chairs, garlands, and a half-constructed archway of boughs. Though all the French doors at the front of the parlor were open and the angry voices of the guests on the gallery came clearly through, the house itself seemed weirdly silent. 'I'm still offering three-to-one odds that your mother-in-law hired agents in New Orleans to prevent Père Eugenius from getting on the boat, six to one that violence was involved—'

'That's a very charitable assumption about my mother-in-law,' observed Chloë, rustling ahead of them to the door of Uncle Veryl's room. 'How do you define *violence* for purposes of the pay-off?'

'I'd give five to three on violence from Florentin Miragouin,' offered Hannibal. 'Unlike Evard Aubin, *he* can't back out if the marriage takes place and Sister Euphémie's share in the family holdings diminishes.'

'What odds are you giving on me?' Chloë tapped at the door.

'Oh, twenty to one at least,' returned Rose.

'I'm flattered.'

'Not at all. You have no children, and I can scarcely see you putting yourself in danger for the sake of your sisters-in-law. Unless you've suddenly developed a consuming passion for Florentin—'

Chloë raised her moth-fine brows with a pained expression. At fifty, Florentin Miragouin had lost most of his teeth and a great deal of his hair, compensating for these shrinkages by the addition of substantial avoirdupois. But she only said, 'It's Chloë, Uncle,' in response to some inaudible murmur from within. Opening the door a crack, she added, 'Benjamin, Rose, and Hannibal are with me.'

'Good.' Uncle Veryl's soft-timbred voice had a note to it of unutterable weariness. 'It will be a pleasure to see someone who is actually concerned for the happiness of the bridal couple, on the day of the wedding. Or what was to have been the day,' he added bitterly.

Entering the room, January saw a newspaper spread out across the foot of the bed – presumably the one Uncle Mick Trask had brought from town – and a plate bearing a slice of roast duck, a stuffed tomato, and some delicately-prepared rice on the corner of the dresser, untouched. The old man had clearly had new clothes made for his nuptials, a swallow-tailed dress coat – January had never seen him in anything other than a rusty and discolored narrow-skirted suit that dated back to the previous century – and two waistcoats of China silk in complementary shades of gray. His only revulsion from modernity appeared to have been the wearing of long trousers, but he seemed to have found a tailor willing to execute a pair of dove-colored unmentionables – they looked new – which he wore with the white silk stockings of his youth.

Selwyn Singletary, in the room's single bent-willow chair, was attired in what had obviously been his best suit since 1803.

'How is Ellie?' Uncle Veryl turned his pale-blue eyes anxiously upon his niece. 'Is she taking this well? Did someone remember to send her a tray of food? Curse this belief in the ill luck of the bride and groom seeing one another on their wedding day – even if it's *not* their wedding day . . .'

'I made certain of it, Uncle. And went with

her Uncle Trask to bear her company while she ate. Infamous of me to leave poor Henri to preside over that dreadful luncheon with Madame Aurelié . . .'

'I simply couldn't face it.' Veryl shook his head again. 'I simply couldn't. I suppose I must go forth on the gallery and reassure my guests that there will indeed be a ceremony on the morrow.' He passed a slightly unsteady hand across his forehead, like a man who strives to gather his thoughts. 'I can't think what can have happened to Père Eugenius. I hope he did not meet with some accident—'

'According to Rose the odds are close to even that Madame Aurelié arranged it.'

'Ah'd put 'em even mesel', or better nor,' put in Singletary, interested as always by any mathematical computation. 'How'd you factor t'lasses, m'am? G'in their inexperience – how would a woman arrange such a delay anyroad?'

'We'll discuss it later, M'sieu,' Chloë whispered, with a warning glance toward her uncle.

'Oh. Oh, aye.' Though deeply fond of his friend – and sincerely good-hearted – Singletary did tend to forget social and personal amenities when confronted with an intellectual challenge.

'In truth—' Rose crossed the chamber to give the bridegroom a niece-like kiss on the temple – 'the entire episode may be a complete accident. Père Eugenius may simply have been delayed by the sudden illness of one of his parishoners – you know how feverish a summer it's been, sir – and missed the boat.'

'Six to one at least against that,' pointed out Singletary, and Chloë – momentarily disregarding

106

the old mathematician's venerable years – kicked him in the ankle. 'Ow, lass!'

Rose turned back to Chloë. 'Is there anything I – or any of us – can do for Madamoiselle Ellie, m'am? She must be devastated – if she isn't fulminating with rage! As I know I'd be.'

Chloë's huge, aquamarine eyes traveled briefly to her uncle's face, with an expression of speculation. Then she seemed to set her first thoughts aside, and said, as if choosing her words, 'She certainly used a number of very un-lady-like expressions about both the steamboat and the river. And indeed, Rose, she seems to share the general belief concerning Madame Aurelié's involvement in Père Eugenius' delay. She is also—' her brow puckered in another frown – 'much troubled about remaining here at Cold Bayou over another night. The gris-gris sewn into her wedding dress upset her very much. Not that she believes that magic could work her ill,' she added, with a glance from her uncle to Singletary. 'She seems to be a very sensible girl on that subject. More sensible than any of my sisters-in-law, for instance. But the fact that someone could enter the Casita, apparently without Valla hearing it, frightens her a good deal, as well it should.'

January drew breath, hesitating over how much of Valla's movements last night he could disclose without getting the maid into serious trouble. The intruder had after all entered the Casita while Valla had been seeing her mistress' guests out the front door, and probably could not have been prevented whether Valla had subsequently tiptoed out or not.

But Chloë forestalled him with, 'Her uncle said he'll post some of his "boys" around the Casita tonight. There are eight of them, nine if the one who was put off the boat sick at English Turn recovers sufficiently to come down here by night-fall. That should at least spare Madame Aurelié the headache of finding a place for them all to sleep. If – good heavens!'

She stepped back, startled, as the French door shutters of the room were opened quietly behind her and the bride in question herself slipped through.

Her hair was still dressed for the ceremony, smoothly parted and with clusters of moonlight-yellow curls swinging enticingly above her ears, but she'd slipped into the frock of striped white-and-yellow muslin that Valla had worn yesterday – probably, guessed January, because it fastened up the front with a row of pearl buttons and wouldn't require the services of the maid. Under the soft tints of rice-powder and rouge she looked haggard, her eye-paint streaked a little with tears.

Veryl sprang at once to his feet. 'My dear Ellie—'

'If anybody tells me one more time—' she pushed the curls back from her face – 'about how I'll bring down bad luck to everybody if the groom lays eyes on me, I'll scream. I can't stand this anymore, Mr St-Chinian! Cooped up in that house not knowing what's being said or done. And Uncle Mick's as bad as everyone else!'

She turned to look up at January. 'Will you go back to town, Mr J?' she asked. Very slightly, he smelled on her breath the heavy sweetness of plum brandy, and heard the echo of it in her soft voice. He wondered if this were something Uncle Mick had provided her with, or whether she had a spare bottle secreted in the bedroom. That would certainly explain why Valla had forbidden him to enter, anyway. 'Go back to town and find out if this priest is on his way here? If he's not, would you fetch him, or another, or *somebody*?'

'He'll be on one of tomorrow's boats, my dearest.' Veryl nudged Singletary sharply and the old man, after a startled look of inquiry, leaped to his feet and let his friend escort the bride to the room's sole chair, in which he'd been sitting. 'According to the paper, the *City of Nashville*—'

'But what if he's not?' The girl turned tear-filled eyes upon him. 'How long are we going to sit here waiting not knowing anything? If for nothing else, what are we going to feed all these people, now that everybody's eaten up most of what Mrs Molina had set by for the wedding? We can't give your sister, and all those elegant folks, pone and molasses, and that's what Valla tells me supplies mostly are, when the family isn't here.'

'There's enough of everything for a reasonable dinner tonight, and a wedding-breakfast tomorrow.' Chloë folded her neat little hands over the ornamental buckle of her belt. 'Missy and Madame Molina are certainly competent to deal with that. I'll write up an order for Duroque – the Viellard man of business in town – if you'd be so good as to drop it off there, Benjamin, if indeed you'd be so kind as to go up. And I'll ask Molina to put out a flag on the landing for the *Sarah Jane* this afternoon.'

Ellie looked as if she were about to make another suggestion that she and Veryl be the ones to go up to town on the up-river boat, but after casting a glance at her bridegroom – and at the formidable Chloë – she merely inquired, 'Is there any chance Père Eugenius got off at the wrong landing? That he might be someplace up-river . . .?'

'He *is* near-sighted,' remarked Rose. 'If he'd broken his glasses . . .?' She blinked thoughtfully behind her own, and Chloë – whose spectacles were like the bottoms of wine-bottles – frowned as if evaluating the possibility.

'Ah've done t' like,' agreed Singletary, nodding – though he was just as likely to get off at the wrong landing even with his glasses on.

'Could someone go search for him, m'am?' Ellie turned to Chloë. 'I just hate to cause this kind of uproar, but . . .' She hesitated again, and January could have sworn he saw fear flicker in her eyes. Then she smiled, with the diplomatic readiness of one who's worked with drunks half her life, and explained, 'Well, I'm sure nobody's comfortable, all crowded in on top of each other.'

'Père Eugenius is near-sighted,' said January patiently. 'But even without his spectacles he's neither blind nor stupid. And he's been in this country for nine years, and down the river a dozen times. Even if he'd never been ashore here, he knows enough to ask someone the name of a plantation landing before stepping ashore.'

'What's more likely,' said Hannibal, 'is that he went ashore with the fellow who took sick – you

110

did say one of Uncle Mick's boys was put off sick at English Turn, didn't you, Madame?'

'Tommy,' agreed Chloë. 'According to M'sieu St-Ives. Surprisingly mild nomenclature, given that the others all seem to have names like the Black Duke and the Gopher. It's very possible, if the young man was taken seriously ill.' Her pale brows knit with some hidden concern. 'Goodness knows a man of their appearance might have difficulty finding anyone to look after him, in a strange country, if a priest wasn't along to vouch for him. I don't think there are any settlements, even of the most rudimentary sort, along the river between here and English Turn, and English Turn consists of no more than a tavern, a wood lot, and a livery stable.'

'An' down-river?' asked Singletary. 'Might there be a priest in t'back country? At this – what? – this Willis Point that's down-river o' here? Or back o' here in t' woods? Would it fash you to be wed by summat less'n a full-blowed cathedral priest in all his tail-feathers, lass?'

He turned to Ellie as he spoke, and Rose put in, 'Madame Molina would know.'

'I'm sure it would make no difference.' Veryl reached across, to pat his bride's hand. 'If the matter can be accomplished this evening. Good gracious, *mignonne*, your little hand is cold! Are you certain *you're* all right?'

And he peered anxiously at her face, which she turned quickly aside before looking at him again with her warm, professional smile. 'Just . . . Just so wound up over this delay, and the terrible things I know your family say and think. Not

111

you, m'am,' she added quickly to Chloë, who like her uncle was studying her face intently. 'Thank you ever so, for coming in to share lunch with me, even though you had all those people here at the house! It just . . . Sometimes Uncle Mick . . .' She colored slightly, though under her rouge January thought – as well as he could judge in the dim-lit bedchamber – that she was indeed looking suddenly pale.

In confusion, she concluded, 'He does go *on* so.'

Chloë's lips tightened. 'Having been *gone on* at myself, dear,' she said in her small silvery voice, 'I would certainly not have left you to face the man alone.'

'And now I – I really must be getting back.' Ellie got quickly to her feet, and shook out her borrowed skirts. Her voice sounded just the slightest bit tinny with strain. 'St-Ives must be done clearing up by now. Goodness knows what that . . . what Madame Aurelié and Old Madame Janvier and all those others are going to say if they find I've put one foot in your bedroom, Mr St-Chinian – and before the wedding, too!'

'Hannibal, see if the coast is clear,' instructed January. 'M'sieu St-Chinian, if you went out onto the gallery with those reassuring words about the wedding definitely taking place tomorrow, that would draw everyone to the gallery and give Madamoiselle time to get far enough from the house that she'll be mistaken for Valla, if anyone sees her.'

Rose promptly removed her tignon, and with a few quick twists wrapped its white folds around

Ellie's golden curls – fair as Valla was, January guessed the mistress could easily pass for the maid at fifty feet from the house. While this disguise was being undertaken he, Hannibal, and Singletary followed Uncle Veryl from the room and threaded their way among the chairs in the parlor to the French doors at the front of the house.

Behind them, Chloë called out, 'I'll have Molina put a flag on the landing . . .'

But within five minutes, January's proposed errand to New Orleans was a dead issue.

As he stepped out onto the shaded heat of the gallery in the old man's wake, January heard a young man yell, 'Traitor!'

'Evard—' pleaded Charlotte, and reached to take her blonde-haired suitor's arm.

Evard Aubin thrust her aside and stepped belligerently toward the taller, slender, dark young man who'd come riding up half an hour before. 'Your filthy Italian dictator was a traitor—' Evard nearly spat the words into Jules's fine-boned face – 'and that nancy son of his who spent his whole life sucking off the Emperor of Austria: *he* was a traitor—'

'And I suppose that fat usurper squatting on the throne is a rightful monarch?' retorted Jules. 'Or his regicide father?'

'Oh, Jules, no—' Charlotte Viellard made another fluttering attempt to get between the two crimson-faced young men, and January wondered how much of the quarrel actually had to do with French politics and how much to do with marrying the (potential) heiress to a share of the Viellard/ St-Chinian holdings.

113

Neither contestant gave her so much as a glance.

'And as for that cheating sneak who calls himself Napoleon these days, hiding in London and kissing the Queen's fat little arse—'

With a movement as quick and casual as swatting a fly, the dark-haired Jules whipped his riding gloves from where they'd been tucked in the bosom of his jacket and struck Evard across the face with them. Everyone on the gallery around them gasped and drew back, Charlotte screamed and sagged, as if fainting, into the arms of her brother Henri (but she kept her eyes open and on the fracas), and Evard, with a snarl like a bulldog, lunged for his rival's throat.

They were young men, and strong, and those closest to them on the gallery were, as it happened, mostly the women of the party: Madame Aurelié, old Sidonie Janvier, Henri's sisters Euphémie and Ophélie. The men were grouped around the lawyers on the front steps. The nearest of them – Florentin Miragouin – made a half-hearted movement to separate the struggling pair, but it was Uncle Veryl who pushed forward, crying, 'Stop it, now! Stop it!' and Madame Janvier's little pug Thisbe, roused to martial fervor, lunged at Evard's ankle.

Though he hadn't the slightest intention of laying a hand on any white man, much less a young, furious, and murderously inclined Creole French gentleman, January surged after Veryl, and so was at Jules' very elbow when the young man broke violently free of the stranglehold, leaped back, tripped over Thisbe and crashed right through the gallery railing. January sprang to drag him to safety – it was an eight-foot drop to the ground – collided with him instead, and Jules clutched blindly at him for support.

January in turn grabbed for the nearest of the pilasters that supported the gallery roof, and missed.

There was a long drop and they both landed hard.

Nine

For one second January felt nothing except the shock of having the breath knocked out of him. He was dimly aware of voices shouting and the wild clatter of feet on the gallery steps, of not being able to breathe and of Thisbe licking his face. Then the pain started as if the Spanish Inquisition were crushing his right foot in a leg-screw, and his breath returned enough for him to give a howl of pain that dignity required him to turn into the worst curse he could think of.

Everyone was of course clustering around Jules.

The Frenchman, apparently unhurt, lunged to his feet and slapped Aubin – one of the first to arrive at his side – with his open hand, shouting, 'Dog! I will meet you tomorrow on the levee and feed your tripes to the catfish!'

Then Hannibal and Rose were bending over January, and he managed to grate through his teeth, 'I will murder the first person who tells me it could have been worse.'

'It will be worse,' Rose informed him calmly, 'when we try to get you back to the weaving house. Where are you hurt?'

'Leg,' said January, under the increasing din that surrounded the white members of the party. He had to clench his teeth hard. 'Ankle, I think.' He flexed his hands, moved his head, and discovered that apparently every muscle in his body was connected to his *medial malleolus*.

'And me without a drop of laudanum on me.' Theatrically, Hannibal patted all his pockets, though he'd given up the drug himself over two years before.

'Madame Molina will have some.' Rose shooed the lapdog out of her way, and stood to search for the overseer's wife in the ever-thickening group.

'If she doesn't, there's some Hooper's Female Elixir in the Casita.'

Whoever it was who eventually fetched some – while most of the whites were re-ascending the gallery stair to the house again – they mixed the opiate with not quite enough water, so not only was the pain dulled when they pulled off January's boot, but he had only a muddled awareness of being carried on a makeshift litter the two hundred yards to the weaving house. This annoyed him, in a distant fashion, for he was well aware that his subsequent instructions to Rose as to how to bandage his ankle were less than coherent. He was also (he thought even at the time) disproportionately vexed that his mother,

116

and several of the other female guests at the weaving house, were far more concerned about the identity of Charlotte Viellard's new suitor, and the prospect of tomorrow's duel.

'That will be Jules-Napoleon Mabillet,' surmised Laetitia, who was among the group gathered outside the open doors of the room that had been given to Minou, Rose, and Minou's little family – no one had seriously considered even attempting to carry January up the narrow ladder to the attic where the musicians had slept last night.

'Heavens!' declared Livia, in genuine surprise. 'I'd heard Marie-Honorine Mabillet was the first mama to pull her son away from Mamzelle Charlotte when St-Chinian's engagement to the Irish whore was announced.'

'She was,' affirmed Solange. 'No, Stanislas, darling, put that down . . . But I can't think what other *Jules* fits Hannibal's description of the young man—'

'I'd heard La Mabillet was obliging Jules-Napoleon to hang out after the Peralta girl . . .'

'Yes, but the only other *Jules* anywhere near the right age is Jules-Joseph Lafrennière, and his whole family are Legitimistes and would *never* get into a fight on behalf of Louis-Napoleon Bonaparte.'

'Do you know what weapon Aubin will choose?'

'He's said to be an absolute demon with a sword . . .'

January closed his eyes and let his head drop back on the pillow. He was dimly concerned that Rose would make an absolute botch of the bandaging but was also aware – like a little dark seed of clear-headedness in a swoony vapor of half-dreams – that in his heart he believed that *everyone* would make a botch of medical matters that he wasn't himself there to oversee. He'd mapped out how he was going to re-bandage the ankle, and what he was going to say to Père Eugenius when confessing the sin of – *does that count as Pride or Officiousness?* – when he drifted off to sleep.

Besides, where is Père Eugenius anyway? Bound hand and foot in his own confessional? Wandering the back-roads of the swamps without his glasses, ciborium in hand, looking for the wedding?

Even in sleep, January felt the sweep of rain-clouds as they passed across the plantation, the wind rattling the young shoulder-high cane and keening around the corners of the weaving house. He heard the sweet lilt of quadrilles and mescol-anzes, Scotch reels and German waltzes, from the attic above him as his fellow musicians rehearsed. *Of course the folks in the big house are going to want music tonight, wedding or no wedding . . .*

He wondered if, with the aid of a crutch and a much more restrained dose of laudanum, he'd be able to hobble over to join them – better than lying here, anyway.

In the room next door – the one grudgingly shared by Laetitia and her widowed daughter with Solange Aubin and her precious Stanislas – he heard voices gently chattering, with now and then words concerning the possibility of dancing at the big house that evening if the wind-squalls died down, 'Which it looks like they're going to,' added Marcellite St-Chinian – Laetitia's daughter – her clear voice youthful though she was in her forties.

'As if that Viellard witch is going to hold any sort of dance for the likes of us,' drawled Isabelle. January wondered if she referred to Madame Aurelié or Madame Chloë.

'Well, even if the weather clears,' pointed out Minou's sweet tones, 'they can't very well hold a dance for themselves in the house without moving all those chairs.'

Piercingly, little Stanislas let out a scream followed at once by a gale of hysterical giggles. 'Now, precious, be good,' coaxed Solange, to little avail.

'It'll clear,' added Livia, her smoky inflection reminding January of her daughter Olympe's. 'But it'll be hot as a Turkish bath and then I shouldn't be surprised if there was a worse storm on the way.'

His mother, January reflected, still plunged in half-dreams like a wreck on the ocean floor, was probably the only woman present who had actual experience of watching the weather in the country. His mother and Rose, who had spent her adolescence on the barrier islands of the Gulf. *Death in the water*. He heard the echo of Olympe's voice in his cloudy dreams. *Death in the fire*.

Death coming for Mamzelle Ellie? In the water, in the fire?

He drifted deeper into sleep.

Heat woke him. His mother had certainly been right about the flittering spookiness of

119

the storm-breezes being followed by the steamy stillness of a Turkish bath. The voices were more audible now, because the long windows of his room stood open to whatever breath might be moving in off the river (none was) and everyone was out on the gallery again. By the light it was an hour or so before sunset. He wondered if anyone had put out a flag on the landing, and who Ellie had gotten to go to New Orleans in his stead.

'—can only consider it a blessing,' his mother was declaring. 'What on earth they're going to do with the little slut in the family I can't imagine. The old man must be senile . . .'

'Well, M'sieu Brinvilliers tells me,' said Nicolette, 'that according to M'sieu DuPage – the Janvier family lawyer, you know – Madame Aurelié and Madame Euphémie have been trying to prove it for the past year – really, ever since M'sieu César died.'

'Now, that's unjust,' protested Laetitia. 'And I'm sure in her better moods Aurelié is perfectly aware of it. My brother is eccentric, of course, but he's perfectly sane. And it's very kindly of him, to look after the education of his nieces and nephews the way he does—'

'*Kindly*?' Livia sounded as if someone had tried to convince her that a cockroach in the oatmeal was a currant. 'Turning Madame Chloë into a frigid bluestocking? The whole problem would never have come about if the girl weren't a cold-blooded ice-princess that no man – let alone a tub of flan like Henri – would get children on.'

His mother had clearly, January reflected,

120

reached the limit of her patience with the crowded quarters of the weaving house – albeit that she was the only person in residence who had a room of her own.

'Maman!' protested Dominique.

'You know it's true.' January could just imagine his mother's great brown eyes turned upon his sister with irrefutable calm. 'Henri Viellard is a perfectly pleasant young man, but even you must admit that he cares more for his dinner and his seashell collection than he does for either of you. And if he's even attempted to get that bride of his with child it's more than I've ever heard.'

'Maman, I will admit nothing of the kind!' It was Minou's genius, thought January admiringly, that her laughing voice turned the whole discussion into banter. 'And *you* will have to admit that in Madame Chloë, Henri has a wife who can talk to him about his frightful insect collections and what birds he's seen and what Julius Caesar said to Alexander the Great at Christmas in 200 B.C. without running *screaming* out of the room—'

'Exactly!' proclaimed Solange impatiently. 'What man in his senses speaks so to his wife? Livia is right, it's Veryl the family has to thank, that Henri's only child is Minou's daughter.'

'That doesn't mean he's senile!'

'What else do you call it,' retorted Livia, 'when a man of sixty-seven starts drooling over some round-heeled tavern slut – and asks her to *marry* him? And buys her those frightful dresses? God knows who she'll be pregnant by, before the end of the year. Yes, girl, what is it?'

121

Rigid with fury, Valla's voice said, 'Madamoiselle sent to ask, is there any of the oranges left from lunch, that got brought over here? M'am Molina says as how there's none left in the kitchen, nor from the white folks' luncheon, but that she had sent over more than a dozen here. Might there be one or two here that you could spare back?'

January turned his head on the pillow and – as he thought he'd recalled – he saw one of the fruits that had decorated the luncheon table on the gallery, lying on a china plate on the little table beside Minou's pallet bed where he lay.

He heard his sister say, 'We have—' but their mother cut her off.

'I'm so sorry—' by her tone she clearly wasn't sorry in the least – 'but we haven't any to spare. I'm afraid *Mamzelle*—' her voice slid with oily sarcasm over the honorific – 'will have to get her little treats elsewhere.'

'*Madamoiselle*—' Valla pronounced the word with painstaking perfection – 'asked me specially, and I see three of them in there right through that door there.'

'*Madamoiselle*,' returned Livia sarcastically, 'can evidently take whatever she wishes away from her sweetheart's guests, so obviously we can't stop her, or you.'

Through the open door of his own room January saw Valla's mouth twist as the girl took a step toward the door of the room beside his. Livia folded her arms and added, 'And I can only hope that *Madamoiselle* is adequately feathering her nest – and that you are feathering yours – against the day when her light o' love wakes up and realizes how far above herself she's gotten.'

Valla swung around upon her, her sapphire eyes narrowing. 'You should talk about gettin' above yourself, woman. First thing my lady's gonna do, when she has a man to help her get her rights, is call in the mortgage money her father lent your master Simon Fourchet, that he never paid back. Mortgage on every slave on his property—' she jabbed her finger viciously at Livia – 'that couldn't be sold nor freed nor turned over to somebody else, until that money was paid back. Then we'll see who's gettin' above theirselves!'

With that she flounced into the next room, to re-emerge an instant later, three oranges in her hands.

Hoarse with shock, Livia gasped, 'You're lying, bitch!' and Valla gave her a spiteful smile.

'You'll see if I am. *Madame.*'

And with a swish of her green silk petticoats, she was down the gallery steps and striding back towards the Casita.

'That's ridiculous,' said Rose, who had followed her mother-in-law and Minou (and half the other women on the gallery – the room could hold no more) into the chamber where January lay.

Then she glanced from his still face to Livia's, and around at the others – freeborn plaçeés, like herself and her own mother, who had never really had to think about the legal complexities of being owned. 'Isn't it?'

January's heart was pounding hard as his mind flicked back over the events of the day. About

123

Uncle Mick and his 'boys' trooping down the gangplank of the *Vermillion* – had it only been six hours ago? – and of the heavy-shouldered Irishman spending a lunchtime quietly closeted with his niece in the Casita.

About Hannibal's casual description, yesterday on the deck of the *Illinois*, of old Fergus Trask: *He owned the High Water Saloon but he was a moneylender and the worst screw on the river . . .*

His mouth felt dry and he felt as if he were shaking all over, and he could see the barely suppressed panic in his mother's face.

'The first thing we need to do,' he said, 'see whether Valla was lying.'

'Of course she was,' snapped his mother, ashen.

January bit back the temptation to add, *And I don't blame her* – a quarrel with his mother was the last thing anyone needed at this point – and said instead, 'I think we need to send Hannibal back to town to check at the Cabildo, to see if any sort of paperwork was filed recording this supposed mortgage. Uncle Mick could be lying,' he went on. 'Mamzelle Ellie could be lying – or could be only repeating what Uncle Mick thinks he can get away with. Let's see what we're talking about, before we do anything.'

'Marianne,' said Isabelle to her daughter, 'run to the big house and fetch Michie Hannibal—'

'Wait,' said January as the girl whirled to set off. 'I'd like to request – I'd like to implore – that none of you speak of this to *anyone* at the big house until Hannibal gets back from New Orleans with that information. Gossip and guessing and putting ideas into peoples' heads are only going to make the situation worse. Will you all give me your word – all of you – that you'll keep this quiet?'

Heads were nodded – *Not that* that's *going to be any guarantee*, January reflected despairingly, as Marianne grabbed up her skirts and darted away down the high steps.

('Walk, darling!' called her mother after her. 'Gentlemen do *not* wish to see a lady run . . .')

'Maman,' he asked, 'what year did you come to Bellefleur Plantation? You were freed in 1803 . . .' He was careful not to say, *St-Denis Janvier bought you in 1803*, knowing that his mother generally presented herself to other plaçeés as a freeborn woman like themselves. Enough of a shock to her, to be revealed as slave-born, without rubbing it in. Even so, he was aware of Isabelle and Laetitia, Solange and Nicolette all glancing at her sidelong, with that curious change in the way they stood, the way they looked.

They were freeborn.

She had not been.

And she had probably claimed the contrary to every one of them.

His mother's face was calm now, but still gray with rage, humiliation, and terror.

Stiffly, as if the truth (if it was the truth) were being forced from her by hot irons, Livia said, 'I don't know. I was maybe Marianne's age—'

With every sang-melée member of the family in the room, he knew she wasn't about to give her real age, nor would he have asked it of her. Even the oldest sugar plantations along the

Mississippi hadn't been established much before 1740, and it was conceivable that Simon Fourchet had borrowed against his slaves well prior to his mother being sold.

'When Hannibal gets here,' he continued, 'I need you to talk to him about exactly what years you were at Bellefleur. Natchez is an old town and God only knows how long Ellie's father was there, or when this loan – if there *was* a loan – was made. Rose,' he added quietly, 'I'd like you to go with him.'

She nodded, not needing to be told.

'But—' stammered Dominique. 'But even if – even if that horrible *salope* was right, and Mamzelle Ellie *does* have some kind of claim over . . . over Maman . . .' She could barely get the words out, and their mother looked aside with an expression that twisted January's heart in unaccustomed pity. 'I'm sure – I *know* – Henri would simply pay her off. That's all she'll want, isn't it? Just money—'

'It's not that easy,' said January quietly. 'If Ellie – and probably Uncle Mick is going to get into this – has a legal claim on Maman—' he found himself, a little to his annoyance, avoiding the words, *If our mother is this girl's slave* – 'it means she legally owns all her children.'

Minou's mouth fell open, in shock and horror.

'And all their children,' he concluded quietly.

And it was highly unlikely, he reflected, that the rest of the family was going to let Henri pull eight thousand dollars out of their joint holdings to purchase slaves whom he intended to simply set free.

Ten

As January suspected, Solange Aubin had two pint bottles of Godfrey's Cordial in her luggage ('Poor little Stanislas suffers so from the colic!'), so January had no trouble in mixing himself a drop of the powerful opiate in a large glass of water ('Are you sure that's going to be enough, M'sieu Janvier? I give Stanislas a teaspoon in half that amount of water every night, and sometimes he is still restless.') ('Which explains a great deal about Stanislas,' sighed Rose, when the woman had left the room.)

The remedy wasn't nearly enough to make his ankle cease hurting, but it did let him, with Rose's help, examine the injury, now grossly swollen, and determine that the lower end of the fibula – the lateral *malleolus* – was almost certainly cracked. During this procedure Madame Molina appeared, with more laudanum ('Godfrey's Cordial, tcha! You might as well drink lemonade'), which January declined with thanks, and her basket of splints, bandages, plasters, and pins. She was, by her own account, the plantation midwife and veterinarian, and seemed to know enough about the surgeon's art for January to trust her and Rose to splint his foot, for by this time he was sweating and sick with pain. ('You sure you don't want some Hooper's Female Elixir, Ben? I wish to God we had some

127

Black Drop on the place – puts Hooper's all to shame!')

Scarcely was she out of the room when Hannibal returned, with the news that both the *Sarah Jane* and the *Phoenix* had passed the landing earlier in the afternoon. In the uproar of Jules Mabillet's challenge to Evard Aubin, and its disastrous sequel, no flag had been flown to signal a passenger to be picked up. There would, according to Mick Trask's copy of the *True American*, be no more boats tonight. The *Louisiana Belle* was due sometime heading up-river tomorrow and, as Uncle Veryl had pointed out to Mamzelle Ellie (*Was that only this morning?*), the only saddle horses on the place were the elderly bay gelding on which Molina supervised the work-gangs in the field, and now Jules Mabillet's tall black saddlebred.

'There was apparently quite a nice saddle mule,' added the fiddler, winding his long hair up like a lady's chignon and fastening it into place with one of Nicolette's tortoiseshell combs. 'But – also in the aforesaid uproar – it, and Uncle Mick's valet St-Ives – both disappeared.'

Rose's eyebrows lifted as she folded up the surplus bandages. 'Searching for Père Eugenius along the river?'

'If he is, he didn't notify Trask of his intentions – or so Trask says.'

'On his way to town,' grated Livia, her fists clenching.

'Well,' agreed the fiddler, 'I can't see where else one would be going, in this godforsaken country: *una selva oscura*,' he added, quoting Dante with arms outflung.

'Ché la diritta via era smarrita.
Ahi quanto a dir qual era è cosa dura
esta selva selvaggia e aspra e forte . . .

'But whether he's decided that now would be a good time to resign his position as Trask's valet, or whether he intends to intercept me on the road – or forstall me somehow in my search of the Cabildo – remains, I expect, to be seen.' Hannibal frowned. 'I wonder how good a shot he is?'

'I expect,' said Livia grimly, 'that, too, remains to be seen.'

Damn it, thought January, his hand tightening on Rose's fingers. *Damn it, damn it, damn it!*

'And of course that topic is as nothing beside the duel tomorrow,' Hannibal went on, as Livia went to the doors to answer Laetitia's motherly enquiries about how January did. 'Madamoiselle Charlotte weeps and flutters her handkerchief but has not yet retired to her room, no matter how frequently faintness overtakes her at the thought of two young gentlemen fighting over her – which I daresay is the case, with all due respect to His Majesty of France and Mr Bonaparte. Sisters Sophie and Ophélie wear expressions of sour dudgeon but have not yet retired to *their* room – since they are of course all three sharing a room with – it would now appear – Florrie Cowley: sorry, Fleurette née St-Chinian, and her daughter Gin.'

'I expect,' said Rose thoughtfully, 'that every dormer in the attic is going to be crammed with spectators and spyglasses tomorrow morning when the duel takes place. I wonder if Visigoth

129

and Hecuba are going to rent out the window in their room? I think it's on that side of the house. One can't get a decent view of the levee from the gallery because of the trees, you know. I expect Madame Chloë will lend you one of the plantation work-mules, Hannibal.'

'Two,' said January quietly. 'I want you out of here, Rose.' He lowered his voice, not that he thought that his mother had ears for anything but the diatribe she was currently delivering to Laetitia on the subject of the shortcomings of Louisiana laws concerning slaves, debt, and manumission. 'And I want you out tonight.'

Rose looked as if she would speak, then only nodded. The French law of Louisiana, under which she had been born free, specified that children inherited the legal condition of their mother, but there was no saying how an American judge would interpret the status of January's sons. From the gallery, Minou's voice drifted like the scent of roses, praising Charmian as they played bounce-ball in the sticky pallor of approaching twilight. The little chamber was like the inside of an oven.

Equally softly, she said, 'I'll warn Olympe.'

'I think it might be best,' said January, 'if I went across and spoke to Chloë about it now. I can't imagine Uncle Mick doesn't know . . . and I can't imagine that a city-born, northern, free man—' which they had ascertained by this time that St-Ives indeed was – 'would choose to escape in the middle of country like this when he could just as easily slip away in New Orleans where he could get passage to the North.' In fact, given the presence of slave-stealers in the ciprière, it was a wonder the man had risked leaving the plantation at all.

He gazed at the ceiling-rafters for a time, trying to clear away some of the cobwebby sensation of being trapped in a nightmare. 'If any of this does come out, Henri can almost certainly protect Minou and Charmian. The more people involved, however, the less likely anyone is going to be to start making allowances and exceptions to rules. I may be able to talk Chloë out of two mules but certainly not three, and with any luck Maman and I can get out tomorrow afternoon on the *Louisiana Belle*. My nightingale, is there any chance you can find me a pair of crutches? Madame Molina ought to have some.'

'I think you underestimate the good-will of Henri and Chloë,' said Hannibal quietly, as Rose hurried out into the brutal glare. 'Between them, if worst came to worst and that *meretrix* Valla was speaking the truth, I can't imagine they wouldn't come up with whatever Ellie and Uncle Mick are going to demand in the way of payment.'

'By my calculations—' January sat up – extremely carefully – and took the wet flannel Hannibal fetched for him from the bedside wash-bowl – 'that's going to be about eight thousand dollars, for myself, Maman, Dominique, Charmian, Olympe, Olympe's children, and possibly Rose's as well, if Uncle Mick should happen to be feeling generous when he bribes the judge before the trial. But even if worst came to worst,' he went on, over his friend's exclamation of disgust, 'if Uncle Mick *doesn't* try to run up

131

the prices beyond what Aurelié Viellard would agree to let her son pay – remember that freed slaves have to leave the state nowadays. Or else Henri – or whoever's name is on the manumission papers – is going to be liable for *another* thousand dollars apiece as bond.'

Hannibal made a comment which was fortunately – since both Charmian and Stanislas were on the gallery and in earshot – in classical Greek.

'But first, and above all, let's see what we're talking about. It's nearly twenty miles to town by the river road, but even if St-Ives is lurking along the way, that's probably a safer way for you to take, than trying to cut across country. To go direct you'd have two river crossings and nearly ten miles of swamp, and most of that's going to be by night. That's supposing I can find a reason good enough to get Madame Chloë to lend me two mules after one has already been stolen. Thank God September is the slow time of year.'

Madame Molina did indeed have crutches among her plantation store, though even the longest pair were slightly too short for comfortable use. Even so, crossing the weedy, uneven distance to the big house was an agonizing journey. As January had suspected, Chloë Viellard was closeted with Madame Aurelié and the assorted family lawyers, and had he simply sent word requesting her to visit him at the weaving house, he guessed she would not have done so until long after dark. Moreover, such a request – from a man of color to a white member of the family, and a woman at that – would have generated more speculation than he cared to deal with.

It was going to be difficult enough as it was, to keep Valla's words from going through the white family like a grassfire.

He wasn't even entirely certain she'd excuse herself from the meeting at the news – relayed by Archie – that he was waiting for her on the back gallery.

'Veryl's gone across to the Casita with his light o' love and that preposterous Englishman,' reported old Sidonie Janvier, seated by herself on the far end of the gallery on the women's side – the downstream side – of the house, with Thisbe panting gently on her lap. 'Poor old Visigoth's being run off his feet, getting supper for everyone, and now looking over his shoulder every two minutes to make sure that pestilent Irish bandit isn't trying to talk Aurelié into selling him.'

'*Selling* him?' The mere word put a chill up January's spine.

The old woman shrugged, and stroked her lapdog's black ears. January had always liked this once-beautiful Frenchwoman; when as a child he'd accompany his mother's cook to the market, Betsy would point her out as they passed through the Place des Armes: 'There's Michie Janvier's Maman.' He'd known even then that Madame Sidonie was friendly with his mother when they met by chance, not ignoring her (as Michie Janvier's pale young wife did), nor treating her with scorn because her son had taken a former slave woman, rather than one of the fashionable *librée* demimonde, for his plaçeé. Later, when as a young man January had played the piano at the various festivities during Carnival season, Madame Sidonie had chatted with him with friendly kindness, accepting him as a distant 'family connection' despite the fact that he was a) absolutely African-black and b) no relation to her own blood. Nearly every other French Creole mama in New Orleans would have berated her son for taking care of his plaçeé's children by another man, and that man an African slave.

When St-Denis Janvier had died, Madame Sidonie had written to January in Paris – a brief note, but asking in evident sincerity if there were anything she could do for him – and upon his return to New Orleans, he had received a similar short but friendly query. His mother, he knew, still took coffee with the old lady on Sunday afternoons.

At any rate, though this was the longest conversation he'd ever had with Madame Sidonie, there was no sense of it being an exceptional event. He had, in his way, grown up knowing her.

'Yes,' the old lady affirmed now, her voice dry. 'And were I Visigoth I'd be insulted at the price Trask offered. Eight hundred dollars! Less than the cost of a field hand! I understand he's made offers on Hecuba and poor old James as well. I've warned Aurelié.' A corner of her mouth curled down. 'The man's strolled twice down to Molina's cottage – that's where they're putting Locoul and that disgusting brother-in-law of his – and I suspect he's going to make some deal with Molina, to buy a few of the field hands as soon as everyone's gone back to town. Molina

134

can pocket the money, and tell Chloë and Aurelié that they ran away. And I don't expect it's the first time.

'It's not my business, of course,' she continued, as January's brows shot up. 'But I shouldn't be surprised if some of the mules they've lost to "snakebite" or "theft" over the past few years didn't go the same way. You can't trust those high-yellows.'

After a moment's startled silence, January said, 'You have enlarged my knowledge of Creole business practices, m'am,' which made her laugh.

'Well, they all steal, you know. I've lost two pillowslips since I've been here – "mislaid", my maid swears! Chloë's had her own suspicions about the number of mules that have died on this place, or been "stolen".' She glanced along the gallery toward the main house, the open French doors shadowed with expostulating forms.

'You need someone you can trust, on a place this isolated. Walking about the place today, I couldn't help noticing the number of hogsheads they've got in the cooperage shop. Aurelié was telling me that Cold Bayou doesn't produce more than thirty-eight hogsheads per season. By the look of the fields it should be at least forty-three. That sugar has to be going someplace. Dear,' she added, setting Thisbe aside and stretching out her long, thin white hands to Chloë as the girl came hurrying along the gallery. 'Is Locoul making a nuisance of himself again? What a voice that man has!'

With a serpentine smile – and graceful tact – Madame Sidonie rose, snapped her fingers to the dog, and retreated to her room, admonishing January to 'Tell your mother to walk over tonight for a hand of picquet,' leaving January and Chloë alone.

'M'sieu Janvier, you shouldn't have walked over here!' protested the girl, catching up the bent-willow chair in which the old lady had been sitting and carrying it down the steps for him. 'Please, sit—'

'I won't keep you but a moment.' He didn't sit, but rested his knee on the chair seat, which helped. 'And I beg your pardon, for having called you out of your conference.'

'Anything that called me out of the presence of Cousin Locoul,' returned Chloë, 'is both a relief and a joy, but yes, I do have to get back . . .'

'I realize it is a monstrous imposition on you,' said January. 'And on Michie Molina, at this time of the year. Particularly now that one mule has been stolen – I assume the sheriff has been notified? But is there any possibility that Rose and Hannibal might borrow two of the mules, to ride back to town tonight? When we left,' he went on, 'Xander – our baby—' Chloë nodded, having already met that lively, sunshiny child – 'was a little feverish, and had thrown out a rash on his stomach and thighs. I didn't think it was serious – I still don't – but Rose thought she'd be able to return this afternoon to look after him. Even before Madamoiselle Ellie asked me to return to town, Rose had spoken to me about putting out a flag on the landing. Apparently Isabelle Valverde told her about a friend's child who put out just such a rash as Xander had, and went on to become extremely ill. Rose . . .' He frowned, with what he hoped was a look of genuine concern. 'It isn't like Rose to become upset like this, but I can't say that I'm easy in my mind, either. Hannibal has offered to escort her back to town tonight, and can bring the mules back tomorrow – and possibly Rose as well, since I know she's very fond of Uncle Veryl, and would hate to miss his wedding. But I just . . . I don't want to risk it.'

'Nor should you.' Chloë laid a small white hand on his, where it rested on the curved back of the chair. 'Thank goodness it's not harvest time. Tell Zach at the barn that I said it was all right for him to saddle the two best mules for them to take, and tell them in the kitchens that they can have whatever food they'll need. If you don't mind – if Hannibal won't mind,' she added, with a slight frown, 'could you ask him to make a note of what they're given? Not that I don't trust him, or Rose, but—'

'But more might disappear than was authorized?'

'Something of the sort.' The girl's pale lips quirked. 'Will Hannibal be armed? I haven't heard of trouble here since that uprising in '35, but there are runaways in the woods, Madame Molina tells me. And there are white men who live by thieving. Captain Chamoflet – who deals in smuggling slaves in through the Barataria – wouldn't pass up a chance to rob a traveler. There used to be a maroon village a mile back into the woods, where it starts to become a genuine swamp; thieves will sometimes hide out in the old huts. I'm told, too, that the river-trader

137

False River Jones is supposed to be somewhere on the bayou tonight, to buy whatever everybody's been stealing here for the past two days . . . So it would pay to be careful.'

'I'll tell him.' January wondered how good a shot St-Ives *was*. For all the man's dandified appearance, there was never any telling. *Are there shooting-galleries in New York or Philadelphia that permit black men to practice?*

'Tell him to speak to M'sieu Molina. The man has a truly fearsome arsenal in his cottage – he's said to be a murderously accurate marksman. Or possibly one of M'sieu Trask's boys has something to spare. They all seem to be armed to the teeth. Now I must get back.' She threw a glance back toward the main house as one of the French doors opened and M'sieu Brinvilliers, stout and white-haired, stepped forth and looked around, presumably for her. January wondered if Henri had been asked to be part of the conference or not.

'James!' Chloë called as, almost at the same moment, the valet emerged from Singletary's room in the men's wing. 'James, can you find Archie and the two of you help Ben back to the weaving house? You honestly shouldn't have come, Ben . . .'

She gathered her pale, plain skirts in hand and hurried up the steps again and along the gallery, like a self-important schoolgirl in the hazy shadow. 'She's right, sir,' agreed James, crossing the yard to January, his white brows lowering. 'You could have sent a message.'

'Ben!' A deep voice called out from another of

the doors on the upstream wing. Basile Aubin – the father, by different mothers, of both Solange and of the golden-haired Evard – emerged onto the gallery opposite. 'Just the man I want to see!'

The wine-merchant hastened down the steps, followed a moment later by Evard himself, punctiliously stylish as any Parisian in a nip-waisted coat of dark blue and three silk waistcoats that must, January reflected, be unspeakably uncomfortable in the late-afternoon heat.

'How is the ankle?' The older man offered a hand to January, and shook it briskly. 'I must say I'm astonished to see you on your feet.'

So am I, reflected January, though he knew better than to interrupt a white man. The laudanum had worn off quite some time ago.

'But at the same time I'm grateful for it. To be honest,' Aubin lowered his voice and glanced around him, as if fearing to be overheard, 'Urbain – that's my valet – tells me that Madame Molina, though I'm sure she's a perfectly capable woman when it comes to birthing pickaninnies and giving enemas to mules, isn't . . . Well, I'd feel safer if someone with better qualifications were to act as surgeon at this duel tomorrow morning.'

He put an arm around his son's shoulders. 'Not that I think my boy's in any danger – I could see the way that simpering Bonapartiste cringed when he heard the weapons were to be cold steel! But I just don't want to take any chances with a wound turning dirty. Viellard tells me you trained at the Hôtel Dieu.'

'I did, sir.'

'Good man! St-Denis was always one to deal

fairly with his family. And since I see you're on your feet and well able to get about . . .'

Had he been speaking to any of the folks in the weaving house, January would have protested that he was not 'well able to get about' – he later regretted not saying this, from the bottom of his heart. But the assertion that this was not so would have required an explanation, completely aside from whatever complications would have ensued from contradicting a white man, and January had no thought at the moment beyond getting Rose and Hannibal on their way as speedily as possible.

So he said, 'Of course, sir,' gritted his teeth against the smart thump on his bicep Aubin gave him by way of thanks – which he could feel all the way down to his swollen foot – and taking James' arm, hobbled gingerly to the mule-barn. Hannibal met them halfway, having been flirting mildly with Sophie and Ophèlie Viellard under the oak trees downstream of the house ('Both of them are ready to kill Charlotte – three of Ophèlie's suitors having backed off in an undignified hurry the moment Uncle Veryl's engagement was announced').

'I'll take care of the kitchen portion of the program,' offered the fiddler, when January had turned down his suggestion that he – Hannibal – assist January back to the weaving house and then make arrangements at the mule-barn. 'By the time provisions are packed, the mules will be saddled and ready to start.'

'And it will be almost sunset.' Leaning heavily on James' shoulder, January scanned the cloud-scrimmed sky. 'Damn that wretched girl,' he added, in Latin, since James understood some English as well as French. 'And bringing up the subject to Mamzelle Ellie will only risk triggering some kind of action from her or that miserable uncle of hers.'

'Veryl would never permit—'

'I don't know that,' said January quietly. 'I *think* you're right. But I don't want to find out that Ellie is capable of being pushed into action by her uncle, or that Veryl is capable of being pushed into doing something he doesn't feel is right, for the sake of the girl he loves. *I can't risk it.*' Leaning on both valet and fiddler, he dragged himself along the broken shells of the path to the barn, as if the very air, the very smell of the river and the whirring of the cicadas in the trees, were a wall he had to climb, over and over again.

'Olympe will know where to hide Rose and the children,' he went on, struggling for balance. 'All of them, hers and mine. After that, we can all do and say whatever we want. But right now, we can't risk even a minute's delay.'

St-Ives – if his intent was to reach the Cabildo records before Hannibal did – already had most of a day's start on them.

Zach, the forty-year-old mule-boy, raised no objection to January's assertion that Madame Chloë had authorized the loan of two mules for overnight, and when January turned to go, backed one of the four remaining animals from its stall and haltered it. 'If Michie Hannibal don't mind the imposition, sir,' he said, 'maybe you can ride Keppy here back to the guesthouse, save yourself

141

a walk? I'll have Abi and Oni here saddled up by time you bring him back, sir.'

'I would kiss your feet,' said January, taking a fifty-cent piece from his pocket and slapping it into Zach's hand, 'if I thought there was any chance I'd be able to get up again once I got down.'

'You-all can kneel next time,' agreed the hostler, gravely magnanimous.

January thought he'd be able to bid Rose goodbye before she left. When he'd lain down on her pallet bed, in the room she shared with Dominique, she put a compress on his ankle and re-splinted it, then pressed into his hand the round silver disk of the compass she generally carried. 'You may need this,' she said, and kissed him in a way that made him wonder how much she believed of Olympe's prophecies after all. But though he mixed his own glass of water and Godfrey's Cordial, and was careful about the amount of the latter, pain, exhaustion, and the stress of the day hit him hard. He was dimly conscious – it felt like only seconds after he'd shut his eyes – of Hannibal's voice somewhere in the room, and when next he opened his eyes it was pitch-dark, and the house silent.

Far off, on the other side of the mosquito-bar around the bed, he heard music – the Lancer's quadrille – from the direction of the big house, beneath the metallic roar of the cicadas. Heat-lightning, far off, briefly illuminated the room.

He wondered if that was what had waked him.

No, he thought. It had been a sound. A night bird's distant scream.

Or a sound from the bayou, where False River Jones the trader was trading for stolen goods with the contraband of survival: fish-hooks, gunpowder, the liquor that sometimes made the difference between death from despair and carrying on another day.

Rose and Hannibal must have slipped quietly away hours ago.

Good, he thought. *Good.*

From beneath his pillow he slid the compass, held it to the shard of moonlight that barely managed to gleam through the French door, and it was as if he heard her whisper his name.

He pressed the metal to his lips, closed his eyes again. And though the Devil appeared to be attempting to chew his foot off he slept again almost at once.

Basile Aubin's valet Urbain – a trim little man who retained Ibo facial structure despite generations of admixture with whites – tapped at the door of his room while darkness still lay on the land. He gallantly turned his eyes aside from the still-sleeping Minou and Charmian, to help January dress, and even offered to shave him, out on the gallery by torchlight. 'I'll take you up on it later,' January said, 'if you'd be so kind.' He mixed himself the least amount of Cordial-and-water he thought he could get away with, and with the help of his crutches managed, with the valet's help, to limp to where torchlight burned on the levee.

Any white woman who exhibited the slightest curiosity about such violent matters as dueling

143

would have been branded at once as an unmarriageable trollop, and every slave and servant on the place was already at work. But every white male guest was assembled in a loose ring on the flat ground at the foot of the levee, and January was well aware that his fellow musicians, and old Sylvestre St-Chinian and his sons, followed him and Urbain, and stood just far enough away from the yard-high embankment so as not to offend white sensibilities. ('Get them damn darkies outta here!' snarled Uncle Mick to his boys, but the musicians simply scattered like cats into the pre-dawn blackness, to return when the attention of the Irishmen reverted to the duel.)

Jules-Napoleon Mabillet stood several inches taller than his opponent, and his sensitive features contracted in a frown of concentration as he warmed up with practice passes in the torchlight. Clouds had moved in. Shifty fragments of warm breeze flattened the linen of the young combatants' shirtsleeves to the muscle of their arms, and rattled the cane in the fields nearby. The torchflames streamed out in orange ribbons against the darkness, then would seem to fall and contract abruptly as the wind drew breath. Once, while the young men's seconds – Florentin Miragouin and Basile Aubin himself – were conferring, a few drops of rain spattered January's cheek.

Evard Aubin, his square-chinned face set in an expression of calm contempt, stretched into lunges also, flexible, light, and very strong.

Henri Viellard came over to January, whispered, 'Are you all right, Benjamin?' The orange light made two neat rectangles of his spectacle-lenses

144

as he glanced toward the seconds, and his plump face creased with distress. 'I've always hated these affairs – barbaric! Evard was gloating all evening about it. Yes, he's my cousin, but Jules' mother is Mama's closest friend! Should anything happen to Jules, I'll be very surprised if Mama will countenance Evard's suit in any case!'

'Which of them would Madamoiselle Charlotte choose, had she completely her own will of it, sir?' asked January quietly. In a way, Henri Viellard was almost a brother-in-law: he had traveled with him, had delivered the daughter he adored. Among all the whites at the big house, January realized he *did* consider Henri almost a member of his own family. 'Or do you know?'

The fat man shook his head. 'Who among us has his own will?' His voice was wistful. Thin, fair strands of his hair flickered across his brow. 'Both of them acted like absolute cads when Uncle's frightful . . . when all this uproar began,' he corrected himself, with a glance across the torch-lit circle at Uncle Veryl. 'Charlotte – and Sophie and Ophèlie, indeed – were very much hurt. The more so because Ophèlie found the note that the Picard family lawyer sent Mama, informing her that Ophèlie's fiancé would be obliged to withdraw his suit if the conditions for property settlement could not be guaranteed. Oh, this entire business is medieval!'

Medieval, reflected January, *was exactly the word for it*. From the meticulous hair-splitting of the family holdings to the two young men now poised in the firelight, the steel catching long slips of burning gold, it all smacked far more of the fourteenth century than of the nineteenth. Atavistic, if not downright primitive . . . except of course for the presence of four lawyers, eager as spectators at a cockfight.

And though the fight was supposedly only until first blood, if the Mabillet boy managed to wound young Aubin fatally, would Basile Aubin really permit his cousin Madame Aurelié to bestow the hand of her daughter on his only son's killer?

Jules Mabillet's face still wore that nearly-studious frown, as if he were trying to remember some half-forgotten lesson. Evard Aubin's narrow mouth framed a tight, cold smile.

There was a quick pass: Mabillet fell back. His parry was uncertain, and it appeared that only his longer legs saved him. A shifting for position, Evard beating a time or two on the foible of his opponent's blade, Mabillet clumsily retreating. The Black Duke – the tallest and most powerful of the Irishmen – called out, 'Run in an' spit the feller, why don't yez?' – fortunately in English – and another – lean and runty and pock-marked – muttered more quietly, 'What you bet Blondie kills 'im, an' to hell with this first blood tripe?' 'Here's hopin' anyways, Gopher,' opined a third.

Then with a spring and a lunge Evard drove in, and with blinding and wholly unexpected speed Mabillet parried to fifth and riposted, blood bright the length of Evard's sleeve as the taller man's point ripped his arm from wrist to shoulder. There was a whoop of delight from the Black Duke and a thunder of Gaelic curses from the others – presumably the Duke had bet against the general impression that Mabillet didn't know what he was doing with a blade in his hand – and at the same moment a voice yelled from the growing dawnlight behind them,

'Michie Veryl! Michie Veryl!'

And such was the note in it that everyone turned.

It was Luc, panting and gray-faced with shock.

'Michie Veryl, you gotta come! In the woods – back of the Casita! They killed her—'

Jules Mabillet, like the others, had turned at the shout, and like the flick of a frog's tongue ending the life of a fly, Evard Aubin drove his blade straight in through his rival's body. The young man let out one despairing cry and collapsed as Aubin jerked his sword free, blood spouting out onto the trampled earth.

Eleven

Luc gasped again, 'They killed her!' and everyone, with the exception of January and Henri, set off in the direction of the Casita at a run.

January yelled, 'Get a torch!' and Henri – nearly as tall as January but almost twice his weight – had to pursue them at a rolling trot.

He called out, 'Stop! We need a torch here! Stop!' as January dragged and staggered to the fallen man's side.

There was enough light in the sky at least for him to see, and he tore open his surgeon's bag as he fell to his knees. Mabillet twisted as he lay on the ground, sobbing in pain. The wound was low in his body, between hip and groin, and January, his own hands shaking with the pain in his ankle, ripped open the young man's flies and pulled down trousers and drawers to expose the flesh. He'd wadded bandages and handfuls of lint over both entry and exit holes, and wrapped them tightly by the time Henri returned, gasping, a brand upraised in either hand.

Immediately behind him clustered Visigoth, Antoine, and Madame Molina, appearing from two different directions. 'What happened?' Antoine demanded, dropping at once to his knees beside January and the injured man. 'I saw everybody go runnin' to the woods like somebody found treasure there.'

'They did,' retorted Visigoth grimly. 'Luc come runnin' past the house yellin' "*She's* dead, she's dead by the Casita", an' every livin' soul in the place lights out like the buildin' is on fire, to see.'

'Dead?' Madame Molina crossed herself.

'I don't think half of 'em even saw Michie Evard run poor Michie Jules through, but I had the spyglass just at that minute.'

In addition to his spyglass, the butler had brought the litter on which men injured in the fields could be carried to the infirmary – January guessed this was why it had taken him as long to reach the levee from the house as it had taken Antoine and Madame Molina to get there from the overseer's cottage. The only white women to actually come to the levee – the slatternly Fleurette, her cowed-looking daughter and Locoul's wife Madame Pepa with no rouge

148

and curl-papers still danging from her hair – were now hastening toward them through the growing dawnlight, and all cried out in horror at the butler's news. But none of them, obviously, could brand herself an incorrigible gossip by racing off to the Casita to look at a murdered corpse when there was an injured man to be seen to, no matter how much more interested they were in the one than in the other.

'Was anyone left in the house?' January asked Visigoth, and the butler shook his head disgustedly. 'Then perhaps,' he went on, with the tactful circumlocution necessary, even in an emergency, when a black man had to give orders to white ladies, 'if one of these ladies might be so good as to run ahead of us to the kitchen, and fetch hot water to Michie Jules' room . . .?'

'I'll do it.' Fleurette gathered her skirts to her knees and pelted for the house like a hare.

By this time all the women from the weaving house – family members and maidservants in a body – had reached them, exclaiming in shock over Visigoth's news and most of them dashing off in the direction of the Casita at once. Solange, Minou, Laetitia and young Marianne remained, to lend Antoine a hand in helping January hobble slowly in the wake of the litter toward the big house. Sunrise had revealed a sky smeared from horizon to horizon with a sticky film of cloud, and the wind still came and went, came and went in a manner that whispered of a storm to come.

Just what we need, thought January, who had been in the bayou parish during hurricane season.

The dream he'd dreamed two nights before

149

coming down here – the dream of flood, of rising waters, of the smell of smoke – had been filled with the smell of storm, with the tension in the air that heralded wind and downpour. More than ever he was glad he'd gotten Rose out of here. And when the *Louisiana Belle* came by that afternoon, he was going to do his utmost to make sure he and his mother were on it – and old Michie Singletary, for he knew he couldn't abandon his patient.

But he had another patient now. He looked ahead, a dozen yards now, where Visigoth and Henri bore the litter toward the house. Maybe two more patients. Veryl would be devastated with shock and grief, and he knew to the bottom of his heart that for all his occasional abstraction, Selwyn Singletary wouldn't abandon his friend.

Damn it, he thought, *damn it.*

If blood's shed – he could almost hear Olympe saying it – *you know who's going to get the blame.* Though how anyone could blame him when he was laid up with a broken ankle . . .

And he could almost hear his sister jeer, *They'll manage.*

Back behind the Casita, Luc had said. How far behind? How had it been done?

He gritted his teeth despairingly, knowing that whoever had killed the girl must have left their marks on the ground, on the trees, somewhere . . . And with the entire population of the big house, the weaving house, and by this time half the quarters milling around to stare, any sign of the true culprit was going to be trampled away, leaving the field open for accusation to fall upon

150

whoever was most convenient to the white folks involved.

I hope Valla didn't go slipping out again to meet her lover.

If he is her lover . . .

He glanced sidelong at Antoine as the slender young houseman steadied him up the gallery steps.

Or if she did sneak out, I hope she stayed with him long enough that it can be proved she couldn't have killed her mistress.

Because as things stood, the one person over whom Ellie held actual power had been her maid. Every member of the St-Chinian and Viellard families had reason to kill Veryl's disgraceful bride, but if they could point to a disgruntled servant and say, 'She did it', they would.

And the Louisiana courts had proved over and over again, that they would far sooner hang a slave than a respectable French Creole.

I need to get out there and look at the place, look at her body.

No! They passed into the big house, threaded their way between the silent rows of chairs still assembled in the parlor and dining room – the ironclad rule about black folk cutting through the front of the house suspended in the face of grimmest necessity. Jules Mabillet had shared the room at the end of the upstream wing last night with the three French lawyers. They had already rolled up the pallets and made the room's single bed ready to receive him.

What you need to do is make sure that Jules Mabillet doesn't die. Ellie Trask is dead. Valla

151

has not yet been accused. You need to focus your mind on the man whose life hangs in the balance now, *whose body-cavity may* now *be filling with blood and waste leaking from a pierced gut . . .*

Archie rushed past him with bottles of laudanum and spirits of wine in his hands.

And you need not to take any more laudanum no matter how much your ankle hurts and it hurts like a million devils.

You can't make a mistake.

The young man was laid on the bed, the French doors open though the room was designed to exclude sun rather than admit it. Visigoth had stripped him and brought in more bandages; Fleurette Cowley squeezed past January with a brass can of hot water. January took the spirits of wine – one of his instructors at the Hôtel Dieu in Paris had sworn by it for cleansing wounds – and rinsed his hands. Marianne held out his satchel to him, and from it he took scissors, ran the blades back and forth through the flame of one of the candles, waited a moment for the metal to cool and then carefully cut the makeshift bandages he'd bound on fifteen minutes before.

And exhaled in relief. It was immediately apparent in the better light that Aubin's sword had gone lower than he'd thought. It had missed the hip joint a scant inch below the pelvic girdle and pierced the inner thigh an inch or so to the left of the testicles.

No involvement in the gut.

Had there not been a marked difference in height between the two men, the wound would have been higher, and mortal.

And without a doubt, January reflected sourly as he cleansed and packed the puncture, the courts – if the matter came to court at all – would simply fine Evard Aubin for 'disturbing the peace' or 'brawling' rather than a calculated attempt at murder. He would argue that he hadn't heard Luc's call, hadn't been aware that first blood had already been drawn . . . that as far as he was concerned, the duel was still in progress.

But from the instant Luc had called out, 'They killed her', Evard had known that Jules Mabillet was the one who stood in the way of his marriage to a substantial percentage of the Viellard and St-Chinian lands.

Behind him, January heard everybody returning. (*Returning after trampling the whole scene of the murder. And if it rains this afternoon, which it's going to – and if I don't die of the pain in my ankle – there'll be nothing left out there to see.*)

He wondered where they'd put Ellie's body. The Casita? Veryl would surely ask him to look at her.

Stop! Focus! Think of this man's life . . .

A wound that pierced straight through – particularly a narrow one like this – often turned feverish.

Then he heard someone say in a sweet, unmistakable voice, 'Oh, Mr St-Chinian, who would have wanted to hurt her?' and he nearly dropped his swab.

???!!!???

ELLIE???

He didn't hear Veryl's reply, and had to shut

153

his mind to the voices on the gallery, as much as he shut it against the pain in his foot. *You cannot think of that right now . . .*

But it was Ellie's voice. There was no mistaking that dove-like Celtic coo.

He'd had to open the wound a little larger, to make sure it was properly cleansed; now he bandaged it tightly, and washed his hands again in the spirits of wine. By the sound of it, everyone in the house was coming and going from the Casita, and he was wondering if he'd really have to hobble out onto the gallery and grab someone by the arm in order to ask for a servant to help him, when shadow darkened the French door.

'How is he?' asked a voice that he barely recognized as Madame Aurelié's, so changed and gentle it sounded.

January turned – very carefully – on the bedside stool on which he'd sat to work. 'It's early to tell, m'am. The gut wasn't pierced, thank God, nor the femoral artery severed, though there is severe bleeding. And of course with a puncture wound there's always great danger of fever.'

Aurelié Viellard crossed to the bed, and seated herself on the edge. She was fully dressed, even to her graying fair hair having been combed and pomaded into its usual thick knot at the back of her head. *She must have risen early to watch the duel.* Her face, in which her children's slightly aquiline nose and receding chin were graced with the haughty hardness of absolute self-confidence, seemed fallen and tired as she looked down at the young man on the bed, and her blue St-Chinian eyes were filled with an unwonted sorrow.

'I shall have to write to his mother,' she said after a time. 'Jules told me last night that his mother was delayed in town – she should have been here yesterday. We were at school together in France, you know. She'll be devastated. He's her only son. Her treasure.'

Gently, the stout woman leaned down to brush the black swatch of hair from the young man's eyes. January saw, almost unbelievably, a tear track down her pendulous cheek.

'Oh, my poor boy.'

The door opened behind her and Chloë stepped in, prim and neat as always but, January observed, with her eggshell-pale hair braided in a long plait down her back. Behind her thick spectacles her pale-blue eyes were grave.

'Is there anything you need, Benjamin?' she asked. 'Anything I can send for? Zach has one of the mules ready to carry you back to the weaving house, any time you say.'

'I kiss the soles of your shoes for that,' replied January. 'And if you can come up with some anodyne that isn't going to make me sleepy or affect my judgement I will pledge myself to work for you for seven years in payment for it.'

'I think if I could come up with that I should make a fortune patenting and bottling it.' The young woman had a pitcher in one hand and in the other, the substantial bottle of Hooper's Female Elixir that January had seen in the Casita pantry. She set both down on the bedside table, and mixed what looked like a well-calculated dose. 'Hélène – my maid – will take over nursing. I've ordered Leopold to spell her on this, and to run and fetch you from the weaving house if there should be any sign of trouble.' Leopold, a middle-aged German, was Henri's personal valet, but it had been clear for four years who gave the orders in that household. She glanced at her mother-in-law and added, 'I've made some enquiries about the state of people's health in the quarters, Madame, and I am not satisfied that Madame Molina is competent to doctor so severe an injury as this. I hope you agree?'

The older woman shook her head wearily. 'Whatever you judge best, child. Odd . . .' She passed a plump hand over her eyes. 'One would hope that the son of one's best friend has a tougher constitution than a field hand, yet when it comes to it . . .'

'One would not wish to say,' finished Chloë tactfully, 'that one did not seek the best-trained and best-qualified help. Leopold!' she called out, and the servant entered, his saggy-jowled face reminding January, as always, of a disapproving mastiff. 'Please assist M'sieu Janvier down the gallery and escort him on the mule back to the weaving house,' she instructed in the man's native language, which January was thankful he also knew.

'Very good, Madame.'

'Have you had breakfast, Benjamin? Would you prefer to have some here on the gallery, or back at the guesthouse? I trust accommodations there have been re-arranged so you don't have to go clambering up to the attic? Minou tells me you shared her room last night.'

There was nothing, January reflected with an

156

inner grin, that Henri's wife didn't forsee and arrange.

'I did. Thank you. And with your permission, Madame, before I return there I should like to have a look at . . . was that Valla who was killed, then?'

The girl made a gesture half of vexation, half of despair. 'God help me – extraordinary how the mind doesn't seem capable of maintaining full concentration on two catastrophes at once. Yes, please, in fact I had meant to ask you to do so, if you feel able for it.' She closed January's satchel neatly, and picked it up. 'Shall I send Hélène in, Madame?'

'If you would.' Madame Aurelié rose, and in her voice January heard, for the first time, the sort of stunned confusion that can overcome the mind in shocked pain. Fleurette and her widowed daughter Gin passed along the gallery, and chattering excitedly about the dress the dead woman had been wearing, and how Madame Molina had said it served her right . . .

Madame straightened her shoulders and took a deep breath, shaking off whatever distress she felt. 'I should like to accompany you, if I may.' And – to January's utter surprise, for today was the first time Madame had so much as acknowledged his existence – she added, 'I have heard so much of Benjamin's acumen in the matter of corpses that I would be very interested in what he should make of it.'

In the few moments it took Leopold to help January to his feet, the maid Hélène was summoned, a lanky fair Frenchwoman a few years younger than January himself. January gave her instructions for what to do should his patient awaken, and, sweating with pain himself, limped after the two Mesdames Viellard to the end of the gallery. At the foot of the steps, Keppy the Mule waited to carry him to the Casita and the grim scene that awaited him there.

Twelve

A sort of tent made of pink mosquito-bar had been erected on the back gallery of the Casita. Through its gauzy walls January saw the maid's naked body lying on that piece of furniture that every isolated plantation had and few mentioned: the 'cooling bench', where those who died could be put until the fluids of their bodies had all leaked out through its open cane-work into pans set beneath, preparatory to washing and preparing for the funeral. Even through the cloudy netting he could see that Valla's caramel-gold hair lay in a loose braid, as it would have been under a tignon. As he had seen Rose's, thick on their pillow, thousands of times.

Her breast, face, and hands had been slashed with a knife. Her throat had been cut.

'Was she dressed when she was found?'

'She was.' Chloë nodded toward a rough willow-work chair that stood beside the pantry door. The yellow-and-white striped dress lay spread over it. A white linen chemise, a corset and the stiff satin petticoat whose rustling had marked all the maidservant's steps. All had been soaked with blood and smeared with mud.

Then she ducked ahead of January as he lifted aside one section of the curtain. Madame Aurelié followed them inside, and turned at once from looking at the poor ruined beauty of the girl, to watch January's face.

For a moment he stood, simply regarding the dead girl. He remembered the spiteful timbre of her voice, and the anger that had bristled around her like the quills of an invisible porcupine. Remembered what Luc had said about her, and how she'd ordered January to fetch charcoal for her mistress, and had demanded that those in the guesthouse surrender their oranges so that Mamzelle Ellie could enjoy them. So that *she* could present them to her, and get credit for cleverness and devotion.

Recalled the silvery rustle of that expensive petticoat.

And felt only pity for her anger, and grief that she'd come to this.

Who *wouldn't* be angry, he reflected, after being a lady's maid in Virginia, to be stuck for a year or more in this sweltering, isolated world of monochrome green? Who wouldn't be angry to be bulled by the overseer and, almost certainly, pushed and bullyragged by his wife, whose hair she'd been obliged to comb every morning and whose chamber-pots she'd been ordered to clean?

Of course she'd done everything in her power to make herself indispensable to Ellie Trask, once the love-struck Uncle Veryl had plucked her from

159

kitchen-work and brought her back to a decent-sized town and new, pretty dresses. Of course she'd been on edge, to encounter once more a former lover and a former rapist. 'How old was she?' he asked quietly, and neither of the Viellard women knew.

'I don't see why it should matter,' declared Aurelié.

'It isn't important. If you will excuse me, ladies, one of the first things I should like to do here is verify whether the poor woman was raped as well as killed.'

Madame Aurelié's face contracted with appalled disgust at the thought, and she turned her back. Her daughter-in-law simply stepped aside to give January more room in which to work, folded her little hands, and watched with scientific interest.

Valla had not been raped. But by the slight bruising around the vagina it was clear that she had had intercourse not more than a day previously. And the struggle with her murderer was written on her body: her nails broken, the single deep stab under her ribs on the right side accompanied by smaller cuts on her palms and fingers, and slashes that made January think she'd been wriggling like a landed fish while her attacker tried to get in a killing blow. There was a deep slash on her left side – as if she'd gotten herself turned facing her assailant – and this may have doubled her up so that he could grab her hair, and cut her throat.

His late-night waking came back to mind, hearing music in the darkness from the big house, and wondering if it was the cry of a night bird that had startled him.

What time had that been?

The musicians were still playing . . .

Valla's muscles had been sufficiently relaxed that someone – probably Hecuba – had been able to undress her. Her neck, jaw, fingers and wrists were stiff. The pale ivory skin of which she'd been so proud showed wide patches of coagulated subcutaneous blood on her sides and the small of her back.

'Who found her?'

'Old Nana,' replied Chloë. 'One of the women in the quarters. She has trap-lines on the bayou and went out to check them when the men were rallied to work. She ran to the work-gang who were just going out to the field only a few hundred yards from where Valla was lying. M'sieu Molina sent Luc running back to tell the house.'

Midnight? One in the morning? Valla's eyes were open, the eyelids stiffened that way before anyone could force them closed. The whites were clouded. Her throat was bruised, not heavily enough to indicate strangulation. *He seized her*, he thought. *Held her by the neck and stabbed her . . .*

He took up her hands, fine-boned but callused, and saw traces of something brown beneath her nails. Even with his magnifying lens, the fragments he tweezed out were too tiny for him to tell whether this was skin – a black man's skin – or the leather of gloves.

Yes, she'd clawed at his hands or arms.

'Can the wench be trusted?' Madame Aurelié

161

had turned around again by this time and was watching him narrowly.

A silly question, he thought, and Chloë said, 'Old Nana? I can't imagine why she'd lie.'

'Don't you?' The older woman's eyebrows quirked upwards. 'They all do. Madame Molina tells me that last night that thieving trader False River Jones was out on the bayou. Half the field hands were sneaking out with goods they'd stolen, she says: the tea I'd brought from town and the good napkins and pillowcases. I daresay this girl was one of them, and the woman who found her may have been on her way back from a rendezvous with the trader as well.' She turned her chilly blue eyes on January. 'Can you tell who did this thing?'

'Not at the moment, m'am, no.' He rose stiffly from his stool and bowed a little as he said it – he wanted to shake her for her nosiness but a lifetime of restraint told him this would not be a good idea – and limped out of the little tent and over to the chair where Valla's clothing lay spread.

Someone, he reflected, had shown a good deal of sense. Folding could have confused the outlines of the bloodstains, rubbed the patches of mud against clean cloth.

No tignon, he noticed at once. Her hair was braided as if she had been wearing one, but many white women – including Ellie Trask – braided theirs before bed. Or was that beautifully-wrapped confection of yellow and white lying somewhere, half-ground into the mud and pickerel-weed?

Huge blots of blood marked the left side where the knife had been driven in under her

162

ribs, and the right side just behind the right breast. That wound was a gash rather than a simple stab, as if she'd turned her body even as it was inflicted. By the rent in the heavy linen of the corset, the ripping knife had been stopped by the corset-bone.

Even the sleeves, where glancing blows had caught her as she'd struggled, were heavily daubed and smeared.

He seized her by the throat from behind, and stabbed her in the side. But she turned, and the blow wasn't mortal. As if he could see her, he knew she'd twisted in her killer's grip, raked at his hands trying to get free. He'd cut at her again, and again, until he landed one strong enough to make her stagger. By the way the cut flesh of her throat gaped, and the pattern of the blood down the breast of her dress, it looked like he'd held her by the hair against him, and cut her throat from behind.

How much blood would that leave on a man's sleeves and breast?

Beside the bench a tin bullseye lantern lay on the floor. 'Was this near her?'

'I don't know,' Chloë said. 'I think so.'

Had the victim been a white woman, reflected January wearily – even Mamzelle Ellie, whom everyone on the plantation had been wishing would be murdered since their arrival – somebody would have made damn sure to observe the place and keep track of things more carefully than this.

'I'd like to see where it happened.' He began to limp toward the back gallery steps. Beyond them, visible past the shadows of the gallery, sudden wind shook the woods, barely a dozen yards from the back of the Casita, with a noise like the pounding of rain. Spectral streamers of Spanish moss groped at the air.

Before January could reach the steps the house door opened behind him and a Hibernian voice called, 'Hey, boy-o! You'll be Ben that's a doctor, then?'

'That'll be me.'

The Black Duke spit tobacco on the gallery planks, said, 'Miss Ellie's askin' after yez.' And he jerked his thumb to the shadows of the house at his back.

January expected to find Uncle Mick at the young woman's side, but he was wrong. Only Veryl sat perched on the threadbare yellow upholstery of the couch where the wedding dress had been draped yesterday. Even the Black Duke disappeared onto the front gallery. Ellie, beautiful in a gown of rose-colored silk, paused in her pacing as January entered. Her face maintained its composure, but was chalky under the rouge.

'Mr St-Chinian tells me you found the men who murdered his nephew a few years ago.'

'I did, yes. I couldn't testify against them in court – they were white – but they were engaged in other illegal activities and came to grief just the same. But I had nothing to do with that, I'm sorry to say.'

'I can – we can . . . Uncle Mick can . . .' She stumbled a little over the words. 'Whoever did this . . . They'll be punished for it, won't they?

164

I mean, it's still murder in this state to kill a slave, isn't it?'

'It is,' returned January quietly.

'I think she really was only killed by accident,' said Veryl quietly. 'They – whoever did this – thought it was you.'

Ellie turned her face quickly aside, and her movement wafted to January, again the reek of plum brandy. His eyes went to the open door of her room. A square cut-glass bottle stood on the table beside the bed. A pong of alcohol hung in the air.

'Even if you were the intended target, Mamzelle,' he said, 'whoever stabbed Valla is guilty of murder, though I doubt that any court in Louisiana will hang them for it. My guess is they'll be fined . . . for robbing you of your property.'

Her eyes went to his at the words, and he tried to read what was in them. But he couldn't tell – couldn't see whether it was in her mind that, according to Valla, at least, she had a claim that *he* was her property. Or had this, if it was even true, been thrust from her mind by grief, terror, and rage?

She looked away again. 'Find them.' She put her hand briefly to her lips. 'Whoever did this . . . They'll come after me next, won't they? Everybody looks at me . . .'

'Whoever did this,' said January evenly, 'was probably appalled to learn that it wasn't you they killed. I suspect they would have dumped her body in the bayou, if False River Jones and God knows how many of his customers hadn't been out there. The bayou's less than a hundred feet

165

from the Casita, behind a screen of trees. Now he – or she – the killer – has shown his hand. You know now that someone is prepared to use violence against you. And that may mean that whoever it is, will hang back and bide his time.'

'Bide his time . . .' she whispered.

'Giving us time to get away,' agreed Uncle Veryl eagerly, rising to his feet and wrapping his arms around his beloved. 'I'm sure Père Eugenius will understand, when he arrives. I'll have the flag put out on the landing for the *Louisiana Belle*—'

As if in answer – or as if the sky were jeering at these plans – the wind snarled suddenly around the corner of the house and somewhere a casement banged loudly. Something – it sounded like a torn-off tree-branch – slammed into the house with brutal force, making Veryl flinch. Ellie's eyes widened at the sound, but she didn't turn and cling to him. Fear seemed to have knocked away all the arts and pretenses she'd used – to whatever degree she'd used them – and January had the impression of seeing, for the first time, the real young woman beneath the veils of sweetness and artifice.

Tougher than the girl who'd shivered and bewailed the death of her worthy and hard-working father. Thoughts fleeted behind those lovely brown eyes, watchful now and calculating which way she'd better run.

'Will boats be running, in this weather?' She looked back at January. 'And if we run – if they are running – won't that mean . . . Well, whoever wants to kill me before I marry Mr St-Chinian

166

will want to kill me even worse after I do it, won't they?'

'*Mignonne*,' pleaded the old man, tightening his embrace. 'Don't say such things! That's what they want you to think! Trying to frighten you! Trying to scare you away!'

'Well, they're succeeding.' Ellie's brow pinched at another thought, and her eyes flooded with tears. 'You don't think – Mr J . . . You don't think they just . . . just killed Valla to warn me off, do you? If like you said all they'll get is a fine for destroying my *property* . . .'

Her voice twisted on those last words, but Veryl put in quickly, 'Surely not!'

The pantry door at the back of the parlor opened, and – to January's startled surprise – Uncle Mick's demure-eyed butler St-Ives entered, bearing a tray of lemonade and some freshly-baked teacakes, presumably prepared in the hopes of a belated wedding today.

His heart seemed to contract in his chest: *what the* hell?

Did that mean Hannibal and Rose were lying dead in a swamp somewhere?

Or . . . *What*?

Not an iota could be guessed from looking at the man's inscrutable face.

Veryl's voice continued, 'It is still murder in this state to kill a slave, especially someone else's slave. I'm going to get you out of here, my child. On the next boat that comes along – thank you, St-Ives, that will be all – and we can be married in town. You'll be safe in town.'

'Will I?' Ellie whispered despairingly.

January thrust aside his panic, forced his mind back to the events that had actually taken place, as Veryl poured the lemonade, pressed the tumbler into the girl's unsteady hands. He had to forcibly remind himself of what he had said yesterday: *Let's see what we're talking about, before we do anything.*

In his mind, January heard his friend, the Kentucky hunter Abishag Shaw, when he, January, had once faced flight with Rose from an unknown killer: *The hunter has all the advantage. Even knowin' your hunter's name – even knowin' his face – in a town the size of New Orleans, you don't know which way he's comin' at you til he's on your back.*

Even in the slow season, New Orleans was a beehive of activity, of busy crowds into which a killer could blend like a fox in long grass. In a few months, winter fogs would cover the city like a blanket.

In New Orleans, a killer could wait.

Counting the slaves in the quarters there were about a hundred and fifty people on Cold Bayou. There were over a hundred thousand in New Orleans. He thought he saw this statistic in Ellie's face, but couldn't say aloud the corollary: *It'll be easier to catch him – or her – if you stay here, and encourage them to try again.*

So he said nothing. Later he wondered if the outcome would have been different, if he had.

Instead he asked, 'Was Valla here when you got back last night?'

Ellie nodded. 'That is, she was asleep,' she explained. 'The dancing went on at the house

168

until . . . I don't know, two?' She turned to Veryl, winced again as another gust of wind slammed some other fragment of debris against the swamp-side windows of the little house.

The old man tightened his hold tenderly about her, and again January saw the slight twist of her body, impatient, as if she really wanted to break free rather than bury her face in his shoulder.

'It was past two,' said Uncle Veryl. 'James and I walked back up here with Madamoiselle, with lanterns. Because of that unpleasantness with the voodoo marks the doors were latched. A veilleuse was burning here in the parlor, and in each of the bedrooms. James went in with Madamoiselle and shone his lantern around the parlor and the bedroom.'

'I looked into Valla's room,' said Ellie. 'She was asleep in bed. Well, the mosquito-bar was down over the bed, anyway, and I could see her through it.'

'Has anything in the room been touched?'

The young woman looked a little surprised at the question, and shook her head.

'May I?'

Ellie and Uncle Veryl followed him to the shut door of the maid's bedroom. The casement banged again as January opened the door, and Ellie exclaimed, 'Oh!' Wind billowed the mosquito-bar over the narrow bed, and through the ghostly white tent of gauze a figure could be made out, and a rumple of blonde hair on the pillow. But even the stormy daylight showed in the next instant that the sheets had been humped over a bolster to counterfeit a body beneath them, and

169

the hair was an assortment of Ellie's false switches, cunningly arrayed. In darkness, and behind the netting, it would have been impossible to accurately distinguish their pale honey-gold from the richer – and only slightly darker – caramel hue of Valla's hair.

January limped around the bed to the window that faced the woods, and caught the casement as the wind hurled it closed again. The sky to the southwest was a gray turmoil of cloud, and warm rain splattered against his cheek, like a white man's derisive spit.

'You know she had a lover here at Cold Bayou?'

'I know Antoine pestered her,' said Ellie, who had not moved from the doorway. 'She said he kept on at her, the way men do: "You used to let me, why won't you let me now?"' She caught herself in the midst of this cynical observation, glanced at Veryl, and swiftly donned the mantle of confused innocence again – widened eyes, slight pucker to the brows. 'That's what all those awful girls said, that lived down the street from Papa.' And she covered her mouth for a moment, the gesture of a schoolgirl who fears she's said something naughty in ignorance.

Judging by Uncle Veryl's face, he gulped that one down like a dog swallowing a lump of cheese.

Even for a white man, that's naïve. No wonder he still thinks she's a virgin.

'You think he might have persuaded her?'

To January's surprise, Ellie's pallor pinkened suddenly into a very genuine blush, and again she looked aside. 'I . . . I don't know,' she whispered. 'I know you . . . I know a girl can tell

170

herself she's never going to . . . never going to look at this man or that man . . . and then you see him again, by chance, and it . . . it all comes back.' She raised her eyes to his, and in those doe-like depths he thought he saw the quick glimmer of tears, quickly blinked away.

'She might have,' she concluded in a tiny voice, and January had the feeling that it wasn't about Valla that she spoke.

He thought of the maid's bruised genitals. Of the way Antoine had waited for her in front of the house Tuesday morning, had caught her arm.

Of the power an overseer had on an isolated plantation like this one.

Rape and consent were always tricky questions, when the woman concerned wasn't truly free. *Pull up your skirts or I'll tell your mistress I caught you sellin' her pearls to False River Jones . . .*

'Do you think she'd have been trying to run away?'

With her hair dressed like a white woman's – rather than hidden by a tignon – Valla could easily have passed for white, once she was out of the slave-states where people looked twice at girls of ivory complexion.

'No!' Ellie's eyes grew wide as if the thought had never occurred to her. 'Oh, no! For one thing,' she pointed out, with a shrewdness January guessed she usually hid from her *inamoratus*, 'none of my jewelry was missing. I mean, Valla's own jewelry – her gold cross and chain, and a gold bracelet she had – those were gone, stolen from her body—' anger momentarily hardened her face – 'but even if she sold those, she wouldn't

171

have got far. But nothing was gone from my jewel box, and I keep pretty good track of . . .'

She glanced quickly at Veryl, who was looking a little shocked at her matter-of-fact tone, and widened her eyes again. 'I remember every single piece you've ever given me, beloved.' He looked mollified.

'Besides,' she added, turning back to January, 'there was no need for Valla to run away. I was going to free her. After the wedding. She knew that.'

January raised his brows.

Uncle Veryl nodded. 'I offered her the choice,' he said. 'For me to pay the bond for her to remain in the state and continue to work for us, or passage to New York and two hundred dollars, for a start in life.'

'And which did she choose?'

'She had made no choice when we left town,' said the old man. 'But she spoke as if she meant to stay. She was very attached to my beautiful mamzelle.' He tightened his hold on Ellie's waist, adoration in his eyes.

'Did you tell her not to wait up for you?'

Ellie's glance flickered back across the parlor to the open door of her bedroom. 'I don't . . . Sometimes I'd . . . I'd rather not be fussed over . . .' She stammered the words, and stopped herself. Looked again toward the bedroom, and January recognized her glance as the tug of longing for a desperately-needed drink.

Rather not be fussed over when you come back late and exhausted from being looked at as if you were a cockroach by all your prospective

172

husband's family? When you really want a couple of drinks before bed, and are willing to forego the services of a maid in order to have them in peace?

'Could you – could you please pour me out a little more lemonade, Mr St-Chinian?' While Uncle Veryl leaped to obey her the girl dabbed quickly at her eyes.

Tears for Valla? Tears of fright at the knowledge that they were coming for her, sometime, somewhere? Of sheer weariness with this struggle to secure safe haven for herself that wouldn't involve bedding a dozen men a night?

More gently, January said, 'Whyever she slipped out – and whenever that was – Valla met someone in the woods. Someone who thought she was you, in the darkness, with only the moonlight on her hair. Was there any reason you might have left the house after you returned here?'

'Of course not!' said Veryl, in genuine surprise.

For a long time, Ellie made no reply of her own. Only looked down and to the side, as if avoiding the sight of some recollection, pushing aside some thought. At last she said, 'No.'

Thirteen

Luc showed January where Valla's body had been found, the field hands having been summoned in as the weather showed signs of worsening. Chloë offered to accompany them, but January took her

173

quietly aside and murmured, 'If you'll forgive me, m'am, and meaning no disrespect, but I suspect I'll be able to question him more freely about anything that might have been going on in the woods or the quarters last night, if a white woman isn't around.'

Particularly, he didn't need to say, a white woman whose family owned not only the plantation, but Luc himself.

To this Chloë agreed, and remained at the Casita playing backgammon with Uncle Veryl and M'sieu Singletary in the parlor while Mamzelle retreated to her room and, it was to be assumed, her bottle of plum brandy. In other circumstances January would have welcomed the incisive little lady's observations, but like a thorn snagging at his sleeve, he recalled that Chloë herself had strong reasons to wish Uncle Veryl's ill-bred bride in her grave. In spite of Madame Aurelié's jeers that Chloë had not and would not give her a grandson, January was far from certain that Henri had not consummated his union with that cold-blooded damsel. It would be just like Chloë to request coitus with her husband for legal reasons, and in any case after the arrival of Uncle Mick, she would probably be capable of murder simply to keep anyone from interfering with the efficient management of the property, whoever was ultimately going to inherit.

Chloë wouldn't be physically capable of overpowering Valla – who stood a good six inches taller and considerably outweighed her – and the maid had almost certainly been killed by a man.

174

So there was no use asking whether the younger Madame Viellard had presided over supper at the big house, though it would be interesting to hear about her comings and goings during that meal.

More surprising, he reflected, as he and Luc descended the Casita's rear steps, would have been to learn that, *if* Henri's cold-hearted bride had indeed been behind the killing, she'd put herself in the power of a confederate. He knew Chloë almost certainly wouldn't stick at murder if she thought it called for – but letting another person hold that knowledge over her would be very unlike her indeed.

In departing, he had remarked on St-Ives's re-appearance, and Chloë had replied, 'Well, if *I* had a clandestine errand of any sort to arrange, I should entrust it to St-Ives rather than any of Uncle Mick's Hibernian baboons.'

Which was a comfort, in its way, given his concerns about the possible fate of Hannibal and Rose.

And speculation was about all he could do, surveying the muddle of torn-up pickerel-weed and sawgrass that lay just at the verge of the ciprière's swaying gloom. Pretty much everyone on the plantation, slave and free, had been through the scene. If murder had been done here it would have to have been before False River Jones set up shop among the sedges and cypress-knees of Cold Bayou, a hundred feet to the northwest. Any later, and half the slaves on the property would have walked smack into the rendezvous, or at least heard her screams.

No bloodstains were visible. The ground which

stretched behind the higher, cultivated land along the river was perpetually muddy and sloppy, and had been churned to a slithery muck for twenty feet on either side of where Luc said Valla's body had lain. Sedge and leaves had been squished into the ooze. Water was already collecting in a thousand little pockmarks where boot-heels, or particularly vigorous bare feet, had stepped.

'Where would she have been going?' he asked Luc, sliding from Keppy the Mule's back at the edge of the rucked ground and staggering on his crutch among the trampled foliage. From the satchel hanging over the little mule's withers – Keppy wore no saddle – January took a stone jar of ginger water that Luc had begged from the kitchen, took a grateful drink. 'What would she have been doing out here? Going to meet False River Jones?'

Two hundred dollars wouldn't go far in New York, even augmented by the sale of a gold cross and a gold bracelet – And where had Valla acquired *those*? Would inspection of whatever jewelry Ellie had left back in New Orleans reveal missing baubles? Or would pieces of the random and outdated silverware of Uncle Veryl's town-house be found to be absent? (*And how would you* tell?)

'Prob'ly on her way to the dead-huts,' returned the young man. 'That old maroon village, back into the swamp. If she was goin' to sell stuff, she'd go that way—' he pointed – 'toward the bayou.'

January considered, calculating distances. 'What time did False River Jones show up?'

'Pretty near moon-set.'

Two a.m. There had been a shard of late moon-light, he recalled, when he'd been waked last night: he'd angled the face of Rose's silver compass to it. The musicians had still been at the big house, playing the Lancer's Quadrille – not that that meant much. Creoles, either French or African, would stay up all night to dance.

Somewhere between midnight and two?

That fit with the state of rigor on a hot night.

'Why would she go to these dead-huts?'

'Ever'body goes there.' Luc shrugged at his ignorance. 'Sometimes to trade, if word's out the pattyrollers is watchin' for traders on the bayou or the river. Mostly to make jass.' He used an African patois term for sexual congress. 'Sometimes just to get away.'

He put one foot on the trailing end of the rein to make a stirrup of his hands, and boosted January back onto the saddle-cloth, then handed his stick back up to him.

'Back 'fore Old Michie Froide cleared the land here for sugar, Auntie Zare tell me when I was little – Auntie Zare used to birth the babies down at St-Roche where the family had its first plantation. She said when this was all woods, and there wasn't enough white men in the county to patrol like there is now, they was half a dozen maroon villages in the swamp. A lot of 'em was where the Indians had villages before.'

He led Keppy around the trampled section of weed, and into the restlessly whispering woods.

'Ol' Michie Alexandre Froide had a house on a chenier back there, 'fore the bayou changed course. The dead-huts is supposed to be haunted, but me, I don't believe it. Mose – our main-gang boss – got a broad-wife over from Malsherbes plantation an' they sneaks out an' meets there all the time. Shanny, too, 'cept Shanny got a new sweetheart pretty much every week. She really does believe all old Nana's stories about the platt-eye devil an gettin' rid by witches, an' she says she ain't never seen anything out there.'

'You think Valla might have been going to meet Antoine?'

'She'd have to,' returned Luc with a grin, 'after she went around all day Monday sayin' as how she wouldn't touch him with a ten-foot pole.'

The narrow trace that wound along the highest ground into the deeper swamp informed January that the dead-huts were visited with at least some frequency. A mile and a half didn't sound far when Luc said it, but he knew from experience that forty years ago, in his childhood, even a few hundred yards, in the woods, constituted another world. A world in which *les blankittes* were foreigners, a world in which a fugitive could hide . . .

And had.

He bent from the makeshift saddle-pad, said, 'Whoa,' and Luc halted again.

'Step off the path,' instructed January, 'and help me down.'

Luc started to protest that they were nowhere near the dead-huts, then saw the direction of January's eyes and said, 'Well, shit.' And did as he was told.

There was too much leaf-mold, too much

178

decaying vegetation, mixed with the muck under-foot to provide a clear impression, but it was obvious that the shod man who'd walked this way last night had done so outbound – headed toward the dead-huts – bearing no burden, and inbound – back again – laden. The deeper tracks overlay the shallower. January judged his burden was about a hundred pounds. The weight of a woman.

Luc said, 'Well, shit,' again, and straightened up. 'Why carry her back to the Casita?'

'I'm guessing,' said January, 'he meant to dump her in the bayou. Once he discovered this wasn't the woman he meant to kill . . .'

He paused, frowning, his mind snagged on a question, but Luc asked, 'You sayin' he'd *want* people to find Mamzelle Trask?'

'Of course.' January paused in his mental tally of the men in the big house . . . and the weaving house, he made himself add. Sylvestre St-Chinian and his two sons stood to lose as much from Ellie's interference as did Evard and Basile Aubin, Henri Viellard, Florentin Miragouin or even possibly Locoul St-Chinian and his American brother-in-law.

Not to speak of their lawyers, he mentally added, though he personally had difficulty picturing either stout Henri Viellard or willowy Aristide DuPage carrying a dead woman a mile and a half through the blackness of swampy woods.

'The last thing any murderer would want is for poor Michie Veryl to spend the next ten years seeking for his vanished sweetheart.'

179

The younger man shook his head. 'If it was me,' he said, 'I'd have just wrote a note sayin', "Dear Veryl, I have runned off with another man".'

'Mamzelle Ellie can't read,' pointed out January. 'Can't write. And people would search if a white woman went missing. A slave girl, everybody would figure she'd just run away. Once the killer pulled back his lantern-slide and says, "Oh, shit, I done killed the wrong girl!" he's got to hide her body. Because now he's shown his hand. Now Mamzelle Trask *knows* that someone's coming for her. Help me back up, if you would – I sure can't make it a mile and a half on foot – but lead Keppy from the side, so I can watch the tracks.'

He didn't expect to see much – and didn't, for the tangled undergrowth made the tracks themselves intermittent. But at least he could look.

'So you think he's waitin' for her out in the dead-huts?'

'He could have got word to Mamzelle at dinner, told her something that he thought would get her out there.' January swiped at a mosquito that whined in his ear; the hot shadows beneath the trees droned with them. 'She obviously didn't go, and it doesn't sound to me, talking with her, that she deliberately sent Valla in her place – not unless she's a more skillful liar than I think she is. She may not have got the message at all, if a servant was supposed to deliver it. Or it may have been something she wasn't about to admit to me, at least not with Madame Chloë and Michie Veryl standing there. But why Valla would have gone . . .?'

'Hell, no secret about that.' The young man sniffed bitterly. 'You don't think them lawyers, an' Michie Flo an' Michie Basile an' that son of his, ain't all been screwin' Shanny an' Ima an' Zandrine here since they got off the boat? That's one place they'd do it, with all their relatives all fallin' over each other back at the big house. *An'* Michie Locoul an' all them Irish trash? Hell,' he said, and turned his face aside, his mouth suddenly hard with anger. 'Valla couldn't'a gone ten feet outside after ten o'clock, an' not tripped over *some* white man out here.'

January said nothing. *But she'd already made love . . . to somebody.*

Didn't mean she couldn't have arranged another assignation, of course, but why would she need to? She was under Mamzelle Ellie's protection.

Unless she was being blackmailed herself . . .

Luc walked in silence by Keppy's head, visibly struggling to retrieve his usual air of carefree cheer in the face of this aspect of his life. The girls that he'd named – field hand girls, illiterate as birds and without the slightest hope of ever doing anything but cutting cane and digging in their gardens in the hope of keeping their families fed – would be friends he'd known since his childhood. Cousins, sisters, maybe sweethearts.

Girls he had to watch when Molina, or some member of the family, or one of the family's guests perhaps, would squeeze their breasts or slap their flanks or bull them – whether they wanted it or not – against the wall of the laundry or the mill-house.

'Whoever he was,' said January after a time, to

break the silence, 'he may not have intended murder at all. He may have seen Valla, and thought it was Ellie headed for the woods, and thought, "She's meetin' somebody and if I can catch her with her sweetheart, that'll scupper the marriage right there". Then he might have thought,' he went on, 'about how blind Uncle Veryl is about Mamzelle, and decided, Oh, the hell with it, let's make sure . . . But if you've never killed a man – not just shot him in the arm from a distance in a duel, but held him against you and stabbed him with a knife – it can be damned unsettling.'

Luc looked up at him, wide dark eyes troubled. In a very soft voice he asked, 'You ever done that, Ben?'

He remembered a dying bandit in Mexico that he'd shot; and the British soldier he'd bayonetted on the cotton-bale barricades in the fog at Chalmette. The way that man's blue eyes had stared into his in despairing disbelief. 'I have. It's not . . . anything that anyone should ever have to do. Sometimes it's hard to keep your head afterwards.'

The young field hand walked in silence for a while, carefully keeping to the longer grass at the edge of the trail, and watching the ground before the mule's plodding hooves. At length he said, 'You ever killed a woman?'

'No.' All the women January had known – like individual flowers in some marvelous garden, each with her own music, her own scent, the bright delight of her eyes – went through his mind and among them the dark eyes, the quiet calm face of Delphine Lalaurie, beaded with sweat and slightly smiling. 'There's one at least that I would have, if I could. But not for money.' The shudder that went through him at the memory of that beautiful lunatic was complex and painful, and his smile was wry when he added, 'Maybe that's why I'm not rich.'

They moved on, the monochrome green of cypress and palmetto closing them in. Down among the trees the hot air was stifling, but looking up, January saw the curtains of Spanish moss flare and twist. Now and then movement threshed in the thick beds of wild honeysuckle and pickerel-weed: otter, rabbits, alligator.

He remembered the little maroon villages that had dotted the swamplands closer to New Orleans as late as a few years ago. Remembered how the men of Bellefleur Plantation, where he'd been born, would disappear into the ciprière, risking savage punishment if they were caught. How they'd sometimes come sneaking back, to visit wives and children still in the quarters. He remembered at least two, who had been caught – one had been beaten to death, and his master had cut the foot off another. In those days it was harder to flee north, and much easier to live as the Indians had lived. Then the country had settled up, the owners of the plantations had hired the poorer whites of the district to ride patrol. Those maroon villages had first moved farther back into the swamps, then vanished. When Cut-Arm, the last of the defiant maroons, had been hanged in '37, the last of those villages had blinked out of existence, like a candle going out.

You couldn't fight The Man.

Sedge and wild grape had long since taken over the garden-plots in the clearing where escaped families had clung for a time to the old ways of distant Africa. Indians had probably lived there before them. January could still make out the broad leaves of squash and pumpkin, the trailing green serpents of beans, among the wilder growth beyond the huts. Four dwellings still stood, round, windowless, surrounded by the broken detritus of those hidden lives: fragments of barrels and boxes, rusted cook-pans, a bleached and rickety ladder. Enormous roofs of thatched sedge and palmetto, now tattered with years of hurricane seasons, over-hung the mud-and-wattle walls to protect them from the bayou country's endless rains. Leaning on Luc's shoulder and stabbing the ground ahead of him with his crutch as a snake-stick, January dragged himself painfully to the largest and most complete. The tracks had long since disappeared in the springier morass of grass and weeds, but the humming of flies, everywhere thick in the swamp, was like the sickening drone of some low-voiced instrument.

Ducking through the door-hole, he knew already what he'd see.

'I guess Antoine wasn't waiting for her here after all,' said Luc quietly. By the sound of his voice, he spoke to keep himself from retching. The boy had seen blood before, of course – you couldn't machete cane, or live in the quarters, without witnessing injuries, childbirth, savage whippings, the occasional fight. But this was different.

184

Valla had quite clearly been knifed here. Had fought for her life, and had lost.

'She may have been waiting for someone.' Signing his companion to stay by the door, January leaned on his stick, propped his other hand on the wall, and dragged himself painfully around the edge of the room to the one place that might, at the outer edges of the definition, have been deemed furniture: a deep, crushed-down pile of moss and boughs, still fresh enough to be fairly green in the dimness.

Clearly, everybody in the quarters came here to 'make jass', as they said. Even with hot daylight outside the windowless room was a foxhole of stink and shadow. At night it must have been pitch-dark. With her lantern-slide closed, Valla wouldn't have known whose bulk had blackened the doorway. Had she whispered, 'Antoine?' Had she lain here with him – or with someone else – and when that lover departed, dozed here still for a time, to wake at the sound of another man's step? Maybe she hadn't even been aware of the killer's real identity. As he had not realized hers, until after she was dead.

He leaned down and picked up the tangled mass of white-and-yellow muslin. Valla's tignon, still folded in its elaborate pattern with yellow silk flowers pinned among the folds. Droplets of blood had sprayed on it.

She'd fought for her life in darkness, knowing only the hard handgrip on her body and in her hair, the cold cut of the knife.

If she'd screamed, would Antoine have come? In his childhood in the quarters at Bellefleur,

185

the protesting screams of women or girls hadn't been so unusual a sound. Like them lawyers an' them Irish, Luc had said. And if a slave heard what was most probably some white man raping the girl he himself loved – a stuck-up girl who treated him like dirt, by all accounts – would he really dash to her rescue and risk the beating of his life?

Pain washed over him suddenly, like a rising tide of sickness. He felt his face and hands turn chalky and cold, and very carefully sank down onto the pile of foliage. From the door, clearly torn between concern and the strictest orders to stay outside, Luc called out, 'You okay, Ben?'

'I'll be all right in a minute.' His voice was muffled by the fact that he'd lowered his head down between his drawn-up knees. 'If you'd fetch me that ginger water I'll be much obliged – come carefully, around the wall of the room.' His eyes were shut but he felt the edges of his mind graying. *Do* not *faint* . . .

The ginger-water jar – warm now – was pressed into his hands, and after a couple of swallows he corked it, and, very carefully, lay down.

'If you would,' he said after a moment, 'could you work your way around the room and check the thatch of the roof, to see if anything's hidden in it?' The walls were barely five feet high, though the poles which rose, teepee-like, from them made the inside of the house into a thatched cone an additional fifteen feet in height, blackened all over the inside with decades-old soot. 'And if you could check the other huts as well,' he added, when the younger man had turned up nothing but a small bag of coffee beans, and – to his combined amusement and irritation – a pair of gloves that he recognized as belonging to Nicolette Charpentier.

Was that what Valla had come here for, on the night when everyone knew False River Jones would be down by the bayou? Not love, but just some salable trinket stashed away?

Whites and librés alike indignantly claimed that all slaves were thieves: *What the hell do they expect, of people who could find themselves torn from their homes and families at two minutes' notice?*

But why would Valla indulge in petty theft nowadays? She had no more need of it than she had need to prostitute herself. And False River Jones – whom January knew slightly – was far too canny a trader to accept anything really valuable, like jewels, even had he the money to pay for such a thing.

In any case, January guessed, by the alacrity of Luc's agreement with this program ('You just lay here, Ben, an' I'll be back in a tick') that the young man, and probably his friends, had contraband of their own tucked away here – gunpowder and quite possibly a gun or two, wrapped in greased paper, bought from Jones or others of his ilk.

Lying on the prickly mass of Spanish moss and dried creepers, in spite of the throbbing in his foot January smiled a little at his own memories. Guns hidden in a place like this almost certainly had nothing to do with the slave revolt or dark revenge that white slaveholders dreaded, much less with murder. On a sugar plantation, with every usable acre devoted to the cash crop, penny-wise owners, like Madame Aurelié and Chloë, bought parched corn by the ton off the Illinois flatboats to feed their 'people'. Most field hands received that, plus a little hog meat and molasses, to keep body and soul together – nothing more.

One of his earliest memories was of his father coming into the family cabin on moonlit nights with a couple of rabbits or possum; of the exquisite savor of fresh meat. The master had searched the quarters regularly for guns and had never found a one.

'You know where Antoine was last night?' he asked, when Luc returned to report that he'd found nothing. 'Does he sleep in the quarters?'

'That he does, sir. In the men's cabin, with Cuffee an' Mander an' York an' me. But he go over to Michie Molina's awful early, to get a fire started in the kitchen there an' draw up water. But you not thinkin' *Antoine* . . .'

'If Valla was coming here to meet him—' January sat up – carefully – and scratched the shards of moss out of his hair – 'he might have seen or heard something. Walking among the huts, you didn't smell anything, like as if a man who'd been waiting here had taken a piss against a wall someplace?'

Luc thought about it, calling small details back to mind, then shook his head.

'When we get back,' said January, 'do you need to get out to the field right away? Or could you maybe do a couple of things for me?'

188

Luc grinned. 'I'm yours, boss, long as I can keep clear of Michie Molina.'

'Well, that's the trick, isn't it?' replied January grimly. 'Could you at least let Antoine know I'd like to see him, as soon as he's able? Was there anyone else Valla might be sneaking out to meet?' Bracing himself against the wall, he held onto Luc's arm as the young man got him to his feet: at nearly January's own great height, he was twenty years younger and nearly solid muscle. 'Molina, maybe?'

'She hated Michie Molina.' The young man shook his head decisively. 'I can tell you that. Once she got clear of him, she'd never go back.'

'What did Molina feel about her?'

'What does any overseer feel 'bout a woman he can have for the takin'?' Luc's mouth twisted again. 'He used to hold it over her – rag on her – 'cause she was lighter than him, musterfino, an' stuck-up because of it. "You think you so white, with your straight hair an' your prissy airs an' your holdin' up your nose 'cause you can read an' figure. But you gotta do what I say." Sure, she played up to him, an' he give her presents. He coulda given her to any of the field hands, you see, if she said no. Shammy tells me, an' Zandrine—'

He made a face as if he'd found dog turd in his porridge. 'He does nasty stuff, Michie Molina. Stuff you couldn't pay a whore to let you do to her, I bet. That's why his wife won't let him touch her. More'n once I seen her – or the other girls – come outta his house with their mouths bleedin', or blood all on their skirts. Or, he coulda

189

had her sold for a field hand. She wouldn't'a been goin' to meet him at the dead-huts, that much I can tell you, sure.'

'Anyone else?'

'I don't think so.' Luc helped January up onto Keppy's back, took the halter and led the mule back toward the Casita. 'Pretty as she was, an' used to be a lady's maid back in Virginia – all the men in the quarters was after her. York for one – that shares the men's cabin with us – an' Rufe in the main gang, even though he's married to Lina . . .'

'She ever say why she'd been sold as a field hand?'

Luc shook his head. 'Her master back in Virginia died, an' his wife had to sell most of the hands, to pay his debts. Least that's what Shanny told me. Myself, I think Valla was a troublemaker. She could read an' write, an' ran away once after writin' herself a pass – I think maybe she stole things to sell as well. Comin' here, I think she took up with Antoine 'cause she didn't want Michie Molina passin' her on to some field hand, just for spite. But Antoine, he was crazy about her. They all was.'

'You, too?'

Luc laughed, his bitterness vanishing in the recollection of that evanescent passion. 'The minute I saw her – an' it lasted all of about a minute.' He made a wry face. 'She was always lookin' out for things to find out, to hold over people. When she learned about Bubba – that's my brother – stealin' nails to sell, she tells him to go on stealin', but he's got to give her half the money he gets for 'em, or she'll tell, she says. Things like that. Anything that'll get her money, or get people to do what she says – or hurt 'em if they won't.'

Things like my mother having been put up as collateral for a loan to Mamzelle Ellie's father?

It crossed his mind to wonder how Valla had found it out – if it was true. Was it the sort of thing that Ellie would have told her? Particularly if, as it now appeared, Ellie had a habit of drinking a glass or two of brandy in the evenings?

Or was there some kind of paper that Ellie had – if Valla could in fact read? A paper that perhaps Ellie herself knew nothing of. And was that paper somewhere in the Casita?

And if so, should he use the last few ounces of his energy in figuring out how to search for it, or in searching for the other thing that needed to be sought?

Pain from his ankle surged again through the whole of his body, and he found himself wishing for nothing but to return to the weaving house and to his bed. *Maybe if I rigged a sling and elevated it, the pain would ease?*

Or maybe if I mixed myself a nice cocktail of Hooper's Female Elixir . . .

Just as they came clear of the trees it began to rain, not heavily, but with huge, scattered drops, the sort of rain that came and went half a dozen times before a storm. He felt giddy and increasingly sick to his stomach, but he could see, beyond the Casita, Veryl's valet James hurrying along the shell-path. The elderly servant straightened up with relief at the sight of him, and left

191

the path to hasten towards him over the uneven ground.

Damn it.

Some development with Jules Mabillet, January reflected bitterly, *that I'm supposed to have a look at.* Uncharitably he wished the young man dead.

'Michie Ben . . .' James panted a little as he caught the mule's halter, squinting up at January against the rain. 'Michie Ben, you got to come. They're gonna kill that poor man.'

Fourteen

Too-ample experience with the quack medical theory that ranged abroad – like a Fifth Horseman of the Apocalypse – in America, made January ready for almost anything as James and Luc helped him up the steps, across the gallery, and into Jules Mabillet's room. Completely aside from medicines which consisted chiefly of poisons like lead and mercury, he had encountered practitioners – well-paid and greatly in demand – who claimed to cure cholera with decoctions of camphor and gunpowder, to banish yellow fever by placing sliced onions under the patient's bed, to restore male 'vigor' by means of warm ale and mesmerism, and to dispell madness by shaving the patient's head and raising blisters on the flesh with Spanish fly. One of the problems he encountered regularly in

America was the nearly-unshakable belief, held by most Americans, that any man was qualified to be his own physician. In his somewhat sketchy career as part-time healer among the librés of the French Town he spent a good deal of his time trying to convince people that just because a medicine was advertised on its label to cure rheumatism, kidney-stones, rabies, fever, and indigestion didn't mean it would actually do so.

As they crossed the gallery January smelled sulfur, and heard from within the room the frightened mewing of a kitten.

Damn it!

He thrust the French door open without knocking, pretty sure what he'd find.

Madamoiselle Charlotte Viellard sprang to her feet from beside the bed, brown eyes flared with guilt, and in doing so knocked against the shoulder of the young woman who sat beside her: Gayla, the maid who looked after all three of the younger Viellard girls. Gayla lost her hold on the struggling black kitten she held, and the little animal turned nimbly in her grip, raked her hand with her claws, and bolted past January and out the door.

'Don't you friggin' knock, nigger?' demanded Gayla furiously.

Shaking free of his two supporters, January limped to the bedside and looked down at Charlotte. The tisane in the water glass she held smelled of honey and sulfur and something else.

'I apologize for breaking in on you like this, Mamzelle Charlotte,' he said, with as much respect as he could manage considering the

193

amount of pain he was in, and the degree of his disgust. 'I hope you didn't give any of that to M'sieu Mabillet?'

The girl looked quickly from him to Gayla, who had likewise risen to her feet.

'And what you know about it?' the maid demanded, clutching her bleeding hand.

Keeping his voice gentle, January replied, 'If it's what Queen Regine makes up to cure all ills, I'd advise you against giving him any, Mamzelle. It's moonflower, isn't it? Zombie cucumber? Mix it with honey and sulfur, and rub it against a black cat?'

'Queen Regine give me this miracle herself—'

'And my sister Olympia Snakebones taught *me*,' returned January quietly. 'And moonflower – datura – has to be used very carefully.' Tactfully, he added, 'Have you ever used this remedy before? It takes a touch—'

'I used it.' Gayla's eyes smouldered. 'An' I knows more 'bout it than you do, sister or no sister.'

'If you mix it too strong,' said January, 'moonflower is a deadly poison.' He saw Charlotte's eyes widen with shocked horror, and Gayla's face freeze.

'That's a damn lie—'

'It's a risk I'd rather not see Michie Jules put to.' His voice reasonable, he spoke mostly to the girl, but kept an eye on Gayla, who wore now the angry look of a woman thrown on the defensive. 'If he were to take an' go into convulsions – which is one of the things moonflower does, Mamzelle – I wouldn't like to have to explain to M'am Aurelié what I found here.'

194

The stout girl sank back onto the bedside chair, clutching the water glass to the pink ruffles of her bosom.

'An' if he dies,' retorted Gayla, 'you don't got nuthin' to worry about, do you? 'Cause no *blankitte* gonna believe the Queen's Royal Blessin' could have cured him. Oh, no! On your hand be his blood, nigger doctor. An' on your head be the Queen's curse, if you breathe a word of this to any. On the head of *any*—' she turned, and stared hard at the terrified Charlotte – 'that speak of what passed within these walls: the tongue that wags will dry an' split, the eyeballs that peeked will scorch up an' run out as blood.'

She spit on the floor at January's feet, shoved James aside from the doorway, and swept from the room.

Charlotte sobbed, 'No . . .' and made as if to go after her.

January murmured, 'I had crosses worse than that put on me, Mamzelle, and taken off by my sister. You have nothing to fear.'

The girl began to cry, and very, *very* gently – the last thing he needed was an accusation that he'd laid a hand on a seventeen-year-old white girl – January removed the water glass from her fingers.

'Michie Jules gonna be all right,' he promised, though a glance at the young man on the bed made his heart sink: his handsome face was flushed, his eyes a hectic glimmer beneath lids three-quarters closed. 'James,' he added, 'would you be so good as to fetch back my bag, that I left at the Casita? Is there water still in that can?

Thank you, good. I think a saline draft will help him, and some barley water when Missy has time to make some up. Mamzelle,' he went on, as the elderly valet hurried across the gallery and away, 'it's early to tell anything, but I promise you, voodoo remedies probably won't help him and may make matters a great deal worse.'

'But she's a great voodoo,' whispered Charlotte miserably. 'A powerful queen.'

'I don't know that one way or the other,' said January tactfully. 'Though I understand it isn't usual for a voodooienne to be a slave woman.'

Charlotte frowned, digesting that bit of information.

'I know Queen Regine,' he added, 'and she's said to be very powerful herself. I respect her powers. But I'm not sure that she'd teach a woman she knew to be a slave.' Père Eugenius, he reflected, would be horrified at this entire conversation, and he had every intention of confessing himself of the sin of conversing about witchcraft the minute he was back in town. But at the moment it was most important to reassure the girl. Aside from dispelling her fright, it was vital to make sure she didn't come slipping back in here with God only knew what kind of Heavenly Root Juice or Conjure Angel Medicine the moment no one was looking.

'She said she'd curse me,' said Charlotte hesitantly. 'If I told. And she's – I'm afraid now she's going to dig up and throw away the . . . the charms she made . . .'

'To get Michie Jules to fall in love with you?'

She flushed scarlet to the roots of her hair.

'You tell Mamzelle Gayla,' said January, 'that I won't go telling on her to M'am Aurelié – or on you, either – as long as neither you nor she tries to give Michie Jules any other kind of medicine. I know your mama would give you all kinds of trouble, and Mamzelle Gayla, too, and I wouldn't do that to either of you. Michie Jules' life is in God's hand, Mamzelle. I think Queen Regine would be the first person to tell you that God is stronger than M'am Erzulie or Papa Legba. Put your trust in Him, Mamzelle. And when Père Eugenius gets here—' a gust of wind hurled another splatter of rain on the gallery outside, as if reminding him of the unlikelihood of any steamboat putting out from the New Orleans wharves in this kind of weather – 'you might think about confessing your doubts to him, and asking for his intercession in prayer. Now I'm going to have to ask you to leave me alone with Michie Jules—' James' shadow had darkened the French door behind her – 'for me to have a look at him.'

Charlotte nodded, and stood for a moment beside the low bed, gazing hungrily down at the young man who had ridden alone from town to take her in his arms. And January reflected – surreptitiously mixing the smallest possible dose of laudanum-and-water for himself from the bag that the valet handed him, because the pain in his ankle was making his hands shake – that in thrusting his sword through his rival, Evard Aubin had probably destroyed whatever chances he might have had of marrying into any share – large or negligible – of the Viellard-St-Chinian holdings.

Unless of course Jules Mabillet did die, in which case Charlotte would be nearly desperate to secure a husband for herself.

And if – and it was a great *if* – the next attempt on Mamzelle Ellie succeeded.

Once Charlotte had taken herself away – presumably to find Gayla and conciliate her into not digging up whatever juju-ball of white wax and honey she'd buried under the room where Jules lay – January unpinned the bandages on the wound. He could understand the girl's terror. The flesh around the puncture looked angry and swollen, and was hot to the touch. The fluid that stained the bandages – where visible around the edges of the bloodstains – had a greenish tinge, and a smell he didn't like. Though he himself felt sick with the pain that had spread from his foot to every inch of his body, he opened the wound, very slightly, with his scalpel, then washed it again more deeply with spirits of wine and dusted it once more with basilicum before wrapping it in clean bandages. Despite his little lecture to Charlotte about voodoo remedies, he took from his bag a twist of paper containing his sister Olympe's sovereign febrifuge – powdered willow bark – and mixed it with the hot barley-water that James delivered to him from the kitchen.

'You look like you could do with some of that yourself, sir,' observed the white-haired valet, after January had administered the draught and laid the young man back onto the pillows.

'I could do with some cold compresses and

about a week in bed with my foot elevated. Has there been any sign of the *City of Nashville*?'

James shook his head, and poured out a second cup of the barley water for January. 'But it's early yet, sir, not even ten o'clock.' He steadied January's hands around the cream-colored Queensware. 'With the weather shaping up as bad as it is, I'm not that sure any boat's going to put out from town today.'

At least, reflected January, *that'll save Père Eugenius the effort of chasing the bridal party up and down the river.*

The next moment, as Archie appeared in the doorway, met his eyes, and then vanished again, the older man said, 'If you'll excuse me, sir. Do you need me further? Michie Veryl sent word for me to pack up his things, and such as matters are we have no way of knowing when or if the *Louisiana Belle* gonna be by up-river . . .'

'Go,' said January. 'In a few minutes I may ask you or Archie to help me get back to the weaving house.'

'Of course, sir.'

January wondered what kind of upheaval was going on there, and how many people were going to go streaming down to the landing when – or if – the up-river boat steamed into view.

He rose from the stool beside the bed, staggered to the bent-willow chair nearby and sank into it, trembling with exhaustion and pain. *And should I be one of them*?

Whatever information there might be in the Cabildo, it would take Hannibal more than a morning to find it.

199

Getting Maman – and Minou – out of here on the Belle *is what I need to do. And if Uncle Veryl is leaving, Singletary is leaving, so in fact it will be my duty as a physician to go . . .*

Beside him, Jules whispered, 'Maman?' in a broken shred of a voice.

'She'll be here presently.' It was a complete lie, but he guessed his patient was half delirious with fever and pain. Like Charlotte, Jules needed reassurance at this point, more than truth.

I'm the only physician in this part of the county – always excepting Madame Molina. Is it my duty to remain?

'I tried,' murmured Jules. 'Maman, I tried. It hurts, Maman, please give me my medicine. I'm sorry, I tried, please . . .'

Having already dosed the young man with about ten grains of opium – as far as he could estimate the strength of Godfrey's Cordial – January wasn't about to ply him with more until evening (*If I'm still* here *in the evening*), but given the depth of the wound and the degree of inflammation, he guessed the pain was still severe. He limped and staggered to the door, hoping to catch James or Archie on their way in and out of the next room: *All I'd need is for Mamzelle Charlotte to come back in and hear him, and decide that he needs more Cordial.*

Instead he saw Old Madame Janvier emerge from her room in the opposite wing – impeccably dressed in the second mourning that she'd worn for over forty years – and signed to her. Many white women would have taken it deeply amiss that a black man would even *think* of summoning

200

them to *him* – and in the men's wing of the house at that – and would have retreated in dudgeon. But Madame Sidonie descended the gallery steps, crossed the yard with Thisbe trotting at her heels, and came to where he stood, though of course it would be unthinkable that she enter the room itself. She looked through the door, however, and asked, 'How is he? Thisbe, *no*,' she added, as the little dog attempted to investigate the sick man's bedside. '*Sit*, mamzelle.'

'It's early days, m'am. It's to be expected he'll be in a great deal of pain, in spite of the laudanum. He's quite feverish, calling on his mother.'

Her lips tightened and her dark quick eyes went to the sweat on his own face, which he knew must be ashen with fatigue and pain. 'And how are *you*?'

'In better case than my patient,' he replied. 'Which is about all that can be said.'

She returned his weary twist of a smile with one of her own, and glanced at the gray, louring morning sky. The rain had ceased and the ground steamed between the long wings of the house.

'I take it he can't be moved?'

'No, M'am. And it is imperative – both because my own injury will quickly render me unable to attend on him as I could wish, and for other reasons as well – that I return with my mother to New Orleans. Is there any physician – any at all – in the parish? I'm told Madame Molina—'

'I wouldn't trust the woman to mix a mustard plaster.' Sidonie Janvier's glance slid sideways to him again and she asked, 'Looking to get out before Uncle Mick locks you up?'

January felt the heat of dread prickle his hair. 'I take it my mother has spoken to you of this?' He was astonished at how level his voice sounded.

'She asked what I could do to protect her, if worst came to worst. She seemed to take it for granted that Henri would be able look after Dominique and Charmian – she's obviously never seen Aurelié when someone's offered her money – and whether your existence slipped her mind in the stress of the moment, or she believes you to be able to deal with any number of Hibernian thugs, I was unable to ascertain: she didn't mention you at all.'

'Excuse me while I find my smelling-salts,' January said drily. 'I think I'm going to faint with shock.'

'I'm perfectly willing to nurse Jules for a day, if you feel it necessary to slip onto the *Louisiana Belle* the moment she pulls into the wharf. *If* she pulls in,' she added. 'Myself, I shall be very surprised if any boat sails from the Balize today. The weather is almost certainly worse down-river, and there's less protection if the storm turns nasty. Any down-river boats will almost certainly stay tied up at Carmichael's woodyard at English Turn until it blows over. And if that piddling excuse for a levee crevasses I shouldn't be surprised if we're all trapped here for two days.'

Death in the water. Olympe's voice, and the memory of his dream, flickered again through his mind.

In the shadows of the room, Jules called out again, 'Maman . . .'

Damn it, thought January savagely. *Damn young fool and double-damn Evard Aubin.* 'I still wouldn't want to be answerable, should he be moved,' he said. 'I suppose I shall have to remain – Uncle Mick or no Uncle Mick.' Mentally, he cursed the Hippocratic Oath. 'If the *Belle* does put in today, might I beg you to get my mother out of here, if you can? I'll send word to Madame Mabillet—'

'Let me write it. I am deeply fond of Marie-Honorine,' she added, when January raised his brows inquiringly. 'But she is a woman of strong character, and volcanic impulse. I wasn't at all surprised to see her son come riding up to the door like Young Lochinvar – it's precisely the sort of thing that Marie-Honorine Mabillet herself would have done, twenty years ago. If Jules feels that degree of passion for Charlotte, despite Veryl disrupting the family over that brass-haired floozy, I'm only surprised that Jules didn't carry the poor girl off over his crupper. Personally,' she went on, shaking her head, 'I wouldn't have thought anyone . . . But there's no accounting for tastes.'

'Since Charlotte seems to feel a like degree of passion,' said January, 'I am afraid, Madame, that I need to beg another favor of you. I don't know any of the sisters well – nor whether any of them can be relied on . . .'

'None of them can. Cretins, all of them. Their father couldn't be trusted to walk down the street without a minder.'

Having heard this evaluation of Henri's father from his own mother, January maintained a

203

tactful silence on the subject, saying instead, 'The fact is that I fear that Mamzelle Charlotte may attempt to implement remedies of her own.'

'Oh, *peste*! Not the filth she gets from that voodoo maid of theirs?'

January nodded. 'When I came here I found them – Mamzelle Charlotte and Gayla – preparing to give him a preparation which I'm pretty sure contains moonflower – datura – jimson-weed, it's also called, which in small quantities can trigger hallucinations, and in larger concentrations can kill. Even in a small amount I wouldn't like to see it given to someone so weakened as M'sieu Mabillet. Judging by Mamzelle Charlotte's distress over Michie Jules' condition, I'm also concerned that she'll simply dose him with more laudanum than is good for him.'

'The girl has the brains of a louse. God knows what Jules sees in her, particularly now that it looks like there'll be far less money in the offing. I shall do what I can.' The old lady shook her head. 'I've told Aurelié more than once to get rid of that maid of theirs. I'll swear the girl can read and write, for all she pretends she can't – she must have something on Aurelié, or on one of the younger girls that will foul their chances of a decent match. No one in their right mind should have a house-servant who knows her letters.'

It crossed January's mind to wonder if this had, indeed, been the reason the lovely Valla, for all her skill as a hairdresser, had been sold as a field hand.

'Not that this absurdity of Veryl's hasn't sent

204

every sensible mama in Louisiana scampering like field-mice for the hills, dragging their sons behind them.' Madame Sidonie looked past him again at the handsome face of the young man, turning restlessly on the pillow. 'And I will minimize the danger when I write to Marie-Honorine. For all her vapors and crochets and fancied ailments – I don't wonder Jules is begging for medicine, she's kept him on a steady diet of laudanum and paregoric since he cut his first teeth – she's just as likely to leap on a horse and try to come down here to nurse him. She thinks she's straight out of a romance herself, you know.'

And in spite of herself, Old Madame Janvier smiled. 'When Claud Mabillet's mother sent him back to France, Honorine – Picard, she was then – cut off her hair, disguised herself as a page-boy, and stowed away on the same ship. Got Jean Lafitte to take her down to the Balize to do it. Jules is the apple of her eye, her youngest boy and the only one she has left now. She would do anything for him. I'll watch him for her – and for you. Now you,' she added, 'get back to the weaving house, and get some rest. That ankle of yours must be blown up to the size of a watermelon and hurting you like the Devil, and if the *Louisiana Belle* does make its appearance, you're going to need all your strength to evade Uncle Mick and get on it.'

January said wearily, 'Oh, joy.'

Fifteen

Unfortunately, rest was not something January was destined to achieve that forenoon, neither at the weaving house nor elsewhere. James got him onto Keppy and across to the rickety structure, and up its tall gallery steps to Dominique's room. But every instinct January possessed told him that to take any sort of anodyne would be the act of a fool, both because Jules Mabillet might take a turn for the worse at any time and require clear-headed assistance, and also because he himself might unexpectedly have to flee from Uncle Mick. Half sick with pain, he instructed Sylvestre St-Chinian and Jacques Bichet in constructing a sling to elevate his foot, and this helped. So did the dish of stew and callas that Minou brought him from the kitchen.

He was not, however, permitted to enjoy any of these items in peace.

'Did you search the Casita?' demanded his mother, coming in hard on Minou's heels. 'You were over there,' she added, in annoyed disgust, when January only stared at her. 'Surely you could have taken the opportunity to slip into that cocotte's bedroom and see if she has any proof of that idiotic claim of hers. Myself, I believe that yellow slut made the whole thing up, out of jealousy of her betters.'

Her taffeta petticoats swished as she paced the

room. In her frock of red India-print chintz and a red-and-gold tignon roughly the size of a watermelon, she gave the impression of an immense and murderous rose. Contradicting herself, she added, 'Where else would that impudent little tramp have gotten that story, except by spying on her mistress' papers?'

'For one thing, Maman—' January reminded himself that *of course* his mother would disregard a mere broken ankle – 'I doubt Mademoiselle Trask would have such papers with her. She's as illiterate as your cats—'

'She could still have told the girl of it. Clearly the *Irlandaise* gave her presents, and that usually means confidences as well.' Rage flashed like silver razors in her voice, but her hands gave her away, twisting at each other and at the delicate fabric of her skirts.

She was terrified.

'For another,' he argued patiently, 'even were I nimble on my feet, which as you may have noticed I'm not, I was with Mesdames Aurelié and Chloë. Uncle Veryl and M'sieu Singletary were in the parlor with Mademoiselle Trask. There was no opportunity for me to "slip" anywhere.'

'Pish.' She dismissed both his reasoning and his injury with a flick of her hand. 'One can always make an opportunity if one wishes. Sometimes I just can't understand you, Benjamin. All you seem to think of is how you'll look to *les blankittes* . . .'

January didn't even bother to contradict this statement or to point out the years of trouble she

207

had taken to learn exactly how to dress, how to paint her face, what wines to order and what literature and music to patronize in order to keep her white protector enthralled. In any case she wouldn't have listened even had he managed to get in a word between hers.

'Up until a month ago the girl lived in an attic in the Swamp, with all her worldly goods crammed in a carpet bag. I don't doubt she still has the habit of keeping anything really valuable where she can grab it before she runs. I should think for your own sake, even if you have no care for me . . .'

'You know I care for you, Maman . . .'

'You don't act like it.'

She averted her head slightly as she made this too-familiar accusation – which January was long used to hearing – and stepped out onto the gallery. Her eyes turned towards the shell path that ran from the Casita to the big house, as January had seen them do half a dozen times as she'd paced. Now she said, 'Drat it,' and he realized she'd been watching the path all morning. 'Stupid bog-trotters are taking her food from the kitchen – the trollop is probably too afraid to stir forth. Who did it, do you think?' The sidelong glint in her eyes made her look strongly like her elder daughter. 'I suppose it could have been anyone . . . That'll teach the little bitch to go about dressed like her betters.'

'Maman!' protested Minou, who had sat all this while on a stool beside January's bed, the bowl of stew and a bottle of ginger beer in her hands. 'The poor girl is dead.' She turned her head, at

208

the sound of Charmian's voice from the next room, where she and the other children played under the watchful eye of the nurse Musette.

'You are being a cry-baby,' the four-year-old stated in her precise accents. 'Crane-flies don't bite.'

Stanislas' voice lifted in a treble wail of horror and there was a scramble of feet running along the gallery.

'What is it, darling? What's the matter?'

Dominique sighed, set the bowl down next to January's low pallet, and slipped past her mother to the door. 'If we don't get out of this place soon I'm going to slap that woman.'

Livia Levesque swung around from the door, frustrated anger flashing in her glare. 'And I suppose *you* don't think any more of this trouble than *she* does,' she snapped at January – as usual directing her ire at her son rather than her beloved quadroon daughter. 'If we all end up on the auction block you'll wish you'd put yourself out a trifle more, for all of our sakes!'

And with an angry swish of her skirts she strode out onto the gallery, just as big, scattered rain-drops began to fall again.

Since at the moment there was no one close enough to call, to discover if the *Louisiana Belle* had come into sight downriver yet, or to send for Luc, January took advantage of the momentary quiet (except for Solange Aubin's voice raised in defensive maternal fury in the next room) to pick up the bowl of stew, for he was by this time profoundly hungry despite the pain. He hadn't eaten more than two mouthfuls, however, when a clumber of heavy boots on the gallery stairs made the whole weaving house vibrate. He guessed immediately who it was and set the bowl down, and, yes, it was Uncle Mick who darkened the French door moments later, followed by his boys. And by Martin Loudermilk, Locoul St-Chinian's American lawyer.

'Can I help you, sir?' January asked, when the Irishman only stood there in the doorway, studying the room and especially the sling that hung from the ceiling-hook above the bed.

Mick Trask removed the cigar from his mouth and blew a line of smoke. 'Just lookin' to see how you're situated, Ben. St-Ives tells me you're sharin' the room with your sister an' her brat.'

'It was true last night,' returned January politely, biting back the inappropriate urge to ask this man where St-Ives had disappeared to last night. 'What arrangements they'll make tonight, I have as yet no clue.'

'She's in the next room,' said the Black Duke, shifting his massive shoulders against the door frame. 'Shall I bring her in? Make sure she don't run for it? The mother, too . . .?'

'With a brat she'll not run. Paddy, Harry – get yourselves down to the wharf an' make sure if that goddam steamboat ever *does* show itself, nobody goes sneakin' onto it. Syksey, you keep an eye on the old wench. Now . . .' He held up his hand, as January drew breath to speak. 'You may think I'm bein' a bit previous, an' maybe I am. But I have to watch out for my niece's interests here, 'specially as there's plenty of folks in that stuck-up family who'll treat her like the

210

goose-girl in some fairytale, an' not give her her due. It would purely make your heart glow,' he added, 'to see the kind of respect even havin' five thousand dollars of your own will bring you.'

January took a deep breath, and reminded himself that in all probability Hannibal was back in New Orleans checking on the truth of Ellie Trask's case. 'I take it there's been no sign of the boat yet, sir?' he asked, as mildly as he could.

'Not the hair on its arsehole.' Uncle Mick shook his head. 'When it does show, the Duke and I'll head back to town to look up the legal papers. What year was you born in, Ben? An' your sisters?'

'1795.' Better, he supposed, than this would-be master coming over to determine his age by taking a look at his teeth. Better for everyone, since he feared the outcome of the attempt wouldn't be good for anyone concerned, broken ankle or no broken ankle. At least, he reflected, the question seemed to indicate that St-Ives hadn't been sent to town last night to look up the papers himself.

Covert study of the man's face still didn't tell him what else he might have instructed his valet to do, if anything. In addition to being five times smarter than any of Uncle Mick's tame head-breakers (the same could have been said of Thisbe), St-Ives had the advantage (for Uncle Mick) of being unable to testify against a white man in court.

He went on, 'Dominique was born in 1811. My wife, in any case,' he added, 'was born a free woman—'

211

'They all sez that,' remarked a bulldog-faced 'boy' whose curled soap-locks, like those of his boss, had been dyed a startlingly youthful black.

'Shut up, Rags,' returned Trask easily. 'No sense actin' like a goddam Englishman about this. An' you're a sawbones, then?'

'Surgeon,' replied January. 'I trained at the Hôtel-Dieu in Paris.'

'Should be good for a couple thousand at least,' put in another of the thugs, a heavy-built man with the scarred ears and cheekbones of a boxer. 'Do they train niggers to be doctors, then?'

'I thought niggers couldn't read,' added Rags.

'You might think different if you could read yourself,' retorted Trask, and turned back to January. 'I understand you own a house on Esplanade Street . . . and your mother has not only a house but a good deal of property. That true?'

'If in fact the woman Livia was a slave at the time the real estate was presented to her,' advised Loudermilk, 'the deed would not be legal . . .'

'It is, sir.' In France, even if he'd had a broken ankle, he'd at least have been free to speak his mind, if not break Mick Trask's face in and throw him off the gallery. In America, January reminded himself, it was quite simply unthinkable. Even if he was legally free here, he had understood from his childhood that in many ways, he was the slave of any white person he met.

He fixed his eyes on the upper-right corner of the French door.

'Who would they belong to, then?' asked Trask.

'The go-between that bought them? Or would they revert to Fourchet, in which case—'

'Here!' Henri Viellard's voice sounded from the gallery, and past Trask's shoulder January got a fragmentary glimpse of the stout young planter trying to shove his way past the boys. They shoved back in no uncertain terms, but Henri, though a gentle-hearted mama's boy who collected butterflies and seashells, was still slightly over six feet tall and weighed three hundred pounds. He shoved again, with such force as to make the boys stagger back, and Trask stepped aside from the doorway with a look of amused surprise on his face.

'Mr Viellard, I was just coming to see you.'

'I'm pleased to have saved you the trouble, sir,' returned Henri, plump cheeks pink with anger. 'And to have spared you a walk which would only have concluded with my servants putting you out of the house.'

'Not a very hospitable attitude to take towards your uncle's in-laws.' The Irishman looked grieved. 'And it'll make for difficulties if in fact you want to purchase Madamoiselle Janvier and her daughter . . .'

'You lay one hand on Madamoiselle Janvier – you speak one word to her . . .'

Trask held up his hands, a smile tweaking his narrow lips. 'Not a finger,' he promised. 'Not a whisper. Martin's going to be doing that for me.' He gestured towards Loudermilk with his cigar. 'And Sheriff Baltard of the parish – who should be on his way even as we're talking. So I hope for everybody's sake, he'll find my

213

property here when he arrives so he won't have to go looking.'

Turning, he strolled from the room, his boys – and the lawyer – following him down the gallery steps.

Henri made to exit also – January guessed he was headed to the next room to speak to Minou – and January said, 'M'sieu, if you please . . .'

The fat man turned. His face was still flushed with anger, but the thick forenoon light showed the tears of terror and dread.

'He may be lying, sir,' said January quietly. 'Bluffing you, to get you to pay him now. I sent Hannibal into town yesterday afternoon to look up the Cabildo records for evidence of the debt.'

'Oh,' said Henri, in startled enlightenment – he'd clearly not thought of checking on the truth or the legality of the claim. 'Oh, that's very sensible! Of course it would be recorded.'

'Simon Fourchet sold my mother to St-Denis Janvier in 1803. If he borrowed money from Fergus Trask after that date, none of this affects any of us, in any way.'

'But he still may be able to take her away,' said the young man quietly. 'Her, and Charmian. His word to that imbecile Baltard would be enough, and there are plenty of venal judges in Louisiana. If it comes to a lawsuit, Mother would never put out money to . . . to save them. Particularly now with the family properties in a state of flux.'

'She may if she needs your vote – and Chloë's – in the family business to counteract that of

Madamoiselle Trask,' January pointed out. 'And the sheriff of the parish may put more store by a planter who owns two prime sugar plantations along the river, than he would in a richer man who's going to go back to town and never vote – or tell others to vote.'

Henri drew a deep breath, and his heavy shoulders relaxed as this information sank in. 'Yes,' he stammered. 'Yes, of course.'

'A lawsuit will be as expensive for Trask as it will be for you,' January went on. 'Let's wait until we know what we're talking about, before we start making threats or opening negotiations or trying to get away from Cold Bayou with a storm coming on. Which brings up the subject,' he went on, 'of how deeply is your sister in love with Jules Mabillet?'

'My sister?' Henri's brow furrowed – the body of the almost-golden-haired maidservant clearly in his mind. 'Why do you ask?'

'Would she for instance try to pay some of the hands to harness up a wagon and try to get him back to town,' asked January, with what he hoped was convincing concern in his voice. 'If she got it into her head that he wasn't getting the care he needed here, for instance. Forgive me for asking.' He could see the younger man, startled at not being asked about Charlotte's part, if any, in murder, visibly lower his guard. 'And please understand that I mean no disrespect. But two hours ago I found Madamoiselle Charlotte trying to dose Michie Jules with a voodoo remedy that I suspect would have done him far more harm than good.'

215

'Ah!'

Clearly, reflected January, watching the young planter's expression relax, it did not cross his mind that Charlotte might attempt to hire – or persuade – someone larger and stronger than herself to do the deed.

Someone – perhaps – like Godfrey St-Ives.

Would St-Ives – a stranger to the district – know about the dead-huts?

Or had he stolen the riding-mule in the expectation of having to flee, only to return it – and himself – when it became clear that he hadn't, in fact, murdered his boss's niece?

With a stately deliberateness, Henri brought up the room's one willow chair (which creaked protestingly under his weight) to the side of the bed. January knew Viellard well enough to know that though the younger man had been well educated and was a formidable autodidact in his chosen field – which had nothing to do with the running of his six plantations – he was in fact not very subtle. His mind relieved of all thought that January might suspect his sister of procuring a murder, he was perfectly happy to give him any information on her motives that he wanted.

'You see,' explained Henri, 'Jules actually offered for *Sophie*, back before all this hullabaloo about poor Uncle Veryl arose. He's handsome, of course, and extremely charming, I suppose, and Charlotte fell passionately in love with him. Then when it first became clear that Uncle's intentions towards Madamoiselle Trask were honorable – that he intended to marry her – his mother withdrew him from the marriage negotiations.'

216

He removed his thick, rectangular-lensed spectacles and polished them carefully on his handkerchief. Without them his large brown eyes had a defenseless look, rather like a good-hearted cow.

'Madame Mabillet and Maman were at school in Paris together,' he continued. 'They've been friends all their lives. Nevertheless they had a fearful quarrel about it, because Maman had already spent five hundred dollars on Sophie's trousseau. Sophie – who has Maman's temper – wrote Jules an extremely cutting letter, which his maman read. That didn't help matters.'

January bit back his first question – *how the hell old is Mabillet, that his Maman still reads his letters?* – and only nodded as if this were the most common thing in the world. He recalled the days, before Henri's marriage to Chloë St-Chinian at the age of thirty-five, when Minou had practiced every sort of subterfuge to communicate with her protector since Madame Aurelié read *his* letters.

French Creole families . . .

Of course, his own mother would have read *his* letters, during the three years after his return from France when she'd rented his old bedroom back to him at five dollars a month.

He wouldn't have put it past Madame Sidonie Janvier, either, now that he came to think of it.

'I gather—' Henri concentrated profoundly on removing the last specks of imaginary dust from his glasses – 'that at that point Charlotte . . . ah . . . wrote several love letters to Jules, swearing undying adoration. Ophèlie told me this only

217

yesterday, after Jules came riding up like something out of a Scott novel. He's always been such a spoilt care-for-nobody that his appearance here rather surprised me, you know. I had no idea Charlotte's – er – *passion* was reciprocated, for they really have nothing in common . . . except of course their intense mutual admiration of Jules Mabillet.'

And he smiled, his shy quick smile.

'But Ophèlie and Sophie were aware that he'd written her back – they all steal and read each other's mail, you know, even the letters Gayla sneaks in to them, and they're forever fighting about it. And of course Charlotte's ecstatic over having scored over her sisters. Girls . . .' He shook his head, distressed at this illogic.

'And where does Evard Aubin fit into all this?' asked January, in a voice of idle curiosity. 'He didn't come riding up like Lancelot, but he *did* accept Michie Jules's challenge . . .'

'Evard accepts anybody's challenge. He genuinely enjoys duelling and I gather he's very good at it.'

January remembered the young man's supple eagerness, as he'd practiced passes on the levee. *Was that only this morning?* It felt like years ago.

'And his Uncle Gustave is some sort of official in Louis-Philippe's government, so he takes criticism of the House of Orleans very ill. But he simply enjoys getting into quarrels and duels. He's kept his distance from Charlotte – I think on the advice of his father. I gather he's been courting Marie-Felice Picard, who Chloë says is a tremendous heiress. But I've noticed here that

218

he's also been keeping poor Charlotte on a string. In case the Picard match doesn't work out, I suppose.'

With finicking care he replaced the spectacles on his nose, and frowned again in thought. 'So yes, I would say Charlotte does love Jules Mabillet. But as for hiring some of the field hands to smuggle him back to New Orleans, I doubt she'd know how to go about it. Euphémie would.' His brow puckered deeper at the thought of his eldest sister. 'It was Euphémie, you know, who paid Gayla to put all those hexes on Madamoiselle Trask's wedding-clothes. At least that's what Charlotte tells me. I gather Euphémie's husband has been giving her no peace since the wedding was announced and has been talking about suing the Viellard family for false representation, though they've been married now for nearly twelve years. Charlotte is a little afraid of the field hands, you know, and very much afraid of getting caught.'

He gazed for a time through the glass of the French door, out toward the heavy gray clouds above the river, a lumbering, overdressed dandy who would have been profoundly happy to have been left alone to collect butterflies and marry the beautiful quadroon girl who was the mother of his only child.

A little sadly, he added, 'Sometimes I think Maman likes Chloë as well as she does, because Chloë will stand up to her. None of the rest of us will. It's a damnable thing.' He shook his head. 'I am truly glad to see Uncle Veryl so happy, but . . .'

He broke off, and January finished gently, 'One

219

doesn't like to say it. Because your uncle has done the honorable thing. Or what would clearly be the honorable thing, had Madamoiselle Trask been other than what she is.'

Henri turned his moist brown gaze upon him, and January could read in his nearsighted eyes the other thing that nobody – not even Henri – would or could say: that what he felt to be the right and honorable thing with regard to Dominique was even more unthinkable, because Minou was what *she* was.

Black.

'I'll do everything I can for you.' Henri rose, with a slight puff to his breath. 'In spite of Maman. I promise. And Chloë likes you. Oh, damn it,' he added, as he reached the door. 'He's got one of those filthy Irishmen posted at the bottom of the gallery steps! Of all the—'

'Do you see anyone else nearby, sir? Anyone who can take a message for me?'

'I can take one.' He turned back from the door. 'To whom do you need to speak?'

'Thank you,' said January, genuinely touched. There were few enough white men (and even fewer planters) who would even have considered going on an errand for a man who should, in the opinion of many, have been cutting some white man's cane.

But he doubted that Henri even knew Luc by sight. Luc was a field hand and had probably been sent back to the cane-patch by Molina. So he said, 'If Uncle Bichet – the old musician with the country-marks on his face – is somewhere in the building, I'd like very much to speak with him. If you can't find him, might you send someone to fetch either James or Archie, if they can be spared?'

Neither Uncle Veryl nor Selwyn Singletary, he calculated, as Henri's lumbering tread retreated along the gallery, would require much assistance in the way of packing. Even with his new-found importance in the family, Veryl was a man of extremely simple tastes, and Singletary still wore the clothes he'd bought (or more probably that his now-long-deceased mother had bought for him) when he'd gone to whatever dissenting academy it was that had fostered his bizarre mathematical genius. January would have trusted any of his fellow musicians – fat Cochon Gardinier, handsome and hapless Philippe duCoudreau, genial Jacques Bichet – with his life or the lives of his family, but of them, only Uncle Bichet, in January's experience, could be trusted to keep his mouth shut.

Whether the old man could undertake the task – and find the information – that young Luc could have done so easily, January wasn't certain. But it was a long distance to the laundry, and he cringed from the thought of hobbling all that way, even if he could have come up with some reasonable excuse to give the laundress for asking if any of the men had deposited a shirt.

And it was interesting, he thought, lying back and shutting his eyes, that Evard Aubin would have put himself in the danger of a duel – whether he enjoyed the sport or not – for the sake of a match which offered so little return. Or so little return, as matters stood at present.

221

In the next room the voices of Solange Aubin and Isabelle Valverde rose shrilly, debating the relative imbecelities and offensive personal habits of each others' offspring, by the sound of it. Out on the gallery, rain splattered, then slacked. The air felt hotter in its wake, like wet towels. His ankle, elevated in its sling, still throbbed and he felt nearly sick with exhaustion, and somewhere in the building he could hear Jacques Bichet playing the flute.

The same reasoning applied, of course, to Jules Mabillet.

Both were young men, and handsome. Surely handsome enough to feel they had a chance of enticing a pretty young woman, who was about to wed a man old enough to be her grandfather, into meeting them at the dead-huts.

He remembered the rider bursting from the woods, black hair whipped by the wind of his speed, sliding from the saddle to swoop Charlotte in his arms. *Yesterday*. He shook his head, and closed his eyes. Time seemed queerly telescoped with his exhaustion. As if he were sorting cards in his hand, he tried to put together the events of yesterday and today: the limping, agonized quest for mounts for Hannibal and Rose, his conversation on the gallery with Sidonie Janvier.

On a plantation this isolated, you need someone you can trust . . .

The yellow-and-white tignon on the floor of the dead-hut.

Trask's schemes with Molina to steal Cold Bayou slaves.

222

The way Antoine had caught Valla's wrist, and the smell of plum brandy in Ellie Trask's room . . .

Thunder woke him, hard on the heels of lightning whose flash left the room dark in its wake.

Dark?

He turned his head toward the French door.

It really was twilight – or else this was the worst storm-overcast he'd ever seen.

Rain pounded the walls, and the violence of the wind made the weaving house shake. The slap and smash of torn-off branches and leaves was like the rushing of the sea.

He fumbled for his silver watch, but found he'd completely forgotten to wind it the night before. His leg throbbed diabolically.

How long was I asleep?

'How long was I asleep?' he asked Minou, about thirty minutes later when, wrapped in an oiled-silk cloak, she finally slipped quickly through the French door. Like many plantation buildings in the French and Spanish Caribbean, the weaving house – when it had been partitioned to be a guest residence – consisted of entirely separate chambers, each entered from the gallery that ran along the front of the building and not from each other.

'*Hours*, darling!' She bore a candle, her hand curved protectively around its flame. This she carried to the little table that she used as a dressing-stand, where a small porcelain vielleuse stood. 'It's nearly seven o'clock and poor Visigoth's just in *despair* between taking the wedding decorations

223

down *again* and trying to come up with dinner for everybody!'

'Did the *Louisiana Belle* ever turn up? Or the *City of Nashville*?'

'Not a sign of either one, P'tit.' She touched the candle-flame to the wick beneath the night light's little teapot, and a thread of sweetness from the scented oil drifted on the gloom. 'I suppose that's just as well because one wouldn't want Père Eugenius coming all the way down here in this awful weather. Poor Henri was in conference with M'sieu Brinvilliers for just *hours*, and had Leopold watching the river like that poor girl in the fairytale, whoever it was, who ended up getting murdered . . . determined to get us away the *minute* the boat appeared, in spite of everything Uncle Mick and those horrid hooligans of his can do.'

She rustled to the door and peered out into the lashing twilight. She'd removed her tignon in the heat, and her long, curly dark hair lay half-unravelled from its braid over her slim shoulders. Bronze silk over dark ivory.

'And I hope those *awful* Irishmen are still standing on the landing getting soaked, and that *dreadful* man he had at the bottom of the gallery steps also, not that I think that any of them can stand up to a little rain! Uncle Veryl and Mamzelle Ellie, too, and Maman and I don't know *how* many others, just waiting to get out of this *horrible* place. Is it true that even if Henri pays Uncle Mick what he wants, then he can't . . . can't set me and Charmian free?' She came to the side of his pallet bed, sank to her knees beside it and took his hand. 'You don't think that awful man would . . . would sell me to somebody else?' Her voice fell to nearly a whisper.

'Nobody would buy you,' pointed out January in his most matter-of-fact voice. 'They'd be buying a lawsuit with the Viellard family. And we don't, any of us, know if what we're talking about is real or not.'

'And we can't even ask that miserable girl if she was telling the truth!' Minou's fist clenched, then relaxed almost at once. 'I'm sorry – I know I shouldn't speak so of the dead. And I *am* sorry . . . It was a dreadful thing. Chloë says she was cut up just *frightfully* . . . Chloë's offered to go spend the night with Mamzelle Ellie in the Casita, so she won't be alone. I know I'd be frightened to *death*! Because whoever did it – whoever killed Valla – is still out there, isn't he?'

'He's out there,' said January quietly. 'And I'm pretty sure he's going to try again.'

Sixteen

Something was hidden in the dead-huts.

In his dream, January searched them patiently, probing his hand into the half-rotted thatch: *It's got to be here somewhere . . .*

He found three of his mother's napkins (*She's going to be furious!*), Nicolette Charpentier's lavender gloves, the packet of colored chalks that his Paris friend Aristide Carnot had lost back

225

in 1829 (*So* that's *where they were!*), and the Holy Grail (*Wonder what that's doing here?*). He ducked through the low door of the hut, walked briskly to the next hut, grateful that he seemed to have gotten over his broken ankle, and noted that this wasn't the dead-huts at all, but the maroon village which had existed out in the ciprière behind Bellefleur Plantation in his childhood. Runaways from all over Orleans Parish would come there to hide. The huts were much the same, a hasty version of wattle-and-daub – not much mud and just bare sticks and branches on the inside – but all with the tall African roofs that made the huts look like enormous mushrooms and rendered the interiors cooler in the sweltering heat. He couldn't find the thing he sought (*What the hell* is *it, anyway?*), so he fetched the broken ladder from the rubbish-heap outside and propped it up against the eave of the largest hut.

I should have remembered to tell Luc to do this. As a tiny child, Olympe always hid things in the thatch at the top of the huts, where it was less likely to be found.

He was halfway up the ladder when he heard children crying wildly in one of the huts, and looking down, saw that the river had risen in flood.

Steel-gray and silent, the waters had rushed among the broken-down little dwellings, rising, inexorably rising. Trees floated in it, ripped from their moorings by the current. Whole lengths of fence; chicken-coops and the roofs of houses.

Valla's white-and-yellow tignon floated past,

like an unravelling serpent. Yellow silk flowers dotted the water, like vagrant stars.

Somewhere he smelled the smoke of a fire . . .

Heard Olympe say, 'Blood . . .'

He woke, to find the roaring howl of the wind had eased. But by the way the old weaving house rocked and shifted on its tall piers, he could tell that yes, the river had surged from its bed. The waters had risen in the swamps, inundating the cane-fields. The night light's tiny gleam barely outlined the shape of Dominique's empty bed – with Chloë spending the night in the Casita, Minou had taken the opportunity to slip across to the big house for a few hours with Henri. At the bed's foot, Charmian slumbered in her low cot, and beyond that, cramped into a corner, a dark braid on the pillow of a still-lower pallet (and a soft but pronounced snore) announced the presence of the nurse Musette.

January guessed it was Stanislas screaming in the next room. A second wail rose – Isabelle's daughter Marianne. The girl cried out in terror, 'Maman! Maman!' and though January was pretty sure that it was just the fear of a girl who'd never been caught in a flood before – the levees in town having been raised and strengthened since January's childhood – January carefully extricated his leg from its sling, found his crutch, and limped to the French door.

Outside was black as pitch. When he opened the door he could smell the water as well as feel it, surging and pushing gently at the pilings of the house. So clear was the recollection of his dream that for a few minutes he stood inhaling

227

deeply, trying to smell the smoke. Strained his eyes to probe the darkness, to locate that wild speck of orange flame.

But no sign of conflagration showed anywhere. Isabelle and Solange rushed past him along the gallery like unseeing ghosts, and the candles in their hands showed him the water, tiny glints flickering momentarily on a world of black silk, still a yard below the gallery. Now and then a branch or a broken length of fence would knock hollowly against the pilings or the stair.

The slaves in the quarters would be on their roofs. Well January recalled such nights – and days, too, sometimes – spent waiting for the water to go down. If Michie Fourchet had any warning whatsoever of a levee breach he would lock everyone in the sugar mill, lest any take advantage of the confusion, and of the rising waters that would obliterate their tracks. Since nobody in the quarters owned much in the way of possessions, it was little loss if their cabins were engulfed. The drowning of the garden-patches was a far worse calamity. Depending on the damage, it could mean no relief from grits and molasses for months. His father, he recalled, hid his rifle in the cabin's rafters for that reason, as well as because *les blankittes* seldom thought to look above their own eye-level.

A heavy storm further down-river, he thought. The wind brought him no whiff of smoke, but rather the smell of the far-off Gulf. *And the waters prevailed exceedingly upon the earth, and all the high hills that were under the whole heaven were covered . . .*

For a moment his thought went to Noah, and the shudder in the timbers of the Ark as it lifted from its stocks. Did the old man hold his breath, wondering if the overladen vessel would hold together? Did his sons' children cry out in terror in the darkness?

In the next room Solange whispered, 'It's all right, my sweetheart! Maman's here. Here, darling, go back to sleep, it can't hurt you . . . Look, Maman's got something to make you sleep . . .'

And Isabelle's candle appeared in the doorway, and her soft voice said, 'Here, *ma chou*, come and see . . .'

The stout plaçeé and her daughter emerged onto the gallery, and after a moment, came and sat on the bench beside January, who said comfortingly, 'The only time I've known this parish to flood deeper than six feet was during that hurricane four years ago, and this doesn't look nearly that bad.'

'Lord, no.' Old Laetitia emerged from her room, white braids hanging over her shoulder and a candle, shielded, in her hand. 'When I was a little girl, it would flood in town something dreadful, before they got the levees raised.'

'I remember that!' said January, laughing.

She chuckled in reply. 'You could paddle down Rue Royale in a boat. I remember how, in a bad flood one year, all the coffins washed up out of the cemetery, and went floating down the street to bang on windows—'

'Gave a new meaning,' grinned January, 'to the phrase, "Grandma's coming to visit",' and beside him on the bench, the little girl clapped her hands over her mouth and giggled.

'Oh, be still!' hissed Solange from within. 'Oh, my poor little boy . . .'

Lowering his voice, January said to Marianne, 'I was here when the hurricane hit this parish in '35. The only place I could climb onto was the roof of a shed, and when I looked around, this alligator the size of a dragon—' he stretched out his arms to illustrate – 'had climbed up on the other side of that roof with me.'

The girl laughed again, and for a time in the darkness he and the two women traded flood stories, diminishing the child's fear. And incidentally, keeping an eye on the level of the waters. With the sky like ink it was difficult to estimate the time. He held his watch close to Isabelle's lantern, and saw that it was three thirty, an hour at least before first light. There would be a mighty to-do, he reflected, if Henri didn't either get Minou out of the big house, or find some way of accounting for her presence there – *Conceal her in the attic, perhaps? Smuggle her food until the waters went down?* This fanciful thought amused him, but he guessed that if she did put in an appearance, though Madame Viellard and her daughter Euphémie would undoubtedly make poor Henri's life – and Minou's – miserable for as long as the waters stood high around the house, nobody would be very much surprised. And Minou, like Hannibal, could turn pretty much anybody up sweet.

It was of course out of the question for anyone to try wading through the floodwaters, even if

230

they crested at lower than chin-height. All those creatures about whom January had always wondered, when the good fathers at the St Louis Academy for Young Gentlemen of Color would relate the story of Noah – poisonous snakes and coldly-grinning alligators – would have been flushed from their holes and be swimming at large in the swirling waters, along with the great nine-foot gar-fish, which would attack pretty much anything they thought they could swallow. Once daylight came, it was a good bet that poor Antoine would be given the task of dragging a raft of foodstuffs – gators or no gators – out to the weaving house, and another one to the Casita. January recalled the flood during which one of the Bellefleur housemen had been killed at such a task, when he'd run onto a copperhead swimming in the brown waters. There had been a small rowboat among the brick piers of the big house, he recalled, and wondered if anybody had thought to get it out in time.

First light showed him they hadn't.

He pointed out to Marianne – and to Charmian, who had joined them, like the older girl angelic in a white nightgown – the dark shapes of Visigoth and Archie on the big house gallery, looking down at the water. Like spectators at the theater, he, Isabelle, and the little girls sat on the bench and watched Archie – under the dumb-show of Visigoth's objurgations – strip to his drawers and gingerly slip into the water, which had stopped rising at about four and seemed to be holding steady a few inches below the level of the galleries. 'Didn't you say there's snakes

231

in the water, Uncle Ben?' inquired Marianne worriedly.

'There are,' returned January grimly. 'That's why no white men wants to go in.'

'The poison ones are copperheads and cotton-mouths,' reported Charmian, in her precise little voice. 'Can they come up here, too?'

'They can,' said January. 'That's why every-body's going to have to be very careful where they step.'

Thisbe ran out onto the big house's front gallery and barked excitedly at the flood.

The big house, the Casita, the weaving house and the overseer's cottage sat upon the waters as if they floated there; the glassy yellow-gray surface stretched westward as far as the eye could see. January called the children's attention to where the top of the levee would be, now no more than a long patch of uneasily stirring water over the submerged ridge. Beyond it, far off under the wind-ragged gray sky, a few dollhouse islets like their own marked the plantation of Malsherbes, on the other side of the river, and three-quarters of a mile beyond that, dark, tiny trees dotted the glossy surface of the flood, even as they marked the siprière to the east. Charmian and Marianne surveyed the desolation with round eyes, caught between fear and the amaze-ment of the first major adventure of their young lives.

The quarters was an archipelago of roofs, on which dark shapes moved. A little further off, the stone mill-house rose, like an island cliff, crowned with an uneasy frieze of chickens. Narrowing his

232

eyes January could make out movement in its upper windows.

'What happened to the mules and M'sieu Mabillet's horse?' asked Marianne. Three of the barn cats had slipped indoors already past January's feet and those of the children as they'd come out onto the gallery; it was a good guess their brothers and sisters had taken refuge in the rafters of the barn itself.

January replied, 'Zach will have turned them loose when the waters started to rise. At least that's what the mule-boy on our place always did. Animals know where to find dry land and shelter. When the waters went down, everybody would spend days rounding them up again.'

'Antoine says,' reported Charmian – and January wondered what the nurse Musette had had to say about her charge trading words with the overseer's house-man – 'that in floods the animals always run away to this old house in the ciprière that Old M'sieu Froide built. How do they know?'

'God tells them,' said January. 'God looks out for animals, because they can't think like people can.'

'Oh, look!' cried Marianne. 'M'sieu Molina has a boat, too!'

Indeed, a larger rowboat was setting out from the overseer's cottage, heading for the sugar mill. January made out the overseer's stocky form, massive in his threadbare blue coat, bending to the oars. Antoine manned the other set, and like the overseer – January smiled to observe it – kept on the short jacket that marked

233

him as a house servant and not one of the ragged field hands.

'Are they going to bring the people in the sugar mill to where it's safe?' asked Marianne.

'More probably count them,' returned January, 'to make sure nobody ran off. They'll take the people off the roofs in the quarters, and take them over there. The sugar mill's probably the safest place to go in a flood.' And when he recounted how – and why – his master had locked the slaves up in the mill during floods, they turned those wondering eyes upon him, as if such a predicament could never come their way in their lives. Considerably later Solange took him to task for telling the two girls about slavery. 'Thank goodness little Stanislas was asleep when you spoke of it! It's not something children need to know about.'

Pray it won't ever be, January thought.

But at the moment it was simply a part of this strange adventure, and the girls watched with January as Archie emerged – evidently un-masticated by gators or snakes – from beneath the house, towing the recalcitrant boat, which he tied to the balustrade. Charmian asked softly, 'Will Maman come back here in that boat, Uncle Ben?'

'She will,' said January. (*And well before Madame Aurelié opens her eyes this morning, if Henri has anything to say about it*.) 'But first they have to go over to the Casita and make sure Madame Chloë and Mamzelle Ellie are all right.'

'I like Madame Chloë,' confided Charmian.

234

'She's funny. She's teaching me how to play cards. Were they afraid of the flood?'

'Mamzelle Ellie might have been,' said January. 'I don't think Madame Chloë is afraid of anything.' The wind sharpened again, still smelling of the sea and of more storm to come, and a vast crescent of hurrying ripples smote the water as if with an invisible arm. In a confidential whisper, he added, 'I suspect hurricanes and floods are afraid of *her*,' and both girls giggled again.

'Look . . .' He pointed to the Casita's gallery. 'There's Hélène.' The queenly shape and formidable lace cap of Chloë's French maid appeared, and the tall woman leaned on the rail of the gallery as the rowboat from the big house crept nearer. He guessed his little niece was watching for her formidable friend, and shook his head inwardly again over that unexpected mènage of husband, wife, husband's mistress and mistress's beautiful child.

And then frowned. Neither Chloë nor Ellie appeared on the gallery.

Ellie, it was true, from what he had learned about her yesterday, could very easily have begun drinking out of sheer funk and be at the moment incapacitated.

But he couldn't imagine Chloë sleeping when there was the faintest trace of light in the sky. Nor could he picture her passing up the opportunity of observing a flood at first-hand, any more than Rose would let such a chance go by.

There's something wrong . . .

He watched the little craft dock. Hélène, instead of turning back to the house to call out

235

the obligatory, 'Madame, the boat has arrived from the principal residence', was at the gap in the railings before it touched the gallery edge, and in her posture January read no trace of her customary hauteur when dealing with any member of the African race. He saw Visigoth's startle of alarm, and the glance that passed between the butler and the valet. Read, more clearly than anything else, the gravity of the disclosure in the way the haughty Frenchwoman snatched up her skirts to lead the two men into the house.

Isabelle's glance crossed his, she reading, too, something amiss. January flipped open his watch and noted the time – five past six – and it was thirteen minutes before the three of them emerged.

Too much time to simply rush into a bedroom and cry, 'Oh, my God!' at some scene of horror . . .

Thirteen minutes meant they'd at least cursorily searched the house.

Only the three of them emerged. And Hélène got into the boat with the two servants.

January whispered, 'Damn it,' as the boat started its painful journey back toward the big house. He picked up his stick, limped agonizingly back into his room, stripped out of his nightshirt, and began to wash in the tepid water that remained in the ewer.

He knew Henri would be on his way.

Seventeen

'Heard anything, Monsieur?' Hélène Fischart's pale brows snapped together with indignant anger at January's question. 'And how does one contrive to hear anything, with such a din, in such a ramshackle house? As well ask it of one who has been nailed in a crate and pushed down a flight of steps.'

He saw she was trembling.

She led the way across the gallery and into the Casita, the parlor lit now by the stormy silver light of the morning that had broken above the tumult of cloud-cover.

Henri hurrying at his back, January went first to the little chamber where Valla had slept, its minute dressing-table now adorned with Chloë's plain, neat toiletries: ivory-backed brushes, a tiny box of rice-powder, the rouge without which no Creole lady – French, Spanish, or African – felt completely dressed. A glass carafe of water and a tumbler, a larger ewer to wash in, with its bowl.

The bed had not been slept in. An evening frock of rose-colored silk, cut severely as that of a schoolmistress, lay over the room's chair, with two modest petticoats – even a woman who dressed as simply as Chloë did customarily wore three in the daytime, five or six or seven in the evening. A pair of evening-slippers to match the dress had been neatly set outside the door to be cleaned from

237

the walk back from the big house, and a glance inside the small armoire showed January a couple of clean chemises folded on one of the shelves, along with a plain nightgown, two pair of clean stockings, and a corset cut for evening wear. Another chemise – also neatly folded but clearly worn – lay on the armoire floor.

Of course Madame folds her dirty laundry . . .

'When Madame changed for dinner,' he asked Hélène, 'did you carry her day-frock up to the attic? Is it still there?'

'It was left here,' reported the maid. 'I helped Madame change her dress before dinner and then went in to assist Madamoiselle Trask. Madame instructed me to stay out of this room, as she did not wish anything to be disturbed. Madame had often made this request of me, when she is engaged in her studies.'

'And I take it the dress she changed out of needed no assistance, to be resumed?'

'No frock,' returned Hélène in chilly accents, 'can look its best when donned without professional assistance. But given her natural slightness of figure, Madame is well able to dress herself, should some pressing reason exist to do so. But I was upstairs all the evening, and there is a bell in the parlor which rings into the attic room where I slept. I can conceive of no circumstance which would have precluded Madame's summoning me. She is always meticulous in her appearance, and would never venture forth in a . . . a *slip-shod* condition.'

'What was she wearing before she changed for dinner?' January turned back to Henri, who simply

238

looked baffled by the question. Not, reflected January, having been married for nearly ten years to a dressmaker. 'Still the green sprig-muslin?'

Henri could have distinguished a crow from a grackle on the wing, by the shape of the tail, or identified an orange butterfly as a checkerspot or a fritillary at a glance. He now said, 'Uh . . .' casting his mind back with an effort.

Hélène said, 'With the white collar, yes, sir.'

'And you didn't see her after you helped her get ready for bed?'

'I did not help Madame prepare for bed.' Something – the first signs of distress to break the woman's marble calm – flickered across her face. 'Until I came downstairs this morning I thought that Madame had remained with Monsieur—' she acknowledged Henri with an infinitesmal nod – 'and had been constrained to remain there by the storm. The noise, you understand.'

Her lips tightened, and she seemed for a moment to struggle with how to organize the events of the previous night.

'And you thought Madamoiselle Trask had remained at the big house after dinner as well?'

'I thought so, yes, when no one rang.'

Together, the three of them passed from the small bedroom into the parlor again, and January couldn't keep from glancing to the little covered loggia of the back gallery, where Valla's body had lain twenty-four hours previously. He'd guessed it had been moved – even the cooling-bench was gone – when Minou had told him that Chloë was going to keep Ellie company at the

239

Casita last night, and made a mental note to ask his mother or old Madame Janvier about it when he had the opportunity.

He stopped, holding to a corner of the secretaire for balance. Through the French door he could see, approximately where the cooling-bench had stood, a puddle of vomitus, half-diluted by rain and spreading in a watery mess almost to the edge of the step. At the same moment Henri said, 'Good Lord!' and January looked around him at the parlor itself, seeing it as he had not done when first the distraught Henri had hustled him to the room that had been Chloë's last night.

Quickly January's eyes went to Hélène's. 'Did you hear anything downstairs last night?'

The room had been searched. It hadn't been ransacked, but he saw now that two of the drawers of the little secretaire on which he was leaning were open, that a paper or two had been dropped on the floor. He picked them up: a menu for the wedding-breakfast in a scribbled hand (Madame Aurelié's?), an inventory of the kitchen supplies, with a rough tally – labelled 'B' – in a different and uneducated-looking scrawl. Another scrap bore a tiny circle with what looked like a face scrawled in it, and a rude hieroglyphic that could have been a dress.

'I did, sir,' said the maidservant quietly. 'As I said, it was difficult to distinguish sounds, up in the attic with the noise of the storm, but at about ten o'clock I heard – or I thought I heard – someone moving about downstairs. I expected momentarily for someone to ring the bell, but no one did. Then I realized that there were no voices,

240

as there are when the gentlemen will escort a lady from the main house. A lady will always ask the gentleman in, at least for a moment.'

Not if she's ill to the point of vomiting, she won't.

Or, he thought, *drunk . . .*

He looked back at the disordered desk and saw a faint, dirty mark on the polished surface where something had been set. By the shape, he guessed it had been a lantern, and guessed also that it had been made last night. Visigoth's wife Hecuba had charge of keeping the Casita clean, and whatever she might think of Uncle Veryl's ill-bred bride, she had her standards. She'd have worn any housemaid out with a cane-stalk for leaving such a smudge unwiped.

A woman entering the parlor and feeling herself taken sick might well set her lantern down here as she rushed through to the back gallery. *Though wouldn't it make more sense to take the lantern with her?*

And wouldn't she have summoned the maid?

Unless of course, he thought, the maid had been looking down her cold French nose at her and visibly restraining her criticism from the moment she and her mistress entered the Casita.

His eyes went to the floor, criss-crossed with the faint, muddy smudges of footmarks.

I'll have to compare them with Mamzelle's shoes, and Chloë's.

'Does your attic door lock?'

'It does not,' said the woman. Her voice remained matter-of-fact, but January saw in her eyes what he himself saw: Valla's slashed throat

241

and blood-soaked dress. Still in that same calm tone, she went on, 'I was afraid that if I moved about, my own footsteps would be heard by someone downstairs – if there *was* anyone downstairs, of which I . . . I could not be perfectly certain. I knew I would be able to hear it if someone ascended the attic steps, so I covered my bedroom candle with the ewer – the shape of the pitcher permitted sufficient oxygen so that the flame would not be extinguished – and I . . . I waited.'

In the darkness, thought January. In the storm, behind a door that did not lock. A hundred yards from the main house and as isolated as if she were in a tiger's den a hundred miles from help. He understood why Chloë would appreciate this lanky, unglamorous woman as her handmaid.

'At one point—' Hélène brought the words out with stilted difficulty – 'I did hear the stairs creak. But then there was nothing. No one came up, but you will understand, messires, that I did not like to go down. There was insufficient light to read my watch, but it felt like hours, and this building does creak a great deal. Only with first light did I finally descend, and found things—' she gestured toward Ellie's room – 'as you see them.'

Ellie's room had definitely been searched. Gesturing his companions to stay at the door – and out of the melange of scuffed tracks – January limped inside – carefully. There were at least two sets of tracks, maybe three, crossing and re-crossing between door and dressing-table and bed.

The drawers of the dressing-table gaped open

and their contents – pots of rouge, switches of false hair, silk stockings, exquisite gloves – were stacked roughly on a corner of the bed. The three jewel boxes were open and their contents, glittering darkly in the silvery gloom, scattered the table's surface in a sticky puddle of plum brandy whose reek filled the room. The decanter had been tipped over and only the dregs remained. The glass on the nightstand hadn't been touched, a trenchant hint as to Mamzelle's drinking habits when she felt herself unobserved.

There was no sign, in the chamberpot or anywhere else in the room, that its occupant had been sick before the apparently comprehensive convulsion on the back gallery. Yet the bedclothes were creased, as if she had lain down in them in her clothes. 'Do you remember what Madamoiselle wore to dinner last night?' asked January, looking around him.

'Turquoise silk with cream-colored lace embroidered with gold. I do not see it here.'

'Did you take her day dress up to the attic when she dressed for dinner?'

'I did, sir. I will check that it is still there, but there was no occasion on which she could have come upstairs and fetched it. The dresses are all stored in the outer attic, outside my room. I would have heard if someone came up there, and I think I would have seen lantern-light beneath my door.'

'I think you would have, too.' Sitting in the blackness of her attic, her eyes must have been riveted on the crack beneath her door for terrifying hours.

Holding onto the tester for balance he studied

243

the dented coverlet on the bed, the swatches of powder and rouge that stained the pillow. A little brandy had been spilled here, too, and he frowned at the smell of it. *Not brandy only.* He knelt with difficulty, and leaned until his nose was almost against the embroidered linen. There was another smell to it, bitter and half familiar . . .

'*Did* no one escort the ladies back here?' He straightened, and Henri helped him to his feet. By a heroic effort January did not add, *And how drunk was Mamzelle?*

If whatever she'd consumed at dinner – and God knew what she'd surreptitiously shared with Uncle Mick afterwards, if he'd had a flask on him – had hit her that hard, no wonder she was in a hurry to return here.

But from what Hannibal had told him of the young woman, he had formed the impression that she could drink like a hole and not be much the worse.

Henri blushed a bright pink at his question and stammered, 'I . . . I don't know. It was . . .' He pressed a fist against his lips for a moment, brown eyes sick with guilt and grief, and January remembered suddenly what had been at least one result of Chloë spending the night here instead of at the big house. 'That is, I had . . . I left the company early . . .'

Only his love for Dominique, thought January, would have taken this man from the joys of coffee and dessert.

Of course he wouldn't have known when his wife left the assembly in the main house.

'Of course,' he said gently, and Hélène threw

244

a glance at her mistress' husband that could have stripped the paint from a door.

'Because of the storm we all ate dinner indoors, you see.' Henri took a deep breath, steadying himself, though his face was taut with misery. 'The . . . the circumstances were extremely awkward.'

Even clearing all the chairs from the still-unachieved wedding from the dining-room and parlor, calculated January, there would still have remained the problem of where one would seat twenty-seven guests in the small space of a plantation-house designed more as a field-office than a regular dwelling. And that wasn't even counting the American lawyer Loudermilk (*Did they put him out on the back gallery*?) and Uncle Mick's boys.

It went without saying that those who had rooms in the big house would disappear into them with their coffee – and whoever they felt was congenial company – as soon as they could, rather than listen to yet another harangue by Locoul St-Chinian on the subject of his father's injustice in disinheriting him, or a lecture from Gloyne Cowley about the lawsuit he was bringing against the family over his wife Fleurette's inheritance. Not to speak of Madame Aurelié's icy snubbing of Evard Aubin for harming the son of her dear friend, and Charlotte's desperation to return to her beloved's side.

He shuddered to think what Uncle Mick was like after dinner with a couple of whiskies in him.

Of course no one was keeping track of who was in which room when.

And Uncle Veryl, January was well aware, was just as likely to sink into one of his long scientific discussions with Selwyn Singletary – *his* most congenial companion – only to surface two hours later with the vague assumption that had Mamzelle Ellie wished to return to the Casita, she had only to ask one of the gentlemen to escort her.

And Ellie, of course, would have been silent all evening among her intended's disapproving relatives.

A piece of paper lay on the floor beside the bed, and he bent carefully to retrieve it. A page torn from a ledger, he thought, unfolding it.

Printed in pencil were the words: *Dead-huts. Midnight.*

'What is it?'

Heedless of footprints, Henri rushed to his side, took the paper from his hand. 'Dear God,' he whispered. 'What time did the flooding start?'

January shook his head. 'Later than midnight,' he said.

'How much later?' Henri gazed from the printed words into his face, his pendulous cheeks ashen. 'If she started for the dead-huts, and Chloë heard her, and followed her . . .'

Behind them in the parlor the French door slammed open, and the thunder of feet – before January even turned – sufficiently announced the arrival of Uncle Mick and his boys.

'*Bastard*!' The Irishman stormed into the bedroom, grabbed January's arm and swung him around, the torque and pressure on his ankle dropping him to the floor with a cry. Uncle Mick's grip dragged him up, and with his other hand the

Irishman struck January a brutal punch like a hammer. 'Filthy nigger bastard—'

Even without the 'boys' present January knew better than to strike back, though the pain in his ankle made it hard to think. He brought his arms up to protect his face, and Mick's fist drove twice more into his ribs, before he thrust him to the floor and began to kick him, shouting curses. It took Henri several moments to wade into the fray (*Is he taking off his spectacles*? January wondered in distracted exasperation) – above him, January heard the planter saying, 'Here, now, stop this! Stop it, I say—'

Uncle Mick smelled of whiskey and January curled himself tighter, praying the boys wouldn't all wade into him and weirdly, in a tiny corner of his mind, wanting to yell at them, 'Don't tread on the footprints!'

'Stop this at once!' Hélène didn't raise her voice, but her words were like the lash of a whip.

The kicking stopped.

'Explain yourself, sir! How this man can have had anything to do with your niece's disappearance—'

'How?' Mick Trask was nearly spitting with rage. 'He was goddam well on his goddam feet a minute ago, now, wasn't he? Him and that bitch mother o' his. Just waitin' for the chance to get my poor girl, sneakin' Nubians! An' her wid her dress wet from the storm an' soaked to the knees with the flood. Didn't think o' that, did yez, boy-o?' This to January, who had cautiously, agonizingly sat up again. ''Tis the first thing I did, when I'd heard my poor girl had been done

247

for – went through the rooms of every one o' them that'd wish her ill, lookin' for who'd been out in the rain! Lurin' her out of this place, like you lured that poor wench o' hers. Sneakin' witch! I'll live to see the pair of yez hanged!'

Eighteen

'It's ridiculous!' Livia Levesque jerked on the chain padlocked around her wrist. 'It's a lie, and this is an outrage, an obscenity, to keep me imprisoned in this way!'

'I hope by that you mean <u>us</u>, Maman,' said January wearily. His ribs ached sickeningly and the whole left side of his face had swollen from Mick Trask's blows, to say nothing of the blinding throbbing in his foot. He wanted nothing more than to lie down on the floor, stack chunks of wood high enough to elevate his ankle – the only room above water available as a prison was the loft over the wood store – and go to sleep, something he knew he must not do.

He wondered if, as suspected murderers as well as potential runaways, anyone was going to feed them, particularly given the issue of rationing in the flood-locked plantation.

Somebody has to come, who can take a message . . .

'When did you go over there?'

'*Really*, Benjamin—'

'Maman,' said January patiently, 'we have very

248

little time to figure out what actually happened in the Casita last night and according to Uncle Mick—'

'You would believe that lying Irish swine over your own *mother*?'

'Was your dress wet from the storm? And soaked to the knees?'

'The fact that a – a swindling, camphorated bog-jumper should have the temerity to search the rooms of the other guests in the house . . .'

'That was very quick thinking on his part, actually. Did you search Mamzelle's rooms for papers about Fourchet's debts?'

'I think I was very well justified in doing so, given that brassy-haired hussy's lies.'

'When? While she was still at dinner?'

His mother emerged from behind the stack of logs that separated them. Each had been chained to one of the several kingposts that held up the roof; stacked billets of wood lined the walls and here and there piles were heaped where exhausted work-gangs had dropped them. Neither January nor his mother had a chain long enough to reach to the open trap in the middle of the room, through which January could see brown floodwater, bobbing with more wood, almost to the level of the loft floor. *Just what we need. A copperhead or an alligator coming to take refuge . . .*

At the end of the long room an opening in the wall, shaded under the ten-foot eaves, let in the dappled reflection of gray morning light.

For a long time his mother only regarded him, her fine-boned face – of whose nearly-European features and mild cocoa-colored complexion she was ferociously proud – closed like a pair of shutters, admitting nothing.

She's afraid, he thought, returning her gaze. She knew the life she faced, even were she not executed for the heinous crime of killing any white person, let alone one legally deemed her master. She had spent thirty-six years as a free woman – a woman of a certain amount of wealth and property. She owned her own house, had slaves of her own (whom she had, in the past, taken down to the Cabildo to be whipped by the City Guard for allegedly padding the household bills). In her early sixties now, she had not the stamina to survive in the fields, nor the temperament that anyone in their right mind would take into their household.

She would fight, with words or lies or whatever weapon came to hand, to the last. But he saw the terror in her eyes.

At length she said, 'Did that other hussy steal the jewels?'

'What other hussy?'

'I don't know.' She turned the shackle on her wrist: the light, small sort that dealers used on 'fancy goods'. The links tinkled in the wet still-ness. 'Whoever it was must have seen the light in the attic and knew the maid was up there, and would be too afraid after that brass-haired bitch's murder to come down if she heard any noises. Cold-faced hag. I daresay she helped herself to the jewels—'

'The jewels were still on the dressing-table,' said January.

For one second his mother's face relaxed in

relief; then she frowned sharply, as if at a house-maid's neglect of some task. 'Well, *really*!'

He knew the only reason they hadn't gone into *her* pockets was because she knew they'd be recognized when she tried to sell them.

'So you went over there while everyone was at dinner,' he went on, 'knowing the storm would cover whatever sounds you might make. You searched the Casita . . . and someone else came in while you were there?' He thought there had been at least two noticeable sizes of track on the straw-matting of the bedroom floor. Possibly, he thought, three . . .

'I'd searched the bedroom,' admitted his mother grudgingly. 'I found nothing – not in her dressing-table, not in her trunk, nowhere. I'd glanced in that small room – though even that *cocotte* wouldn't have been so stupid as to conceal anything where Valla could have laid *her* thieving hands on it – and was about to start on the pantry when I heard someone open the French door into the parlor. I covered my lantern at once and stepped into the attic stair, and pulled the door to behind me. I listened for the sound of the bell up in the maid's room – it was dark enough that I could have slipped out onto the back gallery if I had to – but there was no sound, only someone moving about the house for an unconscionably long time. I thought it might have been that cold little witch of a wife Henri's got, trying to find some evidence against the girl, though God knows what it would take to pry that senile fool Veryl away from her. If it were her, it would make sense she wouldn't touch the jewelry I'd

251

left on the table. Nasty, gaudy stuff – I'd have blushed, if poor St-Denis gave me stones like those.'

Her eyes narrowed, piecing together recollections of events, and January hid a smile at the lie.

You wouldn't have blushed, you'd have worn them for him with a dazzling smile and sold them before his body was cold.

'Was there a dress on the bed in Madame Chloë's room?'

'Rose-colored silk. And I must say I was a bit shocked at that maid of hers, for not putting it away. For all her airs . . .'

'Rose-colored silk.' January turned the meaning of that over in his mind. Trying again to picture the faint, shadowy tracks on the scrubbed cypress of the parlor floor, of the straw matting in the bedroom; cursing Uncle Mick and his boys.

'And you left . . . When?'

'Good heavens, Benjamin, I didn't look at my watch! After that sly little hussy left I went through the parlor and the pantry pretty thoroughly – though I doubt the girl even knows what a pantry is for. Except to hide liquor in. Three bottles of plum brandy – nasty, stinky stuff – and enough Hooper's Elixir to put an army to sleep, I daresay. *No* woman gets the cramps *that* bad! By that time it was late. I was in the parlor when I saw a lantern on the path from the big house, and guessed it was Little Mamzelle Virginity on her way. I slipped out the back and kept within the woods where my lantern wouldn't show. The wind was frightful by that time and it was hard to get along, and the water started coming up before I reached the weaving house. And as for that Irish scoundrel searching the rooms of his fellow-guests—'

'Where did you hide your wet clothes?'

'Under the top mattress of the bed, Benjamin.' She went on, her voice changing, 'What are we to do? I hated that vile ninny but you know I'd never have raised my hand against her.'

January didn't know anything of the sort, if his mother thought she could have gotten away with a murder, but was reasonably certain that it was not, in fact, the case now.

'Do you have your notebook on you? If I can get a message to Old Madame Janvier, I know she'll stand my friend. Surely she won't believe I had anything to do with what happened. Of course nobody will believe that ice-faced *galette* Chloë was in the house—'

He recalled what Olympe had said about who would get the blame if Ellie Trask was murdered before the wedding, and shivered. *We already have blood, death and water . . .*

'I have a hundred dollars in gold,' his mother went on, and extended her hand. The kingposts were far enough separated, and the chains that held them short enough, that they could not touch, but sure enough, the cindery daylight showed him a small stack of ten-dollar gold pieces nested in her palm, and on top of them, a half-dozen silver dollars. Seeing his expression of surprise, she added tartly, 'A fine thing it would be, if I didn't think to have a bank sewn into my corset. Ever since that stripe-eyed *pichouette* sounded

253

off her mouth about us I've kept it full. I daresay that sneak of an overseer would sell us five minutes alone with the key: I saw that silk dress his wife was wearing when she came down to the levee Tuesday, thinking to meet Père Eugenius! Thirty dollars it must have cost, with that lace – and that cameo was Italian work, twenty-five dollars at the least! She can't have things like that on an overseer's—'

'*Don't*,' said January quietly. 'Don't even think it, Maman. You think the man isn't going through your luggage even as we're speaking here, looking for whatever he can find? You think, if you even *hinted* that you had money on you, that he wouldn't search you to the skin for it?'

She fell silent. He could see the glint of irritation in her eyes as she rebuked herself for even thinking that an overseer could be trusted.

'Someone will come,' said January.

He knew this was likely, but in his heart he didn't believe it.

It was in fact Henri who arrived about an hour later, pasty with shock and accompanied by the aenemic-looking lawyer DuPage. The men who rowed them up to the outer window were, January knew by their voices ('Mind yer step, sorr . . . Not that way, yer bletherin' Frenchy gobshite, you'll have us over . . .') to be some of *the boys*.

'I refuse to believe, absolutely refuse, that you had anything to do with . . . with whatever happened.' Henri knelt at January's side and began pulling pads of linen and bottles of things like spirits of wine and basilicum powder out of a willow basket he'd brought. His hands shook so badly he kept dropping them, and – perhaps surprisingly for a man whose devotion to meals was amply attested by his fifty-four-inch waist – of course he hadn't remembered to bring anything to eat or drink. He kept his voice low and glanced repeatedly back at the wide square of yellow-gray water and daylight, against which the heads of the Black Duke and Gopher were silhouetted, though at a guess they spoke no French.

'You have to *do* something,' the planter begged, as January took over the process of making a compress for his eye. 'What can have happened to them? We've had . . . I've sent parties into the woods, but we've only two boats, and the water is six feet deep, nearly as far as town, I think. Poor Uncle Veryl is almost ill with grief and anxiety, and Maman is . . . I've never seen her like this! Chloë . . .' He pressed his fist to his mouth again, unable to go on.

Beyond the piled wood January heard the clink of chain-links, and his mother's incisive voice: 'I trust you're not going to lock me into an attic somewhere? Or does that pox-raddled Irish pirate propose to hang me out of hand?'

She, and DuPage, emerged from around the woodpile, Livia Levesque liberated from her bonds and stiff as an outraged queen, and be damned to breaking and entering the Casita in the middle of last night.

'You're to remain at the weaving house, Madame,' said DuPage, escorting her tenderly toward the wide window. 'It is part of Madame

255

Janvier's agreement with Trask that this gentleman
– M'sieu M'Gurk—' he gestured to the weasel-
faced Gopher – 'remain with you there for the
time being, until the floodwaters recede sufficiently to permit the arrival of the Plaquemines
Parish sheriff—'

'That *estragot*? Stupid as a basket with a hole
in it. If he's in charge of finding what became of
that good-for-nothing strumpet we might as well
call Père Eugenius now for last rites, not that
he'd come.'

She barely glanced at January as the Black
Duke clambered into the loft, and DuPage assisted
the widow Levesque into the rowboat, then
climbed in himself.

'I'd advise yez don't try nuttin',' growled the
Duke as he settled himself just inside the window,
drawn pistol on his knee. 'Gopher M'Gurk can
plug the eye outten a rabbit at a hundred yards
by moonlight, so he can, drunk or sober.'

'How *ever* did you arrive at the information
about the latter state?' replied Livia, glancing
him up and down before averting her face in
contempt.

'Madame Janvier posted a bond of eight
hundred dollars with M'sieu Trask,' explained
Henri, as the boat was rowed away. 'Trask is
demanding fifteen hundred for you, and Maman
. . .' He stammered, and flustered again with his
plump hands. 'I'll see she puts it up,' he went
on after a moment. 'I swear it. And of course he
won't listen when I tell him that even if you *had*
plotted to murder Mamzelle Trask you couldn't
have walked the distance from the weaving house

to the Casita! "He looked to be walkin' just fine when I seen him there" . . .'

'I was "walkin' just fine",' responded January drily, 'because I'd gotten there in a boat. Listen,' he went on. 'I need you to do several things for me, sir, and I need them very quickly, as soon as . . . who's going to bring that boat back here, if Michie M'Gurk is going to stay at the weaving house and keep an eye on Maman?'

'DuPage – though I believe he considers it beneath his dignity to act as a waterman.'

'As soon as you have the boat at your disposal, it is *imperative* that the Casita be locked up and kept locked, until I can look at it. Can you do that?'

'Of course.'

'No one is to enter for any reason. That paper we were looking at when we were interrupted – you don't have it with you now, do you, sir?'

Henri looked baffled for a moment, as if the incident had entirely vanished from his mind, then said, 'Oh, the paper! *Dead-huts, midnight* . . . No, I . . . I must have dropped it in the scuffle.'

'Bring it to me here, if you would be so good.'

'I'd forgotten all about it,' admitted the planter, straightening his spectacles. 'But of course the dead-huts are the first place the . . . the search-parties will make for. According to James, everyone in the Parish uses them as a rendez-vous for everything from love-trysts to receiving-offices to the commercial exchange of stolen goods. You don't think . . .' His brow crumpled again. 'You don't think Mamzelle Trask was lured to the place, do you?

257

And Chloë set off after her and . . . well . . . encountered whoever it was who . . . who sent that note . . .'

January opened his mouth to reply, thought about it for a moment, then changed his answer to, 'I'm reasonably certain that Madame Chloë returned to the Casita, changed her dress, and left again before Mamzelle Trask left the big house.'

A look of guilty pain returned to Henri's eyes. 'But why?' Clearly he saw himself slipping away from the candle-lit dining-room to his own room, where Minou waited for him.

At the window, the Irishman belched, and spit into the water below. Past him, January could see the overseer's larger rowboat, Molina in his shabby blue coat with patches to its elbows, crossing toward the sugar mill. Provisions for those trapped there were piled in the boat's stern.

'I don't know. Bring that note to me, and then, if you'll forgive me, sir, I'm going to have to ask you to do something so disgusting that I wouldn't request it of anyone, if there were any way that I could perform the task myself. But I can't. I'm sorry. The lives of Madame Chloë and Mamzelle Ellie may depend on it and my life certainly does. I need to know as much as I can about what happened in the Casita last night if I'm going to have even a guess about what became of Madame and Mamzelle Trask.'

'Of course.' Henri propped his spectacles on his sweating nose. 'Anything.'

'Last night someone was very sick on the back

gallery,' January said. 'The vomitus has been diluted by the rain that splattered in past the abat-vent but . . . I'm going to have to ask you to sniff it.'

'Oh!' Henri's unexpected expression of pleased enlightenment reminded January of his own days of learning medicine at the Hôtel Dieu in Paris. No disgust (*Well, the man* does *collect and classify cockroaches*), but the startled realization that information could be derived from cast-up stomach contents. 'Of course!'

'You're looking for the smell of liquor. Madame Chloë isn't a heavy drinker – I believe Mamzelle Trask is.'

'Oh, yes, like a stung pig.'

'I also have reason to believe she was lying on her bed drinking when she came in last night, before she went out – for whatever reason she went. I just need to know. And if you can, take one of these bandages—' he shook free a small pad of linen from the basket – 'and soak it in whatever is left in the decanter by the bed. Bring that back to me, too.'

'All right.'

'And don't let *anyone* know what you're about. It's remotely possible that Mamzelle went out to meet someone who isn't staying here at Cold Bayou, but the odds are very strong that if she was lured out, it was by one of the guests here – either white or colored. Or, just possibly, by one of the slaves.'

'One of the *slaves*?' Henri drew back with an expression of puzzled disgust. 'Why on earth would she—?'

259

'*We don't know*,' repeated January. 'We don't know what she was told, or by whom, or what she thought was going on. But whatever happened – whatever *is* happening – we don't know who's responsible. And we don't know what that person or persons would do to keep from being found out. Please, sir – don't tell anyone. Not even Minou.'

'Oh, Minou can keep secrets . . .'

'I know she can.' He smiled gently. 'But I also know that my sister is impulsive – and I think you'll agree with me there, sir.'

The younger man's smile trembled into being, at the recollection of some of Dominique's more impulsive acts.

'She wouldn't tell secrets,' went on January, 'but neither you nor I has the slightest idea what she might take it into her head to *do* with any given piece of information.'

By Henri's smile he, too, was recalling some of the courses of action which had made sense to Dominique over the years. 'She'll never forgive me.'

'Oh, I think she will. And if you can, sir,' he finished, as the rowboat knocked gently at the wall beneath the window and the Duke yelled, 'About fookin' time!' – 'even before you set about trying to get me out of here so I can examine the Casita myself, could you manage to get me something to eat?'

260

Nineteen

Fifteen minutes after Henri's departure January heard the knock of another boat against the wall below the window, and Archie's voice saying, in English, 'Now, you step careful there, sir . . .'

Selwyn Singletary climbed carefully into the loft, and to January's almost tearful delight, leaned back out through the aperture with the incomprehensible Yorkshire admonition, ''Ug yon skep careful nor like,' and lifted in a substantial basket of food. 'If I ever knowed one like our Henri,' the old man added, shaking his head as he crossed to January. 'Rowed straight off for yon bitty oyl, an' poor Veryl nigh rigwelted wi' not knowin' what's come of two that he loves wi' the whole of his heart—'

'I'm afraid that's my fault,' said January. 'And I beg Michie Veryl's pardon. But it's imperative – I cannot overstate how imperative – that the Casita be locked up until I can get free to see it.'

'Bait yoursel', for God's sake.' Singletary pushed the basket at January, who unwrapped the little bundle of hoecakes and head-cheese and fell on them like a starving wolf.

'What hast found?' the old man asked, when the meal was done – which it was, January estimated, in record time.

'Nowt,' January replied solemnly, in the mathematician's own dialect, which made Singletary smile. 'Precious little, anyway. At least two other people were in the Casita last night, besides the young ladies: searching it, I think.' Since Singletary spoke to almost no one except Uncle Veryl there was little chance that he'd blab secrets, but he'd certainly pass along whatever he heard to his friend . . . and there was no telling who Veryl would tell, in his grief. Best keep the name of Livia Levesque out of it.

'None of the doors or windows looked as if they'd been forced – I'll know better when I've had a chance to go over it carefully. And someone – either one of the young ladies, or one of the intruders – or just possibly someone else – was sick on the back gallery. How did Miss Trask seem last night at dinner?'

'Fashed, poor little phummock.' Singletary shook his head. 'O' course, wi' that poor lass o' her'n kilt in mistake for her an' knowin' t' killer's yet out yon someplace – if he wa'nt i' t' very room wi' her. Quiet as a mouse she was but goin' fra one window t'next lookin' out into storm. So fashed was she, an' so noisy t' room, wi' that scoundrel nuncle goin' on about t' heathan Chinese beatin' sailors that's tryin' to sell opium in their country, an' how dare they, that I tried to get up a chess game in t'office. I won twice – Veryl's a fair player, but he's that careless wi' movin' his queen, an' in t'fourth game caught me fair an' square atween his queen's pawn an' t'bishop . . .'

'And where was Miss Trask during all this?'

Singletary frowned, his mind clearly far more occupied – as it had undoubtedly been the

262

previous night – with the logistics of queen-side castling than the whereabouts of a young woman whose life was threatened by a murderer who had already killed once.

As Veryl had been, thought January, angry but at the same time exasperated. Veryl – and Singletary – were what they were: two eccentric old men whose wide-ranging interests were generally incompatible with the role of knight-errant.

It would have been funny, he thought, were it not for the ransacked Casita, for the dead girl who now lay (he had found out from his mother) in the tiny attic-loft of the kitchen behind the overseer's house. In the clammy heat, he could not keep from wondering about what sort of insect life – if nothing larger – was making a feast of poor Valla's body.

'Ah recollect that nuncle o' her'n called her to t'office door,' said Singletary at length. 'Happen he told off a couple o' them wild Irish, to see her safe back.'

'Happen,' agreed January glumly.

Questioned further, Singletary had no clear idea of what time this conference with Uncle Mick had been, or whether Ellie had returned to the office after it or not.

Archie, at least – called in after tying the rowboat to a rake-handle wedged in the open window – provided him with information about the fifteen slave families who had been trapped on their cabin roofs by the rising waters: they had indeed taken refuge in the sugar mill after freeing the mules and horses. 'Most folks in the quarters don't keep no pigs nor goats, sir. Antoine

263

tells me, Michie Molina taken more'n one pig, so now nobody keeps 'em. Leastwise not here they don't. Zandrine says, some folks keeps pigs out in the ciprière, on the mound where old Michie Froide's house was, up Cold Bayou. It stands through most floods, she say, an' the beasts know to flee there.'

But of the movements of any particular slave during the previous night the young man knew nothing. Purchased the previous year, Archie was a native of coastal Georgia and knew only what French he had gleaned in town since his arrival; certainly nothing of the three-quarters-African cane-patch patois spoken by the country slaves. He promised to get word to Luc, to come to January as soon as he could – just as soon as he, Archie, could get access to a rowboat to get him to the sugar mill.

'It look like it stormin' again later,' he apologized. 'Lightnin' over the woods. Water's still high, an' there ain't but the two boats, 'cept for a couple pirogues some of the men got hid in the woods, they says. An' 'fore God, I wouldn't want to try swimmin' in that water. There's *things* in it!'

Having seen at least two alligators pass silently beneath the trap in the floor, January couldn't argue with him there.

Did Noah have these problems, in his forty days and forty nights when the waters stood upon the earth?

Some half-hour after Singletary took his leave, January heard the splash and creak of many oars, and Antoine's voice – 'We come get you when

264

we loaded up' – as the prow of the bigger rowboat knocked against the wall. Then, 'Whoa, nigger, watch your step there!' as Uncle Bichet, the oldest and, in January's opinion, wisest of his fellow musicians scrambled over the sill.

He, too, bore a split-willow basket of food – 'Anybody think to feed you, Ben?' – and several stone bottles of ginger water. 'You all right? M'am Levesque said as how Old M'am Janvier put up bail money for her, but Lordy, that Irishman they sent to keep an eye on her! Thinks he's too good to use the same pisspot as black folk.'

'He can have the leaky bucket they left for me, and welcome,' grumbled January.

'So they figured out how *you* had a hand in killin' that poor l'il gal?' The old man drew up a chunk of wood to sit on, his thick spectacles flashing softly in the rainy daylight. 'Every member of the family wantin' her dead an' you laid up with a broken leg. '*Course* it was you that done it!'

'They found anything? Or anything of M'am Chloë?'

'Not a pig's whisker. But I think it's clear what happened, don't you, Ben? Somebody did for the girl, an' maybe M'am Chloë as well?'

January nodded, but added, 'I'll know more when I can look over the Casita myself. That—' He bit off a description of Uncle Mick that he'd probably have to confess next Wednesday – *'if I live til next Wednesday*!'

'Uncle Mick and his boys came storming into the Casita like pirates sacking a town and hauled me off here before I could take a look at the

265

tracks, but there were tracks all over the place. It had been searched, and I *think* – I'm not sure – that somebody put something in Mamzelle Ellie's brandy.'

'I heard tell there was a note,' said the old African. 'Lurin' her out to them old huts out on the bayou. Why poison her, if you was goin' to kill her out there?'

January hesitated again, then said, 'Maybe get her out of the house. She was a strong girl, and it could be someone wanted to slow her down.'

'It would account,' agreed Uncle with a slow nod, 'for her leavin' the dinner the way she did, if she planned to get herself out to them dead-huts by midnight. She was mighty twitchy, all through that little soiree they had us up for, after dinner. That uncle of hers was all over her sweet as honey, holdin' her hand an' tellin' us to play all her favorite songs, "Greensleeves" an' "Cuckoo in the Grove". An' small blame to the poor girl,' he added. 'With her maid killed that way only that mornin', an' knowin' every person in the room, just about, wanted her dead.'

'How did she leave?'

The old musician frowned, the deep V's of the 'country marks' that had been cut into his face in boyhood pulling deeper with his thought. He was in fact the flautist Jacques Bichet's great-uncle, rather than his uncle, and had been a man of full years when he'd been brought to America, and a scholar of some repute. Pretty much everyone of African blood in the French Town turned to him for advice, for he was observant, and – in common with the voodoos – expert at

266

piecing together bits of information that others regarded merely as chaff.

'She was watchin' for her chance to go,' said Uncle after a time. 'They split up after dinner, the way white folks do, the men sittin' at the table drinkin an' arguin' politics, but there was really no place for the ladies to go to but M'am Viellard's room – M'am Aurelié – an' there was too many of 'em for comfort, even if every one of 'em hadn't been cuttin' poor Mamzelle Ellie dead as if she didn't exist. Cuttin' that M'am Fleurette – old César's daughter – an' that daughter of hers, an' Michie Locoul St-Chinian's trashy wife. But for all that, those three hadn't a word to say to Mamzelle neither.'

January grimaced, knowing how, even without the impetus of family struggles over power and control of money, any gathering of white folks in New Orleans would split along social and political lines. The Legitimistes ignored the Orleannistes, the Orleannistes turned up their noses at the Bonapartistes and all of them cold-shouldered those whose families had favored the Revolution. White French folks, he corrected himself. None of those groups would have anything to do with an American animal.

'They came on back into the parlor whilst we were still setting up,' the old man continued. 'M'am Aurelié shut the men up pretty sharp. While everybody was takin' seats an' talkin', Mamzelle Ellie kept walkin' over to the French doors out onto the front gallery, which stood open on account of the heat. Someone – I think it must have been one of them wild Irish, but I

267

didn't rightly see – came up to her there, and it looked as if she'd have gone out onto the gallery. But M'am Aurelié an' her oldest daughter, an' Old M'am Janvier, an Pepa St-Chinian, all looked at her like she'd piddled on the floor, an' her uncle went over to her an' pulled her away.'

'And where was M'am Chloë during all this?'

'She'd left already,' returned Uncle. 'Slipped out quiet. Came out of M'am Aurelié's room with the other ladies an' went straight on out onto the gallery. Didn't even look around for Michie Henri, which was a good thing,' he added, 'seein' as how Michie Henri disappeared 'fore we even come in with our instruments. I seen him tip-toein' along the back gallery an' in through Michie Singletary's room, that connects on through to his own.' His cocked eyebrow did horrific things with the cicatrized flesh above it.

'I can't say I blame the poor girl for wanting someone to talk to. And M'am Chloë didn't take anyone to escort her when she left?'

Uncle Bichet's eyes narrowed as he called the scene back to mind. He had, of course, been playing the bull fiddle while all this small-scale drama had been taking place in the parlor, but January knew that all of the musicians – himself included – derived considerable entertainment from watching such drama, and were past masters at following events. It was, Hannibal said, better than the bill at most theaters – *And in any case we're completely invisible to them, you know.*

'Unless it was James or Archie – who I saw later playin' cards in the pantry. Visigoth an'

Jacques-Ange, an' Michie Aubin's Urbain, was all helpin' with the coffee an' sweets. Mamzelle mighta gone with some of the Irish, but I doubt M'am Chloë would do such a thing. It might so be she minds it more than she lets on,' he added in a lower voice, ''bout Michie Henri an' Mamzelle Minou.'

'It might.' January thought of the long, dilapidated shell-path, that led from behind the big house, a hundred yards over broken ground past the house's kitchen-garden and chicken-runs, to the Casita, isolated on the edge of the woods. Chloë St-Chinian Viellard was a girl of diamond pride. The haughtiness that held most of the world – probably including her husband – in such unthinking contempt that his keeping a mistress didn't really bother her. She was honest enough to admit that she was incapable of making any man happy, and was genuinely delighted that Dominique could do so.

But that was not the same, January knew, as the awareness that Henri was absent from a family gathering because he was meeting his mistress *that night*. That hour. Under her own roof.

And part of the cauldron of power and anger was fuelled, January knew well, by the fact that after four years of marriage, Chloë still had produced no heir to the Viellard/St-Chinian fortunes. Henri's mother was not the only one in the family to have commented on the matter.

Whether this troubled that coldly diminutive lady or not, it was difficult to tell. And Uncle Mick's presence alone – bellowing his opinions about how unfair the representation in Congress

269

was against the Southern states – would be enough to drive anyone from a room.

Personally, he would have fled the parish to avoid it.

'So whatever the case,' he said at length, 'Mamzelle Ellie was on her own.'

'She was. An' she looked like she'd got the worst of it, among the women.' Uncle shook his head, pity in his dark eyes. 'Her uncle, an' Michie Veryl, kept close by her, while we was settin' up. But Uncle Mick got to slangin' with Michie Locoul St-Chinian an' that good-for-nuthin' brother-in-law of his, an' Uncle Veryl an' Michie Singletary took her away with 'em into the office – playin' chess, I think, which got to be like watchin' paint dry, unless you're crazy for the game yourself.' The old man shook his head again.

'Pretty soon Mamzelle come slippin' out, an' through the dinin' room an' out onto the back gallery an' into the dark. I doubt Michie Veryl even seen her go. I only saw her 'cause I happened to be lookin' that way.'

'And she asked no one to walk with her?'

'Not 'less she had one of them wild Irish out back waitin' on her, or maybe that stuck-up pussy-foot valet of her uncle's.'

She could have, thought January. Certainly, aside from Uncle Veryl and Singletary – and Henri, who had been otherwise occupied – he could think of no gentleman in the house with whom Ellie Trask would have felt comfortable walking a hundred yards in darkness.

Not after Valla's murder.

And perhaps, he thought, that was what she'd

been doing in the French door earlier, exchanging whispered words with someone on the dark gallery. Asking one of her uncle's boys to escort her, despite the inevitable gossip this would stir among the ladies of her betrothed's family.

As for St-Ives . . .

A thought came to him and he frowned.

A question to be asked . . .

But he wasn't certain, at this point, of whom it would be safe to ask it.

Maybe no one. Maybe the answer would lie in the Casita, among those scuffed and smudged tracks, or somewhere in Mamzelle Ellie's luggage.

So he asked after the inhabitants of the weaving house, and how Michie M'Gurk was faring on guard duty ('He does play the fiddle very fine, and for all his finicking 'bout the washing arrangements he's gettin' Cochon an' Philippe to teach him the airs from St-Domingue.'), and whether Isabelle and Solange had killed each other yet.

The loaded rowboat arrived from the kitchen store-loft, with much grumbling about the quality and quantity of food available for the slaves trapped in the sugar mill ('Least we gonna get sugar with our hoe-cakes.'), Michie Molina sweating, and glaring at January with sharp suspicion in his eyes. At the same time January heard the men call out greetings to Archie, and to 'Michie Henri,' and three of them good-naturedly helped the fat man over the windowsill and into the loft, before the supplies boat – and Uncle Bichet – took their leave.

'Did you find the note?' he asked, as Henri turned from the aperture.

'No. It's gone.'

'*Gone*?'

'Everything's gone.' Henri wiped his sweating face. 'The floor's been washed. The jewelry you said was on the night table has been washed off and put back in the jewelry box – still wet, the water collected on the bottom of the case. The decanter by the bed is gone, the back gallery has been mopped, things inside have been tidied back into the drawers—'

'Who by?'

The planter shook his head, his cow-like, near-sighted brown eyes stricken. 'Nobody will say. I'm sure some of the servants know but none of them will admit it, they just . . . You know how it is, when everybody in the place knows something and nobody's going to tell you.'

January knew it well. It was the way slaves protected one another from retaliatory beatings.

'What can we do?'

'Get me out of here,' said January quietly. 'Whoever did this may have missed something. Other than that, all we can do is wait til the waters go down.'

Twenty

The chain that ran from January's left wrist to the kingpost of the wood store's roof was about six feet long; enough to permit him to use the latrine-bucket set in a corner of the wood piled along the walls, not enough to let him get close to the loft window. Part of that Thursday afternoon he sat at the full extent of the chain, three feet from the window, and watched the two rowboats – large and small – move between the big house, the stone tower of the sugar mill, the overseer's cottage, (presumably) the weaving house – which was on the other side of the wood store – and (January hoped) the quarters, also out of his line of sight. From his own childhood experiences he guessed that those families that had been trapped on the roofs of their cabins were transported gradually to the sugar mill – he himself would not have wanted to try swimming in the floodwaters. Luc confirmed this, when late in the afternoon the young man arrived with a party of men under Michie Molina, to collect wood to boil drinking water.

'You let him alone!' Molina swung around at the sound of Luc's voice, and gave a threatening crack of the six-foot horsewhip he carried in his belt. 'You get on with your work, Luc. You, Ben, you move back and you don't go tradin' gossip with men who're working.'

January moved back obediently. Even as a child he'd known that nothing *ever* came to good from riling an overseer.

Not if you were black, and chained to a kingpost.

He watched the way the men moved, passing the wood from hand to hand and thus through the window and into the boat. Quick and cautious, and always keeping a surreptitious eye on that sturdy form in his coarse jacket of blue tweed.

273

Despite the ferocious heat in the loft he kept the jacket on, as if he would not put aside this badge of command no matter how uncomfortable he was. January had seen this kind of thing before, in men of color who supervised the work of slaves: *I'm not black. I'm not a slave. Don't you go thinking I'm anything the same as these men*.

It was widely said among both blacks and whites, that the men of color who owned plantations – like Sylvestre St-Chinian – were harsher masters than the whites, though January didn't know this from his own observation. Certainly at no point had Sylvestre – always attired in coat and cravat – ever been invited to socialize with the white planters of the family.

In any case – he shook his head inwardly at the reflection – he himself, if he had business in the American section of New Orleans, would swelter and suffocate in a jacket and a cravat rather than go in his shirtsleeves and risk being mistaken for a slave. And not, he had to admit ruefully, entirely because of the danger from slave stealers.

But Molina twice lashed his whip at the legs of men who were clearly doing their best, as if to establish beyond question his right to do so. And the overseer's hard, turquoise-gray eyes had a defiant gleam, as if daring any of the men under his lash to claim kinship.

A man whose anger was rooted in fear.

January was conscious, also, of the way the three field hands kept glancing at him, and remembered old Madame Janvier's words about slaves who 'ran away'. To slave dealers like the

274

local smuggler Captain Chamoflet, who evaded American and British navies to sell Africans illegally to the sugar planters, it would be just as easy to buy a man from an unscrupulous overseer and re-sell him in Galveston, now that Texas was an independent republic.

How easy would it be to claim that an accused murderer – and a man who feared enslavement to the likes of Mick Trask – had somehow managed to break his chain and flee across the waters, never to be heard from again?

Olympe was right.

And every time I set foot out of the French Town, I'm sorry for it.

Molina left him a jar of water, and a pone of cornbread. When the work-party had left January smelled the water, and though it was far from clean it had none of the half-bitter, flowery smell of opium. Nevertheless he set it aside, and the cornbread also, having taken the precaution of hiding some of the food Uncle Bichet had brought earlier. Five minutes after the men had gone, the rats re-appeared, dozens of them, lurking among the wood and watching him and his food.

Every rat, in fact, he reflected wearily, who inhabited the wood stores, and the attics of the cabins, and the woods, in company with (he counted) four raccoons, three muskrats, five or six squirrels, several rabbits, and a snapping-turtle, all flushed out of their homes and, like the folks in the sugar mill, seeking a dry and alligator-free place to wait out the flood. By the sound of it, more were assembled on the roof. (And by the sound of it, he reflected, they were dancing quadrilles.) To entertain himself, he gathered a number of the smaller billets of wood from the piles within his reach, and practiced flinging them at his fellow passengers in this makeshift ark, but they quickly ascertained his range and afterwards disregarded him.

Their bright red eyes in the dusk said, *You gotta fall asleep sometime.*

Mostly, his foot hurt him too badly to do anything but lie on his back with his leg propped on a pile of wood, and think.

About Ellie Trask.

About the dead-huts.

About all the little that he'd seen of the Casita that morning.

About last night.

Fitting information together, like pieces of a child's 'geography puzzle'. Recalling a few words here, a fragment of story there.

Flurries of rain alternated with periods of gray stillness, through which he could hear music from the weaving house: Cochon, Jacques Bichet and his bespectacled old uncle, and handsome Philippe duCoudreau. 'Gumbo Chaff' and 'Rose of Allendale', the Lancers cotillion and the ballet of the mad ghosts of dancing nuns from Robert le Diable.

Then during one episode of splattering rain he heard the unmistakable creak of oar-locks, and a few moments later a girl's voice: '*Hush*! Just *hush*, and do what I say if you know what's good for you!'

It sounded like one of Henri's sisters.

Not Euphémie. The voices of the younger three were pretty much alike, shrill and hurried . . .

Charlotte, he thought.

And it was.

Stony-faced with disapproval, Visigoth helped her over the windowsill and the girl marched determinedly over to January – who had risen, stiffly and in agony – and, taking a pistol from one skirt-pocket and a key from the other, she said, 'You had best do what I say and no questions!'

January said, 'No, mamzelle.'

Jules must be growing feverish. Men often did with the coming of evening.

'Visigoth,' she ordered, and the butler stepped grimly forward, took the key, and unlocked the spancel.

'There's no need to hold a pistol on me, mamzelle,' said January gently. The weapon wasn't cocked and he wondered if it was loaded. 'I have spent much of the day worrying about Michie Jules—' (a complete lie – between his concern about Chloë Viellard, and his concern about himself, his mind had touched on Jules Mabillet for all of about twenty seconds, once) – 'and I wondered if you would have the courage to come and release me.' (*No harm in laying it on with a trowel.*)

'They wouldn't let me.' Charlotte drew herself up and her chin came forward as much as it was possible to do so; her shortsighted brown eyes blazed. 'Maman, and Euphémie, and that horrid husband of hers. And it's no good even trying to ask Uncle Veryl, he just lies in bed and moans.

277

And you're coming straight back here afterwards, so there's really no harm done.'

'As you wish, mamzelle.' *Plenty of time to see about* that. 'You didn't happen to have someone fetch my bag from the weaving house, did you?'

She looked stricken, but Visigoth said, 'We've been bringing in every bottle and packet of medicine, from all over the house an' the Casita too, an' everythin' that everybody had in their baggage, all day. For all the good it done.' He bent his back to the oars as January, sweating with pain, gingerly lifted his hurt foot to the gunwale rather than place it on the seat next to Charlotte, who would almost certainly have considered it an unacceptable liberty. 'I hope that does you.'

The shutters in the big house had all been closed during the storm. The flash of rain had ceased again, but the wind rattled them, as Visigoth rowed them across, and around into the long center of the U between the house's two wings.

Leaning on the stick he'd provided himself with from his prison, January limped across the gallery and into the room assigned to Jules Mabillet. The pallet bed had been removed – presumably the three French lawyers had found accomodation elsewhere – and the small table from the parlor that had been set in its place was, indeed, lined with an informative array of medications. Six bottles of Godfrey's Cordial (besides the one on the nightstand beside the bed), three of McMunn's Elixir of Opium, a packet of Pow-Ness-Sa Uterine Wafers, two bottles of Hooper's Female Elixir, a box of Old Sachem Female Pills, a bottle of Dr Bateman's Pectoral Drops, a bottle of Fowler's

Solution for ague (a mild arsenic solution, January knew), several phials of mercury digestive pills, and four pots of assorted wrinkle and freckle creams.

On the bed, Jules Mabillet lay, tossing feverishly and muttering in fitful spurts of words; gently opening his eyelid, January saw that even in the dimness of the shuttered room the pupil of his eye was contracted to a pinprick. He glanced at the bedside table, estimating the levels of medicine in the various bottles he'd seen there the previous afternoon, then frowned.

'The medicines you brought here,' he said, turning to Visigoth.

The butler waved a disgusted hand at the collection on the small table. 'If you'll excuse me sayin', sir, there's not a thing here that improves on what you were giving him yesterday.'

January turned his eyes back to the bedside bottles, reckoning them up, then to the butler again. 'You didn't bring over any of them from the table to the bedside?'

'No, sir.'

'Mamzelle Charlotte?'

The girl shook her head, eyes wide and filled with tears. 'You have to help him . . .'

'You haven't given him anything from those at all?'

'Only from what's beside the bed,' she whispered. 'And only when he seemed to be in . . . in such terrible pain. Please, give him something . . .'

'But you have been dosing him from these?'

'Only this afternoon,' said Charlotte, picking up one of the two silver spoons that lay among the bottles of Godfrey's Cordial and Kendal Black Drop. 'He was sound asleep all morning – I sat beside him. He never stirred until past noon . . .'

I'll bet he didn't.

January felt his heart quicken with anger as he looked at the bedside bottles, and with something else: the sharp anticipation that he felt, when part of a problem fell into place.

'Then when he got restless I gave him some of the Cordial, but I didn't give him any of that Black Drop stuff because I don't know what it is.'

'It's a good thing you didn't, mamzelle,' said January, keeping his voice steady with an effort. 'Black Drop is the strongest opiate on the market. It might easily have killed him.' He took the spoon gently from her hand, and turned it over in his powerful fingers, then held it up with the other one, comparing them. 'Visigoth, can you get me some hot water and bandages, please? I think the best thing we can do for him now is change his dressing.'

'I have hot water here,' said the butler, 'in the veilleuse.'

There were bandages still, folded up beside the bottles on the nightstand where January had left them the day before. Also, to his relief, his own packets of basilicum powder and willow-bark. Charlotte held Jules' hands and turned her eyes modestly aside while January removed the old dressings and washed the wound. The inflammation had visibly abated, and such fluid as hadn't been obliterated by the blood on the bandage was clear and nearly odorless. Jules flinched and moaned, whispering, 'Maman! Maman, please . . .'

'Can't we give him even a little Cordial?'

'I dare not, mamzelle. I don't know how much laudanum he's had, between what you've given him, and what others might have given – were you here with him last night?'

Charlotte shook her head. 'I came in this morning.'

'Hecuba came in an' checked on him, every hour or so,' reported Visigoth. 'Even with all the storm goin', he slept like a baby. If she'd give him anythin', she'd have told me, but she said he never stirred.'

'Maman, please,' breathed the young man on the bed. 'I'll be good. I swear I'll be good. Just please let me . . . Just please let me have . . .'

'Get all this rubbish out of here.' January motioned toward the tablefull of Cordial, Elixir, and Vegetative Skin-Food on the other side of the room. 'Lock it up in the pantry – this, too.' He passed his hand over the bottles on the night-stand. 'Is there still a little hot water there? Visigoth, could I get you – or Hecuba – to make up a little draught with this? It's willow-bark, the main ingredient in a saline draught. It should bring down his fever. If you would . . .'

He extracted his notebook from his pocket, and the stub of pencil he always carried, checked his watch, and asked Charlotte, 'When was Jules last given Cordial? Just after the last rain started? That would have been . . . what? Four thirty? And how much? Good girl. You've done just exactly right. Visigoth, if you would be so good . . . Put all the cordials, everything, under lock and key, and don't give poor Michie Jules anything until nine tonight. He'll be uncomfortable,' he added, turning to Charlotte. 'And he'll probably beg you for some. Distract his mind, hold his hands, put cold compresses on his face, whatever you need to do. You'll need to be brave.'

Her eyes flooding, the girl nodded.

'He's had too much. Someone gave him more – a lot more – than is good for him. We have to let some of it pass out of his system before he can have another dose. After that . . .' He showed her what he'd written. 'No more than that, at those times. Not before. Can you do that for him?'

She took the paper and brought it to within an inch of her nose – she was as near-sighted as her brother – and sniffled. 'I'll try.'

'Good girl.'

'Did . . .?' She clutched his sleeve, as he made to hand the bedside bottles to Visigoth. 'Did somebody try to poison him?'

He half-opened his mouth to reply, *Only you, child*, and then closed it again. Thinking.

Thinking about the people in the house. About the people who'd come to Cold Bayou. And the reasons they had come.

He said, 'I'll know more about this when I've been able to have a look at the Casita. You don't happen to know who ordered it cleaned up, do you?'

Charlotte shook her head, mousy curls bobbing, plainly baffled by the question. But glancing beside him, he saw Visigoth's dark eyes narrow:

282

the expression of a man who also sees a piece of a puzzle fall into place. Maybe only the fact that none of the other servants would say who had ordered it.

Maybe something else.

'If I'm to learn what happened – why it happened—' he made a gesture that could have implied that someone attempting to poison Jules was connected to what had passed in the Casita last night . . . As indeed, he was beginning to think it might be – 'I need to see the inside of the Casita. Visigoth, would you take me across?'

A man who was in on the scheme would, January thought, have hesitated for an instant – or have answered with immediate assent. As it was, the butler frowned, tallying who he'd get into trouble with. Charlotte pulled the pistol from the pocket of her dress, taking nearly a minute to do so (*Thank God the thing isn't cocked!*), and handed it to Visigoth. 'Bring him back here,' she instructed. 'Don't let him take the boat and run away. I'm sorry,' she added, looking back at January. 'I'm sorry, but I can't let you leave! Jules needs someone who knows what he's doing—'

'I understand, mamzelle.' Behind the bars of the jalousies, the daylight was fading. January was ready to agree to nearly anything, to reach the Casita while daylight lingered in the sky.

Visigoth still looked doubtful, but took the pistol in one hand, and picked up the lamp from the sideboard with the other. 'What M'am Aurelié's gonna say, I don't know.'

'Stay with Jules,' said January to Charlotte.

283

'And follow my instructions about the medicines. We'll return, and tell you what we've found.'

And hope to goodness, he reflected, limping painfully from the room in Visigoth's wake, *that I can find something – anything – that means something over there.*

Other than the absence of anything that means anything.

Neither Visigoth – climbing into the boat with lamp and pistol – nor Charlotte, bending already over Jules again, noticed that January pocketed both spoons.

Twenty-One

'That thing loaded?'

'Oh, hell, no!' Visigoth paused in his rowing as the sinuous mottled shape of a copperhead slipped by them in the water. The rain had ceased, but the silver-gray sheets of cloud overhead still spoke of storm. The wind tasted of the sea. Far off, above the flooded ciprière, a thin line of smoke marked where some swamp trapper or slave stealer had found an Indian mound high enough to support a dry camp. 'You in the house last night?'

'I was not, sir. I couldn't have made it there before the flood, and afterward, there were only the two boats that didn't get taken out until first light.'

'Your Mama was.'

'My Maman,' returned January, 'did a very stupid thing, but I can understand why she did it. Yes, she went in and searched the place, thinking Mamzelle might have had whatever notes her daddy had got from our old master, Michie Fourchet, about that loan that might or might not even have taken place. She says someone else came while she was there, so maybe Michie Fourchet wasn't the only person Daddy Trask had the goods on. Who cleaned up that house?'

'Savoy.' He named Florentin Miragouin's valet. 'And Reinette.' Reinette, January recalled, was the prettiest of the housemaids Madame Aurelié had brought from town.

'Who told them to do it?'

'Nobody. Savoy says, he just saw what a mess the place was, with vomit on the back gallery and mud tracked all over the floors—'

'And a *valet* – who probably cost Michie Miragouin nearly two thousand dollars and who's done nothing for the past eight years but polish Michie Miragouin's boots and iron his cravats – just sort of spontaneously looked at a puddle of puke and muddy boot-tracks and thought, "Oh, gracious, I gotta go find me a mop!"'

Visigoth said nothing, but paused in his rowing. His gaze, dry and skeptical, held January's.

'And a little gal who'll be the first to yell for a houseboy, if somebody should suggest *she* mop up where the dog pee'd,' continued January softly, 'rushes to fill up a bucket an' lend a hand. Like my aunties always said, that sort of doesn't listen right to me.'

'Not to me, neither. But that's what both of 'em say.'

'They afraid?'

'Who ain't?' The butler's voice was quiet. 'I worked in the house all my days – yeah, moppin' dog pee an' clearin' up where somebody couldn't hold their liquor sometimes, but polishin' silver, an' keepin' track of wine, an' makin' sure sheets get washed, by somebody who's not me, thank God. I'm sixty-two, an' I know damn well I could end my days in the cane-fields, if I get some bukra pissed off at me for somethin' I maybe didn't even do. I kept secrets in my time. I got a wife, an' I got two daughters, an' for the thirty years I worked for M'am Aurelié I been lookin' for word of the daughter an' son I had when I worked for Michie Picard before her, sold when I was sold, an' I never heard one word of 'em yet. So you bet I keep secrets. An' you bet I'm afraid.'

January nodded, as Visigoth bent his back once more to the oars.

'You happen to know when it got cleaned up?' he asked, as the rowboat nosed against the Casita's front gallery and the butler climbed out to make the painter-line fast. 'You, Michie Henri, James, and I were here just after first light. Uncle Mick and his boys came in about half an hour later in the other boat – somebody must have told him Mamzelle was gone, just after you and James brought the boat back to the big house. After they took me and Maman to the wood store, do you remember who all came across to the Casita, before it was cleaned?'

'Just about everybody in the big house.' Visigoth

286

unlocked the shutters of the Casita's front parlor, led the way inside, and lit the lamp. 'For a while there it was like Antoine and Archie was runnin' a ferry. Only ones I didn't see go across were Old M'am Janvier – who said she was too old to go scramblin' in and out of a rowboat – an' Mamzelle Charlotte, who wouldn't have moved from Michie Jules' side if the house caught fire.'

As he spoke he picked his way through the deep gloom of the parlor, unbolting French doors, opening them to unbolt the shutters. Even so, with the lateness of the afternoon and the grayness of the day, the light added little to the weak glow of the oil lamp, and January, leaning on the secretaire, felt a kind of despairing exasperation. It crossed his mind, too, to wonder if this was the proper moment to dart back across the gallery, leap into the rowboat, and make his escape.

Leaving Maman behind to face a charge of murder?

Do you think either *of you is going to stand a chance in a court whose only alternate choices are influential white French Creoles*? He could almost see the mocking glint in Olympe's dark eyes.

All right, then . . . supposing my ankle gives out on me before I even get to the French door, I go down screaming and don't have a chance to even look for whatever Savoy and Reinette might have missed?

And after I leap into the rowboat and paddle away . . . In which direction? Toward that plume of smoke, which is far more likely to be slave smugglers out looking for runaways than it is to be members of the Underground Railroad waiting to whisk me to safety? And after I've rowed around in the woods for a couple of days and the water goes down, where am I going to walk to? New Orleans?

Hannibal will be coming downriver on the first boat.

Or the second.

(Along with Père Eugenius? Olympe's voice jeered in his mind.)

He turned back to the room as the tall butler came back to him.

'For a couple of people who don't mop floors as a rule,' he said bitterly, surveying the rucked-back straw mats by the wan light, 'Savoy and Reinette seem to have done a peach of a job.'

The only tracks that remained in the parlor were indeterminate crusts and crumbles of mud, and a few fragments of shell, caught in the folds of the braided straw. The room's sparse furnishings, like everything else in the Casita, were at the end of their lives. January recalled quite clearly, from his childhood on Bellefleur and his subsequent visits to plantations around New Orleans, that chairs, carpet, silverware, dishes, even the very pots in the pantry, had all been purchased new for use in the family townhouse in New Orleans, and relegated to one or the other of the family plantations when they wore out or grew too old-fashioned to be endured. From the big house they'd migrated, like poor relations, to the over-seer's cottage, and only when too dilapidated for even the overseer, had they gone on to the Casita.

He could tell at a glance that it would be

288

impossible to measure any of the tracks, even had Uncle Mick's boys not added their own marks to those of his mother and . . .

And who?

Leaning heavily on his stick, he limped into the larger bedroom.

Someone who is in a position to threaten Savoy and Reinette.

That additional piece of information still left pretty much everyone in the Viellard/St-Chinian clan. Even Locoul, despised by the rest of the family, could almost certainly find some way of talking Michie Florentin, or M'am Aurelié, into thinking they needed to get rid of the valet and the maid. Even a minor lie could go a long way against a slave, as witnessed by the Biblical tale of Joseph and Potiphar's wife.

Someone white.

I don't have to prove they did it, January reminded himself. *I just need enough proof to establish that Maman didn't.*

But what that proof would be, particularly under the scrutiny of a white jury, he had not the smallest idea.

The brandy decanter was gone from the night-stand – in fact he established that it was nowhere in the house. Dropped off the gallery rail into the flood . . .

The nightstand itself had been wiped. Not the faintest whiff of that slight, acrid, vegetable smell, that he thought he'd detected, remained in the wood.

The jewel box was gone, too. At a guess, M'am Aurelié had secured that.

Someone who didn't want the jewels. Who would that be?

It was in any case the best argument he'd seen so far that Ellie Trask hadn't intended to simply run.

All Mamzelle's clothes – even her night-things and her overnight-case – were gone, probably bundled up and removed to the attic. By the sound of it she'd come back to the Casita after escaping from a nightmarish dinner, lain down for enough time to have a number of drinks, then risen once more and staggered out to the rear gallery, where she – or someone – had been very sick.

Maman left the Casita at the sight of an approaching lantern. The waters had begun to spill from the bayou and ciprière not long after that; Mamzelle may have had to hike up her turquoise-and-gold skirts when she descended the back gallery stair. Anyone who entered the Casita after her would have left a sodden trail of dribbled water, not scuffs from the shell-path's mud.

Maman saw no vomit on the back gallery. Drunkenness?

If the girl had been poisoned – if the intruder his mother had heard had entered with the intention of putting something like hemlock or oleander in the brandy decanter – Ellie could have staggered, or fallen, down the back gallery steps after she'd vomited. Then she'd lain at the bottom until the floodwaters rose over her, drowning her while Chloë's maid huddled in perfectly understandable terror in the dark of her tiny attic.

But she didn't ring the bell. If she went out

simply because she was sick, why not ring the bell for the maid?

Fear of Hélène's scorn?

Understandable. Ellie was far from insensetive to the contempt of those around her.

And as for the note . . .

While these thoughts passed through his mind he opened and closed every drawer of the night-stand, the dressing table, and the armoire, held the lantern up and down so that he could peer beneath the bed (Reinette had been *very* thorough in her sweeping) and into the darkest corners of the room. Visigoth followed him, looking also.

Someone put poison in the brandy. Of that he was nearly certain. Unfortunately, the only people on Cold Bayou who *wouldn't* have done so would be Uncle Veryl and Selwyn Singletary, Uncle Mick and his boys. Even Mick's lawyer Loudermilk, who had originally been in the pay of Locoul St-Chinian, might turn his coat yet again if given sufficient incentive.

Someone, clearly, had spoken to Mamzelle Trask through the French doors of the parlor, to get her to return to the Casita.

It was difficult to picture Sidonie Janvier hobbling all the way out here in the storm to set a trap, though the old lady was, January knew, tougher than she looked. Between the musicians and Visigoth, he could probably put together at least some general idea of who'd stayed longest in the parlor last night, who'd been gone an hour or two before the rising of the floodwaters; whether Euphémie Viellard Miragouin had been with her sisters in their room, and what time

Evard Aubin had retired with his hopes that a) something would happen to prevent the wedding and b) that Jules Mabillet would die in the night. *Chloë* . . .

She came out here before anyone. Had changing her dress – and ostentatiously leaving her dinner frock on her bed – and going out into the storm been some way to establish that she was *alibi*? A foolish one, if so, and one that had backfired with the rising of the floodwaters. Was it Henri himself, for that matter, who'd ordered his brother-in-law's valet, and his mother's maid, to wipe away all evidence of who'd been in the little dwelling? Had he found some bit of irrefutable evidence against someone he would endanger even Chloë to screen?

In the little bedroom which had been first Valla's, then Chloë's, all trace of occupancy had been smoothed away. Chloë's rose-silk dress no longer lay on the bed, probably bundled up in one of the trunks in the attic, along with Mamzelle Ellie's things, and goodness knew what besides.

Chloë herself could have poisoned the brandy at any time. He limped into the pantry. *She was staying here.* Rats darted to safety; an affronted corn snake retreated under the table.

Why sneak in on a night when she'd have left tracks for Henri to force a couple of servants to tidy up?

As Visigoth had said, every bottle of medication had been removed from the Casita to the big house. But anyone, he reflected, could have acquired poison from the girls' maid Gayla.

And if Chloë were not herself the poisoner,

why *had* she slipped away from the big house early, changed her dress, disappeared into the darkness?

Dead-huts. Midnight.

Had the note been for *her*?

In his mind he saw again the coarse yellowish paper, faintly lined with blue.

Saw Valla's body, riddled with knife-wounds, lying on the cooling-bench, her corn-gold braid trailing to the floor.

Saw Mamzelle Ellie's wide brown terrified eyes as she whispered, 'Will I?' when Uncle Veryl assured her she'd be safe in town.

Why would she have left the Casita at all? At midnight, in the dark, in the storm? When she first felt the grip of sickness clutch at her belly?

Knowing that the man who killed Valla was out there somewhere in the night?

No sign of the note.

'I need to have a look through all the things that were taken from here up to the attic,' said January.

Visigoth's mouth twisted. 'An' leave you down-stairs here with the boat?'

'And where am I gonna row to?' retorted January.

'Old Alexandre Froide's broke-down house up the bayou.'

'And from there I'm going to walk to New Orleans?'

'Many men would crawl to town,' said the butler quietly, 'rather than find themselves sold as a slave. Or burned alive, or their balls cut off, for killin' a white woman who was – or might

293

have been for all they knew – their master. And you might not be all as lame as you're lettin' on. I'm sorry, Ben. Mamzelle Charlotte's a good girl, an' I know she's grateful to you for comin' to see Michie Jules, but if I come back without you she's bound to tell M'am Aurelié, an' word'll get to that Irish animal Trask, an' then I'll be the only one around to catch hell.'

'And my Maman.'

'I *met* your Maman,' retorted Visigoth. 'Aside from the fact that Old M'am Janvier won't let nuthin' happen to her, for all I know you'd be happy to leave her standin' in a little mud. I sure would.'

Dammit . . .

And the longer he stood arguing with Visigoth, the greater were his chances that, if someone had seen their boat crossing to the little house, word would get to Uncle Mick. Loath as he might be to the idea of tamely returning to the wood store loft, January was well aware that this could be the lesser of several evils.

Thus he suffered the butler to tie his hands behind him with a strand of clothesline rope, as he sat in one of the bent-willow parlor chairs, and bind his feet to the chair's legs. Thus he waited while Visigoth climbed the attic stairs, taking the lamp with him and dropping the parlor into gloom. Waited, and sorted through names in his mind, circumstances and possible circumstances. *Poison is a woman's weapon – a knife, a man's.* Or did he only use poison because Mamzelle Ellie had been warned of a knife? *But if the knife had been his first choice, had he brought poison as a second line of attack? Why hadn't he used it as a first line?* He thought he knew where the poison had come from, but there were several pieces of this puzzle-map that were missing still.

Yet he could almost see them, as if they'd been scattered to some dark corner of his brain.

The moment Visigoth went upstairs, rats emerged with gleaming eyes from their hiding places, sniffed the air warily. Only a silvery dimness came through the windows now, and the wind, finally, seemed to be dying down.

And thus he was sitting, listening to the butler's firm tread on the floor of the attic above, when he saw the flash of a lantern in the windows and heard the creak of oar-locks . . .

Damn it, damn it, damn it . . .

And Uncle Mick's dark shape silhouetted against the last of the failing light.

'Black bastard!' The Irishman crossed the parlor in two strides and struck January with such violence that his head swam. 'And here's where you come after all your pleas about what an innocent lamb y'are!'

Another sickening backhand swat. January tasted blood in his mouth and nose.

'Bastard – bastard to kill my girl!' Mick reached behind him and one of his boys handed him a club, such as the soap-locked toughs carried ostensibly as walking sticks. January ducked his head and hunched his shoulders, as two more blows smoke his neck and back. He knew that at this moment nothing he could say would be heeded or possibly even heard, except as further

295

provocation. He had learned as a child to take beatings in silence, until whatever buckra was dealing them out had worn out his first rage.

Take them and just hope you live through them.

Mick kicked the chair over, struck him twice more, then grabbed the top rung of the chairback and dragged him toward the French door to the gallery, screaming curses at the top of his lungs. January was peripherally aware that Visigoth stood in the doorway that led through to the pantry and the attic stairs, a great bundle of fabric in his arms, his eyes stretched in horror but saying nothing. Not the first time, January guessed, the butler had watched a man killed, knowing there was nothing he could say or do . . .

'Look in the bundle!' January yelled in English, as the infuriated Irishman hauled the chair out onto the gallery and across it to its edge. 'The bundle Visigoth found in the attic!'

Those words got through, and Mick stopped, and flung the chair from him, so that the jar of impact with the gallery planks was like the blow of a sledgehammer, felt through every bone of January's body.

Gasping, January said, 'There was a note – there might have been more. Somebody cleared it all away—'

Trask kicked him, but the first incandescent blaze of his rage was spent. He turned and stalked back into the parlor, where the light of Visigoth's lantern, and the lanterns borne by two of the boys, flung monster shadows around the walls. Black Duke and the Gopher, who'd followed their boss out onto the gallery to watch him heave

January, chair and all, into the floodwaters, started to follow, but January called softly, still in English, 'Who got off the steamboat at English turn?'

The two men stopped. Looked at one another, then came back to him.

'Nobody,' said Gopher M'Gurk.

'Couple o' French biddies,' said the Duke.

January looked up at them, faces invisible in shadow, enlightened and aware of the lie. More pieces fell into place. 'Rich or poor?' he asked. 'The French biddies.'

'What's it to yez, chimney-chops?' demanded the Gopher.

'Rich,' said the Duke. 'La-di-dah hats an' their own niggers carryin' their carpet bags.'

'Old or young?'

Gopher merely kicked him – hard – but the Duke pushed his hat forward to scratch his head, and asked, 'What's it to yez?' He bent down to drag the chair upright. 'Damn, yer a heavy nigger.'

'It's the weight of the world on my shoulders,' said January tiredly, and the man laughed.

'I think one of them may have had something to do with what happened to Miss Trask,' he went on quietly. 'I came here looking for further clues.'

'Aargh, tell me another one, daddy,' urged M'Gurk scornfully.

Duke said, 'Arrh, shove it up yer arse, Gopher,' and looked back at January with his head cocked a little, inquiring. 'What makes ye think so?' With his pockmarked face turned a little to the light he wasn't an encouraging sight.

'Little things,' said January. 'I think somebody came into the Casita last night and put poison in the brandy bottle beside the bed. I think Miss Trask became sick and disoriented, and staggered outside into the storm. I won't know anything until her body is found, because someone came in and cleaned up all marks and traces—'

'Yeah, someone like you . . .' jeered Gopher, and stepped aside as Trask emerged onto the gallery again.

'There's no note in there,' said the Irishman quietly. 'Nuttin' at all. Nor would there be, my friend. Me girl couldn't read.'

January said, 'I know.'

Twenty-Two

There wasn't room in the larger rowboat for Uncle Mick, all the boys, and their prisoner as well, so Visigoth was left at the Casita while the Irishmen redistributed themselves and January – his hands bound before him and supported by Gopher M'Gurk and Black Duke Monohan rather than by the stick he'd used in his bedside visit to Jules Mabillet – in both vessels. The Duke searched him, but when January cautioned, 'Don't touch the spoons – they may have poison on them,' the big man let them be, without asking how he knew this or where he'd acquired them.

He did, however, help himself to January's silver watch.

Visigoth's lantern glimmered on the porch next to his tall form in the darkness as the little Hibernian armada made its way back to the wood store. From all January could tell by that faint flickering glow, the floodwaters had not begun to subside by so much as an inch.

Gopher went into the loft first with one of the lanterns and January heard him exclaim 'Gah!' in alarm and disgust. 'Somebody been in here, boss!'

Trask, the Black Duke, and the other two thugs followed, dragging January clumsily after them. Their lantern-light wavered over the design wrought of black chalk and brick-dust on the floor around the kingpost, where January's chain still lay coiled.

Trask said, 'What the hell?'

'Voodoo,' said January shortly, with a grimace of annoyed distaste. 'It means nothing.'

'It some kind of curse, then?' Gopher asked hesitantly. 'For killin' Miss Ellie an' M'am Viellard?'

'I didn't kill them,' retorted January. 'Let them curse. To a Christian it means nothing.' He took care to back off, not touching the wide band of scribbled symbols – snakes and crosses, eyes and valentine-hearts, with arrows pointing outward, to the four points of the compass – as the Irishmen hesitated to come near.

'Those designs in black,' he added after a moment in a careless voice, 'they're the summons to Ogon, the god of war and violence. That thing that looks like a file, that's his footprint. The red are curse marks, to trap the soul so that Ogon may come on him for vengeance.' He pointed.

299

'Those two red arrows, those are the gate, through which Papa Legba, the father of magic, permits the curse to enter. The black arrows in the other three directions are gates that are closed.'

Gopher and Rags crossed themselves. Somewhere in Heaven, January supposed, the priests who'd schooled them in childhood cried aloud in astonished beatific joy. Trask raised a heavy brow, and said, 'As a good Christian man, you got any objection to sittin' down on that thing?'

And he walked across it, to pick up the spancel and chain.

Black Duke and Gopher, supporting January on either side, would clearly rather not have stepped on those interlinking paths of sigils, but January limped deliberately over to the kingpost, forcing his attendants to follow. Leaning his back to the thick oak, he sank to the floor, feeling as if he'd been run over by a wagon. The blows from Trask's fists and stick, on top of the bruises left by his fall from the gallery, had begun to swell and throb and he felt giddy from the pain in his much-maltreated ankle.

Trask locked the manacle around his wrist before cutting free the clothes-rope.

'I am flattered,' said January wearily, 'that you consider me worth taking all those precautions.'

'Ah, Ben.' The Irishman smiled with a deadly glitter in his eye. 'You think I don't see you're the kind as lays low and waits his chance, like a fox waitin' for the hounds to run by? On the ship for Australia I strangled a warder in me chain, after playin' so sick he thought I didn't bear watchin'. I took the key off him so me mates

300

and I could take the jolly-boat two days' rowin' back to Castletown, an' I don't trust you far as me boys can throw you.'

'Do you trust me enough to drag over a couple of pieces of wood for me to put my foot up on?' asked January tiredly. 'And maybe to have Molina send over something to drink and a couple of pones of cornbread in the morning?'

Trask snapped his fingers, and the Black Duke rolled a stumpy chunk of wood toward them, across those enigmatic lines of red and black.

'Any thought on who'd think you'd done the deed?' he asked. 'That would put such a *mallacht* on a Christian man like yoursel'?'

January shook his head. 'You,' he pointed out, and Trask's grin widened.

They took the lanterns, and left him alone in the darkness. He listened to the creak of their oar-locks retreating across the water, and wondered if any of them would think to row back to the Casita for Visigoth.

Then he waited, listening to the scratch and scurry of rat-feet in the dark.

Death in the water, Olympe had said.

Death in the fire.

If I try to flee now morning will bring pursuit, and, almost certainly, death. He knew he couldn't talk his way out of it twice.

But the night, he knew, would be long.

At length he judged it safe to fish the stump of candle from an inner pocket, and the little box of friction-matches from another. By the wavery light he studied the ring of black and red designs which surrounded the kingpost.

301

They had, of course, absolutely nothing to do with curses. He scarcely needed the gridwork symbol of Ogon – the blacksmith-god in his more peaceable moods – to tell him that a file had been cached in the piled wood, pointed at by the two red arrows. And though he was fairly certain that the stylized drawing of a boat in another corner of the 'vévé' didn't indicate an actual boat, he *was* fairly certain that something which could be used to paddle away from the wood store floated just under the floor of the loft.

All the musicians knew his sister was a voodoo. They'd know he could read these signs.

Propping himself on a billet of wood, he dragged himself to the area indicated by the red arrows and yes, there was a file, tucked in between the cut branches stored up for the winter's *roulaison*. As he was turning back toward the kingpost his eye caught the fact that the latrine-bucket, which he'd left standing a foot or so from the wood not far away, had been moved. Pushed deep into a sort of niche formed by the uneven lengths of the logs.

Moving it out, he found a second file, shoved under the wood at floor level. With it were two gourds of water, a knife, and a small sack containing about two dollars in assorted coin.

The Cold Bayou slaves might not know the formal signs of the loa, he reflected, smiling. But like the loa, they, too, looked after those who needed help against The Man.

The question was – he lay down again, propped his foot on the chunk of wood – whether to run or not.

How far can I get in a night? Not to New Orleans, that's for sure. Nor to anyplace where there'll be friends to help. He still had Rose's compass, strung on its slender ribbon around his neck, but more likely than not theciprière was stiff with the slave stealers who prowled the swamps, just waiting for slaves to risk escape in the confused conditions of a flood.

How long before steamboats start running again on the flooded river?

Fairly soon, despite the hugely increased danger from snags and tow-heads. *Every merchant in town knows that after twenty-four hours, everybody south of English Turn will be willing to pay triple prices for foodstuffs, not to mention for passage north to higher ground.*

He closed his eyes against a wave of faintness and pain.

Is waiting for Hannibal – with whatever information he may have found, which Trask may or may not dispute – safer than setting off in darkness into the swamp?

The days were past – thankfully – when he'd have wondered whether Hannibal would choose this particular occasion to go on one of his whiskey-and-laudanum benders.

He would be here as soon as it was humanly possible, that much January knew.

If Trask learns tomorrow that one of his jailers found only the cut manacle, he'll have his boys out searching in earnest. Then God help me if I'm caught.

The thought of the sheer physical exertion involved in flight – of both the pain and the likelihood of unforseen complications from his lack of mobility – nearly nauseated him.

On the other hand, God preserve me from whatever scheme is going to come into Uncle Mick's mind after half a bottle of bourbon following dinner tonight.

It comes down to this, thought January wearily. *Can I trust a) fate or b) white people?*

With a sigh he sat painfully up, removed his foot from its improvised stool and set his shackled wrist on it, and started filing.

This turned out to be a fortunate decision. He'd cut more than halfway through the manacle – the cheap iron was relatively soft, and rusty as well – when he heard, through the distant throb of cicadas and bullfrogs, the creak of oar-locks across the water. He snuffed his candle instantly and slipped both files into the pockets of his jacket. He had not the slightest idea what time it was – he couldn't have gotten near enough to the window for a clear look at the sky, which was partly overcast and in any case hidden by the eave – but the sounds from the big house had ceased some time ago. Now and then voices still drifted from the weaving house, indistinguishable with distance, but he knew his colleagues routinely stayed up half the night.

Coming to get me?

There were only two boats on the property – not counting whatever his colleagues had hidden under the loft floor for him to escape on – and no whites were going to leave one of them anywhere for the convenience of the Other Side of the Family.

Charlotte? Is Jules worse?

But from what he could see through the window, no flakes of lantern-light splattered the dark surface of the waters even as the boat drew closer.

Moonlight through the clouds. But Visigoth – or whoever Charlotte would have blackmailed or threatened to be her galley-crew – wouldn't be likely to steer by it if they had a choice.

Looking out into the steely darkness, one shade lighter than the black of the loft, he thought he could see movement.

Then the blazing glare of fire, the reek of burning pitch, and a fireball was hurled in through the window with such violence that it rolled clear across the loft floor and into the wood piled at the far side.

'Shit—'

January pulled the file from his pocket, scraped – twice – at the deep groove he'd already hacked in the spancel, but it was terrifying how swiftly the flames spread. They licked through the heaped wall of wood, spread onto the rafters – evoking a stream of rats, raccoons, lizards, and squirrels down the far wall and out through the window – and the air smote him with an oily heat.

Somebody heard I'd been out to the Casita, poking around . . .

Smoke poured from the wood, burning his eyes and his lungs. *Minutes, only*, he thought . . .

He laid his shackled wrist on the wood again, dug the second file from his pocket and angled both files so that they formed a V through the ring, like scissors. He bunched his shackled fist tight, partly to further wedge the two pieces of

305

steel but mostly to protect his fingers, raised the stout chunk of wood he'd earlier used as a crutch, and smote the large end of the V, driving the two ends of it apart.

Nothing, except that the blow nearly broke his hand. Streaks of flame raced over his head along the rafters; sparks rained down onto the floor. *Put a block of wood between the ends of the V . . .*

And hold it in place with your teeth?

He settled the two files, braced himself, and struck again, like Ogon striking the iron in his forge, and this time the two steel files proved stronger than the rusted iron of the bracelet. The manacle snapped, and, gasping in the heat, January crawled across the floor to the open trap. And yes, there was a rope, nearly invisible in the darkness, wrapped around the top of what had been the ladder from below, that hadn't been there the day before.

A shower of sparks fell on him as the roof-blaze spread. Holding to the rope (*and I'd better find something on it besides somebody's snagged-up laundry!*) he tried to inhale, coughed on smoke and burning air, and slid down into the water. The surface lay a foot beneath the rafters holding up the floor; in the red flare and blackness it was difficult to make anything out clearly. A desperate rat scrambled onto his shoulder; holding the rope, January submerged and felt it swim free. The underside of the floor – the ceiling-beams of the wood store below – swarmed with frantic cockroaches, and every bobbing log that filled the water around him seemed occupied with

306

livestock: rats, raccoons, squirrels. Beady inhuman eyes reflected the crimson light.

You had better, he addressed his musical colleagues, *have run the guideline clear out through the wood store door, if this is going to work . . .*

They had. The line in his hand was joined to a small pirogue, not much more than a hollowed-out cypress log. He was afraid, as he pushed himself and the little vessel toward the barely-visible bar of reflected firelight, that he wouldn't be able to get it under the lintel of the ground-floor entrance without swamping it. The space beneath the loft floor was nearly solid with floating wood as well, impeding his progress. Heat beat on his face, and he feared that the lintel and its framing would be in flames by the time he reached it.

At least the fire should scare away any gators . . .

He was well aware that alligators were particularly fond of underwater caves, such as the wood store had become. Also that alligators were pretty stupid and might well fail to notice the upper-works of their latest 'cave' burning over their heads . . .

Virgin Mary, Mother of God, get me safe out of this . . .

Saint Florian – conveniently the patron saint of both fires *and* floods and of the New Orleans First Municipality Volunteer Fire Company as well – *get me safe out of this. I'd light a candle for you but you've already got the whole wood store going . . .*

307

He emerged, gasping, into the muggy air of night above the water just as the roof caved in. Lights swarmed like fireflies along the gallery of the weaving house and when he'd pushed himself a little further from the blazing walls, he could see candle-flame in the windows of the big house as well. The brightness of the fire behind him now, and of those lights and their reflections, made it hard to make out whether the rowboat which had launched the attack was still in the vicinity. At least, he reflected, the lights oriented him. When first he'd begun sawing at the chain on his wrist he'd feared that in the dark of the half-overcast night he'd become confused, and find himself out in the river and being swept along toward the Gulf.

He kept one arm over the gunwale of the pirogue and let the vessel support him, rather than trying to clamber in. The water around him was filled with debris, not only of the burning wood store but of the flood as well: fragments of fences, uprooted trees, now and then the bloated body of a horse or a cow. He prayed that Cochon and Uncle Bichet would whisper to Minou and Charmian, *It's all right. We snuck him a file and a pirogue . . .*

(*And where the hell did you boys get that pirogue?*)

He wondered if his mother was watching, from the attic of the big house where she was comfortably confined.

Or did she know, or guess?

Did she even waken?

The prospect of being incinerated in his prison

308

had rendered him somewhat philosophical about the possibility of alligators (*Just who* is *the patron saint to invoke against alligators*?) in the dark water around him, but he was nevertheless extremely glad when he finally glided among the first of the cypress trees, and felt safe enough to haul himself up into the boat. By the sound of the scuttling in the stern, he wasn't the only passenger, but was so exhausted at that point that he scarcely cared. His fellow musicians had remembered to leave an oar in the vessel (*That must have been Uncle Bichet*), and though his arms hurt as if he'd been beaten by an enraged Irishman with a stick, he paddled in among the trees, the dry fingers of Spanish moss scratching gently at his face, until he lost sight of all but the smallest twinkle of the fire.

Then he pushed the pirogue up against the side of a tree, stretched out on the bottom, and in spite of wet clothes, burned hands, and pain all over, fell asleep.

Twenty-Three

Waking, he smelled smoke.

For a moment he thought he was back in his own house, dreaming of the flood.

Then he remembered yesterday evening, and the sight of a thread of smoke above the trees of the ciprière. *Swamp trappers or slave stealers or, just possibly,* he thought now, *someone else . . .*

But between the big house, and half the Cold Bayou slaves camped in the sugar mill – not to speak of the blackened ruin of the wood store – it was actually pretty difficult to tell.

Old Alexandre Froide's broke-down house up the bayou, Visigoth had said.

He half-closed his eyes, remembering where he'd been in relation to the Casita when he'd seen that line of smoke, and its approximate direction. Ravenously hungry and half-numb with exhaustion and thirst, it was hard to make himself do anything. But a glance around him showed him that the waters had retreated some six inches during the night. It was almost light enough that he knew that search parties would be out probing the woods, in quest of some sign of the missing women.

At least whatever small stowaways had accompanied him out of the burning wood store last night had abandoned ship and scrambled up into the tree in the small hours. The only creature remaining on-board was an enormous king snake, basking in the tepid grayness of early dawn in the stern. 'I'd take it kindly in you if you'd put in a good word for me with Damballah Wedo,' he addressed it, and the serpent turned a wise gold eye toward him and flicked its tongue in enigmatic assent.

Hell, that might be *Damballah Wedo . . .*

He took Rose's compass from its ribbon around his neck. Contact with its round silver shape was like touching her hand. *While I've been running and hiding like a rabbit in a field,* she's *been in hiding as well, not knowing what's happened.*

In the inner pocket of his vest, his fingers sought the blue beads of his rosary – which the Black Duke *hadn't* stolen – and he whispered a prayer for her, for their sons. *Holy Mother of God, let me see them again . . .*

He paddled, cautiously, west.

It didn't take him long to sight the stronger light where the trees ended. He knew that without a compass, men could become lost in the swamps, starving or dying of thirst while they struggled with the changeless, featureless sameness of identical trees. With the flood upon the land the situation was worse, and he blessed Rose for leaving him with the compass and the Black Duke for not checking anything besides his pockets. Carefully, he paddled closer to the trees' edge, noting again how the waters had sunk a little, with the ending of the storm in the Gulf. To the north of him he saw the tall roofline of the weaving house, and identified where he was.

The temptation was strong to go to the dead-huts, to look for what he was fairly sure was there, but he didn't dare. They were too close to the house, too close to the man who'd tried to kill him last night. Instead he turned swampward, as they would have said in New Orleans. Awkwardly – it was difficult to paddle with his legs stretched out in front of him, instead of sitting on his knees – he made his way north eastward, where he had seen the smoke. When the sun came up, the heavy gray air grew brighter, but it was still impossible to tell direction in this sullen green cathedral of cypress and half-drowned tupelo. He checked his compass

311

constantly, and he sipped cautiously at his water-gourds, as rivers of sweat ran from his face.

He passed shell-mounds, where the Chaouachas or the Colapissa had raised their villages on the high ground along vanished bayous and branches of the main river, lines of oaks and loblolly pine now standing barely clear of the surrounding waters. Cattle and pigs, released from their pens as the waters came on, looked up at January as he paddled by. On one chenier he thought he recognized his old friend Keppy the mule. On another, surely that was Jules Mabillet's handsome black gelding.

He smelled smoke again, this time with sufficient strength that he could turn his pirogue in that direction. His hands and his bruised back smarted from the paddle. Dizziness turned him sick.

Turtles regarded him from half-submerged logs and alligators slid wetly from the banks, or regarded him with eyes like black-and-yellow beads. On a branch over his head two dozen white egrets watched the movement of the water below, like a choir of ghosts.

Clearer light beyond the trees, and the glimpse of something gray that wasn't a tree trunk. January backed his paddle, approached more cautiously. Yes, definitely what had been a house, on top of a chenier and surrounded by oaks. There wasn't much left of it and the islet-space was severely reduced now, the remains of the brick piers standing in a half-foot of water and the higher ground behind it crowded with three mules and two cows. Most of the roof had fallen in – years ago, it looked like – and the plank walls had been half-stripped by whoever needed lumber in the years since Alexandre Froide had sold the land to the St-Chinians. It had no gallery, and the upper floor, jutting out on both sides over the lower, had begun to sink down as the rafters yielded themselves to destiny and decay. In ten years, thought January, it would be utterly gone.

Smoke puffed fitfully from a chimney at one end. Also from the windows, which did not auger well for the state of the chimney nor the breathability of the air indoors.

And indeed, as January watched from the concealment of the trees, a man emerged onto the broken steps. Young, tall, and wide-shouldered, his red shirt and tucked-in trousers, the gaudiness of his waistcoat and the bedraggled strings of what had once been stylishly-curled soap-locks all announcing that this was the Irishman who'd gotten off the *Vermillion* – sick, Hannibal had reported second-hand – at English Turn.

The young man looked about him at the waste of water that still surrounded the chenier with an air of weary vexation, and turned to call some remark back to someone in the house behind him. Probably, reflected January, 'Fooken water's still up to our chins out there . . .'

A shadow moved in the house, then emerged onto the step behind him.

It was Chloë Viellard.

'In me heart I always knew, I'd rather see her dead than wed to another man.' Tommy Kildare rubbed tired hands over his rather long, square-chinned face. 'T'was all I meant at the beginnin', gettin' off the boat as I done. I just couldn't stand it.'

He was a redhead – dark auburn, like polished mahogany – but his eyes were a Spaniard's, chestnut-brown and fringed with long black lashes. Without five days' growth of scrubby beard he'd have been boyishly pretty, save for the strong set of his mouth.

'And 'tisn't I didn't know what that fookin' louse father o' her'n had made her do, from the time she was twelve years old. I never got the chance t' kill him, but if ever one man died of another man's prayers that he'd do so, that man was Fergus Trask. There's more than one time that I've kissed the leather of her pretty shoes. But I was sixteen, an' had Ma an' me sisters to look after, an' none to keep the roof over their head 'cept what I could bring 'em. Old Fergus said he'd kill me if I so much as touched her hand. But her marryin' . . .'

He shook his head, glanced across at Chloë – perched on the ruination of a bent-willow stool just within the house doorway – and then back at January, who sat on the step below him.

'I couldn't face it. I couldn't.'

He kept his voice soft, though the woman who lay on the bed behind him – in that portion of the downstairs parlor that wasn't hazy with smoke from the malfunctioning chimney – lay unmoving, her closed eyes smudgy with fatigue and with her struggle for life. When January had checked her pulse, and drawn back the lid from

314

her eye, Ellie Trask had recognized him and smiled a little, stretched out one hand to touch his arm.

Then her glance had gone past him to Tommy, and the smile had deepened and warmed.

'I thought seein' you here was a dream,' she'd whispered, her soft voice cracked, and she'd sipped a little of the water Chloë had been boiling.

She slept again now, and January guessed that she was going to live.

'I only meant to talk to her.' Tommy's glance again crossed Chloë's, drawing January's eyes after it, but behind the thick lenses, the young woman's eyes were expressionless as aquamarines. 'On the boat from town me an' the boys heard talk from the engineers, about that old camp or village out in the woods, where the runaway slaves had hid, poor bastards. I told St-Ives to send me word, to let me know from seein' her wid his own eyes, if she was happy wid this senile old Frenchman the Boss was after pushin' her to wed. How . . .'

He hesitated, and looked again at Chloë.

'How Madame here guessed I'd be there—'

'It was elementary.' Chloë shook her head, her spectacles flashing. 'Fleurette – Locoul's wretched sister, who is so grateful for anyone's notice that she'll reveal the secrets of her bosom in the next breath after "Hello" – mentioned that one of M'sieu Trask's boys got off at English Turn, sick, which started me wondering. It seemed to me a very curious thing, you know, for a man to forsake his transportation an hour's paddle from a destination where he could be sure of a bed, in favor of the amenities available at a settlement that

315

boasts of little more than a wood lot and a livery-stable.'

'It did to me, also,' agreed January. 'I take it that's why you left dinner and returned, alone, to the Casita—'

'Well, I couldn't very well ask Hélène to assist me,' Chloë reasoned. 'With the storm blowing up, she'd never have let me go out alone. I'd sent St-Ives out Tuesday night to English Turn, with a note for M'sieu Kildare—'

'St-Ives never did like the Boss treatin' Ellie as he did,' reflected Tommy. 'An' he never trusted him not to sell him off, for all he's a free man an' knew a fair few secrets about him.'

'I told Madamoiselle Trask after dinner that Tommy would be at the dead-huts. They were the only place where an assignation could reasonably be arranged, since they're really the only landmark in the woods that can easily be found. This place—' she gestured to the ruinous structure above and around them, half-swamped in wild grapevine and smelling of smoke and rot – 'is far too far back in the ciprière, and there isn't a clear path to it. I only knew of it because I used to come to Cold Bayou as a girl, when Uncle César had the running of the place. After Valla's death,' she went on more quietly, returning Tommy's sidelong glance, 'I had the feeling that Madamoiselle Trask might . . . might feel differently about a suitor from among her uncle's *comitatus*. But I wanted to meet with him, first.'

She hesitated, as if considering a hand of cards. 'I wanted to be sure I was doing the right thing,'

316

she said at length. 'I do try to, but I'm never certain what the right thing is.'

'You thought in fact,' said January, 'that arranging a match with someone else might be the only means of saving Ellie's life.'

'And so 'twas.' Kildare's heavy brow knotted over those oddly womanly eyes. 'Wid the rain comin' an' goin', an' wind weepin' like the souls of the damned, we come to fear she'd lose her way in the woods. So we took me lantern an' walked back toward the house, an' that's where we found her, lyin' on the path about half a mile into the woods, cold as mackerel an' throwin' up blood.'

'Had I known there was the slightest chance you'd be accused of the deed—' Chloë laid a small hand on January's arm – 'I should probably have tried to get her back to the Casita. But the flood was already rising. We brought her to the dead-huts, where at least she'd be dry, and wrapped her in a coat Tommy had found there, thrust into the thatch of one of the ruined huts. Tommy had a horse – it's that gray out behind the house, one of Thierry Chiasson's that runs the livery at English Turn. By the time it was clear we were going to have a full-on flood, it was obvious to me that she'd been poisoned. On the whole I thought she'd have a better chance at survival if we didn't go back to Cold Bayou, at least not until I had a better idea of who was behind it, and how many people were in on it.'

'I think,' said January thoughtfully, 'that I know who that might have been. But it'll be hard to prove – and I doubt there's anything we can do about it.'

317

Chloë's eyes narrowed. 'Hmn. In any case by that time,' she added, 'I knew that Valla's death had nothing to do with her.'

'It did—'

They all turned, at the hoarsely-whispered words from within the dimness of the house. Kildare sprang to his feet at once and hastened inside. '*Acushla*, you shouldn't . . .'

January turned himself on the doorsill where he sat, in time to see Ellie Trask raise her face to the young Irishman, a look of wondering disbelief in her eyes, and then clasp him tight as Kildare's strong arms went around her.

'So it weren't a dream,' she whispered. 'Tommy, *mavourneen* . . .'

'I'm here,' he murmured, after their lips parted from a kiss. 'I'll always be here, if you'll have me—'

'Always—'

'Your uncle—'

'The devil can swallow my uncle sideways.' She pressed her face to his chest. 'Tommy, I thought you'd turned from me . . .'

'Never.' Another kiss. 'Never! But how was I to come to you, when this rich old Frenchman would give you everythin' your heart was set on . . . includin' gettin' away from Uncle Mick . . .'

'We can get away,' she breathed. 'You an' me. Somehow.' She moved shakily toward the light of the doorway, and January saw, draped around her shoulders, a man's short-skirted tweed coat, of a yellowish mustard tweed.

A coat crusted with dried blood.

His eyes went to Chloë, and she nodded as she

318

got to her feet. 'You should lie down,' she said gently, touching Ellie's arm. In the morning light the taller girl looked ghastly, her wheat-gold hair hanging around her face in muddy strings and the turquoise-and-gold silk of her dress unspeakably soiled. 'You've been ill . . .'

Ellie looked out across the yellow-brown waters that stretched on all sides, and her eyes widened; she looked quickly around her, brushing the hair back from her face. 'So that weren't a dream neither,' she murmured. 'Where am I? I thought I was at them dead-huts—'

'We brought you here, when the floods started comin' deep,' said Tommy. '*Mo chroí*, I feared I'd lost you – and I think I'd have died, to lose you a second time.'

'Never. Not now.' She shook her head, still clinging to his shoulder, and her eyes went to Chloë. 'Not ever. You said . . . What happened to me? After you talked to me on the gallery I – I made up me mind to go . . . But then I felt sick, I think . . .'

'You were poisoned,' said January quietly. 'Someone broke into the Casita earlier in the night and put poison in . . . in a drink they knew you'd take.'

Ellie looked aside quickly, and blushed. To Tommy, she murmured, 'Brandy. An' I swear to you, darlin', I've been polishin' off half a bottle an' more every night, since I told Mr St-Chinian I'd be his wife – pourin' it down even as I was thinkin', What the hell am I doin'? What am I doin' to myself? An' when Valla was killed—'

'Valla's death had nothing to do with anyone

319

making an attempt on your life.' January got to his feet, and coming close to the couple, moved his hand toward the crusted bloodstains on the jacket. 'You found this in the dead-huts, Michie Kildare, I think you said? Pushed into the thatch?'

'High up. Where the floods wouldn't pull it loose, I think.'

'It's Guillaume Molina's. The overseer,' January added, when Ellie looked blank. 'I think when we go back to the dead-huts and search the thatch of those huts to the very top – which my amanuensis didn't think to do, when I was there Wednesday morning – we'll find whatever proof Valla had come across, that Molina was cooking the plantation books.'

Rather than surprise, Ellie's pretty face registered only relieved agreement. 'I knew he had to be,' she said. 'I saw all those barrels in the cooperage there, far more than what I knew a plantation this size should be puttin' out each year. An' that cameo Mrs Molina was wearin' when she came down to the landin' to greet poor Father Eugenius – wherever it is *he* ended up – an' that silk dress of hers, that's got to have cost twenty-five dollars if it cost a silver dime . . .'

'You made a note of it,' remarked January, and, surprised, Ellie nodded.

'Just 'cause I have no writin' doesn't mean I can't take note of what I see.'

'An' she's got her numbers, right enough.' Kildare gave the girl's shoulders a proud squeeze. 'Hell, she was keepin' the books for the High Water tavern since she wasn't tall enough to look

320

over the bar.' And in a quieter voice he added, 'I think I loved her then . . .'

'Well, you was for always pullin' my hair,' retorted Ellie, with a rare, relaxed grin at him. 'An' him lookin' like a garden-rake covered in spots, an' just over from Ireland with no more English than M'am Janvier's dog.'

Her lips pursed tight suddenly, and she looked aside.

'But you're wrong, Mr J,' she said softly. 'Wrong when you say poor Valla's death had nuttin' to do with . . . with what happened to me. With what everybody was hopin' an watchin' would happen to me.'

Her brown eyes flooded with tears. 'When they found Valla – for whatever reason she was killed – all anybody could talk about was, that they had to protect *me*. It was all as if Valla had been like a dog tied up outside the house, an' the dog got killed by someone who was comin' after *me*. Can you understand that at all?'

White and haggard, she turned her face from Chloë to January and then back. 'They were all: "Oh, we're so sorry your dog got killed but we need to protect *you*." Even the ones who really *did* want to protect me,' she added. 'It's like Valla was . . . was just somethin' that got stepped on by accident.'

'But in fact,' pointed out Chloë – who had a great deal in common with Michie Singletary – 'it's what they all did think.'

'That didn't make her less dead!'

'No,' said January softly.

'That's when I knew. That's when I thought . . .'

321

Ellie shook her head. 'I knew I had to get out of there. Not just because someone there was after killin' me, but because . . . because someone had killed *her*, an' it looked to me like no one was noticin'. Not her, an' really not me, except for poor Mr St-Chinian. An' I thought: *I can't do this. I can't live among these people.* Not 'cause one of 'em – or pretty much all of 'em – wanted me dead . . . Not 'cause I was afraid. Not really. I was angry. An' sick of it to me back teeth.'

In silence January looked down at that beautiful averted face, that had seemed so child-like when she gazed at Uncle Veryl. *She was kind to me*, Hannibal had said of her, *even when she could see no profit in it.*

'However it may be.' The girl sighed, and wiped her eyes. 'When M'am Chloë come to me at the window after dinner that night, an' whispered that Tommy was here and Tommy would be waitin' for me at the dead-huts, I knew me mind was made up. I knew starvin' to death with him – an' likely we *will* starve, on account of we have to run from Uncle Mick – an' breakin' poor Mr St-Chinian's old heart, was better than livin' always either lookin' over me shoulder or wipin' peoples' spit off me skirts. I'm sorry, m'am,' she added, taking Chloë's hand. 'They're your family an' I shouldn't speak ill of 'em. But one of 'em *did* try to murder me, if Mr J is tellin' the truth.'

'And yet you didn't take any of the jewelry Uncle Veryl bought for you,' said Chloë.

Spots of embarassed pink flared on Ellie's pale cheeks. 'I ain't sayin' I'm no angel with a halo

322

on me head,' she admitted. 'Sometimes it's either lie or starve. An' I'll be the first to tell you I bought many a dress with the wages of sin.'

She glanced shyly at Tommy, who hugged her again and said, 'Lord, Ellie, you want to sit down some night an' discuss each other's sins over a bottle of brandy I'll have you runnin' for the door.'

'I just . . . I couldn't take them from Mr St-Chinian. He loves me. He really does. That's the hardest part,' she added after a moment. 'It'll hurt him so bad.'

'But possibly,' said January, 'prolong his life – since another attempt might not involve only one of you.'

She – and Chloë – stared at him, Chloë with eyes like glass calculating-beads behind her thick spectacles, Ellie with her lovely mouth open in shocked protest.

January produced two silver spoons from his pocket, and held them up to Chloë. 'Who has spoons of those patterns?'

'The acanthus-leaf pattern is one of the ones from the dining-room here,' said the girl promptly. 'They were Granmère Duquille's. French – Robert-Josephe Auguste – you can see the hall-mark here. I think part of Uncle César's quarrel with Cousin Locoul was that Locoul supposedly sold about half that set to pay his gaming debts – that's what the rest of them are doing here, along with that horrid Sheffield stuff that my mother got for her wedding that nobody in the family would have in their houses.'

She took the other spoon, turned it in small

thin fingers like a child's. 'This looks like the townhouse silver from Madame Mabillet's.'

Twenty-Four

Madame Marie-Honorine Mabillet was at her son's bedside when January and Chloë reached the big house at sunset.

'What did I tell you?' said Old Madame Janvier, after she'd embraced Chloë and cried out her thanks that she was safe, and had sent her maid running along the gallery toward the main house where everyone was assembling for dinner. 'Absolutely intrepid! She will let nothing keep her from her son's side.'

January said quietly, 'So I apprehend, Madame.'

Chloë raised an eyebrow, and said nothing on that subject.

It was Charlotte who met January at the door of Jules' sickroom, her chinless, earnest face drawn with anxiety. 'Will he be all right, Ben? She brought her own medicine – she won't listen to me . . .'

'Good Heavens, child, I should hope not!' From within the room, the mother's voice came low and musical as she rose from her chair beside the bed, her movements too graceful to permit her tall, wide-shouldered form to be called 'lanky'. Dark-haired, like Jules, and like her son possessed of Byronic dark eyes and a ferociously aquiline nose. 'One day you'll understand, dear

324

child,' she added in a caressing voice, and crossed to put a strong hand on Charlotte's cheek. 'You're seventeen; you have no experience in such things. Life will teach you.'

Turning to January, she held out her hand. 'I so much appreciate your efforts on behalf of my son, M'sieu. Of course you did as you thought best. Sidonie tells me you trained at the Hôtel Dieu in Paris. How shocking you must find Louisiana, after such experiences! But I have been accustomed to nurse my son for many years, and have an exact knowledge of his constitution. He is . . .' Her dark brows tweaked in pain. 'His nervous system is extremely sensitive, for all his great strength. He suffered *agonies* as a child.'

January's eyes went to the satchel that stood open on the bedside table. Another thick square bottle of Kendal's Black Drop stood beside it – like the one which had appeared so mysteriously on the bedside table Wednesday night – and though the twilight had only begun to gather a dozen candles glimmered on the necks of the bottles inside. Then he glanced, very briefly, at the hem of her skirt, splashed and damp, as if she'd stepped from a boat to the front steps of the gallery. 'He is fortunate to have such a mother,' he replied. 'You must have come on the wings of the wind.'

'Men don't understand.' She shook her head with a sigh. 'Have you a child, M'sieu? How could you not fly to his side, the moment you heard of his need?'

'I'm frankly astonished that you *did* hear,' said Chloë. 'I take it the boats are running again?'

325

'It wasn't a proper steamboat from town,' provided Charlotte. 'Just one of those keel-boat things, with food—'

'It is as I said.' Old Madame Janvier's voice was filled with pride in her friend. 'Nothing can keep her away.'

Not even, apparently, reflected January – though he had the good sense not to say it – the fact that there was no possible way for this handsome, energetic woman to have heard of her son's injury, and to reach his side today, had she not known already that he had been hurt.

No way, had she not been one of the 'French biddies' who disembarked at English Turn at the same time as Tommy Kildare had – and Tommy's description of her that morning had been quite accurate, down to the color of her dress. The woman who had encouraged – if not ordered – her son to ride like the hero of a Walter Scott ballad to propose marriage to a girl whose inheritance wouldn't be assured until Ellie Trask was dead.

At least, thought January, watching the white-haired old lady clasp the hands of her younger friend, that was the logical sequence of events. Though his leg still felt like it had been put through a pair of cane-rollers, he forced himself to limp across the little room to Jules Mabillet's bedside, to check the young man's pulse (slight), breathing (shallow and irregular), pupils (he'd seen bigger eyes in needles) and to block Madame Mabillet's view of the bed while Chloë had a quick look at the bottles in her medicine case.

Not that it mattered. His testimony wouldn't

326

be admitted in court against any white person, let alone against a French Creole matron of spotless reputation. He'd gone up against members of that species before and was lucky he'd come out of the encounter alive. And no one would care . . .

Feet thundered on the gallery and January, seated in the bent-willow chair beside the bed, braced himself. 'Where is she?' roared Mick Trask's hoarse voice, over Thisbe's challenging soprano bark. 'What has that cold little bitch done wi' my girl? If harm's come to her—'

Chloë got quickly to her feet, but it was Madame Mabillet who blocked the doorway with one splendid arm, who faced the clot of angry Irishmen on the gallery like a Byzantine empress staring down a parcel of beggars.

'*Be silent*! My boy is ill – dying, maybe!'

She was closer to the truth than she knew, thought January, but he also guessed that she'd said so mostly for effect. It pulled Trask up short, and before he could draw breath Chloë went to the doorway, cold and prim as ever despite her sweat-streaked face and bedraggled dress.

Behind Trask, Uncle Veryl pushed his way through the Irishmen and stretched out his hands. 'Chloë!' and old Mr Singletary struggled forward after him, as if ready to single-handedly pummel the boys to death.

'M'sieu Trask,' said Chloë, in her precise English. 'So far as I know, your niece is well. Please . . .' she added, as her uncle, weeping with the sudden release of his fear, would have embraced her. 'Let's go inside. Benjamin . . .'

Since nothing he could do or say would have had the slightest effect on keeping Madame Mabillet from killing her son with pain medicine, January got painfully to his feet again, picked up the stick he'd been using all day as a crutch, and limped to her side. Trask's face twisted with rage at the sight of him and he grated, 'You!' but Chloë held up her hand again.

'Please, M'sieu,' she said again, and led the way into the next room along the upstream wing of the house, which happened to be Singletary's. The gallery was by this time jammed with further spectators, crowding from the main house and all talking at once, Thisbe darting among them with excited yelps. January heard someone ask, 'Did they find her body?' And Euphémie responded in her trumpet of a voice, 'I don't see anything in the boat.'

All the boys crowded into Singletary's room with their boss. Singletary would never have thought to offer the little chamber's single chair to a lady but brought it up for January.

Chloë remained standing, barely taller than Trask's top waistcoat-button.

From the pocket of her skirt, she brought out a folded piece of paper, and handed it to Veryl, and her cold blue eyes stopped Trask's effort to snatch it out of the old man's shaky grasp as if she'd turned him to stone.

deer Mr St-Chinian,
pleese forgiv me I canot mary you I am
in love wit someone els who is good and
who loves me. wen they kilt Valla I saw

I wud never be hapy but always afraid. pleese tell Uncle Mick it aint anybodys falt an not to go look for us we wil be alrite. pleese pleese find someone els an be hapy an do not be angry wit me. I wil always be yor true frend.

Ellie

The name was written in larger characters, straggling and uneven, and Veryl's eyes flooded with tears at the sight of it, even as Uncle Mick plucked the paper from his fingers.

'Tommy,' he snarled. 'That's his way o' printin' – worthless bog-trash bastard! The cat eat his bones an' the devil eat the cat! Who o' yez knew o' this?' He whirled on his boys, who all backed up a pace, and he lashed out with his open hand, knocking Gopher sprawling into the wall and drawing blood from Syksey O'Neill's nose. The Black Duke took the blow without flinching, though the print of his boss's palm stood red on his pockmarked cheek as he replied.

'For all I could see – for all any of us could see – he was sicker'n a horse when he got off that boat. You saw him, Boss. An' you heard him when he said, wasn't necessary for none of us to stay wid him—'

'Don't you tell me what I saw an' what I heard!' bellowed Trask.

'Mesel',' added the Duke, 'I thought it might even be for the best, if he wasn't to see Ellie – Miss Trask,' he corrected himself. 'I knowed he was always sweet on her.'

Trask struck him again. 'An' it never crossed

329

your flea-size brain that him bein' sweet on her might mean he was fixin' to go ashore an' convince her to run off wid him? Jesus wept! An' him widdout a pot to piss in, an' her throwin' herself away on a pot-lickin' turf-cutter. Where'd you find this, girl?' He swung around on Chloë, and for a shocked instant January thought he'd strike her, too.

After a moment's silence, in which she merely regarded him with her huge bespectacled eyes, Chloë replied, 'I found it in the dead-huts – those old runaway shacks in the woods a mile behind the Casita. I woke Wednesday night to find Mamzelle gone. I was afraid she'd gone to the dead-huts – she'd told me that afternoon that she thought that the clue to find Valla's killer might be there. She was most upset – devastated – at her maid's murder, and she said several times that no one seemed to want to know who'd done it. That people seemed to be afraid of that information coming out.'

She blinked innocently up at Uncle Mick, and January saw that the black rage that passed across his eyes was no longer directed at her, but at those who'd turned up their noses at his niece.

In point of fact, during the long, tiring paddle back through the swamps from where they'd left the runaway lovers (and Tommy's rented horse) on the more-or-less dry ground just above English Turn, January and Chloë had agreed that absolutely nothing was to be gained by any account of Ellie being poisoned. There was no evidence of who had put what into Ellie's plum brandy – notwithstanding the clear signs that after doing so, Madame Mabillet had paid a surreptitious visit to her feverish son, had dosed him to within an inch of his life, and had left a bottle of Kendal Black Drop and a spoon behind her.

Uncle Mick growled, 'She always was a head-strong little thing,' and the anger was gone from his voice.

The Black Duke answered, with a reminiscent half-grin, 'That she was, Boss. An' kind. Who'd a thought she'd get that put about over the killin' of a nigger wench?'

Those brooding blue eyes turned back to Chloë: 'Go on.'

'Well, I found this note at the dead-huts. It was raining hard, but I found one of her hairpins—' Chloë had prudently taken several from Ellie when they'd parted, and one of these she held up in corroboration – 'where there's a sort of path leading deeper into the ciprière. There's a broken-down house several miles deeper in the woods, you see, and it looked as if she were on her way there, to meet this . . . this man she speaks of. I think she must have heard of the place from Valla, who spent several years here. With the storm, I was most afraid she'd get lost, so I tried to follow her there, calling out for her. Then the water started coming up. I made it to the house, where I found another hairpin, and evidence that a meal had been eaten there – bread-crusts and eggshells and a couple of empty ginger-beer bottles. They'd left – forgotten – some of their provisions, but I didn't find those until daylight. If it wasn't for that I think I'd have starved, when the flood trapped me there.'

Outside the French doors the clamor of voices was louder, Madame Aurelié's trumpeting, 'Nonsense! I must and will speak to that ridiculous man . . .' and Henri's, pleading, eager, 'But she's all right? You saw her and she's all right . . .'

Uncle Mick turned, opened the door a crack, and bellowed through it, 'Shut up out there! Go eat your fooken' dinner!'

'And save some for me,' suggested Chloë.

'An' save some for M'am Viellard!' He slammed the door, turned to January. 'And where do you fit into all this, boy-o? We thought you roasted, night before last, when the wood store burned down. You set that fire yourself?' His voice was conversationally inquiring; January shook his head.

'I managed to get out,' he replied noncommittally. 'I had – I've always had – the idea that Valla wasn't killed in mistake for Miss Trask. That whoever murdered her, did so for his own reasons. And yes, your niece was right – I found the evidence for this at the dead-huts. It was daylight by then and I saw smoke from deeper in the ciprière, and I thought it might well have been either Madame Viellard, or Miss Trask, or both. I'd heard about there being a house somewhere back there on a chenier—'

'You swim there?' inquired Trask mildly. 'Or ride a water-pookah like the leprechuans do?'

'I paid an alligator to carry me.'

Under the tuft of black mustache, a tooth gleamed. 'Musta been a big one.'

'It was. How's my mother, by the way?'

'Your mother . . .' Syksey O'Neill's voice almost trembled with loathing, but he caught his boss's glance, and he fell silent.

'Your mother is well,' returned Trask. 'Syksey's been guarding her. She's had tea a couple of times wid Old M'am Janvier and plays whist wid the ladies over at the weaving house.'

January glanced swiftly at O'Neill and said, 'I hope to God you haven't tried to play cards with my mother!'

'Not more'n oncet.'

It was dark outside by this time. When the French door opened onto the gallery, January could see that the level of the floodwater, which had been slowly sinking all day, was down to the fourth step from the top. Everyone in the house, from Madame Aurelié to the Viellard girls' maids, crowded the gallery, shadowy forms in the reflected glow of candlelight from the windows in the house's main block. Chloë went out first, and while Henri was desperately embracing her ('Really, Henri, I'm quite all right . . .') January said softly, 'M'sieu Trask?'

The Irishman turned.

'I'd take it as a great favor if neither you nor your men spoke of what I said about the girl Valla's murder. Tomorrow I'll get word to the parish sheriff – he's got to be making rounds along the river, now that the water's going down – and I'd rather we took the killer by surprise, rather than let him get away.'

'Suit yourself,' agreed Trask, as amiably as if he hadn't come within inches of drowning January on the previous morning. 'Anybody we know?'

333

'Probably not well.'

The boys nodded assent, and pushed their way out onto the gallery. January, turning back, saw that Uncle Veryl had remained sitting on the end of his friend Singletary's bed, his narrow shoulders bowed, still holding the note in his hands. Singletary, standing beside him, fidgeted awkwardly – a theorist who had never in his life known what to say to other people, how to share joy or express grief.

January limped back to the two old men, put a hand on Veryl's shoulder. 'Can I get you anything, sir?' he asked.

Veryl shook his head. After a long time, he said, 'I wish she'd taken the jewels. They'll need money. She and her . . . her friend.'

'I think maybe she didn't want you to think worse of her, sir,' said January. 'To think she would take the gifts you gave her, and give them to another man.' There was a word for women who did that, and though it had probably been an accurate enough description at periods in Ellie Trask's life, it wasn't one that he'd speak to the bereft old gentleman before him.

'Would there be any way of getting in touch with her?' asked Veryl softly. 'Of hearing if she's . . . she's all right?'

'Would that help you?'

'I think so.'

He glanced after the last of the retreating boys. 'Then I'll do that,' he said. 'When Uncle Mick calms down a little and isn't ready to blow the man's head off.'

It was in his heart to say, 'This has probably

334

saved her life', but he didn't. *He's lost his beloved. Why take from him his family as well?*

Taking up his stick, he limped out onto the dark gallery.

Twenty-Five

There was just enough water, January calculated, for him to paddle back to the weaving house, whose gallery blazed with candles and cressets in the last of the twilight. The pain in his ankle wasn't less than it had been, but the joint itself felt stronger. He supposed the water was too shallow for gators or garfish now, but nevertheless he had no desire to wade.

As his oar dipped into the opaque gray water, he glanced again toward the Casita, and the dark line of the ciprière behind it. 'Anybody we know?' Trask had asked, mildly curious and no more than that.

'Probably not well,' he had replied.

And who DOES know them? They're a part of the plantation, like the sugar mill and the mules. The Family comes and goes. Stays in the big house sometimes at roulaison, *to make sure things are being done properly. But on an isolated plantation like this, it's a penance, or an exile, for men like César St-Chinian whom nobody in the Family wants to deal with any more than they have to. Beyond that . . . You stay down here in the swelter and the cane-rats, you whip as much*

335

work as you can out of the slaves, you get the crop in and you send us the money, and let us know when one of the slaves dies so we can replace him as cheap as we can.

Why not *cheat them?*

And if you're a good-looking young woman who's been used and traded like a piece of meat all your life, who can blame you for—

The crack of a rifle tore the hot stillness, and splinters from the pirogue's gunwale ripped January's right hand. He flung himself sidelong off the boat and into the water as a second shot (*he's got two rifles . . .*) smacked the water just beside him. The bullet, he guessed, would have gone through his head. His arm flung over the pirogue's side to keep it close enough for protection, he tried to guess where the shots had come from. *If I swim towards the weaving house he'll get me in the water . . . If something in the water doesn't get me first.* He felt – or thought he felt – something pass beneath his feet, and kicked against the water, driving toward the distant weaving house.

The new-risen moon was three nights from full, bright in the nearly cloudless sky. Another gunshot drove a bullet into the side of the pirogue and he realized there were two of them – one on the offside of the pirogue and one, now, somewhere behind him and to his right. A bullet grazed his elbow like the stroke of a red-hot rod and he flung himself back from the little boat. *Of course,* he thought, *they're both in it . . .*

Cameo. Silk dress. Not placatory gifts for bulling the housemaid. Her share of the proceeds.

336

Is Madame Molina as good a shot as her husband's supposed to be?

He floundered, feet touching the bottom, and saw the match-light flicker of a muzzle-flash against the dark silhouette of the Casita. *If I can turn the pirogue over I can use it as a shield . . .*

But right now they know I'm close to it. They can see it, *if they can't see* me.

From the corner of his eye he saw a dark shape slide out onto the darkening water from the big house, and there was movement on the roof of one of the half-drowned slave cabins. Another gunshot, and he ducked aside from the pirogue as a bullet struck it; stumbled with the shock of pain through his ankle again, fatigue as much as pain dragging at him.

Then the crack of a rifle from the oncoming boat, and the form standing on the slave cabin spun half-around and fell.

A moment later the boat came up to him and the Black Duke's voice came out of the gloom, 'Gimme your hand, Ben.'

And Trask said, 'Get him in the pirogue and take him to the weaving house.'

The Duke obeyed, stepped across to the smaller vessel and with a certain amount of inevitable difficulty, dragged January up into it.

'Didn' I tell yez, the Gopher can shoot the eye outten a rabbit by moonlight? Fair drove the land-lord's gamekeepers mad, back home.'

As the Irishman paddled for the weaving house January watched the larger rowboat surge steadily toward the Casita, dark on the darkening water.

'She's got to have a boat of her own,' said January. 'They'll never catch her.'

'Her?' The Duke sounded startled and a little offended.

'At a guess,' said January, lying back in the pirogue and trying to keep his voice steady against the agony in his ankle. 'Madame Molina. It's the only person it could be.'

'Molina the nigger overseer? *He* killed Valla?'

'Who else would have reason to fear a black girl's testimony? Or a black man's.'

When January woke the following morning it was to the smell of coffee, and the sound of Hannibal Sefton's voice. 'And is that the card you picked?'

'How'd you do that?' asked Isabelle Valverde disbelievingly.

Marianne added in a worried tone, 'Sister St-Anthony at the convent says there's no such thing as magic.'

'The good Father Clooney back home always said the same thing. Now, pick a card . . .'

January groped painfully for his trousers, which lay across the foot of his bed, and his stick, but the creak of the pallet's mattress-ropes must have alerted those on the gallery outside to his movements. A moment later Hannibal, Dominique, and Cochon Gardinier all appeared in the open French door, Hannibal tucking a deck of cards into the pocket of his threadbare coat.

'Good to see you alive, Ben,' said Cochon, and Minou rustled to his side and knelt in a sursurrance of petticoats.

'Don't get up, P'tit. I'll have Bergette fetch hot water – thank *Heaven* there was wood that stayed dry in the sugarhouse! Oh, Benjamin, what *happened*? Bergette tells me Chloë is back at the house, and that Mamzelle Ellie has run off with one of those *horrid* Irish boys, which one can't but be thankful for, and they've locked up M'sieu Molina in the sugar house and Madame Aurelié is just fit to *scream* with vexation and is swearing he had nothing to do with the wood store burning—'

'Who locked him up?' asked January. 'He's alive, then?'

Minou looked startled at the suggestion that it could be otherwise, but Hannibal said, 'Badly wounded with a rifle-ball in his side. Madame Aurelié expressed her severe annoyance, when I arrived this morning, that you were still asleep, and told me to inform you that you were expected to extract the ball at the earliest possible moment. *Medice, cura te ipsum* . . .'

'Who shot him?' Minou's eyes were round. 'That wasn't *him* last night, shooting at Benjamin—?'

'Hannibal,' said January, and squeezed his sister's hand to quiet her – not that anything had ever succeeded in quieting Minou for long. 'Two things, before anything else. First: did you find any record of Simon Fourchet's debts to Fergus Trask?'

'Plenty,' said the fiddler. 'Fifteen hundred dollars borrowed in April of 1807, paid back in December of the same year at twenty percent interest; three thousand dollars borrowed in July of 1813, paid back in two installments in January

339

of 1814, and December of the same year. "Neither a borrower nor a lender be, for loan loseth both itself and friend" – not that Simon Fourchet *had* any friends, so far as I've heard . . . Evidently Fergus Trask,' he added, 'came to the United States in 1805 – two years after your mother acquired her freedom and moved to New Orleans.'

He coughed, holding his hand to his side. Though his long hair was braided in a neat queue down his back and his old-fashioned chimney-pot hat sat at a jaunty angle, he still bore every mark of a tiring journey and a couple of very long days of searching through papers at the Cabildo.

'Well, you can't blame a man for trying.' January had heard the clump of boots on the gallery while his sister had been speaking, and now Mick Trask stood framed in the doorway, waxed cotton gaiters buckled on over his calves and dripping with muddy water, a stout stick in hand. 'How are you feeling, my friend? 'Tis good to see you well.'

January suppressed the urge to fling his own walking stick at the Irishman – who would cheerfully have sold him as a slave had he been able to manage it, not to mention two beatings and an attempt to throw him into six feet of gator-infested floodwater tied to a chair – and replied, 'I'm well, sir. Did you come to this country with your brother?'

'No, I came in '99 – shortly after the French made such a sorry batch of their invasion. Fergus stayed on with Emmett until his uprising was crushed, then got out on a smuggler-run to

340

Brittany, and so to New York, and couldn't have done that had I not been toilin' for five years in Five Points to raise the ready for him. Greedy parcel of cut-throats, the French.' He shook his head in deep regret. 'Incompetent, too.'

January refrained from any observation on the subject of greedy cut-throats, and asked instead, 'So that was indeed Guillaume Molina who was shooting at me last night? And presumably who tried to fire the wood store while I was chained there.'

'He swears 'tis all a lie – an' swears that as a white man your testimony can't be held against him . . .'

'A *white man*?'

Trask grinned. 'His complexion, he claims, comes from Portuguese ancestry, an' a Chickasaw grandmother, an' that he's no more African than Madame Aurelié. He doesn't mention who he inherited that hair from.'

'Personally,' remarked Hannibal, as Minou fetched in a tray from the gallery with the remains of the morning's coffee, 'I should give much to see him put that argument up in court.'

'You'll have the chance,' promised January drily. 'M'sieu Trask, if you and your men care to take a pirogue out to the old Froide house on Cold Bayou, you'll find a parcel up the main chimney: Molina's yellow-brown tweed coat, which anyone on the plantation can identify as his, with blood on the breast and right sleeve, from where he cut poor Valla's throat. With it will be two of the plantation's account books, containing the accurate records of income and

341

expenditure for the past five years. More accurate, I believe, than the ones to be found in the plantation office in the big house and in the overseer's house.'

'Ah,' said Trask. 'So that's the . . .' He visibly bit off a remark about who might be hiding in a mythological woodpile, coughed, and finished, 'I think I sense an Irishman concealed in the fuel supply, as it were,' and January grinned.

'How Valla knew where the real books were hidden I don't know. But since she worked in Molina's household for two years – and since she was far from stupid, as well as literate and burdened with a sense of grievance – it's no surprise at all that she guessed what was going on. Even your niece, with no background of plantation economics, figured out that Madame Molina had dresses and jewelry that her husband couldn't have afforded on his pay, and Molina had given Valla trinkets that she recognized as expensive.'

'So when they came back here,' finished Trask, 'she thought she'd ask for her cut of it, did she?'

'You can't blame a girl for trying.' January quietly handed his words back to him. 'She knew where the books were hidden, and she knew where to hide them after she stole them in her turn: in the thatch of the dead-huts, up at the top, where flood or animals couldn't get them. Luc searched the thatch for me, but only as high as he could reach. I was in such pain at the time that all I wanted was to get back to the weaving house – which was probably just as well. Molina sent Valla a note on Tuesday, arranging a meeting at

342

the dead-huts at midnight. I knew perfectly well that note couldn't have been to your niece—'

'She's a dear girl,' sighed the Irishman, 'and a damn sight smarter than you'd think, but her own name was the extent of her book learnin', an' that's the truth.'

'Maybe Molina guessed Valla would hide the ledgers somewhere near the dead-huts – they seem to be a locus of contraband goods. Maybe it was just a convenient place for a rendezvous. He almost certainly planned to dump her body in the bayou – probably with her belly slit to keep her from floating—' Trask nodded, evidently long familiar with this post-mortem disposal procedure – 'but the presence of slaves lurking around to meet with False River Jones meant that he couldn't risk being seen, not even for a moment.'

'How *horrible*!' cried Dominique. 'It could be that he heard someone coming, you know – Bergette tells me that simply *everyone* in the quarters goes out to trade things with that awful peddler – and he must just have dropped the body and fled.'

'Did he mean to come back for her?' Cochon, seated next to her on the nurse's pallet bed, helped himself to several brown lumps of sugar from the platter on the tray, blinking his little round eyes as if listening to a tale of derring-do.

'He certainly meant to come back for his jacket. He hid it in the thatch of one of the huts, along with the gloves he had on at the time. They got bloodstained as well, by the way, and had welts scratched into them by Valla's nails. Valla's gold

343

cross, and gold bracelet, are in the jacket's pocket. It's likely he searched the thatch while he was at it, but since he didn't know there was a ladder over near another of the huts – there was a storm coming Tuesday night, and the sky was nearly pitch-black – he only searched as high as he could reach. And maybe he feared he'd be discovered there as well.'

'Why did he kill her before she'd gotten the books for him?' asked Dominique, like Cochon enrapt, as if at an adventure by Scott or Cooper. 'I mean, if that's why he lured her there . . .'

'Perhaps they quarrelled,' theorized Hannibal.

'Were I a lass,' remarked Trask, lighting a cigar, 'and I'd somethin' a man wanted, who'd treated me as he had her, I can't say I wouldn't have quarrelled with the man meself. Who knows what a girl'll say?' He shrugged. 'But that old nigger wench findin' the body must have put paid to his comin' back to dump her in the bayou, and with the storm comin' in Wednesday and gangs goin' out to the field an' comin' back in again, he couldn't well get out to the huts to fetch his coat. How'd you know it was there, boy-o?'

His blue glance slid sidelong to January. 'If 'twas stuck low down in the thatch, the flood would have taken it before you got there to find it—'

'I knew it was there,' said January, side-stepping the question, 'because I knew Molina didn't mistake Valla for anybody. Completely aside from the fact that Molina was waiting there for her, I found her tignon there. He would have known her for a woman of color even if he

344

couldn't clearly see her face. So I knew I was dealing with someone who set out deliberately to kill Valla, not your niece. Kill her, and conceal the body, so that everyone would assume she had simply run away. Your niece found the note the following day, in Valla's room, probably. If you look at one of the "official" ledgers that Molina kept for inspection by the family, you'll find a page torn from the back. The paper's the same. Most likely you'll find the ink matches that in the overseer's house.'

'What I'll be more interested to see,' put in Hannibal, cutting neatly past Trask's indrawn breath to follow up on this discursive side-track, 'is whether the "official" ledgers were all written at one time – whether the ink is *consistent* – or whether the ink differs slightly from line to line, as it normally does on accounts that are kept daily.'

The Irishman – whose eyes had narrowed in suspicion as he'd sensed the discrepancy in January's explanation – dropped the thought and turned to regard the fiddler with interest.

'You sound like a man who knows something about the noble art of screevery yourself, sir.'

Hannibal widened coffee-dark eyes at him. 'Only what I learned at Oxford.'

Trask laughed, then leaned down to clap January on the shoulder, and dug in his pocket to produce January's silver watch, which he dropped onto the bedclothes. 'No hard feelin's?' he said.

'None in the least.' *Sometimes it's either lie or starve*, Ellie Trask had said. January hoped he sounded at least as convincing as she had.

* * *

345

Hannibal, quite sensibly, had packed a pair of waxed-leather gaiters for his return to the flooded parish. He set forth with Uncle Mick and his myrmidons just after ten, through the knee-deep water, to retrieve the account books, gloves, and coat that January and Chloë had secreted in the chimney on their way back from setting Ellie and Tommy on their way. Hot water was brought for January to wash himself and shave. Dominique fetched him breakfast ('Chloë tells me that they were asking *five cents* for eggs from that horrid keel-boat!'), along with the news that the *Louisiana Belle* had been spotted down-river and that Antoine and Luc were already ferrying Isabelle, Nicolette, and Solange, with children and baggage, to wait on the levee. 'Of course the Aubins, and the lawyers – well, the *real* lawyers—' by which January knew she meant Brinvilliers, Gravier, and DuPage, not the American Loudermilk – 'are all going across just when the *Belle* is coming in, so they won't have to wait long on the levee. The sun is absolutely *ferocious*. Euphémie and her sisters, and Madame Janvier, are going to wait for the *Illinois*, which will be along after lunch, they say, now that the river is going down a little.'

'The levee looks just like a snake,' provided Charmian, standing on the other side of the bed with a glass of lemonade for her Uncle Benjamin. With her immense brown eyes, and her soft brown curls immaculately glazed with sugar water, she looked not a whit the worse for having been trapped in the weaving house for two days: every inch Dominique's daughter. 'The water in the

346

river is up almost to the top, and on this side it's way down. But Papa says nobody should walk in it because of snakes.'

Henri, January gathered from the froth of his sister's discourse, would remain for another night at Cold Bayou, with his mother and her dear friend Madame Mabillet. 'Poor Jules is less feverish, but his maman insists he should be taken back to town to what she calls a "real doctor" – the *nerve* of the woman! And Charlotte begged with *tears* to be allowed to go with him, and will remain at his side . . . if Madame Mabillet had a tail she would wag it, she's so pleased, now that Ellie's out of the way. Uncle Mick is looking just *thunderclouds*, but honestly, P'tit, I think there's something very beautiful about Ellie deciding, at the very last minute, that she loved this whatever-his-name-is . . . Tommy? Loved him enough to run away with him, after she's had silk dresses and jewels and they're going to practically starve, but she doesn't care . . .'

January wondered whether Dominique, who as far as he could ascertain loved Henri Viellard truly and deeply, would love the young planter as much were he suddenly bereft of the family whose fortune and influence provided her with silk dresses and jewels, not to speak of an annuity of twelve hundred dollars and a comfortable cottage on Rue Dumaine.

His mother, he gathered, was also leaving on the *Illinois*. Later that afternoon he was to witness her tender farewells to her daughter and grand-daughter, but she forgot or neglected to take her leave of him.

Now he asked Minou, 'What about Uncle Veryl?'

Her delicate brows pulled together. 'Oh, P'tit! I can't but be glad that Ellie chose to run off with someone she loves, but it's so terrible to see him this way! He just sits there looking at the jewelry she left, and the gloves he gave her, and her wedding dress. The *poor* old man! He doesn't even weep! M'sieu Singletary is there with him, but he won't speak – Uncle Veryl won't – and James says he's afraid he'll . . . he'll do himself a mischief. He won't, will he? You don't think?'

January sighed, and set the breakfast tray off his lap. 'Would you hand me my clothes over there, Minou? And get one of the boys—' he gestured towards the gallery, where the musicians were gossipping with Sylvestre St-Chinian about further up-river boats – 'in here to help me dress? I'm not sure he'll do anything foolish . . . but it doesn't sound like he should be alone.'

He didn't reach the big house until after lunch, owing to the fact that his mother had commandeered the small pirogue of his escape (Old Nana's, as it turned out) to take herself and her luggage to the levee, and had paid Antoine fifty cents to pole her to the landing. 'I'm sorry 'bout that, sir,' said Antoine, as he navigated the little craft – at long last – toward the big house, through a sloppy landscape of sodden trees, half-submerged chicken coops, and deadfalls occupied by copperheads and gators. 'But you know I can't turn down any chance to get . . . well . . . something.

348

'Specially now that things'll be upset for awhile, 'fore they gets a new overseer.'

'I understand.' January handed him the small sack of coin that he'd found in the wood store with the file, and the knife. 'Will you see these get back to their original owners?'

'I will, sir.' He turned his face quickly away, and the tension in his naked bronze shoulders prompted January to ask, 'Did you know Valla was blackmailing Molina?'

The stiffness left the young man's body with a sigh. He still would not look back.

Nor, for a time, did he reply.

At last he said, 'I told her not to do it.' His voice was a barely audible croak. 'I told her it was a fool idea. No man gonna let a girl get away with somethin' like that.'

A shudder went through him, and January realized he wept. Crazy about her, Luc had said.

In a voice wrenched with sorrow, he went on, 'I told her I had a little money hid away. I been savin' . . .' He struggled to control his voice. 'He a bad man to cross, Molina. You ain't the first man he's tried to put out of the way, sir. When they lock you up in the wood store, Luc an' me an' the boys, we knew he'd get you. It's why we left the file an' things, even 'fore your friends paid Old Nana for this boat. Valla . . .'

He paused in his poling, and the little craft glided of its own momentum between the island formed by the overseer's kitchen, and the charred, soggy ruin of the wood store.

'Valla said, Mamzelle gonna free her. You know with her looks, she could pass for white in the north. But without money, she said, she'd end up like all them white girls in the north, that hang around the taverns where the sailors go . . .'

He remembered the yellow-and-white striped dress, the neat leather shoes. 'Wasn't Mamzelle going to give her money as well?'

'Two hunnert dollars.' Antoine looked back at him then, tears running from his eyes. 'Enough to set up a little business on her own. Not enough to buy me free.'

'Buy you . . .' January stared. Remembered the way Antoine had caught Valla's arm. How he'd waited for her, followed her steps . . .

'I told her to leave me behind. Told her I'd get out some way, an' come to her in the north.' He turned back to his poling, sun glinting on the glaze of his sweat. 'When she left, back in July, she said she'd come back for me. Then when she did, she said she knew stuff about Molina, stuff to make him let me go. She said, Molina "lost" so many "runaways" from this place, sellin' 'em to smugglers like Chamoflet, he could just as easy "lose" one who really did get away. I couldn't make her see different. I tried – I begged an' I swore. She said, he hadn't no power over her now.'

He fell silent for a time, guiding his little vessel, like Charon's barque, through murky waters in which a thousand secrets were drowned. 'I try not to think of it, sir. I was with her that night. If I'd had any idea – any thought that that's what she was up to – I'd have kept her by me, somehow. Held onto her. Kept her from goin'.' He shook his head again, like a tethered horse tormented by flies, and steered the pirogue around

350

a sodden grove and into the long U between the wings of the house, toward the weed-draped steps of the upstream wing.

'You think you could have?' asked January softly. 'My sister called her a *pichouette*: headstrong. Fierce. A bobcat. She didn't mean it kindly, but I think it was true.'

Something like a smile of memory flicked the corner of the young man's mouth and he poled the pirogue to a stop at the steps. 'That it was, sir. Valla . . .'

He shook his head, reached with his pole to brush a coiled cottonmouth off the lowest step, so that January could disembark.

Quietly, he finished, 'It was our only chance, she said. I begged her to let it go. She wasn't 'fraid o' nuthin', Valla.'

Marie-Honorine Mabillet emerged from her son's chamber as January, assisted by Antoine, dragged himself up the steps to the gallery. 'It was kind of you to come, sir,' said that beautiful, dark-haired woman, surveying January condescendingly. 'But Jules's fever seems much improved now. We'll be taking him to town tomorrow, to see our own physician.'

She had assumed, January realized, that he had come to see Jules. Not to comfort a man half out of his mind with grief.

'I'm very glad to hear it, Madame.'

Through the French door he glimpsed the young man lying still as death on the bed, the mosquito-bar draped up to reveal Charlotte, plump and plain and devoted as a spaniel, at his side. A horrifying array of bottles on the bedside table testified to the depth of young Mabillet's rest – and to the range of the lady's portable pharmacopia. It would be, January assumed, no great task to prove that Madame had disembarked at Carmichael's woodlot at English Turn, rented a horse from Thierry Chiasson's livery, and ridden down to Cold Bayou on the night of the storm, though she'd probably gotten rid of her riding-clothes by this time.

No serious effort either would be needed to prove that she'd had poisons in her satchel, as well as enough opiates to stupefy a rhinoceros. Or that the silver spoon he'd found in Jules' room on Thursday morning came from her house. Any jury in the country could put together the sequence of events: that she had urged her son to press his suit with Charlotte, and had followed him down-river – almost certainly without his knowledge – with the intention of making sure that the Viellard/St-Chinian holdings remained intact and unsullied by Hibernian interference. Hearing, probably at the livery stable at English Turn, that her son had been injured in the duel, she had gone to him after putting hemlock or fools-parsley into the bedside brandy bottle in the Casita.

It was only good luck – born of Tommy Kildare's devotion, and Ellie Trask's heart – that the lovely blonde girl hadn't been found dead on the Casita's back gallery, or in her bed after that.

But what, reflected January, *would be the point of proof?*

No jury in Louisiana would convict a respected French Creole matron, on a black man's testimony.

Pressing the issue would probably cause her – or her family – to seek another culprit from among those in the Cold Bayou weaving house that night.

Death in the water, Olympe had said. *Death in the fire.*

Death waiting at Cold Bayou like the smell of smoke.

He watched as Aurelié St-Chinian Viellard emerged from one of the back doors of the big house. Never a handsome woman, her sandy hair nearly all gray now, still there was the confidence of power in her heavy-featured face. Her friend Marie-Honorine hurried to meet her, and in the clasping of their hands January saw the devotion of which Old Madame Janvier had spoken; the kindness of an older girl who had looked after a younger one. The affection of an intrepid child toward one who has been like a wise elder sister.

He heard Madame Mabillet exclaim, 'Well, it really is for the best, you know! Doesn't he *see* that?'

'Honestly!' Madame Viellard shook her head. 'He just sits there, and stares without a word. I always knew Veryl wasn't quite right in the head – I said from the start that the match should never have been permitted. But no, nobody would listen to *me* when I so much as mentioned that he should be confined for his own protection. At least it's over.'

And she cast, January thought, a probing, side-long glance at her friend.

'And there's no trace of the girl?'

'Well, apparently the story is that she's run off with one of those horrible Irishmen.' Madame Aurelié shrugged. 'So I suppose we can be doubly thankful that she couldn't wait til she was married to start kicking up larks. I found this.'

And from the pocket of her puce foulard frock she drew a folded piece of paper – what appeared to January, at that distance, to be the folded page torn from the back of a ledger.

Madame Mabillet unfolded it and held it at the length of her arm, while her friend, still with a look of queer intensity, studied her expression. 'From this Irishman of hers?'

'I presume so.'

'So it looks as if she planned to betray Veryl all along.' Marie-Honorine dropped it over the gallery rail, and taking Aurelié's arm, walked slowly with her toward the house. 'Dearest, I *must* congratulate you – or felicitate you, I'm not sure which it is – on having raised such a loving, loyal-hearted girl as your Charlotte. It was *quite* wrong of Jules to have run off from town as he did to propose to her, but seeing them together, one cannot but be struck by the passion of their love . . .'

Through the French doors January could see Jules, still profoundly unconscious beneath the weight of his mama's medications. But Charlotte's face, half turned towards him, radiated the ecstatic glow of martyrdom.

Which she'll certainly experience, he reflected sadly, *once she starts living under the same roof with a drug-dependent mama's boy and his beloved parent.*

'Will you help me here?' he asked Antoine quietly, and with the slave's assistance, lay flat on the gallery the moment the two older women were out of sight, and leaned down to the fullest stretch of his arm, to pick the floating paper from the water.

It was, as he'd suspected, the pencilled note from Molina to Valla, which he'd last seen in Ellie's bedroom in the Casita.

Twenty-Six

'Did I do right?' Chloë was waiting for January just outside the French door of Veryl's room, on the front gallery. The floodwaters were sinking. Barely enough remained to float the flat-bottomed boats that were being loaded with baggage and passengers bound for the landing, where the summons-flag whipped in the Gulf breeze. Chattering, three of Chloë's sisters-in-law descended the front gallery steps – January caught a series of catty remarks about the absent Charlotte's 'romance' with her unconscious swain – followed by Gayla, swishing her skirt self-importantly, Euphémie's maid Etta, and Visigoth laden with baggage. Against a cloud-swept sky, a line of 'family' dotted the levee. The bell of the *Illinois*, on its return journey up the river, chimed faintly in the air.

The bedraggled fragment of a wedding-garland swung from a corner of the gallery roof. From the fields, the voice of one of the gang-bosses – standing in as overseer – echoed faintly on the heavy air.

January glanced back into the gloom of the bedroom he had just left. Singletary, white head bent, had gone back to his book. The chessboard on the little table before him stood, its ivory ranks untouched.

Veryl, sitting on the bed, had disclaimed any desire to play chess, or backgammon, or fox-and-geese. No, he did not want to read, or to talk, he had said. No, he did not wish to bid his family goodbye, as they took their leave.

Nor did he wish to leave Cold Bayou himself. Not just now.

He didn't know what he wanted to do.

Would they all just leave him alone, please?

'In helping Ellie run off with Tommy Kildare? If you hadn't, I doubt either Mamzelle's life – or, possibly, your uncle's – would have been worth an hour's purchase.'

And January outlined to Chloë his near-certainty concerning Madame Mabillet's scheme to marry her son into a family whose wealth was uncompromised.

'I could probably prove it, in a court in any country but this one,' he finished. 'When you get back to town, I'd appreciate it – Rose would appreciate it – if you'd keep an eye on both him and them. I apologize for eavesdropping, but I

356

overheard your mother-in-law speak of having Veryl confined, to keep him out of the hands of any further encroaching females. In the state he's in now it probably wouldn't be difficult to establish grounds for it. And you might,' he added, as Madame Aurelié and Madame Mabillet appeared on the gallery to bid the young ladies goodbye, 'speak to Mr Singletary, and to James, about . . . about keeping an eye on who has access to his food.'

Chloë glanced at him sidelong, with those cold unsurprised insectile eyes.

'If they can't lock him up,' she opined after a moment, 'that would be the logical step, wouldn't it? I took this from Madame's medicine satchel.' She held up a phial. Sniffing it, January recognized the smell of one of Olympe's more deadly concoctions – water-hemlock or cowbane. 'All the other bottles and phials in her satchel were full. This was as you see it.' An inch or so of the greenish distillation had been poured out . . . somewhere.

'I'm fairly certain it was my mother-in-law who had the place cleaned up,' she continued quietly. 'From things she's said, I think she realized almost at once that it was her friend Marie-Honorine who had been in the Casita that night. Do you think Uncle Veryl will be safe?'

January thought for a time before he replied. 'If someone keeps an eye on him,' he said slowly. 'Particularly now, when he . . . doesn't seem to want very much to live. I'll visit daily, when I get back to town.'

'Thank you.' Chloë pocketed the phial.

'It might be well if he left New Orleans for a time.'

Henri emerged from the French doors of his own room, and seeing his wife, made a move to join them. She raised one little white hand, and he disappeared like a jack-in-the-box. 'I'm staying on here, for a time,' she added. 'Until we find another overseer. Euphémie flatly refuses to let Florentin bring their family down here – and of course Florentin has his own importing business in town to run – and nobody in their senses would put Locoul or that worthless husband of Fleurette's in charge of that much sugar and this many slaves. We're looking into employing one of Laetitia's sons. Or possibly Sylvestre St-Chinian's younger boy.'

She frowned again, behind her thick spectacles, and glanced again toward her uncle's darkened room. 'I meant it for the best,' she said. 'I didn't think he would be so . . . so *devastated*.'

January shook his head. 'I'm only surprised that she did it,' he said. 'Mamzelle Ellie was frightened by Valla's death – frightened and angered. But she never impressed me as a woman who would let her heart rule her head. She was ready to go through with it, and with Uncle Mick in the background I can hardly blame her. I could see her eloping with a lover – and I'm afraid that your mother-in-law was right, when she spoke of her concerns about Mamzelle's later faithfulness to poor Veryl – but not with a penniless man. I stand rebuked for my opinion of her.'

'Well . . .' Chloë looked up at him. 'Not entirely. He wasn't penniless, you see. As I'm

358

sure he told her, once they were well and truly on the road to town. That's where I was Thursday night after dinner – why I walked out to the dead-huts to meet M'sieu Kildare before his rendezvous with Mamzelle.' She shrugged. 'I did what everyone in the family should have had the wits to do in the first place. Once I heard from St-Ives that Mamzelle Ellie had a suitor of long standing among her uncle's entourage, I sent St-Ives to him at English Turn, with word that I'd give him a draft for a thousand dollars if he'd elope with her.'

She frowned, and propped her spectacles on her short little nose, watching the rowboat being towed by a half-dozen slaves towards the levee. Watching the tall red smokestacks of the *Illinois*, that seemed to float against the sky.

'I must say I was a little surprised that she actually did start out to meet him, after I told her he was waiting for her there. That's why he and I started back to the Casita . . . and had she not started to walk to the dead-huts, I think we would have found her dead in her bed. So loving this young man – going to him the way she did, *without* knowing he had that draft – did in fact save her life. I'm only sorry that it seems to have broken my uncle's heart.'

Thanks to the falsified ledger, the bloodied coat, the gold cross in its pocket and the note – which did indeed prove to have been torn from the back page of one of the faked ledgers taken from the overseer's house – Guillaume Molina was tried that fall for the murder of Valla Tyler, of

Plaquemines Parish and Virginia. Molina's protests that he was half-Indian – and therefore actually white as opposed to black and not subject to a black man's testimony – were easily disproved by the records of Jefferson Parish, where he had been born in 1798. Testimony against him by another free man of color being perfectly acceptable in the Louisiana courts, he was hanged early in 1840.

Olympe said, 'I told you so.'

Antoine Froide, for whose freedom Valla had put her life at risk, remained a slave on Cold Bayou Plantation until his death from pneumonia four years later.

Charlotte Viellard and Jules-Napoleon Mabillet were married at Christmastime of 1839, and returned to Cold Bayou, at Charlotte's insistence, as overseers, as a means of getting away from Jules-Napoleon's mother.

Rose Janvier, who had emerged from hiding with her two children the moment Hannibal ascertained that no danger to the childrens' liberty existed, opened her boarding school on Rue Esplanade that fall. Both Hannibal and January taught there, and as his health improved, Selwyn Singletary also began to instruct the girls in mathematics, a subject offering for which the school was almost universally criticized as being useless to young females of color.

In addition to teaching music – and playing, as always, for the various festivities of Christmas and carnival, including for Mamzelle Charlotte's wedding – January was increasingly employed as a personal physician not only to Selwyn

Singletary, but to Veryl St-Chinian, who never really recovered from the events at Cold Bayou. The old man deeded all his interests in the family business over to his niece Chloë, retreated into his crumbling townhouse on Rue Bourbon, and was seldom, after that, seen on the streets of New Orleans.

Though January inquired diligently as to the whereabouts and fortunes of the beautiful Ellie Trask and her lover, nothing more of them was ever heard.